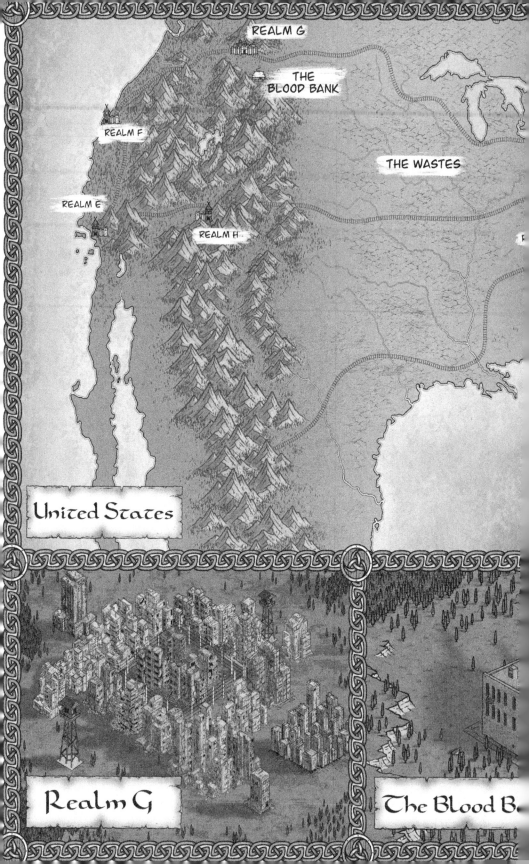

A

NEW YORK
(BELVEDERE CASTLE)

REALM B

REALM C

New York

Belvedere
Castle

Immortal Prince
Age of Vampires #2
Copyright © 2019 Caroline Peckham & Susanne Valenti

Interior Formatting & Design by Wild Elegance Formatting

Immortal Prunce/Caroline Peckham & Susanne Valenti – 2nd ed.
ISBN-13 - 978-1-914425-90-5

This book is dedicated to all those who blush when their book boyfriend says 'you're mine' or declares you their property, but in real life would SLAP any motherfucking man who daaaaaaaared speak those words in your direction.

I see you.

I am you.

I love you.

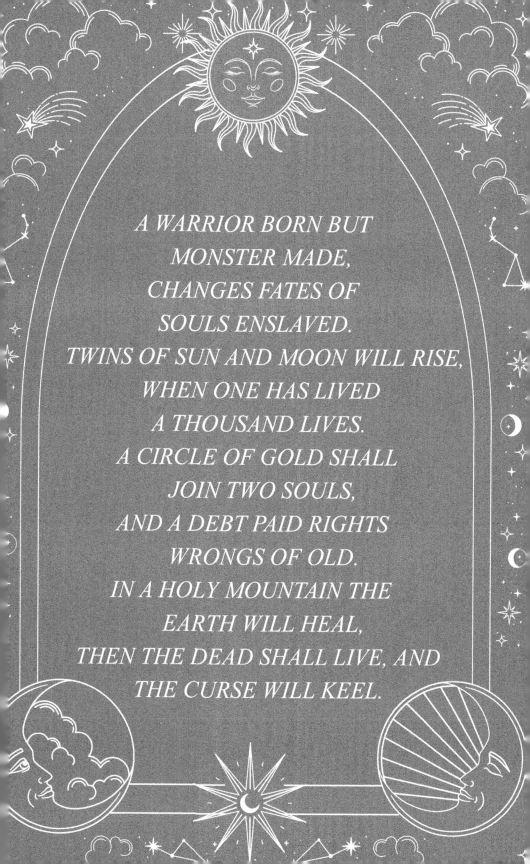

*A WARRIOR BORN BUT
MONSTER MADE,
CHANGES FATES OF
SOULS ENSLAVED.
TWINS OF SUN AND MOON WILL RISE,
WHEN ONE HAS LIVED
A THOUSAND LIVES.
A CIRCLE OF GOLD SHALL
JOIN TWO SOULS,
AND A DEBT PAID RIGHTS
WRONGS OF OLD.
IN A HOLY MOUNTAIN THE
EARTH WILL HEAL,
THEN THE DEAD SHALL LIVE, AND
THE CURSE WILL KEEL.*

ERIK

CHAPTER ONE

1300 YEARS AGO

I tilted my face toward the sinking sun, drinking in its inviting warmth as I bathed in the cool stream. Summer was in the air, but the first kiss of it had yet to bronze my skin, the long, dark winter still staking its claim on me.

My village was far enough away that I could no longer hear the chatter of my people, and the peace here was a balm upon my soul.

"Hey wanderer, why are you off on your own again?" a soft voice called to me.

I turned, spotting the beautiful Kyla on the riverbank, stripping out of her clothes to reveal her inviting bare skin, the fullness of her breasts and the tempting curve of her hips.

"I'm not on my own." I grinned as she joined me in the stream, sliding her hands around my neck. Her auburn locks brushed against my shoulders as she leaned in for a kiss, and I wound my hands around her hips, drawing her flush to me, feeling the graze of her hardened nipples.

"You know we're going to get caught one day," I said, evading her kiss with a teasing smile.

Her eyes sparkled with mischief and my cock thickened in response. "The Earl has five wives, he won't miss one."

"But you are his most prized wife." I gave up on the pretence of holding back, dropping my mouth to the silken skin of her neck and dragging my teeth across the sensitive spot above her collar bone.

"Don't pretend you care," she laughed, and I nipped her skin as she arched into me.

People rarely came to this part of the stream. It ran into a larger pool further into the trees where most of the village washed. Despite that, Kyla guided me further upstream behind an outcrop of rocks, her eyes darting about like she really thought someone might catch us.

"You're worried," I remarked.

"Earl Haver is in a foul mood today," she said, but her hands roamed further down my body, telling me she was willing to risk it. As always.

"The Earl is always in a bad fucking mood."

"He knew I wanted you," she whispered, digging her teeth into her lip. "He married me out of spite."

I frowned at her words. I'd never really thought about taking a bride. It always seemed like something men did for power in my clan. But Kyla would have been my first choice if I'd ever wanted to settle down. Earl Haver had taken that choice away from me, like he did to many men in the village. He took the beautiful women for himself and killed anyone who challenged him.

His son, Fabian, was the only decent man in his family. He was like a brother to me, but his father had never liked me. I questioned his rule, never bowing too low or agreeing too easily. If he hadn't been a drunk, I might have respected him more.

I was on the verge of losing myself in Kyla's soft skin when someone shouted my name, "Come out, Erik! Quick!"

Clarice's voice filled the air and Kyla's eyes widened in alarm. I snatched her hand, tugging her after me as we waded out of the stream. Clarice thrust our clothes at us, not giving a damn about seeing us naked. She was one of the few people I trusted implicitly, and I knew she'd never give away our secret.

Today she looked fierce, her golden hair wound into a tight braid and her dark armour in place. She was one of the strongest shield-maidens in our village, and when she was dressed for a fight, it usually meant there was one coming.

"What's going on?" I demanded, dragging on my clothes despite instantly soaking them through.

I picked up my sword as Kyla pulled on the last of her clothes and took out a knife.

"Our parents have gone insane," Clarice spoke directly to me. "They're ransacking the village. They say someone is coming for us. And they're looking for something they say will appease them," she said, her beautiful features pinching.

"What?" I blurted in confusion.

"Who's coming?" Kyla asked, equally baffled.

Clarice shook her head. "They speak of the gods. And they have a fear in their eyes like nothing I've ever seen." She quickened her pace to a jog, and I hurried after her through the trees, the chaos in the village sounding from up ahead as we climbed the steep path.

I took the lead as we arrived among the first houses and Kyla scampered off, not wanting to be seen with me. It didn't matter though; Clarice had been right. The place was mayhem, and no one was paying attention to us.

Miles sped out from the nearest house, jogging toward me half dressed with terror in his eyes. "Erik, my father's lost his mind. All of them have."

I gripped his shoulder, my heart pumping harder. "What do you mean?"

He pointed across the village, and I spotted my own father tossing a woman's things out of her house into the dirt.

"Father!" I shouted, sprinting toward him, and sheathing my sword.

He was in a frenzy, muttering to himself as he broke apart a jewellery box and rifled through the contents. His long black hair had come loose of its usual braids, and there was a madness about his expression that had my pulse rising.

"Stop." I grabbed his arm, yanking him back, but his elbow smashed into my nose as he threw me off.

I stumbled, fury snaring me. "What the fuck are you doing!?"

He turned to me with a wild glint in his eyes, eyes the exact iron shade of mine. "Where is it? Andvari demands it. He's found the gold. He knows what we've done."

"What have you done?" I growled, grabbing his shirt in my fists and pulling him close.

He tried to shove me off, but I wouldn't let go. Over his shoulder I spotted Earl Haver in a similar rage, his oldest wife Talia on her knees beside him as they smashed apart a wooden chest.

Their son Fabian was next to them, staring around at the madness in dismay. His eyes locked with mine and I released my father, marching toward him with intent.

Miles and Clarice ran to join me, and I spotted their own parents interrogating a group of children by the remains of the fire.

"Fabian, what's happening?" I asked.

"Our parents have scorned the gods," he spat, terror marring his handsome features. "They say they stole Andvari's gold. Hid it in a mountain to the south. Now he says a piece of it is missing."

I shook my head just as fire bloomed to life in one of the houses. *My* fucking house.

I stormed toward it, hearing a cry from within. Ripping the door open, I squinted against the roaring flames and hurried inside, lifting my shirt to cover my nose.

"Erik!" cried my younger sister and I turned over the table she was hiding beneath, dragging her out by the arm.

She clung to my side as I hauled her out into the fresh air as fast as I could. "Did you start a fire, Meredith?" I scolded, checking her over to make sure she was alright.

Her hair was singed, and her skin was flecked with ash but apart from that she was remarkably okay. She gazed up at me with a fierce expression. "No, it started out of nowhere, Erik."

"Fires don't start themselves. Why were you even in there?" I asked, trying to curb the sharpness of my tone.

I glanced over her shoulder as the small wooden structure I'd called home for years went up in smoke, my throat thickening at the sight.

"Mother sent me to look for gold." She shook her head and shrugged her small shoulders.

Some of the village people appeared with pails of water but I knew it was too late. The roof was already caving in, but anxiety gripped me as I sensed this was the least of my worries.

I held onto Meredith's arm, scouring the village for my mother, spotting her on her knees, weeping on the ground, her ebony locks in a mess around her shoulders. "Please give us more time. I know where it is."

At her words, the parents of my friends stormed towards her, and my father was quick to follow. I kept Meredith close as I hurried after them, my arm locked around her shoulders protectively.

My mother was a strong woman and I'd never seen her like this, openly crying, speaking to someone who wasn't there.

"Mother, are you alright?" I asked, pushing past Miles' father and dropping to my knees.

She lifted her chin as I rested a hand on her arm. "Erik...you must find what he seeks. You *must*."

"What are you talking about? Who is seeking what?" I begged, needing to end this insanity.

"The...ring." Mother convulsed, falling into the dirt, her eyes rolling up into her head, and my stomach clenched with fear. Meredith wailed and I was forced to release her as I dropped to Mother's side, gripping her arm.

"Wake up," I gasped.

My father barrelled into me, dropping to her side and yanking her away from me, cradling her in his arms. "My love, is Andvari close?"

"He's here," my mother rasped. "Stop, please stop, Andvari," she choked, jerking again in my father's arms.

"Help her," I commanded as Meredith started sobbing.

Father turned to me, his eyes wide with terror. "Son, gather the men and saddle the horses. We must run."

"Are you mad? What's happening?" I reached forward and pulled Mother firmly into my arms. She slowly stopped fitting and finally fell still, opening her eyes. "It's alright, I've got you."

"Oh Erik…" Her gaze shifted over my shoulder, and she gasped in horror. "No... he has come."

"Who?" I growled, but my question was answered by an ominous voice behind me that planted a seed of dread in my soul.

"I have. Your god is here. Bow to me or face the consequences."

I turned, finding a man behind me in brown robes which were so long they brushed his bare feet. His eyes were blank and nearly white; his hair was a dark tangle of weeds and his face was a ferocious yet beautiful thing.

Fear crackled through me as I absorbed the sight of him, the ethereal way his features moved, how he seemed to hold the power of the earth in his fist. This was no man...

He raised his arms and a harsh wind seemed to blow from his fingertips, forcing my entire village to their knees.

I clutched my mother tighter, looking for Meredith and spotting her between Miles and Clarice. Their own siblings had appeared too, Miles' brother Tamrin and Clarice's brothers Markus and Frond holding swords as they were forced to the ground.

"Who are you?" I breathed, though I knew in my bones that he was a deity; his body gave off a powerful aura that sank deep into my bones and wrapped around the essence of all I was.

"Andvari," he purred. "Do you not even recognise me, human?" His hand whipped out and my mother was wrenched from my arms, rolling violently across the earth. Panic seized me as Andvari advanced on her, reaching out a hand and causing her to choke.

"Stop!" I roared, somehow unable to rise, to go to her or do anything at all as she writhed on the ground beneath him.

Andvari turned to me with a cold smile and terror clogged my lungs. "Son of traitors. Your mother and father have deeply wronged me. What is the name of the boy who would stand against a god?"

My throat tightened as his power relented and I rose to my feet, sensing my father crawling closer to me on the ground.

"Stop," Father rasped, but I would do no such thing.

"Erik Larsen," I answered the god's question, though a tremor burrowed through to my core. "What is it they've done?"

"Not just them, Erik Larsen," Andvari snarled, his cold gaze shifting to others in the village. Miles, Clarice and Fabian's parents all cowered on their knees, their faces haunted with guilt.

"They have stolen from me," the god continued, pointing at each of our parents in turn.

"We gave you back the gold!" my father cried. "We just need a little longer to find the final piece."

"Your time is up," Andvari snarled. "You have wronged me too deeply. I shall find it myself."

"No – please!" begged Miles' mother, Neela, her golden hair hanging in a sweaty mess down her back. "One more day, that's all we ask!"

"You think returning the ring to me would be enough?" Andvari slashed his hand through the air and Neela's head wrenched sideways, her face marked with a red palm print. The sight of such magic sent a shudder through me. I had worshipped the gods my entire life, and yet I had never witnessed them or their power.

Earl Haver stepped forward with a sword in his hand and Fabian strode behind him looking equally forbidding, his gaze moving to mine. I nodded, confirming I would stand with him.

"You wish to fight me?" Andvari mocked, punching the air, and forcing them to the ground with his power.

Fabian and his father collided in a tangle of limbs, scoring a path through the dry earth as they were blasted back and my fingers hesitated on taking hold of my own sword.

My heart tripled its pace as I tried to decide what to do. How could we face a god? We were only men, and he was all-powerful, built to rain chaos upon our kind if he so wished it.

Clarice ran to her parents' sides, shielding them with her body in a bid to protect them from Andvari's wrath.

"We'll do whatever you want," Miles said, pulling his brother and my sister behind him. "Just leave our families alone."

Andvari started laughing, the sound so cold it sucked all warmth from the air. "Such loyal children..." His gaze snapped to my father, and I side-stepped towards him, ready to fight and die at his side if I had to.

"I believe we can come to some arrangement here."

"Yes, anything," Father said, staggering upright.

He clutched my arm, trying to force me behind him. But I would not be shielded like a child, I would dive into battle and seek the blood of our enemy. I spotted my mother gaining her feet and my heart lifted a little at knowing she was alive, and energy surged through my veins as I prepared to defend her.

"Bring all of your children to me, Viking scum," Andvari commanded, and a painful silence followed.

The people of my village were still on their knees, but weapons were in many of their hands. One word from the Earl and I knew they'd fight Andvari to their deaths. But that word never came. Earl Haver shakily ushered Fabian and his older sisters toward Andvari, making my stomach hollow out at the cowardly act.

"Father?" Fabian questioned, but Haver didn't answer, grinding his jaw and avoiding his son's gaze.

Fabian moved toward Andvari with his siblings and slowly, Miles, Clarice and their brothers came forward too, urged on by their own parents.

Meredith hurried toward me, and I clutched her in my arms, turning my gaze to my mother as fear pounded through me. I couldn't let anything happen to my family. I would die before I saw them suffer.

"Please don't hurt them," Mother begged, but Andvari ignored her, directing us all to stand in a line before him.

I kept my hand around Meredith's as I took my position, glaring at Andvari and brushing my fingers over the sword at my hip.

Andvari eyed me curiously, seeming to sense my indecision, but I slowly drew the sword, pointing it at him. "We haven't wronged you. And I will fight to the death if you lay a hand on any of us."

"A pointless threat. You would be dead before the tip of that blade was a yard from my chest, boy."

I ground my teeth and my spine straightened as I prepared to die in the name of those I loved.

"I am no boy," I spat. "I have twenty-eight years in this life, and I will give up all of them to end you."

Andvari eyed me with interest then chuckled softly. "Go ahead." He stretched his arms wide, and I felt Meredith tugging on my shirt.

"Don't," she begged, and I turned to meet her deep blue eyes, shining with strength.

Fabian lifted his own sword, gritting his teeth as he threw me a nod.

As one, we moved, a silent decision flowing between us, and I charged forward with a bellow tearing from my throat, my sword lifted high.

Andvari twirled a finger through the air and my legs moved of their own accord. I lost all control as I turned and aimed my sword at Fabian instead, the god's power rolling through my body and latching onto me. He cried out, parrying the blow at the last second, stumbling from my ferocity, and I cursed, desperately trying to regain power over my own body.

"He has hold of me, Fabian," I cried, and Fabian's eyes widened before he came running at me, his own sword swinging towards my head.

"He has me too, brother," Fabian gritted out, his muscles bulging in an effort to hold off the blow, but I was forced to swing my sword up to block the strike, the clash of metal ringing out across the village.

Andvari moved us like puppets, raising his hands in the air and crashing them together.

Fabian swung his sword once more, aiming to slice it into my side, and I darted back to avoid the blow, my hands forcing me to stab at him again. Fabian just managed to avoid the deadly strike and my chest tightened with the horror of nearly killing him.

I fought back with all my might as Andvari made me lift the sword above my head once more, and as Fabian came at me again, I was forced to kick out his legs.

He hit the ground and I brought the sword down in a deadly arc, his eyes wide with the oncoming tide of his death, and there was nothing I could do to stop it.

"No!" he yelled, and I cried out for Andvari to free us from his game.

My sword was an inch from Fabian's face when my arms jerked to a halt, and I released a heavy breath of relief.

"Forgive me," I murmured, and Fabian swallowed hard, knocking the sword away from his face as Andvari's power withdrew from him. The dark taint of his power retreated from my own body, and I shuddered as it became mine again.

"It was not you," Fabian muttered as I reached down, pulling him to his feet.

Andvari smiled widely, showing too many teeth, his eyes flickering with untold strength. "Back in line," he hissed.

Fabian gave me a grave look, turning to re-join his siblings and as I moved too, a sharp tug pulled the sword free from my hand. Fabian's flew through the air as well, and Andvari caught each of them in his outstretched palms, disarming us as easily as that.

With a ring of laughter, he raised them above him, and they began to melt from the blade down, dripping to the ground in a mess of molten iron.

Andvari observed us with a cool expression, tossing the hilts into the liquid remains of our blades. "Enough of this. It is time penance is given."

He circled his hand through the air and a wicker basket weaved itself from nothing until it hung from his arm, a glimmer of gold winking inside it.

"I have thought long and hard on this punishment," Andvari said with a dark smile that filled me with dread. "And today I have decided I will not punish those who have wronged me...it will be their children who pay the price."

My heart juddered in my chest, and I pulled Meredith closer, needing to guard her from whatever fate was coming our way.

"No!" Mother cried.

Andvari forced her into the dirt beside my father, and though they struggled to get up, it was futile.

My mouth grew dry as reality closed in on us on all sides. Andvari was impossibly strong. There was no way to fight him, no way out that I could see at all.

Andvari's long fingers trailed over the basket, and he plucked a round object from within it. A golden apple was clutched between his long nails, and I eyed it with unease even as saliva pooled in my mouth, the fruit more appetising than any meal I had ever laid eyes on. Its power called to me in a way that went beyond all reason, this simple fruit so tempting that I knew there were few things in this world I would choose above it.

"Idun's apples were quite difficult to come by. However, not all of these are the fruit of the goddess..." His smile was a twisted thing as he walked toward us with an ethereal grace, then held out the apple to me.

"Take it," he commanded, and I reluctantly reached for the golden fruit, knowing I had no choice.

It seemed to shine with hidden rays of the sun, its skin unspoiled and gleaming. When Andvari offered the next one to my sister, I lurched out and tried to knock it from his hands, but the god flicked his finger in my direction. My arms locked tight, so I was unable to reach it, only my grasp on my own apple remaining firm as Meredith took the fruit from the monster before her.

"Meredith, don't eat it," I ordered under my breath, and she gave me a small nod, her eyes twinkling with tears. My chest crushed at the sight. I was unable to help, to do anything to stop this.

When all of us had an apple, Andvari watched us with mirth in his gaze. "Eat," he ordered, but none of us moved, that simple command as certain as a death sentence.

Our parents started screaming, begging for mercy, but a wave of Andvari's hand silenced them.

The village was terrifyingly quiet and nothing but the summer breeze rustling the leaves sounded around us. The sun was low on the horizon, turning the sky to a dusky blood-red, and I wondered if it was the last sunset I'd ever see.

"Eat!" Andvari demanded once more, raising both hands, and my arm lifted under his power, the urge to bite into the fruit overwhelming me.

I battled as hard as I could, but my shaking hand raised, and the gleaming apple met my lips. Meredith sank her teeth into her own, her eyes clouding with fear and remorse at being unable to stop.

No, don't eat it.

I was forced to take a bite, and the sweetest juice I'd ever tasted seeped over my tongue, sugar and power washing together, enchanting me. I chewed through the soft pieces, suddenly unable to stop, intoxicated by the flavour and needing more. So much more.

As I swallowed, Andvari's power released me, and I threw the apple to the floor with a wrench of determination. Meredith discarded hers beside mine, but unlike mine, it turned ashen grey and rotted away before our eyes.

She fell forward with a whimper, and I caught her with a cry of fear, dropping to my knees as I held her.

Others were falling too, but I could only see my sister, my heart tearing in two and leaving me raw.

"What have you done!?" I roared at Andvari, but only his cold laughter came in reply.

Meredith jerked in my arms and foam spewed from her mouth while pain ripped through the core of me and left me barren. Her eyes rolled back into her head and blood joined the mess around her lips as death came swooping down on her.

"No, stay with me. I'm here, I've got you," I promised, shaking her to try and stop her eyes from closing. But slowly, she stilled in my arms and her eyes fluttered shut before a rattly breath left her lungs.

"Meredith," I begged, my voice cracking, grief crushing my heart in its unyielding fist. "Don't go."

But she was already gone, the stillness of her body barely pressing down my lap like she suddenly weighed nothing at all.

My throat tightened and pain captured my soul in its grasp, the suffocation of her loss too much to bear.

My body spasmed violently, and I was certain death was coming for me too, grief ripping through my throat. I turned to find that Clarice, Miles and Fabian were the only ones still alive, their siblings dead at their feet or trembling in their arms in the final throes of death.

Clarice screamed her pain as she clung to her brothers and Fabian stood in shock, taking in his fallen sisters with a roar of utter agony leaving him.

A force struck me like nothing I'd ever felt before, causing me to buckle forward, my hands pressing to the dirt. Electricity coursed through my veins and thrummed through my muscles, leaking a powerful energy into my body that felt akin to a fire eating through my bones.

My mouth ached; my canines grew and sliced into my tongue, then a hundred scents flooded me all at once, everything from the campfire to the earthy smell of the dirt beneath me. Sounds grew louder, pounding into my skull, and a scream tore through the air, making me wince with the sharpness of the noise.

Andvari had released my village from his spell and chaos descended around us, but I couldn't turn my head to learn why.

Above it all was the slow, dying thump of my sister's pulse, still barely clinging to life. It called to me. Surrounded me. But as that sound finally fell quiet, I lay Meredith on the earth, crawling away from her, battling the horrifying sensation taking over my body.

The grief fell away, taken hostage by a growing need at the base of my throat, a need that went beyond all logic and reason. I desperately wanted something. I *hungered* for it more than I hungered for air in my lungs. It was a need so fundamental that it defied all other human needs I possessed, becoming the sole purpose for my existence.

My vision shuddered, growing keener until the world before me was alive with colour, so bright, it was as if I'd never seen the world clearly before. But one colour stood out above all else. Red.

Blood was flowing from Neela's neck. Miles was atop her, ripping into her throat with his teeth. His own mother. And as the scent of the blood hit my senses, a burning thirst carved through my throat that demanded quenching. I lost myself, spiralling down into a dark pit within me and losing grip on who I was.

The people before me suddenly meant nothing, just moving bodies which housed the one thing I needed to sate this hunger. I rose to my feet and ran toward a man with long black hair. He tried to scramble away, but I caught him by the throat and pinned him to the ground with a snarl tearing from my lips. My instincts told me what to do and I wrenched his head sideways, biting into his neck until blood poured into my mouth, and relief slammed into my chest over seizing this prize.

Nothing existed to me but that taste. It was metallic, sweet, and set my mind rushing with a monstrous need for *more*.

I drank until there was nothing left, and the man stopped begging. As he fell still, he muttered to me, "My boy...I'm sorry." For a second, I half-remembered who he was, a thousand memories of my father hovering on the edge of my senses. Regret and terror found me for a fleeting moment, my shaking hand reaching for his face, but in the next moment, all emotion fled again, leaving me in this ravenous state with a single need I had to satisfy.

I moved through the village, ripping out throats, drinking from everyone I caught and finding I could move with the speed of the wind. I killed without care. And I was so fast, no one could evade me as I hunted them down and let my fangs pierce their soft, breakable flesh.

I tore into a girl's throat with auburn hair and skin as white as pearls, the scent of her rousing a familiar tug in my chest. She called my name and begged me to stop, but I didn't know that name any longer. I didn't have the will to stop, and I didn't care to either. All that mattered was blood, and this creature possessed it.

When the girl lay lifeless beneath me, I lifted my head with an animal-like snarl, scouring my surroundings for my next prey, her blood spilling over my lips.

I must satisfy this need. I must drink every drop of blood I can find.

The village was burning around us, smoke billowing from the houses and coiling toward the red sky, and Andvari walked among it, bathing in the carnage as every man, woman and child was cut down around him by Clarice, Fabian, Miles, and me.

Soon, the four of us were the only ones still living, and I stood above my final kill with blood soaking my clothes and dripping down my chin, gazing across the devastation. No breath moved through my lungs; no guilt reached my heart. I was nothing but a monster in the aftermath of a frenzied slaughter, and still I craved more.

Andvari approached me, and my thoughts slowly began to realign, memories slipping back to me along with the clarity of who I was. Of what I'd done.

Emotion slammed into my body, and I blinked heavily as I became me again, reality painted so cruelly before my eyes that I released a noise of utter agony.

I lifted a trembling hand to my blood-soaked lips, the metallic taste of my entire village flooding my tongue.

"Gather," Andvari commanded, and my friends moved towards us, their eyes haunted as they awakened from the bloodlust. Miles and Clarice held onto one another while Fabian clawed a hand over his face and stared at the blood on the ground in horror.

They were the same people I'd known my entire life and yet, they weren't. Their beauty was startling, their features enhanced and any blemishes in their skin smoothed out. It was more than that; they radiated an aura now that was like birdsong on a spring morn, the inviting lull of it drawing me to them in a way I had never felt before.

Clarice reached me first and she gazed at me in fright before eyeing her own bloodied clothes. "What's happened to us?" she whispered, her shoulders shaking.

I wanted to comfort her, but there were no words spoken in this world that could soothe the pain of what we had all done. The regret and loss burrowed into the depths of me, finding a place where they could torture me forever more.

My mother...my father...my sister...Kyla. They were all gone.

"You are undead creatures of the night," Andvari announced, looking between the four of us. "Immortal beings who feast on the blood of the living and cannot stray into sunlight."

"We're not alive?" Miles asked, resting a hand on his heart as if to check.

My own hand moved to my chest and no reassuring thump came in response, the profound silence sending shock twisting through my bones.

"You will be frozen in time, living but not alive. Dead but never at peace. Everything about you is designed to tempt humans, and you will always hunger for their blood. This is your curse in payment of your parents' crime against me," Andvari snarled, dark flames flaring in his eyes and an echo of power lining those words.

Fabian clawed at his long hair, snapping out of the shock which had left him frozen. "No! No, you bastard. Take it back!"

He lunged at Andvari with a furious roar, but the god knocked him back with a single waft of his hand. Fabian came crashing into me and I steadied him, our eyes meeting and our bond sharpening within our shared torment.

"That, I cannot do," Andvari purred. "But I will give you a single way to break the curse."

"How?" Clarice demanded, her hands trembling as she gazed across our devastated village.

Miles looked to me, and I drew him closer by the arm, gripping the back of his head and resting my forehead to his. I had little comfort to give, but I could be here for him. My friend. My brother.

"Erik," he croaked. "I cannot bear it."

"Silence," Andvari snarled, and a powerful energy tore Miles and Fabian away from me, forcing us to stand and listen to him.

"Tell us the way to break the curse," Clarice snapped, a sob catching in her throat, but even now she let no tears fall. Or perhaps we were no longer made to shed them.

I was on the verge of breaking just as my kin were, of going mad with the horror of what we'd done, but if there was an answer, I had to hear it.

The full moon was rising in the evening sky, gazing down on us with its watchful eye, judging the monstrosities Andvari had caused.

The god started chanting a riddle, and the air pulsed with the power of his words.

"A warrior born but monster made,
Changes fates of souls enslaved.
Twins of sun and moon will rise,
When one has lived a thousand lives.
A circle of gold shall join two souls,
And a debt paid rights wrongs of old.
In a holy mountain the earth will heal,
Then the dead shall live, and the curse will keel."

Andvari fell quiet, but the words echoed on in my mind, making no sense at all.

"What does it mean?" I growled.

"The answer lies within the riddle," Andvari laughed lightly as if this was all some game. "If you decipher it, you shall return to your human forms."

"How? It doesn't make any sense!" Fabian cried, his hands curling into fists, his need to fight clear. I felt it too, that roaring warrior in me who had fought and bled at the side of my brothers and sister, and who ached to do so now. But this was a battle we could not win.

Andvari turned, ignoring him as a snarl twisted his features into a demonic glare. "Idun! I know you are here!"

From the smoke winding its way through the village, a beautiful woman emerged with golden skin and fiery eyes. She was clad in a silken white dress which seemed to float around her willowy body, and her golden hair fanned out behind her in a wind that wasn't there.

Idun, goddess of immortality. A deity I knew from the tales of old, yet seeing her in the flesh was something else entirely. Her gaze was unnaturally probing and slid over all of us, her fury evident as I felt it strike me like a lightning bolt.

"What have you done?" she spoke softly to Andvari, but her tone held a strength in it that made the air shudder.

"I have borrowed your power to avenge myself," Andvari said, the coldness to his voice revealing his dislike of the goddess.

Idun's face contorted with rage. "I have hunted for you, Andvari, and now I find you have done the unspeakable with the fruit of my immortal tree. I will never forgive this."

Her eyes fell on me, and a power slid through my body like vines curling around my heart. I crumpled to my knees, clawing at the dirt as my organs squeezed. I was surely dead, the pain too immense, the crushing of my lungs assuring me they were about to burst, yet through the agony I remained.

"You cannot kill them," Andvari spat. "They have your gift now."

"Undo it," Idun commanded, her voice causing a furious gust of heated air that blew out the fires devouring the houses around us.

"By the gods," Miles gasped, his hand clasping Clarice's.

"Erik," Fabian called, reaching for me though Andvari's power held him at bay.

Idun's cruel magic released me, and I gasped for a breath that wouldn't come, finding I didn't need to breathe at all. I scrambled to my feet, my movements agile and the pain from her attack lost to me already. I was death embodied, this skin nothing more than a prison for a trapped soul.

"They are bound by the curse; nothing can undo this except the answer to my prophecy." Andvari stepped toward Idun and lifted his palms, fire scorching the earth between them in a wide line, warning her off.

Idun opened her mouth and sharp teeth were revealed, marring her beauty. "You are altering nature for your games, Andvari. Take back what you have done."

"I cannot!" Andvari bellowed, and a tremor rocked the ground beneath me, the earth cracking from the power that flowed from his being.

I eyed the others, and they gave me a desperate look. We had to run. We had to get away from these monsters.

"Then I shall destroy what you have made," Idun whispered, but she didn't come for us as I expected. Instead, she turned and disappeared into the smoke, cast away on the wind as if she never was.

Andvari's form rippled as he faced us once more, half here and half not at all. "If you do not break the curse, blood will be your payment. You will hunger for every human you meet until the sun bakes the earth and you are turned to dust."

He vanished and all that remained was the hollowness of my soul, the smoke weaving its way around our broken home, and the tang of my family's blood on my tongue. A taste I knew I would never be rid of.

MONTANA

CHAPTER TWO

A storm was rising in me. A burning need. A single cause.

"We have to get them out."

Callie's voice.

I tried to reach for her, and the more I focused, the clearer the world became around me. An overturned carriage. My hands bound in chains, bashing against a barred window.

The vision shuddered and I was in the arms of a powerful man with long hair hanging around his face. His golden eyes captivated me the most. His mouth was just inches from mine. The moonlight shimmered around us, and something felt so incredibly right about the closeness of him.

"-what do you expect me to do? I can't fix every problem you make for yourself, Erik," Clarice's voice jarred through my thoughts, and the dream fell away from me, the protective aura of the stranger dissolving with it. I jerked fully awake, my arms yanking against the torn sheet tying me to the headboard, reminding me of my miserable reality.

My wrists were bruised from hours of fighting to get free, and I was sure I'd only fallen asleep out of exhaustion in the end. I must have gotten just a couple of hours rest – though I'd hardly call it that.

The door was shoved open, and Clarice walked in with Erik at her back, the princess looking like daylight while the prince was the darkest of nights tracing her footsteps. Her gown was lemon yellow today, falling right down to the floor and hugging her curves like liquid satin. Her eyes fell on me, and her lips parted in shock at the sight of my tethers.

Erik was dressed in a crisp white shirt and fine trousers which hung from his slim hips. His eyes were brighter today than I'd ever seen them, seeming more like molten silver than the harsh iron tones I remembered.

"Erik," Clarice snarled, rounding on him, shoving her hands into his chest, sending him stumbling back into the wall.

He snarled at her, and suddenly they were just two wolves with their hackles raised, Erik prowling toward her in a promise of a fight.

"She tried to escape," he hissed.

"And apparently, I will rue the day I ever did so," I drawled, quoting his own words from last night.

Erik's eyes snapped onto me, all murder and hellfire, but Clarice forced his attention back to her.

"There is no excuse for this," Clarice snapped, an air of true power about her that even Erik seemed inclined to take note of. "You are meant to safeguard her."

"She is safe," he said darkly. "She's right there, and unless the mattress decides to grow teeth and devour her, I don't believe she will be in any immediate danger."

"How do you expect her to choose you at the ceremony if you treat her this way?" Clarice lowered her voice, but I caught every word.

Erik shot me a look that told me to keep quiet, but I didn't plan on outing his secret plan for me to spy on Fabian. Not yet anyway. It was still the only chance I had of either blackmailing him or fulfilling my promise to him, securing the deal we'd made. Besides, I got the feeling Clarice wasn't the right vampire to rat him out to. She was clearly close with him despite their differences. No, I reckoned my best bet would be telling Erik's target, his rival, the vampire he was trying to use me against. Because I didn't think Fabian would take to it kindly.

"Perhaps she's into bondage," Erik said, trying to turn my capture into a twisted little joke, but not even Clarice was swallowing it.

"This is not a game, you reckless fool," she said so seriously that it made my heart pound. And my eternal questions clawed at me over why they had created this ritual at all. "Erik, you have chosen her, and you *must* honour that. Is it too much to ask to treat her with civility? She is human, as you once were. Or have you forgotten what it was like to be one of them?"

Erik's jaw ticked, his eyes crawling over me again like I was the most infuriating thing he had ever laid eyes on. "Yes, I still recall what it was to be human, but I am perfectly certain that I was nowhere near as insufferable as this creature before me."

"No, you're doing great at the insufferable thing, I promise," I said, and Erik stepped toward me, all growls and rage.

I couldn't picture him as a mortal, with imperfections and the flush of blood in his cheeks. It was impossible to imagine him as anything but a timeless being with a hollow heart.

Clarice shot into his way, planting a hand against his chest, shielding me from his wrath, and I wasn't sure how to take that. My value to these monsters seemed to be growing every day, and I couldn't for the life of me figure out why.

"Erik," Clarice said, then dropped her voice to a whisper I simply couldn't catch the words of.

Erik's hard features softened a touch, and he inclined his head, giving in to whatever she had said.

"Fine," he gritted out. "I will untie her."

"Thank you, brother." Clarice swept forward with a smile, reaching up to wrap her arms around him, and he pulled her close for a second. Then she moved past him, exiting the room and leaving me there with my own personal nightmare.

My hands curled into tight fists as he kicked the door shut behind Clarice with a sharp snap, his eyes never leaving mine.

He clucked his tongue, regarding me with cold distaste. "Why didn't you tell her about my plans?"

I wet my mouth, realising how achingly thirsty I was. "I'm tied to a bed like a tasty little vampire snack. Seemed like a suicide mission."

"So you would have done so had you been in a better position to escape?" he asked, his grey eyes full of threat.

"No," I admitted. "I'd prefer to blackmail you with your secret and get what I want."

He released a breath of amusement, then lowered down to sit on the bed, angling his powerful body toward me. "What a clever little human you think you are."

"I try."

"Hm."

I eyed him warily as he shifted even closer.

"I'm going to untie you now," he said. "I would prefer if you don't thrash and make a pointless scene of it. I believe I have made it very clear how easily I can catch you, and I promise you, rebel, I will find you wherever you may run to. Now be quiet and lay still."

"I have a question," I said immediately, and his lips twitched in frustration.

"Yes?" he asked curtly, clearly working hard to play nice with me. Or at least be civil like Clarice had told him to be.

"What exactly is going to happen now? Last night, you said I'm your prisoner and made a bunch of angry threats. Now you're untying me. It's a little confusing, don't you think?"

"I think you are a fool to believe a scrap of material around your wrists makes you more of a prisoner than without it." He reached over me, his body pressing down on mine as he grabbed my binds and tore through them with barely any effort at all.

He didn't immediately move away as my hands dropped to the bed, and my heart jolted as his mouth came all too close to mine, reminding me of the kiss we'd shared last night. Of how deeply I'd wanted it when our lips had touched. He was a cruel temptation brought to life, and I had fallen for the seduction of him. But that was all he was, a trap set to confound me, nothing more.

The scent of cypress and falling rain made me inhale, drawing that enticing smell of his into my lungs, and his eyes lowered to my mouth.

"You taste like candied sin, rebel," he whispered, and my throat thickened. "And oh, how easily that taste was claimed."

He drew away from me in a blur of speed, and I sat upright with my hand swinging for a strike I couldn't land. "Well, you taste like tar, asshole. Keep your mouth away from me."

"Alright, but don't blame me for refusing you when you come begging for another kiss," he chided.

I growled as I launched myself out of the bed, unsure what my intention was, only that I wanted to hurt him.

He was gone in a flash, the door slamming shut and the lock clicking behind him, leaving me there with only my rage for company.

I huffed out a breath and stalked into the small en suite, brushing my teeth and scrubbing away the memory of his taste until it felt like my gums were going to bleed. Then I stripped off, tied my hair up in a messy bun and strode into the shower, turning the heat up so high that the water nearly scalded me. But I needed it, to feel the blaze of warmth running over my skin and making me forget the cold touch of the vampire who'd laid his hands on me last night.

By the time I was back in my room with a towel wrapped around me and my black hair hanging loose around my shoulders, I felt stronger, ready to face whatever came my way today.

"-sire, you really must hire a professional stylist, I'm just a maid!"

Erik strode into the room dragging Nancy behind him, and any hope I'd had of being left alone today flittered away before my eyes.

"You just got promoted," Erik announced, and Nancy shook her head in desperation.

"Please, sir, I really must insist-"

"Enough." He took Nancy's shoulders, angling her toward me. "See all the hair sticking up on top of this human's head?"

"Y-yes," she stuttered, and I gave him a flat look.

"Tame it," he commanded. "And make that pouty face fit for royalty."

"Erik?" I said lightly.

"Yes, rebel?" he answered formally.

"Stop being an ass." I reverted to my usual sour tone, figuring it was best to pretend nothing had ever happened between us. Between my failed escape, the kiss, and him tying me up and leaving me there all night, I wasn't going to let him get the better of me.

"Noted," he muttered, a smirk twisting his lips which almost made me smile too, but I stamped that motherfucker down.

Erik was a vampire. And no matter what I'd felt toward him in that fleeting moment of madness, it didn't matter. Because humans didn't fall for bloodsuckers, they just got trapped in their snare. But I wasn't going to be some creature in his trap, just waiting for him to come make a feast of me. I'd be ready with teeth and claws of my own.

"What's this for?" I asked.

"You will be spending the day with Fabian, remember?" Erik said, an edge to his tone. "And you'll behave, won't you?"

Behave was code for 'stick to the plan'. I nodded, and he gave me a searching look that said he didn't quite believe me. But I guessed he had no choice but to try.

Erik seemed like he wanted to say something more, but instead, he turned to Nancy and murmured, "Good luck," then headed out of the room.

The tension in the air disbanded and I soaked in the relief at being apart from him again. He was too intoxicating up close. I needed to focus on getting through my day with Fabian. Nothing else. I had to figure out if betraying Erik to Fabian was even viable, or if the prince who apparently ran the Realms was as brutal as his reputation.

Nancy moved towards me cautiously, pointing me toward the dressing table. "Take a seat and let's get started."

I yawned as I moved to comply, last night's strange dreams coming back to me as I perched on the stool before the mirror. I'd seen Callie, felt the closeness of my twin, and I swear at moments, it could have been real. As if we had found our way to each other through the dark, but I knew that was just a mirage I wanted to believe in.

I gazed at myself in the gilded mirror, my eyes heavy with dark circles and my lips overly pale. Frankly, the lack of sleep showed, and I looked like shit.

Nancy started combing my hair and I put my faith in her, her magic powders and array of fluffy brushes to make me fit for this day. Because if I was going to get Fabian interested in me, then I needed to look like an immortal vampire with flawless skin instead of a sleepy-ass human.

Nearly an hour later, Nancy - for all her monstrous faults - had done it. I was primed for Fabian with my face painted to perfection and my dark hair coiling down my spine in loose waves. There was no trace of the tiredness around my eyes, and I had to marvel at Nancy's skill, even if I would never speak a word of admiration in her direction.

"Lovely," she announced, threading her fingers through my hair as she arranged it over my shoulders. "It's so good to see you smile, Montana."

I glanced at myself in the mirror in surprise, discovering that she was right. I was smiling, but it wasn't a cutesy little puppet of a smile, it was a wicked thing that spoke of the rush I felt at having a plan up my sleeve. Or at least, that was how it appeared to me. To Nancy, it probably looked like I was delighted with my new look. *But you don't know anything, Nancy.*

When I didn't reply, she gave me a knowing look like she understood something. "Prince Erik is quite the catch."

My smile faltered at her insinuation and her belief that I was just a giddy moron who had fallen for the prince.

"Is he? I hadn't noticed," I said coldly. "He's not really my type, being a hungry, blood-sucking demon and all."

Nancy's soft features skewed with hurt. "We're not all bad," she said gently.

I could have sworn those emotions in her eyes were real, and they made my gut tug, urging an apology to my lips. But I'd be damned if she was going to get that from me. I wasn't going to say sorry to a creature who would happily drink a cup of my blood if I handed it to her.

I quickly changed lanes. "This stuff is wild." I circled a finger around my face. "I don't look like the undead now."

She laughed softly, moving closer. "Actually, I'd say the opposite. The undead are the hottest thing in the New Empire." She headed across the room and searched through the closet, examining the dresses before picking out a long, green gown the colour of General Wolfe's cloak.

"Not that one," I growled, and she frowned.

"Fine. You pick one," she said, planting her hands on her hips.

I moved to the closet, rifling through the dresses, wondering what the best option was for today. I had to grab Fabian's attention, so looking appealing was high on my priority list, even if it made my skin crawl to do it. My fingers halted on an ebony gown with thin straps, a low-cut neckline and a slit up one leg. I'd never cared about the clothes I wore back in the Realm, not beyond choosing whatever was most practical. But with the options I faced here, I started to see why the vampires liked their finery. If you didn't have to think about where your next meal was going to come from, or how you were going to make it through another cold winter's night, I guessed you'd have more time for dressing up and prancing about the place like a carefree dipshit.

I took a slow breath, making my decision as I plucked the dress from the rack, ready to embrace my carefree assholeness. Or at least the illusion of it.

Nancy helped me into it, then stood back, admiring the flowing gown which gripped my waist and ass like it was made for me.

"Does it look okay?" I asked Nancy. "Do you think Fabian will like it?"

Her eyes sparkled, and her face went all glowy as she clearly thought I wanted to impress her prince.

"See for yourself." She guided me toward the large mirror on the wall and I fell still as I spotted my reflection.

The dress was striking and even made my cleavage look fuller, the slit between my tits dropping almost to my belly button. If this thing didn't grab Fabian's attention and kick him in the dick with desire, then nothing would.

"Enjoy your day." Nancy bowed her head then hurried to exit the room, leaving me to my thoughts.

Nerves pooled in my stomach as I waited, the minutes ticking by as I expected Fabian to come for me, but the next person to step through the door was Erik.

"I just wanted to check you hadn't decided to dress in rags." His eyes slid from my head to my toes, and I felt like I was being skinned alive. Heat sparked at the base of my spine as I awaited his conclusion, folding my arms and jutting up my chin in a way that told him I didn't give a damn what he thought of me.

When he didn't find any words to give me, I prompted an answer from him.

"Are these rags alright, Prince Boring?" I asked dryly.

Erik cleared his throat, and his voice was gravelly when he spoke. "Passable."

"Good enough to draw your brother's eye?" I pressed.

"His attention is easily won, keeping it will be the challenge," he said, adjusting the cuff of his sleeve, though there didn't seem to be anything astray with it.

"I'm sure I can think of a thing or two to say to keep his attention if all else fails," I said airily, and Erik's gaze sharpened.

"You are playing a very deadly game," he warned. "If you think outing my plan to him is a good idea, I assure you, you will regret it. He will show no mercy to you, no matter what he might promise. You will be far better off following our original plan, then I shall see what I can do about your family."

"So you still haven't done anything?" I hissed, and his demeanour darkened in an instant.

"Play your part, rebel. And it will be done," he barked, making my heart lurch in my chest.

"Fine," I said bitterly. "But I will revert to plan B if you keep me waiting much longer."

He scored a hand down his face, composing himself in the face of the frustration I was clearly causing him, and I couldn't help but take a little pride in that.

"So. Fabian," Erik clipped. "Do as he asks today, but feel free to tease him in your usual way. I suspect he will fall for it hook, line and sinker."

"Did you want me to ask him anything specific?"

Oh fuck. I'm actually going to do this.

"Not today. You must earn his trust first." He stepped closer and offered me his arm. "I'll walk you to his room."

I didn't take his arm, so he took mine instead, locking it in place with his elbow.

"Another shackle," I murmured

"Well, you are my prisoner after all," he said, dropping his head to look at me, and amusement danced in his eyes.

A smile tugged at the corner of my mouth, like we were sharing in some fucked-up joke, and perhaps we were. My heart beat harder under the fierceness of his attention, but I didn't look away, caught in a dare of who would submit first.

Erik turned, towing me from the room as he set a fast pace.

"Did you sleep well in your coffin?" I asked coolly. "Oh, wait. Do you even sleep? Or do you lay awake all night counting your blessings? There must be so many of those here in your fancy castle."

There was some true curiosity in my question, to be fair. I'd heard hundreds of rumours about vampires in my lifetime; I didn't know what was true and what wasn't.

"Yes, I sleep. But only every few days. We don't need as much as humans. And my blessings aren't quite so many as you would believe."

"Uh huh," I said blandly, stowing away that truth, along with the rest of the information I'd gathered during my time here.

We drifted along a bright corridor with beautiful paintings of the grounds hanging on the walls, and all I could hear was my pulse thrumming musically in my ears.

"How did you sleep?" Erik asked after an age, and I looked up at him in surprise, unsure why either of us were keeping up this ruse of civility. But I supposed it beat being tied to a bed.

"I keep having strange dreams," I admitted. "I saw my sister."

"The fugitive?" he asked, and I nodded, scowling at the word. "I ordered my men to bring her here when she's found."

I stopped walking, gazing up at him in relief. Not that this castle was a great place to be, but it was better than dead or strung up for your blood to be harvested.

My nails dug into his arm as desperation filled me. "Here?"

"Yes." Erik nodded stiffly, his gaze glittering with a promise I hoped he'd keep.

"Why didn't you mention this before?"

"Because you were being mouthy. You see, I reward you when you're behaving."

His hand pressed into the base of my spine, making my stomach knot as he drew me closer. I stood inches from him, taking in the sharp line of his brow, the shadows that lay in the depths of his ash grey eyes, speaking of some wickedness I couldn't even put a name to.

"Let's not keep my brother waiting," Erik murmured, but he made no move to continue walking.

"I don't plan to," I said. "It's you who's holding me here."

"Mm," he grunted, unspoken words seeming to thicken the air between us, though I wasn't entirely sure what they were.

Erik took my arm again, encouraging me along the corridor, and as we walked, hope expanded in the centre of my chest. If he was telling the truth, at least Callie wouldn't end up in the blood bank if she was caught. And that meant I might be reunited with her soon, though truthfully, I hoped she'd continue to evade the vampires. If anyone could survive out in the harsh world beyond the Realm, it was my sister.

Erik tugged me to a halt again as we arrived outside a black wooden door. He lowered his head, talking into my ear as all the vampires seemed to do when they didn't want to be overheard. Although this time, it felt more intimate than convenient.

"Only kiss him if you have to, rebel." His breath floated over my neck, and I shivered, fighting away the urge to lean into him.

My thoughts tangled as I tried to decipher the intention behind his words, unsure if it was a tactic he wanted me to play or if there was some deeper meaning I couldn't be sure of.

Taking my wrist, he pulled me in front of the door, rapped his knuckles on it, then disappeared in a flash of movement. I glanced around, shell-shocked at his abrupt departure which had left my dress fluttering around my legs, the asshole long gone already.

The door opened and I came face to face with Fabian. He was dressed in a black suit, looking godly with his dark locks pulled up into a neat bun on top of his head. His eyes were two rusty coins, gleaming with interest. "I was about to come and hunt you down."

"I guess I hunted you down first." I tried out a smile and it wasn't too hard. Despite what I knew about Fabian, his aura wasn't nearly as oppressive as Erik's.

"That predator instinct will serve you well here." He stepped into the corridor and offered me his arm.

I took it, the firm muscle of his bicep flexing against my hand, and I glanced up at him with narrowed eyes, sensing he'd done that on purpose. I guessed I was meant to be impressed by that, so instead of wrinkling my nose, I fluttered my lashes.

"Do you have to work at keeping in shape or is it a part of your general…monstrosity?"

He cut me a sharp look at that word, but then his lips twisted into a smirk. "I look the same as I did the day I was turned."

"You were turned?" I asked in surprise.

"By the gods," he said grimly, then hurried on as if he didn't want to talk about that. "My brothers, sister and I were the very first of our kind. I was a Viking warrior back then, blood and death almost as much a part of my life as it is now."

I recalled the stories Dad had told me about the past, and my mind reeled at how long ago that must have been.

"So you were always built for violence," I stated, bitterness coating my tongue.

"Violence, power, greatness," he agreed, and my heart stammered at the savagery that clung to those words.

"Are those things you value, Prince Fabian?" I asked, heat scoring a line up the back of my neck.

My temper was already simmering, and I knew I needed to find out the truth as to whether he truly was responsible for the Realms, or if Erik had just been lying to shirk responsibility. Either way, the blame lay with these royals, and I ached to hold them accountable.

"Of course," he said, reeling me closer. "But they are things to strive for, not things to be savoured."

"And what do you savour?"

"Beauty…" He carved his finger along my jaw, then ran it down to my throat. "Blood…" His fingers curled around my neck, squeezing gently and making my heart race. "And fucking."

"Which do you long for most?" I whispered, his thumb stroking the pulse point in my neck, and I sensed the beast in him was near.

"Blood," he exhaled with a shadow in his eyes. "There is never anything I desire more than that, it is impossible. The thirst transcends life and death itself."

"It sounds horrible," I said, and he dropped his hand, his brow lowering as if he had been reluctant to do so, and I was relieved to be out of his hold.

"Yes." He frowned. "The thirst is a terrible thing, but once quenched, it is euphoric. A high like no other." His fangs glinted at me, and he wetted his lips. "Come, speak of something else, you are making me hungry."

We began walking through parts of the castle I'd not seen, my focus captured by a beautiful music room and a hall of tapestries before heading into a conservatory that overlooked the huge garden, the grass stretching away from us under a grey sky, the morning dew still glittering on each blade.

Breakfast was laid out beside one of the windows and Fabian guided me toward it, pulling out a chair at the table and gesturing for me to sit.

Thanking him, I dropped into it and eyed the selection of food with a growl in my stomach. Crescent-shaped breads sat beside pots of coloured jellies and a slab of butter, all of it far too much for just one human.

"Croissants," Fabian announced, sitting opposite me, and spreading himself out in his seat. "A food humans like, apparently."

"I never saw anything like this in my Realm," I said with false confusion, wondering if he might comment on why we were given so little food. And certainly nothing that looked freshly baked.

"No?" he questioned vaguely as if he didn't particularly care, and heat coursed up my spine.

"No, our rations were pretty inadequate actually."

He shrugged. "It must seem so now you are here, but not everyone can live like royalty. Are you going to eat, or shall I have them disposed of?" He pushed the plate of food toward me with enough force to warn me that I might be pushing him too far. Though his face remained friendly, I sensed danger stirring beneath the mask.

Keeping my expression neutral, I breathed in the doughy scent and my stomach growled again. I figured it wasn't the worst fate in the world to eat one of these things, so I prised one apart and spread a red jelly on it. When it entered my mouth, my tastebuds went wild. It was sweet, flaky, goddamn mouth-watering.

I moaned and Fabian arched an eyebrow as I took bite after bite, soon left with nothing but the flaky remains scattered everywhere on the table in front of me.

"I told you to eat it, not brutally murder it," Fabian said sharply, and my heart jolted.

He smiled in the next second, but it was a wolf's smile and it set me on edge as he picked up a black and white paper which had been left on the table. *The Royal Times* was printed across the top of it, and I realised this was the newspaper he'd mentioned when I'd bumped into him before.

"No story about Erik's undone fly, I'm afraid, but apparently a flock of pigeons shat all over an Elite," he said.

A surprised laugh broke from my throat as Fabian lowered the paper, and his smile seemed suddenly stitched on, too taut, too much teeth showing.

My throat thickened as he leaned across the table, flattening the paper beneath his large hands. "How do you feel about my kind, love?"

His brown eyes burned into mine and there was no escaping the ruthless allure of him. But there was no lull of safety with him, he wasn't pretending to be anything other than the predator he was now. I knew the truth was dangerous, but I got the feeling he would see right through my lies.

"I've hated you my entire life," I said, unblinking. "Any prey would be a fool to befriend its predator."

"A fool indeed," Fabian said, rising to his feet and unnerving me a little as he walked closer, circling the table and drawing a lock of hair away from my neck. I didn't move or show any sign of the fear that was creeping into me, instead looking up at him and awaiting his next move.

"The difference is, now we're giving you a chance to climb the food chain. And you don't strike me as a prey animal, love."

He swept behind me, finishing his full circle before lowering back into his seat and cocking his head to one side. "You will make a fine predator. And a beautiful one at that. You are a fine thing to behold already, so when you are one of us, you will be perfection embodied."

"And what if I don't want that?" I asked, anger sharpening my voice.

"Then you are the fool you claim not to be," he said darkly. "Life has always been cutthroat, even before the vampires rose to power. When the humans reigned, your kind spilled each other's blood. And not just in war. I have lived many lives, and through them all one thing has remained consistent. Humans do the most terrible of things to one another. At least now we have given the last of you a common enemy. But trust me, given the chance to rise, most of your people would do anything to seize power and not care whose blood they spilled in the process."

"So I suppose I should be grateful," I said overly sweetly, wanting to hurl the whole table at him and more. But I had a part to play here, and we were already way off subject. I had to get back on track because my family was depending on it.

"No, please, by all means despise me, love. I rather like the challenge," he said, grinning wickedly.

I turned away to let him sit with that challenge while I studied the peaceful woodland beyond the conservatory. It looked like the perfect place to get lost, to immerse myself in the seemingly endless stretch of trees and pretend I was in one of the faraway dreamlands I'd once depended on to mentally escape the monotony of my Realm.

"It's called Central Park," Fabian said, bringing me back to the room. "Or it was, before the Final War. Now it's just part of the castle grounds."

"Humans used to live here?" I asked.

Despite having known the fact, it was hard to imagine them walking freely among those trees and lounging on the grass.

"Yes," he replied. "The park was a tourist attraction."

"What does that mean?" I pushed.

He started telling me about the old city, how people would travel from all across the world to visit it. Families would play in the fields and frolic in the woods. It was captivating. He built up such a picture in my mind that I could practically see them out there now, living that peaceful life.

My heart sank as I slowly came back to reality and my expression fell. Fabian was responsible for taking away that freedom. He was one of the reasons we couldn't live that way anymore. And the more that settled on me, the deeper I despised his angelic face and charming tone.

"Come," he commanded, rising abruptly. "We can take a walk out there, and you can tell me what it is you hate about me most."

"I thought we only had a day together? I'd need at least a week to get through all that," I said, standing, and he took hold of my arm, tugging me close to him forcefully and eyeing my face with deadly intrigue.

"Your humour leaves a lot to be desired," he growled.

"Prince Erik finds me quite amusing," I said with a shrug and his eyes sparked at that. Sure, I tended to be the butt of Erik's humiliating jokes, but still.

"Does he now?" he murmured to himself, then half-dragged me out of the room.

We took a short set of stone stairs down to a wooden door and Fabian opened it, leading me into a little walled garden. I shivered in the cold wind and Fabian shed his jacket, sliding it around my shoulders before I could object.

"Oh, I'm fine." I tried to take it off, but he clamped his arm over my shoulders tightly.

"I don't offer chivalry to many humans," he said coolly as if that made me such a lucky little thing.

"Wow," I cooed sarcastically. "You really know how to win me over."

"Even most vampires would kill to be in your place right now, love," he said, his arrogance a special kind of irritating.

The leaves crunched under my feet as we walked, but Fabian barely seemed to disturb those beneath him. I gazed up at the tall trees, eyeing the little birds hopping between the branches, recalling the times I'd watched the birds flitting back and forth above the Realm, going wherever they pleased. More than once, Callie and I had pretended to have wings when we were kids, flapping around our tiny kitchen while Dad laughed. I'd dreamed of what it would have been like to just fly out of that place and go wherever I wanted. Now I was far from home in the most luxurious place I could have imagined, and I felt more like a prisoner than ever.

Fabian told me about the trees as we walked, naming every one of them as if that might be the key to impressing me. Then he spoke of the stream and the birdlife, clearly liking the sound of his own voice and having a willing ear to listen. I happily drank in the information though, stashing away the knowledge of things I could rarely have imagined learning about once.

As we headed through a cluster of oaks, he pulled me to a halt and spun me to face him, the mellow scent of him sailing under my nose. Like honey and orange, sharp and appetising.

It was quiet here, the circle of trees creating a clearing and someone had placed a carved wooden bench at the heart of it. Fabian stalked slowly towards me and I retreated at the same pace, part of me wanting to run, but turning my back on this monster seemed like a bad idea.

I had his full attention now, and knew my plan was working, though his hungry gaze said I was about to be his next meal if I didn't keep him curious.

"I brought you here for a reason," he said, and my breaths came a little unevenly.

"And what's that?" I questioned, glancing away into the shadows between the trees, reminded of the huge vampire I'd seen lurking out here, who had hunted down one of his own and savagely killed him.

My head whipped back towards Fabian, and I sized him up, trying to fit that profile on him, but he wasn't quite as big as that. Unless my mind had been playing tricks on mc, and perhaps I'd overestimated the killer's size. No one I'd seen in this place was as big as the vampire who had murdered so callously in these trees. Either way, it suddenly seemed like a very bad idea to have walked willingly into the deep dark woods with a deadly hunter.

"If you stand still, perhaps I can show you," he said, the dare in his voice clear.

My legs stopped moving, my trust in this situation long lost, but if he had brought me here to bite me or worse, then I stood no chance of escaping either way.

Better to die with your fists swinging than your feet running.

Dad's words. And at the thought of them, I found strength. He had fought with fury and ferocity in the face of adversity, and I would damn well do the same.

Fabian closed the space between us, and his hand came up to cup my chin, his fingers like ice against me. He dragged his thumb over my lower lip, pressing with almost enough force to bruise, but I didn't let him see me wince. "Are you afraid, love?"

"Never," I breathed.

"Liar," he accused. "It's human to be afraid. Your heart flutters, your breaths quicken. I can taste the fear on you no matter how hard you try to fight it. But when you turn…" He took my free hand, lifting it up to place against his chest where no heart pounded, just a hollow silence that felt wholly unnatural. "It all stops."

"If you can't feel, what's the point in living?" I growled, pulling my hand away, and Fabian's grip tightened on my jaw.

"Oh I feel, love," he said, darkness dripping through his expression. "I just don't feel weakness. Instead, I feel strength and immortality flowing through me like liquid power."

"There's a price for that," I said. "One I'd never pay to be a monster."

"There's more to us than you think," he insisted.

"So there's nothing of being human you miss?"

His dark brows pulled together, and he hesitated on answering before finally muttering, "No."

But I didn't think that was the truth at all.

"Now, look," he said, using his grip on my chin to angle my head towards the tree canopy. For a second, I thought he was simply exposing my throat to him, but then I saw what he was trying to show me.

A huge bird sat up one of the branches, two large brown eyes staring at me that were almost the exact same colour as Fabian's.

"He's an owl," Fabian said, releasing me and stepping back, raising his right arm and bending it before him. He shut his eyes for a moment, then the owl took off and a rush of wings and feathers came swooping towards me.

I gasped, staggering back before it landed on Fabian's arm, the creature even bigger than it had seemed up there in the tree, with mottled brown colouring and huge white tufts over its sharp talons.

"He's tame," Fabian promised, stepping closer. "You can stroke him if you like. His name is Heimdall, named after the watchmen of the gods."

I tentatively reached out, running my palm over the owl's silky feathers.

"He's beautiful," I whispered, glancing up at Fabian. "Did you train him?"

"Not exactly." Fabian stroked the owl as he explained, "I can control him. Any animal I bond with will be eternally linked to me. I can see through their eyes, guide them wherever I like."

"Like a spy?" I gasped in horror.

He grinned darkly. "We call them familiars."

"Can all vampires do that?" I asked as a cold realisation hit me. The vampires had always known everything in the Realm. Was this how they'd been able to keep an eye on us?

"Yes, but some are particularly good at it. Like myself." Fabian lifted his arm, and the bird took flight, hooting as it rose into the trees once more. "I have a natural affinity with animals. I prefer them to people. Especially Heimdall."

My gut churned. No wonder the vampires always had the upper hand with us...

Fabian regarded me with a frown. "Can I be honest with you, Montana?"

My own name sent a jolt through me. Erik insisted on calling me rebel no matter how much I told him not to. Hearing my name from Fabian's mouth almost made me feel like an equal. But that was the last thing I was when it came to him. I may have been playing games with this vampire, but he was playing his own.

"Sure," I replied.

"The day you walked into the courtyard, I thought you were trouble. But that's not what I see here standing before me."

My throat tightened at his words. "What trouble could a human really cause?" I asked innocently, tucking a lock of hair behind my ear. *Please don't see through me. What if he's figured out that I'm working for Erik?*

"Precisely. And I see that now. I believe I was playing it safe in choosing Paige, though my first thought was to select you. But you were standing half naked in front of a crowd of Elite with mascara smeared down your face, and I do have a reputation to uphold."

I gritted my teeth. "Of course. I suppose Erik has damaged his reputation in choosing me?" I definitely hoped so.

"Yes, Erik has caused quite a stir; there have been several articles about him and his wild human already. They're calling you the cavegirl."

"Nice," I deadpanned.

"It hasn't hit his reputation quite as badly as I might have suspected, though Erik often dances to his own tune, so it is hardly a surprise to the masses that he has acted rashly. I, however, have a very clean slate and I would not be quick to tarnish it. Though maybe you are worth the damage I might incur. I am yet to decide."

He reached out to tuck the lock of hair behind my ear as it came loose again. His hand on my skin made me stiffen, but I forced myself to lean into his touch instead of recoiling.

"Erik says you run the Realms?" I asked, keeping my tone casual, though adrenaline buzzed through my veins. "That must take up a lot of your time."

"Yes, quite. But I have many subordinates to assist me," he said, pride washing over his face while sickness engulfed me. Erik hadn't lied. This truth was black and white now. And that made me despise Fabian so deeply that it physically hurt.

"Anyway, I am sure all this political talk is going right over your head, so let's talk of something else," he said.

I nodded, giving him a sugary smile rather than the slap I wanted to offer him.

"I still don't understand what you want with us," I said, wondering if I might get more of an answer from him than I had from Erik about the point of the ritual.

"Yes, well, be patient and all will be revealed." He gave me a heated look. "You're shivering."

I was pretty sure I wasn't, but he tugged me closer by the lapels of his jacket around my shoulders, trapping my arms inside it, and my heart pounded frantically as he leaned down.

Oh hell no, is he going to kiss me?

The glimmer in his eyes said he was. As he drew closer, I recalled the female vampire from the bar Erik had taken me to and at the last second, I offered him my cheek.

His mouth met my skin and a devilish laugh rolled up from his chest. "You're fucking with me."

"Am I?" I purred, but my heart crashed against my ribcage with the need to get away from him.

He held me a moment longer, wicked thoughts circling in his rust brown eyes. "One kiss from me and you'll forget all about Erik."

His hold loosened and I ducked out of his arms, dancing away. My heart rate settled a little as I put some more distance between us, but he hounded after me with a hungry look.

"I don't kiss bloodsuckers," I insisted, turning away, and taking a deep breath while he wasn't looking.

"You were all over my brother the last time I saw you," he accused, and my stomach twisted.

"Well Erik is…different," I said lightly, trying to use their rivalry to my advantage. "He's not like other vampires."

I glanced back and saw the challenge spark in his eyes, assuring me I was on the right track.

"Whatever Erik has said to you to make you think he is some saint, I promise you he is coldblooded in every way imaginable. He chose you to make a mockery of the ritual, you're his current entertainment. Nothing more. That is how Erik operates. He is bored by life and seeks pleasure in cruelty. You would do well to explore other options before you become another casualty of his tedium."

I frowned, his words holding a ring of truth to them that I couldn't ignore. As much as I hated Erik, I'd thought I'd seen something in him that wasn't solely driven by callousness and a long-lost interest in life. But that had also been before he'd tied me to my bed and left me there to wrestle with my tethers all night.

"Walk with me," Fabian insisted, shooting to my side and sliding an arm around my waist, giving me no choice in the matter.

We headed further into the woods, and I hesitated before slipping my own arm around his waist too, feeling hard muscles beneath my fingers. He was a feral animal, and those muscles told me all I needed to know about my chances against him if he ever decided to hurt me.

"What's your other brother like?" I asked, aware I'd soon have to spend time with Miles.

"Emotionally unavailable, so he's probably not worth your time pursuing romantically," he remarked, and my eyes narrowed.

"What do you mean?" I asked.

"His bodyguard is his consort," he said simply.

"What does he want a wife for then?" I asked in surprise.

Fabian's posture tensed a little. "It's our duty. We must fulfil it."

I bit back a retort. Duty? What did that even mean? Why take wives if they didn't really want them? Weren't they the kings of the world or some shit?

My mind swam with a hundred questions, and I decided to air one of them as calmly as I could, because I knew for a fact this wasn't the first ritual these assholes had gone through, so that could only mean one thing.

"How many wives do you have?"

Fabian eyed me, seeming unsure whether to answer, then finally gave up the truth. "I have seven."

I sucked in a breath, trying to get my head around that. "What about Miles?"

"Three," he revealed. "And Clarice has many consorts in her harem, although none of them are officially married to her. She wishes to marry for love." He snorted as if that idea amused him.

"What's so wrong with that?" I asked.

Surely of all the things these royal vampires could afford, love was one of them. I'd never had that luxury in the Realm, too afraid of losing anyone I got close to. It was insulting to learn someone as privileged as Fabian could scoff at the idea of it.

"Because if there is one thing that embodies true weakness in this world, it is romantic love. I have known it once and once only. I shan't be tempted into the trap of it again." His jaw pulsed and true hurt crept into his gaze that spoke of the sharpest kind of pain. But it was gone when he blinked, replaced by a void.

"And Erik? How many wives does he have?" For some reason that question made my heart thump harder, and heat rise in my veins.

Fabian's eyes grew colder. "He has none. He's refused his duty to marry. It is not a lie what people have likely told you. You are the first human he has ever selected."

The way he specifically mentioned humans made me desperately curious. "What about vampires?"

Fabian's face flashed with irritation. "He has lovers occasionally. I am yet to see him look at any of them with more than lust." He shrugged. "Let's not talk about my brother."

I longed to know what had pitted Erik and Fabian against one another, or if it was just natural competition that drove them against each other, but it was clear he wasn't going to entertain any more questions about him.

The sound of voices rose in my ears, and I turned, spotting Erik strolling through the woods with Brianna locked under his arm a hundred feet away. She was laughing at something he said, looking beautiful in a peony gown which complimented her flowing dark hair. My pulse drummed in my ears as I watched him shoot her an effortless smile, his eyes full of light instead of the darkness he always offered me. And something about seeing them like that riled up a storm in me that I couldn't make any sense of.

Brianna threw me a small wave and I returned it, catching Erik's attention too as his eyes snapped my way. Coldness descended on his expression as he glanced from me to Fabian, then he tugged Brianna down another path, and I gazed after them with heat rippling through my chest.

Heimdall swooped overhead and called to Fabian with a loud hoot just before an Elite sprinted through the trees, her eyes piercingly green and her brown hair cut short.

As she arrived, she bowed low to Fabian, throwing me an inquisitive glance. "Forgive me for the intrusion, your highness. I have unfortunate news." She gave me another look, seeming uncertain if she should continue.

"Speak freely," Fabian encouraged, and the woman bowed her head.

"Chancellor Torin was found dead this morning. His remains were gathered from his apartment, but we're unsure of the cause. Although..." She eyed me once more and Fabian nodded for her to continue. "There were signs of forced entry."

My thoughts wheeled to the murder I'd witnessed in these woods, and I had to wonder if the violent monster who had killed one of the guards had been involved in this death, or if vampires ended up killing each other more often than I could guess. Either way, I didn't want to voice my thoughts on the matter. Not to Fabian anyway.

"I see," Fabian said tersely. "Thank you for informing me, Constable Mirell."

She bowed once more before hurrying back in the direction she'd come from.

I gazed up at Fabian's taut expression and he sighed, turning to me. "Sorry, love. I have to take a trip into the city. Let's meet for dinner later. I am not even close to done with you."

My stomach knotted at his seductive tone. "Okay," I said quickly, like I couldn't be more willing to spend extra time with this asshole.

"I'll escort you back to the castle."

"It's fine, I know the way back," I said, wanting to be rid of his company as soon as possible.

He observed me for a moment, then nodded. "Alright. But no detours, love. Heimdall will be watching."

The owl hooted at me, and I glanced up at the beautiful creature in the tree, not liking the way his eyes didn't blink. He seemed less cute now that he was spying on me.

Fabian bent down, placing a soft kiss against my cheek without aiming for my mouth this time, and I was relieved he was respecting that boundary. At least for now.

My skin felt singed when he stepped back, then he rushed away after the woman at high speed, setting a wind whipping around me. I stood there in the woods, totally alone, wondering if I should have tried to go with him for the sake of Erik's plan, but Fabian probably wouldn't have let me anyway.

I turned back in the direction of the castle, taking the path Erik and Brianna had disappeared down. Their voices soon carried to me and I quickened my pace, wanting to pass them by as fast as possible. As I broke through the treeline, I found them sitting on a blanket on the lawn beyond the woodland, chatting about something with obvious enthusiasm.

A rustle of feathers above told me Heimdall was spying on all of us, though there wasn't much I could do about that. It wasn't like I was doing anything wrong, but his presence made me feel uneasy.

"Where's Fabian?" Erik shot in front of me so fast that I slammed straight into his chest and Fabian's jacket fell from my shoulders onto the ground. I was damn sure he'd caused that on purpose.

"Fuck. Ow. What is wrong with you?" I snarled, rubbing my nose and trying to step past him.

He used his broad chest to bar my way again, and I pouted up at him indignantly.

"Answer me, rebel."

"He went for a shit, I believe," I said through a false smile.

He barked a laugh, then clapped a hand down on my shoulder and spun me around, making me dizzy. "Then go wipe his royal ass. You are not to leave his side."

"He's busy." I darted off the path, catching Brianna's eye as I tried to run around Erik, but he shot into my way again. She had a look of fear about her, as if she expected him to tear my head off for my behaviour, but he would have done that long before now if that had been an option.

Erik caught me by the waist, wheeling me around to face the

opposite way again, and I growled like a wildcat.

"He's off on some royal duty, Erik. He sent me back to the castle."

He finally let me go, his lips twitching in frustration, then his gaze darted to the trees. I glanced back, spotting Heimdall there, barely visible among the leaves, but he was clearly watching us.

"Fine. Go," Erik muttered, taking hold of my waist and painting on the fakest of smiles. His lips pressed to my temple, and I fought the instinct to knee him in the balls, melting into him instead and letting Fabian see us like this through Heimdall's eyes.

I tiptoed up to whisper in his ear, making it look so very intimate, but my words were dripping with hate. "I'm going to go back to my room and dream about all the ways I'd love to see you die."

His mouth brushed my ear and a shiver darted through me from his ice cold touch. "Well, while you're fingering yourself over my death, rebel, I'll be here enjoying the company of an obedient little human, not thinking of you at all."

He was gone in a flash, his super speed ensuring he always got the last word in when he wanted it, and I realised he'd taken Fabian's jacket with him, so I was left to shiver in the cold. I stalked off along the path, not looking back at him and Brianna, my blood as hot as hellfire.

I made it back to the castle, passing by a couple of guards, but the halls were quiet as I walked inside, and my skin prickled with a strange sensation. I jogged upstairs, intending to return to my room, but the feeling wouldn't subside. I felt...watched. And it wasn't by Heimdall this time. There was no chance that big bird could have followed me in here without me noticing.

I eyed the corridor, searching for the source of the feeling, but there was no one there.

Maybe I'm being paranoid.

Continuing on, I quickened my pace, wanting to put a closed door between myself and the quiet hallways.

Before I stepped into my room, a rat scurried across my path, and I frowned in surprise. I'd seen plenty of the creatures in the Realm, but I wouldn't have expected to find one here in the immaculate castle. I watched as it paused a few feet away, then glanced back, looking directly at me.

"Vermin in the hallways," a malicious voice cut into me like a dagger. "Tut. Tut."

I flinched around, coming face to face with General Wolfe, and my gut clenched violently. His cold blue eyes weren't on the rat, but me.

"What will we do about this infestation?" he mused.

I clasped the door handle behind me, desperate to escape this vile vampire. But the moment I tried to open it, he moved toward me at speed, slamming his hands either side of my head and crushing me to the door.

"Get away from me!" I cried, panic slashing through me as his powerful body pinned me in place.

His hand slammed against my mouth and a wave of terror flowed into my veins as he silenced me.

"No one's here. It's just you and me. And I've been wanting to have this conversation for a while." I hated how beautiful he was, how cruel something so perfect-looking could be. His silver hair was slicked back to perfection, icy blue eyes observing me coldly.

My shoulders trembled, but I glared back at Wolfe with defiance, refusing to let him see me cower.

"I'm going to remove my hand, and if you scream, I'll make sure you regret it," he growled, his lifeless eyes drilling into mine.

I nodded and he released me but kept me penned within his arms. "Five vampires were killed outside of your Realm, human. Your sister was present when it happened, now tell me how that could be possible."

My heart thudded harder as his words unfolded in my mind and I shook my head, having no answer for that. Callie couldn't have killed them. It was impossible.

"I don't know," I breathed.

"Hm," he grunted irritably. "I think you do know. In fact, I think your family are hiding a nasty little secret."

He snatched my right arm, turning it over to study my forearm in the exact same way Valentina had done. He twisted it left and right, inspecting it under his nose.

"What are you looking for?" I demanded, fighting to keep my voice steady.

He dropped my arm, reaching into his robes and producing something wrapped in a sheath of thick leather. Unfolding it, he revealed a curved golden blade with runes inscribed on the hilt, the blade a thing of beauty.

Fear took me hostage and I leaned harder against the door to try and put some space between us, expecting him to strike me with it at any moment.

He can't hurt me. The royals wouldn't allow it.

But the royals weren't here, so how could I be sure?

"Take the blade," Wolfe commanded, offering it to me on the unfolded sheath of leather, not touching the thing himself.

I shrank back, shaking my head, confused by the strange command.

"Take it!" he barked, and I reached for it, having no choice.

I took hold of the hilt and it immediately warmed in my palm, a bright aura humming from within it and calling to my soul. Logic told me I was imagining it, but my heart told me it was real, this blade emitting some untold power.

Wolfe eyed me closely and I wondered what he was waiting for. Did he want me to attack him? Maybe he wanted an excuse to kill me. But why would anyone believe I'd attack an Elite?

The blade hummed, something ancient and natural about the impossible energy flowing from it into me, and I gasped as a strange voice entered my mind. *Nightmare.*

The weapon began to vibrate quietly in my palm and the urge to strike Wolfe overwhelmed me. It was as if it wanted me to fight, like it ached for Wolfe's death as keenly as I did.

But if I fought him, that would equal my end.

"Well?" Wolfe snapped.

"Well what?" I whispered, refusing to tell him what I'd heard or how this weapon *felt.*

"Is the blade hot?" he snarled.

My lower lip threatened a quiver, and the blade seemed to whisper to me, *don't tell him the truth.* I must have been going insane, but that voice seemed so certain, so trustworthy that I couldn't ignore it. And I knew in the depths of my soul I needed to do as it said.

I gazed at Wolfe for a few more seconds, then constructed my face into confusion. "What do you mean *hot*? It's a knife. It feels cold like any knife."

His fingers twitched as if he wished to touch the blade himself, but something was stopping him.

"Do not lie to me." He shoved a finger in my face, his eyes glinting with wildness.

"I'm not," I insisted, praying I was convincing him.

He placed the sheath of leather over his palm, and I could tell how much he didn't want to touch the blade.

"Give it to me," he ordered.

As I handed it over, I purposefully dropped the handle so it touched his exposed wrist.

"Ah! You little *bitch*," he hissed, quickly wrapping the knife in the leather.

I eyed the burn on his wrist with a thrill dancing in my chest. Whatever this blade was, it looked like it was designed to hurt vampires, and that made it my new best friend.

As he stowed the dagger beneath his robes, my heart ached with longing, like it wished to be reunited with the weapon, my fingers tingling from the loss of it and my right forearm beginning to itch.

Wolfe lowered his head, so he was nose to nose with me. "You will show me your arm again in a few days, then we'll see."

My heart nearly stopped as he forced me harder against the door, my back starting to ache from the pressure of his body against mine.

I ground my teeth, refusing to show my pain as his glare willed me to crack. But I wouldn't. Not ever.

Finally, he released me with a growl of annoyance and relief tumbled through my chest.

Wolfe stepped back, lifting his angular chin. "Your sister will be caught soon. If you wish for her to arrive here without any little *accidents* happening, I suggest you keep this to yourself. Tell Prince Erik I questioned you and I'll make sure she is gutted on her journey here."

Fear burrowed into my heart, and I scowled at him, wishing I could hurt him in the way he'd hurt me and my family. If only I had that blade and a chance to drive it into his chest somewhere no one would find his body.

He turned on his heel, marching away, and I half-fell into my room as I twisted the handle at my back. My hands balled into fists and I fought the urge to scream my rage at knowing that piece of shit was on the hunt for my sister.

My forearm continued to tingle, and I observed it for some reaction. Nothing...

I shut my eyes, wishing I understood what had just happened, and light flooded my vision, followed by a glimpse of swaying trees. Birdsong and the rush of wind through a thousand leaves filled my ears. Golden hair danced around my face, tickling my cheeks.

"Callie?" I whispered aloud, then the vision faltered, and I found myself on my knees in a cold sweat.

I gathered myself up, trying to still my racing heart and looking down at my hair. Dark waves gazed back at me, and I blinked hard, feeling a little dizzy from whatever the hell had just happened. Maybe my mind was playing tricks on me, but the feeling of that heated blade had been all too real, and I was sure I'd seen my twin, if only for a second.

I stripped out of the tight dress and changed into some soft pants and a white sweater. Then I dropped onto the velvet armchair, folding my legs beneath me, trying to figure out what Wolfe had been trying to discover, and my mind drifted into a daydream of a sunbathed forest and the sense that I was somehow achingly close to my twin.

CALLIE

CHAPTER THREE

Cold stone walls surrounded me. I was alone, the one beating heart in a room filled with the dead. They stared at me with their too-beautiful faces and eyes full of hunger. They smiled but I could only see the sharpness of their fangs in the gesture. I touched a hand to my neck as if that might protect me from them.

The iron-cold eyes of a stranger found me but instead of feeling fear, my heart leapt with the darkest of thrills. He was like the one solid point in the centre of the room. While the rest of them circled me like a pack of dogs searching for weakness, he stood still, waiting for me. If I could hold on to him then I might just survive.

I ran towards him, reaching for him, but the faster I moved the further he seemed to retreat. And the rest of the monsters were getting closer. They closed in on me, blocking my view of him until I couldn't see him at all, and I instantly forgot what he looked like.

I could only see his eyes in my memory. His iron gaze burning its way through my soul. Trying to burrow into my heart and take something vital from me. So perhaps he wasn't my safe haven at all.

"No!" I gasped as I shoved myself upright, the last dregs of sleep clinging to me.

I squinted around in confusion, trying to figure out where I was. I reached out for Montana like I had a million times before when her bed had been right beside mine and she'd always been so close to me. Now she only seemed near in my dreams.

I dropped my hand to the flattened grass there instead of her bed in our old room, taking a deep breath as I ran my fingers through it. She wasn't there, I couldn't do anything to help her.

I glanced around at the small space Magnar and I had slept in and shivered. We'd made camp under the feeble shelter created by the broken carriage. It was barely big enough for the two of us to lay beneath. But after an awkward evening where neither of us had acknowledged the weird moment that had passed between us and effectively made it a hundred times weirder, I'd escaped into sleep as early as I could.

The last I'd seen of Magnar was when I'd turned my back on him and closed my eyes, willing sleep to take me so that I didn't have to concentrate on the inch of space which separated us.

He was nowhere to be seen now.

I rubbed my skin where the manacles still encircled my wrists. Magnar had managed to cut the chain in two using the axe, but without the key I was stuck with these bracelets for the foreseeable future. The idea made my heart flutter with discomfort, but we had bigger problems to deal with.

"Magnar?" I called hesitantly, wondering if he was having trouble sleeping again.

He always woke before me, and I wasn't sure he'd ever fallen asleep before I had either. In fact, I couldn't really be sure if he slept at all. Maybe lying in slumber for a thousand years meant he didn't need sleep anymore. He'd certainly gotten more than his fair share of it during that time.

There was no reply, so I pushed my coat off and shifted onto my hands and knees. I crawled towards the dim sunlight which shone between the broken axles of the wagon's wheel, seeking its heat, though there was little to be found with the oncoming winter.

A thin tarp fluttered in the wind, lifting a little and giving me a view of the clearing outside. I reached out and pulled it aside, letting more of the frosty morning air in, which chilled me further.

"Magnar?" I called again, looking around uncertainly.

There was still no response, so I crawled out, stepping over the runes he'd scratched into the soil last night, careful not to disturb them. If any more vampires came for me, I intended on leaping straight back under the cart within their protection, especially now that I was weaponless, Fury lost to the grass where I'd been captured. I wondered if the blade was aware of its surroundings, if it felt anything without a master to wield it or if it was simply an inanimate object without my touch to wake it. It was strange to think of a blade having a personality, but I found myself missing it, only now realising how easily I'd fallen into the habit of brushing my fingers against its hilt, feeling my connection to it like being in the presence of an old friend.

Birdsong called to me on the far side of the clearing where dim sunlight shone between the trees, so I headed towards it, wondering if the slayer had gone to check for any signs of more vampires.

I passed the spot where he'd killed the Elite, her robes a blood-stained heap on the ground, Venom piercing the dirt, standing proud like Excalibur, the sword of kings my father had once told me about. I'd watched as Magnar finished her, my eyes drinking in the sight of her demise as he pierced the heart of her decapitated body with the huge, golden sword, striking so hard that he stuck the weapon in the ground.

He'd left it there, striding away before Eve's body had fully fallen apart, the dust she'd become swirling around his legs as he walked through it, not sparing any further looks for me.

I moved closer to the ancient blade, reaching out hesitantly and brushing my fingers against its hilt.

A tremble rocked my core, a deep growl seeming to resonate through the weapon and into me, like a sleeping giant warning me off. The weapon was not welcoming. It served one master and one alone, the deterrent in its energy clear.

I withdrew my hand and continued across the clearing, a shiver rolling down my spine as I left Venom behind.

My mind wandered as I walked, sifting through the details of my dreams. Though trying to do so felt like examining grains of sand. Each piece was impossible to line up with the next. The more I tried to find meaning in them, the more confused I ended up. Sleep wasn't the escape it used to be. My dreams were plagued with thoughts of Montana and the vampire who tormented her. Could Magnar have been right? Could the slayer's mark on my arm have awakened some power deep within my blood which lingered there from my heritage ties to the Clan of Dreams?

If that was true, then the dreams were more than just the ramblings of my anxiety-ridden mind. They were real. In one way or another, they were a true link to my sister, proof she was still alive. The iron-eyed vampire was likely real too. Though even as I tried to focus on him, I found more details slipping from my grasp, my memory of the dream lost to me.

I only hoped that it didn't mean she was being tortured by some psychotic immortal in the blood bank, though the fear I'd felt from her only added fuel to that thought, and her potential fate put me into a sour mood.

I made my way between the trees, pausing as I tried to decide if I should call out to Magnar more loudly, but with vampires still on the hunt and familiars potentially anywhere, I decided against it. My gut prickled with unease as I looked left and right. Where would he have gone? Why hadn't he told me?

A bunch of wide leaves sat to my left, the morning dew gathering on them in little puddles. I stooped low and lifted one to my parched lips, tipping the water into my mouth. It was sweet and cold, sending a chill racing down my spine and quenching my thirst.

I pushed my sleeves back and splashed some more of the water over my face, shuddering against the cold as I rinsed my skin clean, the sting of the wound to my lip and forehead making me wince.

"You should have stayed in the safety of our shelter."

I flinched at his rough voice and looked up to find Magnar standing between two thick pines, watching me with an eyebrow raised in disapproval.

"Holy shit, Magnar, you shouldn't sneak up on people like that!" I pushed myself upright and scowled at him. "Where have you been?"

He stepped between the trees, closing the distance between us before dangling a silver key in front of my eyes. "I thought you might prefer to remove your new jewellery."

"How did you find it?" I asked, my irritation forgotten as I offered him my wrist and smiled widely.

"I merely searched the robes of the dead vampires." He shrugged, taking my arm in his rough palm, his fingers hot against my cool skin. I watched as he tossed the first manacle to the ground, then took my right hand to repeat the process, his skin burning in comparison to my own.

My heart lifted as the iron cuffs left my wrists. I'd been a prisoner for too much of my life and being stuck in the shackles had felt like a reminder of what I'd wanted to leave behind.

As he dropped the second cuff, Magnar turned my hand over, brushing his fingers along the slayer's mark in a move that was so close to a caress that my breath caught. Goosebumps rose at his touch, and I glanced up at him hesitantly, wondering what he was thinking while his attention stayed fixed on my mark.

"Thank you," I said, hoping he could hear how much I meant it. Though I wouldn't have wasted my breath complaining about it, the idea of being stuck in those shackles had been weighing on me all night.

Had he known how much I needed to be free of them, then gone to the effort of making sure I could be? It seemed unlikely. Why would he go out of his way for a mere inconvenience? Then again, I still didn't really understand why he'd come to rescue me at all.

There were still cuts on his body which hadn't healed over after his fight with the vampires, the blood staining his linen shirt, marking them out for me to see.

"It was no burden. I had to retrieve our supplies anyway," Magnar said, releasing my arm with a harsh exhale. "And this," he added, waving Fury before my face.

I snatched it from him without thought and he let me take it, snorting in amusement before turning away, heading back towards the broken carriage.

"How the hell did you even find this?" I asked as Fury sighed contentedly, the blade's thrill over its last kill still vibrating through it, a hazy vision dancing around the corners of my mind, reliving the moment when I'd struck the vampire who had been trying to capture me through the heart with it.

"The blades call to our kind. If you know how to listen, you won't ever lose it."

Fury hummed contentedly in my grasp while Magnar stalked away, and I couldn't even find it in me to dispute that claim, as insane as it sounded. The blade was more than just metal and bloodshed. It had a presence, a…personality. And I found myself liking it.

I shook my head at myself as I pushed the dagger through my belt, following Magnar and noticing the two packs which hung over his shoulder. We'd hidden them before our failed ambush on the vampires and I'd presumed they'd been lost far behind us. I guessed I needed to stop underestimating Magnar's abilities though, as he'd clearly done more while I was sleeping than I'd managed to achieve in the entire previous day. I'd been captured by bloodthirsty monsters, but still.

The silence stretched and I pursed my lips as I considered the thought that had been turning over in my mind between those disturbing dreams all night long.

"So, I've been thinking it might be an idea if I had *some* knowledge of how to wield Fury," I said hesitantly, wondering what kind of reaction I was going to get to my request.

Magnar was gruff and brutish at the best of times, plain rude and abrasive more often than not, and despite him coming to rescue me when it would have been far simpler for him to let the vampires have me, he still didn't exactly seem thrilled to be in my company. I didn't really know what to make of him overall, but I did know what I thought of his skill against the things that were hunting us.

"You want me to teach you how to kill a vampire?" he asked without looking back at me, his tone giving away nothing on his feelings about that.

"Well, yeah. I mean, I know I won't be able to learn much before we get to the blood bank, but surely having one or two moves under my belt would be worthwhile. I mean, it might just save my life. Or yours."

Magnar let out a deep chuckle as if I'd been joking, and heat rose in my cheeks.

"I'm not entirely useless, you know. I saved you before when I threw Fury at that vampire-"

"You missed," he pointed out with a scoff.

"I struck him in the leg, giving you the opportunity to finish him," I replied irritably.

"Oh, you gave me the opportunity, did you? I suppose you got yourself locked up in that cage and endured a carriage crash so that I might have the opportunity to kill the Elite too?" he taunted, and my temper rose further.

"There were twenty of them," I hissed.

"Nineteen," he corrected dismissively.

I hurried forward and caught his arm, forcing him to turn and look at me as I glared up at him. "Twenty," I insisted. "I killed one."

"Did you now?" he asked, his gaze roaming over me curiously.

He took a step closer, and I fought the urge to back up, sucking in a sharp breath as he took hold of Fury's hilt where it was still lodged in my belt, his knuckles pressing against my stomach, making the muscles tighten at the unexpected contact.

I opened my mouth to protest, but a vision flickered around the corner of my eyes, the sight of me making that kill living out again briefly before he gave a soft noise of acknowledgment.

"And there was me thinking you were lying," he said, his breath brushing my cheeks as I fought to hold onto my anger, and he refused to back off at all.

"You're in my space," I hissed, and he smiled, a mocking, taunting smile which only made my blood pump hotter.

"Am I?" His fingers flexed against Fury's hilt, pushing my belt down an inch, sending a lightning bolt through my veins before he released the blade and stepped back.

"I cannot teach you the ways of my kind unless you take your vow," he said with a shrug, making to turn away from me, but I caught hold of his arm and stopped him.

"That's bullshit," I growled, ignoring the way his bicep flexed beneath my hold on him. He was fucking huge. His muscles had goddamn muscles. "I don't need to take a vow to learn how best to strike at one of those things if they come for us again. I'm not asking for your secret slayer training. Just simple 'stab here, slice there' pointers."

Magnar hesitated, seeming to weigh my words before responding, and I held my breath as he finally relented. "I suppose a few *basic* lessons wouldn't go against the will of the gods," he said slowly.

"Really?" I asked hopefully, a smile finding its way to my face.

The idea of coming up against a vampire with a better chance of holding my own lit a fire of excitement coursing through me which was powerful enough to make me forget my irritation with this beast of a man. So it was really fucking powerful.

"Come," he commanded in that bossy way of his, finishing his walk to the broken carriage, plucking Venom from the ground along the way as if it weighed nothing at all.

"Draw your blade," he instructed as he unclasped his cloak and hung it over the side of the carriage, dropping the packs beside the broken carriage wheel.

I pulled Fury into my hand, and it hummed with excitement, like a little yipping puppy dog, hoping for a treat.

"Move quickly, strike for the heart. Try not to overthink things. Let the blade guide you; it knows what to do." He removed Tempest from the sheath on his back and placed it alongside Venom on the rear of the carriage too.

Magnar stooped and retrieved a long branch from the ground, swinging it in his grasp as though getting a feel for the weight of it.

"What's that for?" I asked, frowning at the stick.

"The vampires carry swords. Imagine it's a sword." His eyes danced with amusement, and I bit my lip as I began to wonder what I was getting myself into. He was going to enjoy this, I could tell. And I was pretty sure that meant I wouldn't enjoy it at all.

"Why don't you just use one of your blades instead of a stick then?" I asked.

"Because a blow from one of my blades could cut you in two, and I'd sooner avoid killing you because you made a misstep and impaled yourself. You're too pretty to end up in pieces this early in the morning." His mouth twitched and I was struck with the desire to wipe the smile off of his face.

I frowned down at the blade in my palm, sure it was responsible for the violent thought. Then again, maybe I just really wanted to kick his ass.

"Shouldn't I use a stick too?" I asked.

Fury was much smaller than his blades, but it was sharp enough to skin an acorn. I was sure getting stabbed by it would be no fun at all, especially as he'd instructed me to aim for his heart.

Magnar's reply was a deep laugh, and I ground my teeth as I moved closer to him. Fury wanted to punish him for mocking me and I was beginning to feel the same way.

I stepped closer and he smacked the stick into the ground between my feet. I lurched back in surprise, looking up at him with a frown.

"Stay light on your feet, don't stomp."

"I don't *stomp,*" I objected.

"You make more noise with your feet than you do with your mouth, Callie Ford. And that is saying a lot."

"Don't full name me, asshole," I sniped.

I stepped forward again, but his stick slammed down, crushing my toes. I bit out a curse, but he swung the stick a second time, aiming for my other foot. I hopped back, dancing away as he continued to aim for my toes.

Each time I placed my foot back down, the stick was there; it caught my feet more than once, sending pain racing through me and making me angrier with every strike. I was also endlessly glad that my boots had been in the carriage wreckage after the vampires had stolen them from me and I'd been able to reunite with them before this shit show.

"Why aren't you trying to kill me?" Magnar mocked as he drove me further and further back.

I had no time to even think about the blade in my hand as I tried desperately to avoid the blows aimed at my feet. I cursed more than once as my toes were crushed repeatedly. He moved so quickly, it was impossible to avoid him, and I had no chance at all at focusing on the blade in my fist.

Anger licked down my spine. Fury raged in my palm. As Magnar struck my foot again, I released a hiss of pain.

There was no way for me to avoid his strikes let alone try to attack, unless…

I planted my feet, forcing my attention away from the pain which flared as he hit my left foot and I lunged for him with Fury singing its joy in my fist.

I made it to within an inch of his fighting leathers before he batted my hand aside, almost knocking the blade from my grip.

"Good," he commented. "Now just-"

I twisted towards him again, my movements guided by Fury, which had grown hot enough to burn, though it didn't so much as scald my skin.

I ducked beneath the stick as he swung it for my head and kicked out at the side of his knee. My boot connected with his leg and my ankle buckled from the impact.

Magnar's stick swung out, sweeping my other leg out from beneath me, and I caught his arm, my legs tangling with his as I went down, yanking him off balance.

We both fell into the dirt and Magnar laughed as he caught my arm in his grip, pressing my wrist into the grass so that I couldn't get Fury close to him again while he leaned over me.

He knelt over my hips, pinning me beneath him as he straddled me and smirked.

"That blade is teaching you to fight dirty," he said, though it sounded more like a compliment than an insult.

I struggled pointlessly against his hold, forcing the heels of my boots into the mud as I tried to buck him off of me.

"And you're all about fighting honourably?" I asked with a sigh, feigning defeat as I lay back in the grass. Fury continued to whisper instructions through my mind though, and I glanced at the knife Magnar had strapped to his belt. "Like with that Elite yesterday?"

"You don't approve?" He raised an eyebrow questioningly.

"I just don't think the bloodsuckers deserve an honourable death.

I'd rather do whatever it takes to get the job done than risk my life." I lunged forward and snatched the blade from his belt with my free hand.

Magnar caught my wrist before I could even release the weapon from its sheath, twisting my arm so I was forced to drop it. He caught the small blade and leaned forward, pressing it to my throat, making my breath catch.

His long hair fell around his face as he dipped toward me, devouring the space between us and looking directly into my eyes.

"Nice try," he breathed.

My heart pounded as I stared up at him, unable to form any response as his close proximity sent my thoughts scattering. Magnar was a lot of bad things, but in that moment bad things really didn't seem all that... bad.

Shit, I needed a thesaurus for my own jumbled thoughts, the heat in my veins making my body ache with a desire I refused to acknowledge. He was everything I'd never realised a man could be, and despite his lack of manners and generally irritating personality, my thoughts were very much stuck on the way it felt to have him pinning me down beneath his body like this, and how much better it might feel if he just....

Magnar held my gaze for several seconds, then stood so abruptly that I just lay there blinking up at him. The heat from his body abandoned me, and I shivered as I pushed myself onto my elbows.

"Can I try again?" I asked.

"We need to get moving." He walked away from me and started rummaging in his pack, tossing me one of the apples we'd found on a tree yesterday. A lot of them had been rotten but there had been a few that were still edible, and my stomach growled loudly at the sight of it.

I caught the ripe fruit and stood up, disappointment filling me. I knew we needed to get to the blood bank as quickly as possible but learning to use the skills my ancestors had mastered set something burning in my blood. It felt good. Right. Like it really was what I'd been born to do. Though I tried to dismiss that thought as it rose. The only thing I'd been born to do in this life was stand by my family. They were all that mattered. Nothing would distract me from that fact.

"Today, you can start to hone your skills, if that's what you want.

You can begin by learning to move silently while we travel," Magnar instructed.

"Okay…" I frowned at him as he replaced his swords and cloak on his back before shouldering his pack and heading out of the clearing.

I wasn't entirely sure if it was just an excuse not to talk to me, but I didn't have a good enough reason to object, so I agreed to it. Besides, any skill that I could learn from him might help me when it came to getting my family the hell away from the bloodsuckers.

I quickly retrieved my coat from beneath the wagon and pulled it on, followed by my pack, before racing after him.

"You're already failing terribly," he commented as I crashed my way over broken twigs and fallen leaves in an attempt to catch up with his impossible, and now that I thought about it – *silent* - stride.

"You could have waited for me," I grumbled.

Magnar grunted in place of a response, his attention fixed on the ground as he seemed to assess something in the dirt there. I sighed as I fell into step behind him and focused on keeping my feet silent as I walked, trusting him to lead the way.

I followed Magnar in silence as he stalked between the trees, the day wearing on and the sun high beyond the clouds overhead.

He'd been unusually quiet all morning, which for him meant he'd been silent. I didn't know if he was pissed at me specifically or it was simply his usual demons haunting him, and I hadn't felt like asking. I knew enough of his brutish temperament by now to know that I was most likely to get silence as a response, or him biting at me in reply to any question I might ask. Honestly, I was too damn tired to enter into another spat with him.

Despite my general irritation with the slayer, my thoughts kept hooking on the feeling of his mouth as I'd brushed the corner of it with my lips. I wondered what it might be like to kiss a man like him. He was an asshole undoubtably, but he was so strong, so powerful. The way he'd gripped my hair, the feeling of his arms around me…

No. Bad idea, Callie. No fucking the brooding bastard. It had been a long damn time since I'd scratched that itch, and I was a knot of tension since losing my family, so it was no wonder my mind kept drifting to the idea of stealing a release from him. But I refused to let myself give in to that temptation. No matter how hot he was, no matter if he'd come for me when no one else would have. He was a means to an end. Simple as that. I didn't need any complication to our arrangement beyond that.

The skin on my right forearm tingled at that thought. Okay, so maybe there was one other slight complication, but I didn't care. Magnar had made it clear that the slayer lifestyle was voluntary, and I had a clear life goal in mind which did not involve me offering up my free will in the hopes of vanquishing an enemy that had already won. Two slayers were never going to be enough to take down the vampires, and though I wished Magnar all the luck in the world with his mission to destroy them, his one-man army could remain as it was. My only desire was to see my family free. Selfish or not, the rest of humanity wasn't my problem.

I eyed Magnar ahead of me, my steps far quieter than they had been when we'd started out, my feet finding softer places to land the more effort I put into it.

Perhaps the hush between us was as much my doing as his. I bit my lip as I considered starting conversations about various topics from our families to our hopes and dreams, but I never voiced any of them. It was ingrained too deeply in me to keep to myself, and I doubted I would have been one for small talk even if it hadn't been.

I wondered if I should bring up my plan to head south once I'd reunited with my family. I hadn't broached the subject with Magnar, but I was pretty sure he wouldn't come with us even if I did ask. Not that I was really planning on it. He'd made it clear that his whole point of existence was to kill the vampires, and I doubted that tallied up with getting as far from them as humanly possible.

We were on different paths. That was just the way it had to be.

At least I had Fury back. The strangely comforting blade now hung in a sheath at my hip which Magnar had taken from the clothes of the dead vampires, and I found myself running my thumb along its hilt more than once. I enjoyed the way it felt when I touched it; like a cat arching its back to be stroked. The fondness I felt for the lump of metal may have been peculiar, but it was like travelling with someone who was far better company than Magnar. I knew it had my best interests at heart. It wanted to help me. Wanted to be with me. And I wanted to be with *it* too.

I've made friends with a knife. Pretty sure that counts as insane.

My foot landed on a pinecone, and it crunched loudly as it crumbled beneath my boot. I froze guiltily as Magnar turned his disapproving gaze on me.

"You move with all the grace of a pregnant buffalo," he growled.

I'd quickly learned that his teaching technique was firmly in the tough love camp. Minus the love part.

"Wow, calling me a buffalo really wouldn't cut it? You had to add pregnant to the mix?" I asked, arching an eyebrow.

Magnar folded his arms as he regarded me. "You place your feet with no care at all. If someone was hunting you, they would find you with ease from a great distance. You do not survey your surroundings as you enter them. Your movements are careless and sloppy. If you don't fix these things, then you make yourself an easy target for the monsters who crave your blood. Would you sooner go without my help in improving this?"

I'd sooner not be called a pregnant buffalo.

"Okay," I sighed. "But maybe you could give me some advice rather than just insulting me when I get it wrong."

"You're right," he agreed, his tone flat. "I advise you to move silently."

Magnar turned his back on me and walked away without letting me respond.

I glowered, then stooped down to retrieve the crushed pinecone and threw it at the back of his head. Infuriatingly, he ducked aside before it could make contact. How the fuck did he manage that every goddamn time?

"Next time, try throwing it *silently*." He continued to walk away from me, and I began to wish that he would inadvertently step on a twig just so that I could point it out with as much contempt as he was offering me. But of course, he didn't. If I moved like a pregnant buffalo, then Magnar moved like a gnat's fart on the wind. Impossible to detect.

I ground my teeth as I attempted to stay silent while mentally cursing him in as many ways as I could come up with. He was such an infuriating, pig-headed, frustrating, arrogant, disgustingly attractive son of a bitch. I didn't even know why he annoyed me so much, but he'd wormed his way under my skin, and I was stuck flitting between ways to bite at him, fantasies about rocks hitting him in the back of the head and fantasies which involved a lot less clothes and a healthy serving of self-loathing.

As we moved on, he kept pausing, ducking low to the ground, and pushing leaves aside. The ground had frozen solid in the night, and I couldn't make out any tracks despite his constant observations. I itched to ask him what he was seeing that I couldn't, but I guessed that would mean a failure in my task to keep quiet, and I was determined to prove to the bastard that I could stay silent when I wanted to.

As the day wore on, I began to get better at placing my feet and spotting the things which would cause me to give my movements away. Magnar's insults grew fewer and farther between, and I began to believe that I might actually be adapting in the way he'd directed.

Magnar paused just outside a clearing, staying hidden in the shade of the trees as he peered beyond them.

I crept towards him, stopping a few feet away.

"Better," he announced in a low voice and the almost-compliment felt like the highest praise after a morning of insults. Not that I let it show on my face, but it was difficult not to smirk.

"Am I going to find out what we've spent the morning looking for?" I asked in a whisper.

In answer, Magnar pointed to the clearing, and I leaned closer to see around him. Two large, black shire horses chomped at the green grass by their feet, moving slowly across the clearing, their ears back and tails swishing. They were tethered together by a half smashed contraption which must have secured them to the vampires' carriage before they'd broken free.

Bloody red stripes stood out on their rears, marking the trails made by the vampires' whips. My gut lurched at the sight. It seemed the vampires' cruelty extended to all warm-blooded beings, and I quickly felt a natural affinity to the creatures. They'd been slaves to the same wicked masters as I had, and they'd gotten free too.

"How are you with horses?" Magnar asked in a low voice as I watched the beautiful animals.

"I've never seen one this close before," I admitted. "Occasionally, I would see an Elite riding one when they had to visit the Realm, but I'd always just head the other way, hoping not to attract any attention."

"Then you can consider this your next test. We've tracked these beasts and employed stealth as we approached them. Now it is important that we gain their trust. They will help us cover more ground so that we can get to the blood bank faster. We've taken one hell of a detour, thanks to those bloodsuckers who captured you, and I doubt it's a good thing that the vampires have held your family for so long."

My gut twisted uncomfortably as I thought of them locked in that dungeon. If the horses would mean that we could save them sooner, then I'd do it. I'd sworn to do whatever it took and approaching two beautiful creatures was the least challenging thing I'd had to do so far.

I drew a deep breath and stepped around Magnar, ignoring the way my skin heated as I passed by, the scent of him filling my lungs. I continued to practice what I'd been learning all day, picking my steps carefully and moving silently towards the horses.

The closest horse whinnied softly as it spotted me approaching, and I started to murmur reassurances as I closed in on her. The second horse seemed a little more nervous but that was okay, he'd been through a lot after all.

"Hey, pretty girl," I said softly as I held my hand out in greeting to the nearest beast.

The horse turned towards me, tugging her companion around too. She took a step forward and I stilled. They were *big*.

I swallowed a lump in my throat and made myself take another step, forcing my nerves not to show.

The braver horse shifted closer and pressed her soft nose against my hand. I smiled up at her as I stroked the soft hair covering it and gently rubbed her beautiful face. She tilted her head into my palm, enjoying the attention, and I was able to grasp the leather bridle which encircled her head.

Magnar appeared beside me and reached up to take the reins from her back. I continued to pet her as he cut the broken remains of the carriage away and separated the two horses. The stallion began to feel a little braver as he got used to our presence and he moved close enough for me to stroke him too.

"I take it you can't ride?" Magnar asked me as he hitched a rope over the mare's back before tying his pack in place upon her.

"No," I admitted, wondering what that would mean for his plan to use them to get to the blood bank. If I couldn't ride one of the horses, then how would we get there?

"We don't have time for you to learn. You'll ride with me." He plucked my pack from my shoulders and added it to the mare's back.

"Ride with you?" I asked, eyeing the horses again as I figured out the mechanics of that. "Won't that practically put me in your lap?"

"Come now, drakaina hjarta, you've been looking for an excuse to climb into my lap since the moment you felt my fingers tighten around your throat. This is just the excuse you've been hoping on."

"In your dreams, asshole," I sneered, taking a step away from him. "Just tie the horses together so you can lead mine. I'm sure I can figure out the rest."

Magnar snorted, ignoring my remark as he continued his work with the animals.

I eyed him with interest as he expertly secured our things, then tied a rope to the mare's bridle. Next, he cut the long driving reins from the remains of the carriage and tied them so they could be used to direct the stallion.

Once everything was prepared, Magnar leapt up onto the huge beast. The movement was so swift and precise that I was sure he'd done it a thousand times before. I, on the other hand, had no idea how to get myself onto the mare.

I backed away as the stallion snorted unhappily, chomping at the bit while his nostrils flared, seeming to be having second thoughts about Magnar now that he'd seated himself on his back. The creature stamped his feet as he shifted uneasily beneath the slayer, then tossed his head and reared up.

I stumbled back in fright, a curse escaping me as I tried not to get trampled, backing up so far that I reached the edge of the clearing.

Magnar tightened his grip on the reins, managing to stay in place as the stallion slammed his front hooves back to the ground. The horse snorted wildly, tossing his head as Magnar fought to control him.

My back hit a thick trunk and I recoiled against it as the huge animal continued to protest against its new rider. Magnar gritted his teeth and rumbled some kind of command to the beast which I couldn't make out. The horse reared up again, but through some miracle, Magnar held his seat.

I watched as he wrangled the horse into submission, making it trot up and down in the small clearing, the mare following from the length of her lead rein, seeming much more content with this situation.

I watched them nervously as he continued to make the stallion bow to his commands and the horse slowly gave up on fighting.

Magnar directed the beautiful creature towards me, and I bit my lip nervously as I looked up at him.

"I'm good," I told him. "I'll just run."

"Oh really?" he laughed, and I scowled at him.

"Yes. Really."

I'd seen enough. Horse riding just didn't seem like my kind of thing, and surely without having to carry the pack I'd be able to move a lot faster than I had been.

Magnar smirked in that arrogant I-really-am-going-to-bash-his-head-in-with-a-rock-one-of-these-days way of his as he noted my hesitation and held out a hand. "Come. I won't let you fall."

I scowled at his hand like it was a bomb with a lit fuse.

"Nope."

"Well then," he considered me, lifting a hand to his jaw. "I suppose you'd better run."

I blinked in surprise, uncertain if I'd heard him correctly. That was it? No argument, no taunting, no lecture on all the reasons why he was right, and I was wrong?

I wasn't dumb enough to question his suddenly reasonable attitude, so I simply offered him a taunting grin of my own and turned away, breaking into a run.

I was fast. Years with little to do in the Realm had left me with time for a hobby, and running was a close second to climbing questionable ruins when it came to clearing my head.

The wind tugged at my golden hair, drawing it back and playing with it as I raced away into the trees, feeling freer than ever, nothing but the open horizon waiting before me, a chance at saving my family closer with every step.

The sound of thundering hooves made my pulse skip a beat, and I sucked in a sharp breath as I whipped around, looking over my shoulder and damn near falling over my own feet.

Magnar had a look of pure, ruinous glee on his face as he galloped after me, the stallion thundering closer so much faster than I'd anticipated it would be able to move.

I realised what he intended to do in the same second that I came to the understanding that there was no world in which I could outrun a motherfucking horse.

I screamed as I ran faster, the low hanging branches of a tree slapping me in the face and making me spit leaves from my mouth as I broke into a sprint.

The thundering hooves grew closer, faster, fate closing in on wings far swifter than I could ever hope to escape from.

Magnar barked a laugh as he leaned down and wrapped his muscular arm around me, scooping me straight off of my feet and into the air far more easily than should have been possible.

I screamed to high hell as he pulled me skyward, swinging me up onto the huge animal's back as easily as if I weighed nothing at all and placing me in front of him, sitting in his fucking lap just like he'd told me he would.

"Let me go," I demanded, shoving away from him before recoiling as the move nearly sent me tumbling to the ground.

The horse whinnied from beneath us and I shrank against Magnar's chest as he chuckled at my fear, pulling me tightly against his chest, my ass firmly in his lap.

"I've got you, drakaina hjarta," he assured me, wrapping his powerful arms around my waist. My heart thumped with a mixture of terror and something far less dignified as I cursed him again. "I told you; our fates are bound now."

"Fuck you," I hissed.

He just laughed again, the sound far lighter than any I'd heard him make before, true amusement colouring his voice.

Magnar snapped the reins and clicked his tongue at the horse who continued to gallop so fast that I hardly dared look at the trees which were whipping past us.

I swore at the strange sensation as I struggled to hold myself upright, clamping my legs tightly around the stallion's body while trying to inch away from Magnar.

"Don't fight the motion," Magnar rumbled in my ear, his breath dancing against my cheek. "Let your body move with him."

He tightened his grip, pulling me closer to him so that I could feel his movements too, and fuck him because the heat that sparked in my veins was not what I wanted to be feeling when it came to this motherfucking caveman.

It was clear he wasn't going to be letting me go, and despite my terror and general objection to sitting in his goddamn lap, I had to admit that this form of transport would get us to my family much faster.

I tried to force myself to relax, but it was almost impossible while he held me like that. The lines of his body pressed against mine, heat flooding to my core as his hips rolled in time with the motion of the animal beneath us. I closed my eyes, struggling to keep my thoughts away from him, trying not to notice the way my ass was grinding against his crotch or the thickness of what I could feel pushing against me.

"Better," he commented, though I hadn't done anything other than give in to the urge to press myself against him. My treacherous body wanted to move in time with his, and I was shamelessly giving in to the situation.

"What will you do after we free my dad and Montana?" I asked him, simply because without words, I was going to be thinking about his body surrounding mine far too much and I needed a distraction.

"After?" he asked curiously.

"Yeah. I mean once you've destroyed the blood bank and freed the people trapped there. What then? Are you really planning on going after the rest of them alone?"

Magnar shifted his grip on the reins as the silence stretched and I began to wonder if he'd even reply. *Brooding asshole.*

"I need to find and kill the Belvederes. I have to finish what I started a thousand years ago. Alone or with an army, it makes no difference to my path." I wasn't sure if I detected a hint of regret in his tone or if I was just imagining it.

Some stupid piece of me twisted sharply at the frankness of his words, though I'd always known that would be his answer. After the things those monsters had done to him and his people and were still doing to humans now, I knew there wouldn't be any other choice for him. He'd been on that path since before my great grandparents were born, he was hardly going to turn from it now. He'd already sacrificed everything he'd ever loved in his pursuit of the Belvederes, everything else paled in to insignificance beside that.

We continued on through the trees, heading downhill and moving steadily south. I felt as if the blood bank could be just beyond the next ridge, waiting to end our time alongside each other with a bitter finality.

Good. I didn't want a single moment longer than absolutely necessary with him anyway.

"You could come with me," Magnar said, though he sounded like he already knew my answer too.

I blinked in surprise at the suggestion, wondering if he even really meant it. Was it an offer or a statement of fact? Either way, my answer was a resounding no.

"I have to make sure my family are safe." I shook my head. "We can't head towards the very monsters who want to hurt us. We're getting as far away from the vampires as we can. We have to head south to the sun."

"That's it then. After the blood bank, we'll be heading separate ways," he said, no emotion, no reaction.

I wasn't sure why that hurt, but for some reason it did. I hadn't forgotten what he'd done for me, but I hadn't forgotten what I was expecting of him either. Nobody helped someone for no reason. Magnar's fate hadn't simply aligned with my own. He had a plan for me. Distraction or bait, I wasn't sure which. So I had to be ready for it.

Magnar's grip tightened around me, and his thumb brushed a line along the back of my hand. I frowned as I looked down at the point of contact, the silence between us pregnant again. I wasn't sure why, but it felt like he'd just said goodbye.

ERIK

CHAPTER FOUR

1200 YEARS AGO

Andvari was mocking us, I was sure of it. Any chance of returning life to my body had waned before my very eyes. I had already spent much of my undead life searching for the answer, but the riddle Andvari had delivered to us was maddening.

We were cursed to thirst for blood, to live on this earth as demons and to torture humankind. And I'd had enough. I'd found the strongest place inside my heart and taken shelter there. A place that whispered a promise of redemption to me. My own human death was what I craved. Not even the life before it anymore.

The people of my lands called me Draugr. Vampire. I was a beast feasting on blood. A man turned animal. Only the four of us remained from our long-forgotten village. Clarice, Fabian, Miles and I. Four pillars of stone who'd never fall to dust.

After Andvari had abandoned us to our fate, we had tried all manner of things to restore humanity to ourselves. But no matter how much we tried to resist the call of blood, we always ended up losing our minds for it, preying on people throughout the land until we were feared, a legend whispered as a warning to children.

Eventually, Andvari came to us once more, finding us so desperate and broken that my brothers and sister drank in every word he offered them. He had taught us how to sire humans, to create more vampires, as well as how to sire animals and make them into living spies. He urged us to spread our curse and, the crux of it all, he had promised there might be salvation in such acts if we could come to view our bane as a blessing.

When Andvari left us to our torment once more, my family and I had fought over whether to follow his word. But in the end, they had broken, and I had remained firm. I would not turn a human and inflict this horror on their soul.

Fabian was the first to place this curse upon another, and once it had begun, it did not end. Clarice and Miles followed in his footsteps, and in time, our differences tore us apart.

The others found a way of life, something to keep them sane. They had bowed to the bloodlust and sought power in it, for every human they sired held a fierce allegiance to them. It was another facet of our curse which I had never seen coming, each member of my family building an army of loyal servants, though none of the followers they created ever held the full strength we possessed.

After many more years, the four of us grew distant, each of us taking different paths and heading to the four corners of our lands in hopes that we would draw less attention to ourselves as our numbers grew.

But eventually, some of my siblings started to flaunt their powers...

A hundred years after our curse began, to the south of our homeland, Miles offered eternal life to a select few of those who gave him blood. He had grown a sizeable group of pious human followers who were rumoured to be holding an unending celebration in his name, day and night they danced, and drank, and fucked each other and vampires alike in an orgy of blood and lust.

In the east, men and women flocked to Clarice for her beauty, worshiping her in the belief that she was a deity. Their blood sacrifice was the price of her company, and they gave it willingly, bleeding for her upon an altar of gold.

In the north, Fabian used his animal spies, his familiars, to seek out the vulnerable. Humans who strayed from their towns, the lone travellers, and the outcasts. He took those who wouldn't be missed to ensure he was never hunted down. Fabian's fear of death made him the most cunning of us all. He never caused a stir, only sired humans who could help him gain access to more blood, made deals, and played tricks to keep his name from growing too famous, to ensure no one sought to destroy him.

Through all the years that had passed, I'd remained on the western coast of my rugged homeland where the rolling forests, the fjords and high rivers were a comfort to me like no other.

I had tried many ways to find a place in this world. A manner of living that provided blood at the smallest price. I'd even attempted not to kill for blood, but sometimes the hunger was all-consuming and I was unable to hold back when my victims were at the brink of death. Now, I felt the burden of those deaths weighing on my soul, knowing I could never undo what I had done. But through it all, I had still never sired a human as they lay dying in my arms, for death was a gift in the face of the alternative. To become like me was to tarnish your soul forever, to ensure you never walked into Valhalla, the great hall of the dead, or the eternal resting place of Helheim. That was not a fate I would steal from anyone, and I often envied them of their passage there.

It had been weeks since my last feed. I'd wandered too far inland, roaming the forests of old, praying to the gods, trying to get some answers to my damnation.

My footfalls made no noise as I crossed the mossy ground, following a well-worn path once used by tradesmen. But they'd long since moved on from this area. They believed it cursed, and I supposed I was proof of that.

What would you have me do to end this? I will do it, Andvari.

No reply came to my thoughts. Sometimes the god spoke to me in whispers between the rocks, from shining puddles and stagnant water. He was ever-present, yet always eluding me.

I paced to the still pool between five trees in a clearing at the heart of the wood, the moonlight highlighting a swirling fog between the boughs. The water appeared green beneath the canopy and the pool was formed of several boulders in an exact circle that was unnatural in its perfection. I'd discovered this place long ago. The wind barely stirred the air here, the atmosphere denser, and the forest seemed to hold its breath.

Andvari was near.

"Tell me again." I perched on a boulder, poised in a crouch as I gazed down at the glass-like surface of the pool. Despite the glossy sheen of the water, no reflection was cast back at me, that power of this place crafted by the gods.

A single golden leaf dropped from a branch above, spiralling down and landing on the pool, the quiet so keen that it made me feel like the only creature in the world. As ripples spread out around the leaf, the water changed until my reflection appeared. Andvari always spoke to me this way, with my own mouth. A way of tormenting me perhaps.

My reflection moved, but I didn't. It crept closer on the boulder whereas I remained perfectly still.

"Speak your name," Andvari purred in my own voice.

"Erik Larsen," I breathed.

"You shall be known otherwise one day," he replied.

"Why?" I demanded, my tongue as dry as ash in my mouth.

"There is a great journey in your future," he said, tilting his head to one side, his mouth lifting in a mocking smile.

"Tell me how to break the curse. Tell me again," I begged.

Andvari reached toward the surface of the water and the leaf began to spin in slow circles.

"A warrior born but monster made,
Changes fates of souls enslaved.
Twins of sun and moon will rise,
When one has lived a thousand lives.
A circle of gold shall join two souls,
And a debt paid rights wrongs of old.
In a holy mountain the earth will heal,
Then the dead shall live, and the curse will keel."

I tried to find new meaning in the words, but I could never see the answer. "Please, tell me more. Tell me what it means."

Andvari chuckled and the branches shifted above me in an ethereal wind. "Time is your friend now. You have many years to decipher the meaning."

"I don't want to live this way!" I picked up a stone by my feet and threw it at the pool.

Not a splash, not a ripple. The stone sunk to the bottom and Andvari regarded it with amusement.

"You have no choice," he said.

I thought on the prophecy as I had so many times before, but there was only one part of it I understood. "The holy mountain is Helgafjell. A place of the afterlife. My family and I have already sought it out. We have found the treasure our mothers and fathers stole from you. You know where it is. Is this not enough to pay our debt?"

Andvari sat back on the boulder, regarding me from within the pool. "That is only one part of it, Draugr..."

I scraped a hand through my hair. I was growing weary and so, so hungry. This forest was making me lose my mind; the loneliness, the silence. Sometimes I feared I would sit down against a tree one day and never rise again.

"Blood will sate you," Andvari whispered. "You only need to seek it out."

"The curse...it speaks of a debt," I said, refusing to acknowledge his words. He would try to lead me astray as always. I had to find the answer to his riddle. "If I pay it in hunger, will it break the curse?"

A smile pulled at Andvari's mouth. "Do you believe that is the answer?"

"I do not know." I rubbed my throat, the ache there growing unbearable.

If Andvari wanted suffering, perhaps this *was* the solution. Perhaps it might be enough to return life to my body if I refused to give in to the urges of the curse.

"You will go mad with hunger," Andvari said, his voice as sweet as honey. "That is a high price to pay, Erik Larsen. You will break. You will cave. You will not last a year before the thirst forces your hand."

"I am stronger than you think," I snarled, growing impatient. "If that is the price, I will pay it."

Andvari's reflection started to fade, and I knew he was leaving me to make my own decision on the matter. Was that truly my answer? Could this be the debt the prophecy spoke of?

As the water returned to a glistening pool of dark green, my decision was made.

There was only one way I could stop myself from breaking. I'd find a place which I could seal myself inside and take away the option of submitting to the curse.

I would pay my debt. And pray my heart would beat with human life once more.

I headed north to speak with Fabian. My brother. Or so we called ourselves now. Our true families were long dead thanks to us, so we'd united as siblings instead. But it did nothing to ease the pain at the loss of my real sister, the memory of her dying in my arms still a nightmare that visited me often.

The days merged. Night and day were barely distinguishable. The daylight barely grew to dawn beyond the dark clouds this time of year, and the further north I travelled, the more snow I encountered. Its icy touch was nothing in comparison to my cold body, and it was no more a burden than the winding trails of the forests.

Now, as I stood beneath the heavy shade of an oak tree, a large brown owl landed on a branch above my head.

It hooted to me, and I tilted my head to look at it. It nestled down on the branch, and I realised it was Heimdall, Fabian's prized familiar. Dropping down, I sat with my back to the tree and waited for him to come.

Darkness fell and silence crept across the land as animals took roost, the creatures of the day going to sleep while I remained wakeful, lurking in the night. After a time, an easterly wind swept over me, and I caught the scent of blood on the air. I ran my tongue across my fangs, the hunger in me begging to be sated.

I closed my eyes, willing the urge away, my fangs prickling with the need to pierce soft flesh.

I will not be the monster Andvari made me.

The blood drew ever closer, a group of five humans, at a guess. Their scent was somehow familiar, but the ache at the base of my skull drowned out any chance of me working out why.

They moved near on silent feet. Too silent for humans, I realised.

My senses grew sharper, and I stood up, searching the dark surroundings. My eyesight was keen, and I could see as well at night as I could in the day. The forest at the base of the hill was concealing them, but I knew they were there. I could taste them on the wind.

A rush of noise made me lurch aside, and an arrow embedded itself in the oak tree behind me. I snarled as the group broke free of the trees, charging up the hill clad in fighting leathers.

Slayers.

I had been careless during my journey here, and I hadn't checked if I was being followed. It had been months since I'd last encountered their kind. They were Idun's revenge upon us for Andvari's crime against her. Men and women gifted with the strength to fight us. So, to me, they were the enemy. An enemy I hadn't chosen but was cursed with all the same. Their ancestors had been cousins to my kin once and I'd been welcome in their halls. Now all they saw in me was the monster Andvari had created.

Spilling their blood was a dangerous thing, but I was too hungry to drown out that need as they ran on swift feet in my direction, bringing me the nourishment I craved.

I grew weak in that moment. And I knew, as they crested the snowy hill with battle cries and swords drawn, that the curse was about to claim me once more.

"Stop!" I roared, but they didn't.

Two women and three men.

A man reached me first, just a youth barely past twenty years of age.

He lunged with his sword, and I shifted aside, grabbing his wrist and wheeling him around, trying to snap the bone. He roared a challenge, kicking me in the chest with his godly power and I staggered back, baring my fangs. He was strong, but no creature on this earth was stronger than I, and with the bloodlust warring through my skull and the sound of their pounding hearts all around me, I fell into chaos.

I collided with the man as he took another stab at me with his sword, and I narrowly avoided the strike with a burst of speed, coming up behind him and throwing a brutal punch to his spine. He collapsed to his knees with a cry of agony, then rolled and swung the blade at my legs, the edge of it slicing my thigh before I managed to throw a sharp kick to his head that made him fall still. The burn of that blade made me growl, the blood wetting my leg telling me I had just earned myself a fresh scar.

A second slayer came at me from behind, and I threw my elbow back, catching him in the nose as he tried to drive a dagger into my back. He hit the ground and I twisted toward him, catching hold of him by the throat and lifting him skyward as he lost his grip on his weapon.

A sword came ringing through the air to my right and I shot away with another burst of speed, missing the deadly blow as the other three slayers came for me.

The one in my hold wriggled and thrashed, reaching for another blade at his hip, and with a furious effort, I broke his neck, tossing him into the snow while his kin screamed in horror at what I'd done.

The three of them leapt on me at once, and a searing pain scored into my side as a slayer blade met my skin. The female it belonged to fought with a skill that outmatched the others, and I broke free of the other two slayers as I lunged for her, catching her hair in my fist. She cut it free with her blade, leaving the clump of blonde hair in my grip as she stabbed at me once more.

I cursed, darting aside, the blade skimming my hip and burning like fire. I ran at her full force, knocking her away from me, and she slammed to the ground, her head cracking against a rock and a gasp of shock leaving her lips.

Blood spilled and the madness deepened as I tasted it on the air.

A girl of similar looks screamed as she saw what I had done to the other woman. It didn't matter, because she was my next victim. She fought with fury and heart, but her body was soon slack in my arms as the final man grabbed my neck from behind, bringing his sword around to my throat. Before it made contact, I rammed my head back into his face, dropping us both to the ground.

I felt nothing. I was nothing.

I rolled on top of him and buried my fangs in his throat, taking the drink I so desperately craved, sating the vicious beast who had made a home in my body. The slayer clawed and scratched, his sword fallen to the ground and lost to the cold depths of the snow.

The white world turned red around me. The monster in me fed until it could get no more.

Blood soaked my body and ran down my chin as I spat out the last of my drink. I cared minimally for their loss, but I cared more for my immortal soul. A soul now marred in blood once more.

"Brother!"

I turned, spotting Fabian as he sped up the hill toward me. He was at my side in moments, clutching my arm and pulling me to my feet.

"I heard the fight, I came as fast as I could," he said, shaking me when I didn't respond.

The pain in my back grew sharper and I clutched the deepest wound I had sustained as my body struggled to heal from the cuts of those blessed blades.

I gazed down at the bodies surrounding us in the snow, wishing I'd stayed back on the coast and found a cave to seal myself inside there. But I needed to tell someone my plan. If I was remade as a human, I had to ensure someone could let me out.

"Fabian," I whispered, meeting his dark gaze. "I may have found a way to break the curse."

His rusty eyes roamed over me intently. "Is that so?"

"I wish to rid myself of this hunger by starving it out of me." I hissed between my teeth at the pain in my body. Slowly, it was easing. But it would take a while. The slayer blades were nothing like a human's. They were designed to hurt us, imbued with the power of Idun herself.

"You say this covered in blood." Fabian smiled, dropping to his knees and digging his fangs into one of the women who groaned in protest, the slayer still barely clinging to life.

I watched with cold detachment as he drained what remaining life she had left, wanting to feel something. Anything. But the blood frenzy I had been lost to only left me with a high like no other. Later, the guilt would come.

"I do not wish to be like this forever," I told him as he rose beside me, a glimmer of satisfaction in his gaze.

"Come, stay with me a while, Erik. You can make peace with the bloodlust. There need be no guilt in it. I pick off the weak, that is no crime in our world of hardship. The townspeople will thank us."

"Fabian..." I shook my head sharply. "My decision is made. I will trap myself inside a cave. I want you to be my guardian. To watch over my crypt until the gods return life to my body."

He slid an arm around my shoulders, guiding me down the hill as snowflakes began to fall, fluttering in the air around us. "You are too hard on yourself. Don't be a fool. You will go mad with the hunger."

"Perhaps, but Andvari will be watching, Fabian. This could be the debt he speaks of in the prophecy."

Fabian sighed. "I can see your mind is made up."

"It is. Will you help me?"

He clutched my arm. "Of course, brother. I will do as you ask."

"It could bring your life back too," I said. "Maybe this will be enough of a payment for all of us."

Fabian ground his jaw. "Perhaps," he muttered, glancing away.

We walked on for miles, heading deep into the forest until we arrived at the edge of a large cave which sat on the curve of a river.

"Are you sure about this?" Fabian asked. "At least spend an evening with me first."

I shook my head. "Now, Fabian. It cannot wait another day. My penance must begin before more death is dealt at my hand."

I started gathering large rocks, building a wall before the cave and ignoring the stabbing pain from the cuts across my body. Fabian joined me, helping to build the wall that could hold me in this place until Andvari deemed my suffering enough.

It was nearly morning by the time a small hole was all that remained in the wall, just large enough for me to enter through.

I stepped toward it and Fabian took my arm. "Don't do this, brother."

I cupped the back of his neck and pulled him into an embrace, our familial bond flaring between us. "Let me pay this debt. Do not deny it of me."

He sighed, releasing me and gesturing for me to go inside. "Do as you must."

"Visit me every week," I asked, and he nodded stiffly.

I climbed through the narrow space, wincing as my skin flexed against my wounds. I dropped into the dank cave beyond the wall and fear flickered on the edges of my soul, but I didn't let it seize me. I was born a warrior. And I would die as one too. But not until my human body was restored.

"Fabian!" I called to him beyond the wall. "Do not release me until I am human. Let me waste here until the debt is paid."

"This is madness, Erik," he growled. "I will release you the moment it becomes too much to bear."

"Even if I beg, do not let me out," I demanded. "If you love me, you will do as I ask. I demand it of you as my brother. My kin. Please, Fabian."

He fell quiet for so long that I thought he might have left me there, but then he forced stones into the hole and continued until it was packed solid, trapping me there alone.

I lowered myself down onto a rock, the darkness absolute.

And here, I would wait.

MONTANA

CHAPTER FIVE

Trees surrounded me, swirling like fog. Darkness gripped the world and made me squint as I tried to find something solid to focus on.

A figure came into view in strange attire, looking like a warrior from one of Dad's stories. Tall and roguish with streams of dark hair.

The world shuddered once more, and he was suddenly closer. His eyes shone like molten gold, and my heart stumbled with an ache of longing for his touch.

The world trembled around me and suddenly I was sat on a horse, swaying from side to side. Hills rolled out before me, merging into grasslands and trees.

The sun warmed my cheeks, and the wind toyed with my hair.

Arms tightened around my waist, and I looked down, finding the hands of a stranger holding me tight.

A voice filled my mind as familiar as my own. Callie's voice.

"I'm coming for you."

A cool palm on my cheek stirred me and I jerked backwards as I woke fully, thinking of Wolfe but finding Erik crouched before the velvet armchair I was curled up in.

He extracted his hand, giving me a slanted smile, his ashen eyes warmer than usual. "Good evening, rebel."

Evening? I'd slept all day? Holy shit.

My mind spun with the web of dreams that had poured through my head, a journey alongside a warrior, the roughened touch of his hands. It had felt so damn real...

"What really happened with Fabian? Where did he go?" he asked.

"He had something to do in the city. A chancellor died apparently," I said.

Erik's eyes glittered. "Ah, that makes sense."

I frowned as he rose to his feet, then perched on the bed opposite me. He was still wearing his navy suit from his day with Brianna, immaculate as always, his dark hair styled so perfectly that I had to wonder if it was possible for him to ever look dishevelled.

"Aren't you concerned?" I asked.

"No." He shrugged. "I was the one who had him killed." He smirked darkly, and my heart rate picked up.

"Why?"

Erik pushed himself backwards onto the mattress and lay down on it, not answering.

I stood from the chair, moving forward and tentatively sitting next to him, his expression at ease as if having someone murdered was an entirely common occurrence for him.

"If you're going to reveal that to me, then you might as well tell me why," I pressed.

His gaze narrowed and he reached back to cup his head with one hand, making his jacket fall open to reveal the plane of his muscular body beneath his white shirt. "Chancellor Torin had been prying into my business for too long. I decided it was time to keep his nose out of things for good. Besides, he's not the only one who's been killed lately. My allies are being targeted, so I'm entitled to strike back."

My mouth grew dry as I took in that information. It was strange to know vampires had their own feuds and were even willing to kill each other. I didn't know how much I could ask and was even less sure if

Erik would give me any answers.

"Your allies?" I frowned.

"Those I sired," he said. "There is a certain allegiance that is formed between one's sire and their newly made vampire."

I wrinkled my nose. "Well, I'll add that to the long list of reasons why I never want to become one of you."

Erik snatched my arm, dragging me down beside him, and a breath jammed in my lungs as he rolled onto his side, his gaze cutting right into me. "So mouthy today."

My heart thundered as he lifted a palm and pushed a coil of hair from my face, and for some reason, I didn't push him away. His cypress scent was like a drug I was getting hooked on, but I'd always had strong willpower and I was determined not to get addicted. Especially not to a bloodsucker who had tied me to this very bed and declared me his prisoner.

My thoughts realigned and I asked my next question while he was still in the mood to offer me information. "Did you kill him yourself?"

The vampires were cold, undead creatures anyway, so I wasn't sure if it made Erik a murderer exactly.

He released a breath of laughter. "Of course not. I have people for that these days."

A stretch of silence dominated the space, and I decided it was best to move on from how many people he may have killed in his lifetime, because it was clear he held no objection to bloodshed. "Was this because of Faulkner? Did you find out who killed him?"

"Yes. And no, I haven't. Not specifically anyway," Erik growled, darkness invading his eyes, revealing the deadly creature who lived there. "I am certain Fabian was behind it, though. I sired Faulkner. He was loyal to me and no one else." He ground his jaw, observing me as if considering whether to continue. "Faulkner had been doing some work for me, gathering intel on Fabian's men. I suspect my brother found out and decided to send me a message. I, at least, had the courtesy to end Torin's life quickly. The way Faulkner was killed... it's clear Fabian wanted him to suffer."

I shuddered. I'd sensed something truly dark in Fabian and I was far from trusting him or any of the monsters in this place.

Dad had once said, *'A man who trusts a vampire is a fool. And a fool in this world will eventually be a dead fool'.*

If he could see me now, lying on a bed with one of them, he'd be appalled.

My stomach prickled with guilt, and I pushed myself upright, reminding myself of everything Erik had done up to this moment. I was just his little human confidant, and a pawn in his next play against his brother. It was political, barbaric, and I didn't want any hand in it, not least because if Erik was right about Fabian sending someone to kill his man, then my death could just as easily be in the cards if Fabian ever suspected I was working for his brother.

I moved to get up, but Erik caught my wrist, and I turned in surprise as he sat up beside me. "You're not having second thoughts on our plan, are you, rebel?"

"Have you released my father yet?" I asked sharply.

"I will when you fulfil your part of the deal."

"So you keep saying. But I've played along time and again, and you've done nothing to assure me you're going to stick to your word." I tried to tug my arm out of his grip, but he didn't let go.

"What's going on with you?" he growled.

"I just told you," I hissed.

"No, it's more than that. Something has you rattled."

My throat bobbed, thinking of Wolfe and wondering how the hell Erik could tell I was shaken. I'd thought my game face was pretty sound, but he could clearly sense the change in me.

"Is it Fabian? Did he do something?" he snarled.

"No."

"Then what is it?" he demanded, his fingers squeezing my wrist to the point of pain.

"You're hurting me," I breathed, and he glanced down at his hand on my skin, letting go and eyeing the red marks he'd left there.

"You're so damn breakable," he muttered, his brows drawing low.

"I'm human."

"I am well aware." His gaze moved to my neck for a fraction of a second, then he shoved to his feet, carving a hand over his face. "Did Fabian say something to you? Has he tried to twist you against me? Because if you dare betray me-"

He whirled around and I leapt to my feet in anger, cutting over him. "My family is on the line here. I wouldn't risk their lives for anything."

"Then trust me," he said fiercely. "I have already ensured your sister will be brought here once she is captured, and I will fulfil the rest of my promise once you have fulfilled yours. The moment your father leaves that blood bank is the moment you will have far less reason to do as I command."

"You could always release him and return him once my part is done," I suggested bitterly.

"It is not that simple. Your father broke the law, so his release will have to be done appropriately, subtly. Not to mention if Fabian gets wind of me bending his laws, he will likely grow suspicious."

"So how long am I supposed to wait? I can try and spy on Fabian, I can do all you ask, but where does it end? When are you going to deem my part done?"

"When you are married to him," he said in a severe tone that sliced into my bones.

Silence descended, and his jaw ticked as he watched my reaction unfold. I nodded stiffly, sensing the bars of my cage closing in once more, that fate inescapable.

He took a step toward me, his demeanour suddenly softening. "It's just politics."

I didn't look up at him as I folded my arms, realising how deeply I'd convinced myself it wouldn't have to come to that. But Erik wasn't offering me a path out of this life, that wasn't the deal. Marriage was one thing, but it was going to culminate in something far worse. Being sired. That was a destiny I was going to find a way to avoid come hell or high water.

"Fine," I murmured.

He slid his finger under my chin, tilting my head up to look at him. "I will protect you from him. If he is ever suspicious, or if he hurts you, you must tell me."

"And why would you do that?" I scoffed.

"Because I brought you here, and I have made a vow to keep you safe. That vow will endure even when you are his by law. I will not forget it."

"How very noble." I tsked. "Placing me in danger, then promising to protect me from it."

"I thought this whole thing would be simpler," he admitted, a frown creasing his brow. "I didn't expect to..." he trailed off.

"What?" I pushed, a heated energy rising in the space between us.

"Nothing," he said tightly. "This whole ritual is just fucking with my head."

"You're not the one who has to endure the company of monsters, who has to live with the memory of one of them kissing me," I said, wanting to hurt him after all he had done to me, and his features skewed in anger.

"I assure you, I have no further desire to lay claim to your hateful mouth, rebel. I have spent my day with a woman far more amenable than you, and her kisses tasted far sweeter than yours. I am almost tempted to take a wife after all."

My lungs stopped allowing in air and rage climbed through my skin that went beyond all reason. I didn't even know why those words hurt so much, but they somehow shredded me apart and left me raw.

I was hot all over from his words, embarrassed and angry, hurt and furious with myself for reacting to his venomous speech. I hated him. From the depths of my being to the edges of the earth. I fucking hated him.

My cheeks were betraying me, turning more scarlet by the second.

Erik started laughing, sensing it all from the rising of my blood to the fierce pounding of my heart.

"So you do care," he said, victory gleaming in his eyes.

My teeth ground together, and I cursed myself for reacting the way I was.

"Why *did* you kiss me, asshole?" I blurted, feeling like a toy being made to dance for his amusement.

He tilted his head to look at me, mirth still gripping his features.

"Why did you kiss me back?"

I gaped at him, having no answer and despising myself for it. Maybe I'd been drunk on some vampire pheromones he'd given off, but I knew that was just a lie I was trying to convince myself of. The truth was, I'd kissed him back because it had felt impossible not to kiss him. Like all the chaos in the world had suddenly felt a little easier to bear. Because for reasons that went beyond all sense, kissing one of the monsters who'd haunted me my entire life had felt like the clouds parting and letting in the sunshine. For just a moment, I had stolen something wild and free in that kiss, and I hadn't felt like a creature with no meaning. I'd felt seen, and wanted, and desired. But why did it have to be my captor who made me feel that way?

I didn't let any of that show on my face. And considering his mocking tone, I let a cold front drip over me and offered the words I hoped might cut him in the way he'd cut me. "You're designed to lure me in. I didn't know my own mind. Do you really think I'd want to kiss you if I had any choice in it?"

His jaw hardened. "I only wanted to tick an item off my bucket list anyway."

"What's a bucket list?" My eyes narrowed.

"Something for people who have hopes and dreams. You know, like item number one on *your* list would be pissing off a royal vampire. You can put a big tick next to that one, by the way."

I glowered at him. "Let's move back to the real issue here."

"Which is?" he asked coolly.

"That you can never kiss me again, Erik."

He barked a laugh, annoying me further. "Can I add an escape clause to that verbal contract?"

"Like what?"

"Well...I'll promise not to kiss you again *unless* you ask me to. How's that?"

"Ha," I spat. "Agreed, because that's never going to happen."

He smirked like he knew better. "If I actually tried to court you properly, you'd be begging me to kiss you in a matter of minutes. It would be so pathetically easy that I'm already bored by the mere prospect of it."

"You are so arrogant," I snarled.

"No, I'm simply stating facts. You're so flustered already; I could likely have you on that bed with my face buried between your thighs in less than two minutes if I really wanted you. And you'd be praising my tongue with every stroke against your needy clit."

"Fuck you." My clit betrayed me though, throbbing at the thought of him doing that to me. But my mind was well in control, and I sure as shit was never going to let that happen.

"I'm tired of this argument," he drawled. "Are you going to stay in here all night? Fabian's been waiting for you in the dining hall for nearly an hour now."

My lips parted at his words. "Why didn't you tell me?" The last thing I wanted to do was piss off Fabian, the vampire responsible for a thousand atrocities. Who knew how he might react if I stepped out of line too much? And wasn't I supposed to be pleasing him for the sake of Erik's fucking plans?

Erik shrugged. "I just did."

"God, you're such an ass." I hurried to the closet, grabbing a dark pink gown from its hanger and jogging into the bathroom to get changed.

I slid into the thing which had off-the-shoulder sleeves and fanned out at the bottom in a sort of glittery tail.

"Keeping Fabian waiting will only serve to turn him on," Erik called to me through the door, and it nearly swung into him as I stepped out of the room. It was a shame it missed. "And as much as I'm kind of disgusted with myself for being involved in that, I also know it is essential for him to fall for you."

He caught my arm, forcing me to twirl for him as he took in my dress, his grey eyes full of fire. "Passable."

He released my fingers, and I gave him an obvious look up and down as he'd done to me. "*Ass*able."

He bit down on the inside of his cheek. "You can be quite funny for a blood bag. Now, come on." He took hold of my arm and guided me toward the door. "Let's not make your date wait any longer."

I went to protest but my right forearm suddenly seared with pain and I gasped, rubbing the exact spot that Wolfe had stared at earlier. What the fuck…

Erik followed my gaze, and I quickly dropped my hand, biting down on my tongue.

"What's the matter?" he asked.

"Nothing," I lied quickly. "Just a static shock."

He raised his brows but didn't question me further. I didn't know what the hell was up with my arm but telling Erik about it was a terrible idea. That could lead to mentioning Wolfe, and if I did that, the general would make sure Callie didn't arrive at the castle in one piece. And I wasn't going to do anything that put her in danger.

We took the stairs down to the dining hall where I'd eaten on the first night. Instead of leaving me to it, Erik opened the door and guided me inside, keeping me closer than was really comfortable.

The large table had been removed from the room and four tables were set up around the space instead. Clarice sat at one opposite Hank, his dark eyes flicking to me as I arrived. Across from them was Miles, looking radiant in a white shirt and his sleek blond locks swept perfectly over the crest of his head. He was sat with Paige, who looked stunning in a sky-blue dress which hugged her curves, and beyond them, Brianna waited at a table alone, threading her fingers through her dark hair. Sitting at the final table was Fabian. He didn't look angry as I'd expected, but there was a definite tension in his expression that spoke of the animal lurking beneath his flesh.

Soft music filled the air, the tinkling notes creating a strangely romantic atmosphere that made this whole thing more ridiculous. Were we really supposed to believe these vampires were courting us in any real sense of the word? I just couldn't make sense of it.

Erik squeezed me tight, his eyes on Fabian as he pressed a kiss to my cheek, his mouth just a few inches from mine.

I fought the urge to cringe away, but I was back to being a puppet again, and he was the master of my strings.

"Enjoy your evening. I'll be watching," Erik murmured, then released me and made a beeline for Brianna, filling the room with his dominating aura.

I strode toward Fabian, and he rose from his seat as I arrived, his eyes sweeping over my dress before rising to my face.

"I thought you weren't coming," he growled, seeming offended.

"Sorry, I fell asleep," I said quickly, moving to his side and gripping his arm. Figuring I needed to make up for leaving him waiting, I tiptoed up and brushed a feather-light kiss to his lips. There it was. A commitment to this plan in plain sight that Erik couldn't deny.

Fabian slid his arms around me, pulling me closer and growling carnally against my mouth, making my heart shudder with the power of this beast. I twisted away before the kiss could descend into anything more heated and dropped into my seat with a bullshit smile that was all sunshine and daises. But inside, my emotions tangled into an intricate knot that I couldn't unravel.

I was rolling the dice every day with these devils, and I had to tread carefully to pull this off.

Fabian eyed me like a wolf, then slowly sank back into his seat. "That was an interesting surprise, love."

"It was hard to get you out of my mind once I returned to my bedroom." I gave him a sultry look that spoke of wicked deeds and his eyes sparked with intrigue.

"That so?" His gaze darkened.

I said nothing, but sucked my lower lip, and he sat forward in his seat, resting his elbows on the table.

Erik was suddenly at my side, having used his speed to make it over to us, and my heart leapt in alarm at his abrupt appearance.

"Fucking hell." I held a hand to my chest and Erik grinned, snatching my fingers and laying my hand down on the table.

"Apologies," he said, taking a small box from his pocket. "I forgot to give you this earlier." He leaned down, whispering to me but in no way quiet enough that Fabian wouldn't catch it. "I suppose we were too busy ripping apart that black dress for me to remember."

I blushed, even though we'd done no such thing, but Erik gave me a look of purest lust that made it so damn easy to picture.

"This is my time with Montana," Fabian growled threateningly. "Return to your own courtier, brother."

"Of course. Just as soon as I've given her this." He took a delicate silver bracelet from the box with a rectangular pendant hanging from it, the royal crest on one side and a crown on the other with the letter E within the marking. It was beautiful, and obviously the most valuable thing I had ever been given. The point of it eluded me, just another shiny trinket that was worn to impress vapid vampires, I guessed.

"Are you done pissing on your territory, Erik?" Fabian sniped.

"Quite." Erik stood up, tossing me a warm smile before walking back to his table with none of the haste he had used to come here.

Fabian snapped his fingers at a nearby guard and the woman leapt to attention like she had been stabbed in the ass with a fork. "The courtier will have her meal now."

My gaze trailed back to Erik as he took his seat at the table and promptly took Brianna's hand in his. My gut squeezed at the sight and ignited a fire in me I couldn't stamp out, and I berated myself internally.

A waiter arrived, placing a plate of steaming food under my nose, stealing all of my attention from the parade of assholes in the room. Pasta with some red sauce stared back at me, looking utterly mouth-watering. I happily seized the distraction and started eating, my new bracelet tinkling against the edge of the bowl. Damn, for all its pointlessness, it was stupidly pretty.

The waiter returned with chalices of blood for the vampires, and I fought hard not to wrinkle my nose as Fabian sipped on his.

A light laugh from Brianna caught my ear but I refused to look over at their table.

"Did you have a nice trip to the city?" I asked Fabian.

"Not particularly," he muttered. "Let's talk about something else. It's been a stressful day."

"How come?" I asked. *Come on, motherfucker, open up.*

"More murders in the city. Rebels probably, but maybe not." He ground his jaw, eyes swinging in Erik's direction.

"Rebels?" I breathed, excited by the prospect. Perhaps the royals weren't so secure after all if those rebels were capable of posing a real threat to them.

"Yes, troublemakers," he sighed. "But like I said, I don't want to talk about it."

Shit, how was I supposed to spy on a guy who was clearly never going to tell me anything? I guessed I had to try and build a bridge of trust between us first, but doing so made me seriously uncomfortable.

For Callie, for Dad. I have to do this.

"Okay...so tell me about you. What do you like to do when you're not running the country?"

Fabian relaxed back into his seat, seeming to enjoy having the spotlight on him. "Mostly, I train. I am adept with many weapons."

"Like?"

"Swords, bows, guns. You name it, I am an expert at it."

"I'd like to see that sometime," I said, fluttering my lashes as if I was impressed, though maybe it was a little overkill. His words served to remind me of how powerful these royals were. They could rip off my head with their bare hands, let alone what they could do to me with a weapon.

"If you choose me at the ceremony, there will be plenty of time for that," he said.

"Let's not get ahead of ourselves." I smiled flirtatiously and he regarded me hungrily, his eyes dropping to my new bracelet.

"What do you do in *your* spare time?" Fabian asked, and I realised I should have been prepared for this question.

I tried to think of a hobby I might have enjoyed back in the Realm if I hadn't had the general worry of getting through a day there. I supposed there was one thing I'd done regularly...

"I like walking," I said. *More like pacing the perimeter of my cage.* "And um...reading."

The few books Dad had managed to stow in our house had been read so many times they'd been falling apart. And I'd still struggled with deciphering some of the words, so it was definitely a stretch, but it was a half-truth I supposed.

A prickling feeling in my gut told me Erik was giving us his attention again, but I didn't look over at him.

"Uh huh." Fabian sipped on his blood and red stained his lips before he licked it away.

A pang of nausea made me shift in my seat, but he didn't seem to notice. He started telling me more about his training, and my eyes drifted around the room as he got into the incredibly dull detail of how he cleaned his favourite gun.

Clarice had moved into Hank's lap and my jaw went slack at the way he grinned at her, his hand stroking her thigh and the lust between them clear. What the fuck? He looked thoroughly under her spell, and I wondered if this was how I'd looked last night when Erik had laid his mouth on mine. Was she bewitching him? Or did Hank want this as I'd wanted Erik in that fleeting moment of insanity?

My gaze slid to Prince Miles who was laughing about something with Paige. Both of them seemed at ease, and I wondered if I was the only one left in this place who was still trying to hate these royals. I didn't know if we'd be getting any time together soon, but I wished I could have spoken to them to find out what they knew, what they were feeling. Were these smiles and laughs all fake? Or had the humans really been swayed to the whims of the royal vampires so quickly?

I let my eyes drift to Erik and my heart clenched.

He'd pulled Brianna up to dance and she smiled shyly as he taught her the steps, seeming enthralled by him. They held each other close as Erik guided her movements and his eyes flickered with light. Her fear of their kind had clearly turned to captivation. I didn't know if it was the royals' allure or if she just saw merit in this path now, a way to never return to the horror of the Realms. It wasn't like I could blame her for that.

My throat tightened and I couldn't seem to get in any air as I watched Erik and Brianna, transfixed. In the strangest way, they looked right together, but it was so difficult to marry this light-hearted version of Erik with the one I knew. He was clearly well versed in wearing a mask, and perhaps what I saw of him was just a deeper layer of falsity, the truth of him buried so deep that no one could ever dig it out. Perhaps at the heart of him there was just a bloodthirsty beast who would wield those around him in any way he could to gain power, and the world be damned.

"-broadswords, daggers. I can almost wield a slayer's blade if I wear a leather glove. But they still manage to devour my gear eventually..."

My eyes snapped back to Fabian, his words suddenly interesting me. "Slayer's blade? What's that?"

His rust brown eyes sparkled as he leaned in closer. "The slayers were a group of mortals who tried to oppose us."

My right arm tingled at his words and I nodded, hoping he'd go on, wanting to know more about the slayers after Erik had briefly mentioned their existence. Valentina had once been one of them, so what had made her join the vampires?

"We wiped them off the face of the earth." He grinned maliciously, his pride over that clear.

"Erik mentioned that Valentina was one of them," I said boldly, hoping he might shed some light on that snippet of information.

"Did he now?" Fabian growled. He took another sip of his drink, and I kept my eyes trained on him, willing him to go on. "She has made up for her crimes as a slayer. She came to us many hundreds of years ago and offered to help us defeat her kind."

"Why?" I gasped and Fabian's gaze narrowed.

"I suppose you'd have to ask her that."

Maybe I will...

"So the slayers...they could kill a vampire?" I asked, knowing I was on dangerous ground but desperate to learn more. Anyone who could kill vampires sounded like my kind of people.

"Yes, they had many defences against us. Their strength for one. And their blades were designed to hurt us. We couldn't even hold them without being burned by their runes. But none of that mattered in the end. Now the slayers are all dead." He took a sip of his blood as if toasting that fact.

A thrill buzzed through me. That *had* to be the type of blade Wolfe had given to me. But why?

As I recalled the feel of its warm hilt and the way it had seemed to whisper to me, a longing grew in me again. A dreamy feeling floated over me and I rose to my feet, suddenly filled with an urgent need to be somewhere.

"What are you doing?" Fabian asked and I jolted out of the strange sensation.

What *was* I doing? For a moment, I'd been snared by the desire to find that blade. Like it had possessed me in some way.

I eyed Erik as he swept Brianna around the room. "I thought we could dance," I said quickly to cover my tracks, quietly shaken by the power that had just fallen over me. "Can you teach me?"

"Of course." Fabian stood, moving promptly to my side and pulling me into his arms. "Place your hands like this," he instructed, resting one of my hands on his shoulder and keeping the other in his palm. He tugged me close, resting his free hand on my waist and caging me within the arc of his body.

"Follow my feet," he said, moving slowly as I got the hang of it.

I was clumsy and continually stepped on his toes, but he corrected me every time without anger and soon we were moving around the room at a slightly faster speed. I had to concentrate so much on the dancing that I was able to push the blade from my mind.

As Erik twirled Brianna past us by one hand, his eyes flicked to me. "Perfect," he told her. "You're clearly a natural. Unlike some."

I stepped on Fabian's foot again, cursing myself as I tried to mimic Brianna's grace, but lost my grasp on the steps again.

"You're a terrible instructor, Fabian." Clarice appeared beside him with her hand around Hank's.

"I'm doing just fine," Fabian said firmly, stopping me from knocking into his chest as he tried to guide my movements again.

"Stop pulling her around like a wolf with a bone." Clarice snatched me from Fabian's arms, wheeling me around and pushing me into the hands of Hank, leaving me dizzy.

He raised his brows in alarm. "I don't really dance, your highness," he told Clarice.

"You will when I'm through with you," she said, a ring of power to her voice. "Now take her waist."

Hank slid his arms around me, and the warmth of his skin was so nice in comparison to the vampires' icy touch. It reminded me of home, of living among my own kind. And it stoked a fire in me which I hadn't felt for a long time.

"Hi," I breathed.

"Hey, wild one." His soft eyes sparkled, and I gazed over his cheeks which were naturally flushed with human blood. He was so unlike the royals with their pearly skin and cold touch, and he was going through exactly what I was. Well, maybe not exactly, considering the political warfare I was wrapped up in, but still.

Clarice arranged our hands, moving around us at high speed. She took hold of my waist, stepping close behind me, and I immediately stiffened. "Relax, honey. You're as stiff as a corpse."

"At least I'm not as cold as one," I murmured, and her fingers slid from my waist, one glance back telling me those words had had an impact.

Her beautiful features flickered to reveal something akin to pain, then she was smiling brighter than before, and I wondered if I'd imagined it.

"Lead her through the steps I taught you, Hank," she directed.

I managed to relax a bit, able to concentrate more in the hands of Hank as we moved far slower than Fabian had allowed.

"That's it, now follow us." Clarice took hold of Fabian's arms, yanking him closer, and they started dancing at a slow but incredibly fluid pace.

"Come on then," Miles announced, jumping to his feet and sweeping Paige off her chair and into his arms, dipping her low and making her gasp in surprise. "This party is dead, let's bring some life to it."

"I'm surprised you weren't the first out of your seat," Erik remarked, and Miles gave him a boyish smile, twirling Paige under his arm and giving her little choice but to go along with it.

"I'm not sure even *I* can save this poor excuse for fun," he said, glancing over at Hank and I as we shuffled around in an awkward circle.

Bloodsucker or not, he had a point.

Miles twirled Paige all the way over to the large brown box which was playing music.

"Your highness, please!" she cried as he started thumbing through something on the box while his other hand continued to incessantly twirl her with enough force to keep her spinning like a tornado.

"Oh shit," Miles snorted, tugging her against his hip to stop her, and she dry retched like she was about to throw up. "You good there, Paige?"

She nodded, then retched again, and Miles patted her on the head like that would be any help at all.

"I'm going to take a seat, if you don't mind, Prince Miles?" Paige asked.

"Sure. Do your human thing. Get it all up or keep it all in. Whatever feels right, yeah?" Miles said she staggered away to take a seat, looking queasy.

Miles picked out a song, shooting Clarice a mischievous grin. "You remember this one, Clary? Woodstock, nineteen sixty-nine. We drank so much goddamn blood that night. Pure carnage."

"You thought you got high on that hippy," Clarice laughed, stepping away from Fabian to dance all on her own to the quick tune which was full of drums and passion. She started moving in a new rhythm to before, the sway of her hips and the way she was touching her own body something wholly primal and effortlessly hot.

"I *did* get high on that hippy," Miles insisted.

I frowned at Hank, who looked as disturbed as I did by the story, and we continued shuffling about like idiots, moving far too slow for the song that was now playing.

Fabian dropped back into his seat, manspreading his legs and sipping on his chalice of blood.

"Bet you can't teach them how to dance to rock music," he dared Clarice, and she smirked at the challenge.

"Brianna, Montana, copy me," she instructed, raising her arms in the air, one hand gently caressing its way down the opposite arm while she swayed and rolled her hips in subtle movements that looked so natural on her, yet I knew without even trying that they'd make me look like a potato attempting the limbo.

Brianna followed Clarice's instruction, rolling her hips and running her hands down her body as she followed the rhythm of the music, shutting her eyes as she lost herself to it. She was damn good too, but the vampires shared looks of amusement that told me this whole fucking thing was just another show for their entertainment.

"If you don't wanna move like that, try this," Miles said to me, leaping forward and swiping his hand across his body in a circle like he was playing an invisible instrument. He danced like a complete dickhead, shaking his head left and right, his styled hair coming loose to fall in his blue eyes. "Or this." He jumped up and down in little hops, hands in the air, then coming close to his body, then up in the air again.

Hank released my waist and bounced a bit on his toes, and I waved my hands in the vaguest of ways, sort of hitting the beat. It was pretty embarrassing to be honest.

"How's she treating you?" I whispered to Hank as everyone seemed distracted by the song.

"Fine," Hank admitted, and I gazed up at his dark features and warm eyes. "I thought this place would be hell, but it's not so bad here once you get used to it."

"Do you miss home?" I asked, a longing filling me for my family.

"I miss the people," he said. "Not so much the place."

"Agreed."

He tugged me closer, dropping his head by my ear. "Do the males treat you okay? I worry about the women here..."

"We're all in the same boat," I answered in confusion. "You're in as much trouble as us."

"I suppose..." His eyes filled with some knowledge that I sensed I was unaware of.

"Do you know something?" I whispered.

He nodded but before he could answer, strong hands dragged me away from him and I glanced up, finding Erik there glaring icily at Hank.

"May I cut in?" he snarled before shoving Hank roughly toward Brianna.

I gazed after him, desperate to learn what he'd been about to tell me.

"You're not making much effort, rebel. Look at Miles, this is his favourite song. You'll break his heart if you don't try to enjoy it."

"Boohoo," I said dryly, glancing over at Miles who was now on his knees, head thrown back, swinging around in violent circles. "Wow."

"Yeah," Erik muttered, then grabbed my hands, placing them both around his neck. He tugged me flush against him and started to move my body against his, forcing my hips to roll.

I managed to keep up with each of his prompts, but in the more intimate position, we were pretty much grinding on each other, and if that counted as dancing then it felt seriously wrong to do so with an audience. My flesh started to heat, and I glanced up at him, fingernails biting into the back of his neck as his large hand splayed over the base of my spine, keeping me tight against him.

"It was rude of you to cut in. I was enjoying talking to someone with a pulse," I said.

"I don't give a shit," he said.

I stamped on his foot with purpose.

"Oops," I said innocently, and his mouth hooked up at one corner.

"How clumsy of you," he muttered. "I suppose you can't teach grace."

I ignored him, spotting Miles back on his feet and dancing wildly with Clarice in the corner of my eye. He looked much more friendly than Erik; a constant smile was hung on his lips, and I wondered if spending time with him would be something of a break from pretending to seduce Fabian and dealing with Erik's confounding moods.

"There's a lot to be said for a girl who can dance," Erik said, his eyes shifting to Brianna who was moving fluidly in front of Hank, the two of them finding a rhythm together, even though Hank's steps were a little clunky.

"I must have skipped all those dance lessons back in the Realm," I said, trying not to notice Erik's obvious interest in her.

Erik tightened his hold on me, and his mouth dropped to my ear, his lips grazing the shell and making flames roar at the base of my spine.

"If you'd like a private lesson in my room later, you only need to ask, rebel."

I tried to push away from him, but he held on, fingers curling against my back and fisting in my dress. What was he playing at? Was he mocking me? If he was, I couldn't unravel his words enough to see the joke.

"I don't think dancing is my thing, but if you'd like to teach me how to drive a blade into a vampire's heart, that would be appreciated," I whispered.

He chuckled darkly. "That can be arranged."

My brows arched at his tone, and I leaned back to look up at him.

"Can it?" I asked hopefully.

"Of course, because it wouldn't matter if you were the finest swordswoman in the country, you still wouldn't be able to get a knife in my chest."

"At least let me try," I urged with a grin as dark as his own.

"Perhaps I will." He spun me away from him with one hand, then yanked me back against his body, making me stumble. He was so strong, I couldn't do anything but follow his lead, and suddenly I was crushed against him once more, our bodies moving in sync, and heat spilled through me at how good this felt, despite how wrong it was.

When the song came to an end, Fabian pushed out of his seat, his gaze locked on me as he strode this way.

Erik muttered quickly in my ear. "Come to my room at midnight. It's down the hall from yours, the one with the red door." He released me and I gazed at him with wild, baffled thoughts darting through my mind.

Fabian snared my hand and tugged me into the arc of his body.

He glowered at his brother and tension tangled with the air. "I suppose you heard about Chancellor Torin and the other murders in the city?" he inquired.

"Indeed. What a loss to the world Torin is," Erik remarked coolly.

"Yes, it is quite the blow. One of my finest chancellors has been reduced to dust. Do ensure your chancellors watch their backs, Erik. There is clearly a madman at large, so we must be vigilant."

"Thank you for the warning," Erik said with an arctic smile. "I have already been made aware after the brutal murder of my guard, Faulkner."

"Faulkner?" Fabian frowned. "How terrible."

"Quite," Erik bit out.

Fabian tugged me away and my heart stuttered as he led me straight out of the dining room into the low-lit corridor beyond.

His eyes lit as he pulled me along, and I smiled mischievously back, pretending I was excited about a moment alone with him, even though I felt the exact opposite.

"C'mere, love." Fabian tugged me close and I slapped my hand to his chest, pushing him back with a grin while my heart thrashed harder.

I had to commit to this now. Erik would keep his word to me if I seduced his brother, and I wouldn't shy away from leading him on. But there was no chance of me ever letting this heathen take me to his bed. He was the monster who ran the Realms, the purveyor of our torment, using us in any way he saw fit to provide his kind with an unending supply of blood.

Fabian leaned back against the wall, watching me with intrigue. "Have I earned that kiss now?"

God, I did not want to kiss him. An angry creature had reared its head inside me and it didn't want Fabian anywhere near it. But I had to do this for the sake of my family, even if I despised every second of it.

Closing my eyes, I gave in to the inevitable as I tiptoed up to press my mouth to his, his tongue pushing between my lips in lazy strokes. I bit it on instinct, and he growled like he liked that, his hands roaming up my sides. I tried to relax into it, to let him think I enjoyed it. I took hold of his arms, pulling closer as his fangs grazed my lip and danger dug its claws into me.

It was just a kiss. But it felt like more than that, like a promise of what was to come. This creature owning me in marriage and beyond. He was the ticket to my family's freedom, and I was the price, but how far was I going to have to fall to secure it?

I pulled back when I was sure this had gone far enough, leaving my lips frozen from the icy touch of his.

"Come to my room," he said, gripping my hand, his brown eyes full of sin.

"No," I said immediately, pulling back and quickly recomposing myself. "I like making you wait."

He growled, dropping his mouth to my neck, and I wanted to rip his lips off as he trailed them along my collar bone, but I tilted my head to the side instead, offering it up to him.

"The party is over, brother. It is time you returned to your quarters. I shall escort Montana to hers," Erik's voice sliced the air to ribbons, and I opened my eyes, finding him walking through the shadows like a demon sent straight for the depths of hell. Brianna scampered along at his side, looking to me with worry in her gaze, glancing from Erik to Fabian.

"Fuck off, Erik," Fabian warned, throwing his brother a cold look. "Montana is clearly desperate to remain in my company."

The arrogance of this asshole was unreal.

"Actually, I'm pretty tired." I took the opportunity to slip out of Fabian's arms and half jogged toward the staircase.

I glanced back to find Erik barring Fabian's way, not letting him follow me as I hurried upstairs. A vicious snarl said a fight might be about to break out, but hell if I was gonna be there to be a casualty in it.

I barely took a breath until I entered my room, pressing a hand to my chest where my heart pounded an unsteady rhythm beneath my fingers.

How was I going to go through with this plan? If I picked Fabian at the ceremony, I was going to have to find a way to run before I ever had to marry him. Because there was no chance I was ever going to the bed of the man who was responsible for running the Realms and caging my kind in squalor.

I shut my eyes, despising this whole ritual I'd been wrapped up in. It was sick. And I could see my breaking point cresting on the horizon, because I could go along with this while nothing vital was taken from me. But at some point, I wasn't going to get the option, and it was a price I hadn't even considered I'd have to pay.

The clock on the wall told me it was nearly ten. Two hours until Erik wanted me to go to him.

I shuddered, knowing no good could come of that. Perhaps he simply wanted to lay his claim on me before my body belonged to his brother, but I'd die before I let either of them have me.

I'm staying here until I'm forced out of this room again.

With that, I pulled off my dress hard enough to rip it, then pulled on the silken pyjamas tucked under my pillow. I sat on the bed with my legs curled to my chest, letting my mind slip away to a place no one could find me. Dreams of anywhere else stole me from this castle and offered me some semblance of peace. Or at least numbness.

Midnight came and went, but I didn't try to sleep, remaining in my bubble of false safety, finding it harder than usual to stay within it.

I finally crawled under the covers and rolled over with my back to the door, trying to figure out what to do, hoping an answer would come to me between the fantasies of my mind and the darkness of my reality.

At some point, the door quietly opened, and I shut my eyes, pretending to be asleep.

Get out of my room, Erik.

I couldn't hear him moving, but I was certain he was closing in on me, and my skin prickled as he slid back my covers. I continued to keep up the pretence of sleep, willing him to go the fuck away and get the damn hint.

Something warm brushed my arm. My eyes flew open as heat skittered through my veins, and a strangely familiar voice entered my mind. *Nightmare.*

"Slayer," a cruel female voice hissed, and I rolled over with a bolt of adrenaline telling me to move fast.

My eyes locked on the vampire, her expression as frosty as winter as she lunged for me. I wheeled the other way in terror, trying to escape her reaching hands, but she leapt onto the bed, yanking me backwards and throwing her leg over me so she straddled my hips.

I went to scream, but she slammed a palm down over my mouth, silencing me and crushing me to the mattress beneath her. "The royals will find you gutted in your bed with a slayer's blade in your hand and they will praise my name for assisting them."

Fear scored a path through my chest, and I thrashed furiously, clawing at her hand which felt glued to my mouth.

The vampire took a short knife from her hip, lifting it up, ready to drive it into my heart.

I sank my teeth into her hand before bringing up my fist and punching her in the ribs as hard as I could. She didn't react, my attacks nothing more than moths dashing themselves against her stone exterior.

That deep and warming voice filled my head again, as if coming from the golden blade that lay discarded on the mattress.

Fight or die.

I grabbed the gleaming weapon, the blade singing the name Nightmare in my head once more. It flared with heat, the hilt kissing my palm, urging me on. With a blow that sent a tremor down the length of my arm, I stabbed her in the side with all of the strength I possessed.

She screeched in rage, jerking backwards so the knife slid from her skin, bright red blood spilling over the crisp sheets, giving me another window to strike. It was like the blade was telling me what to do, whispering encouragements while my mind was in a frenzy from seeing a vampire wounded by my hand.

I didn't falter, knowing I only had a mere heartbeat before she recovered from the shock of my attack. I reared upright, raising Nightmare, knowing there was only one way this could end. With her death or mine.

The vampire grabbed my throat with inhuman speed and threw me hard across the room. I wheeled through the air, stomach lurching before I hit the window shutters with an almighty crack, then slammed to the floor.

My breath was knocked from my lungs and pain jarred through me, my grip on Nightmare the one focus of my thoughts. Splinters of wood showered down around me from the broken shutters, and I gazed up at my attacker. Horror seized my heart as she approached me a little more cautiously, still clasping the wound on her side.

"I am a member of the royal legion," she hissed. "If you scream and call your pretty prince to you, he will only punish you for striking at one of his own."

I shoved to my feet among the shattered wood, raising Nightmare and pointing it right at her. But I didn't scream, doubt crawling through me from her words. Erik had warned Wolfe not to touch me before, surely he would punish this creature if I yelled for help?

That very word got stuck in my throat though. Screaming like a hungry babe in need of sustenance didn't appeal at all. In fact, I realised I wanted this fight, like the call of it was thick in my blood. Like I had been made to stand here and face my enemy.

Nightmare burned with the heat of the sun, willing me into the fray, and perhaps it was why I wanted this. Some strange spell cast upon this weapon to bewitch me into believing I was capable of winning. *Stand and fight. End this creature of darkness.*

The vampire came at me, wielding her blade and slashing it through the air this way and that. She was tall and terrifying to behold, her dark hazel eyes promising my death. I surely had no chance against her, but Nightmare seemed to have other ideas, and I was starting to believe it.

The vampire lunged at me in a sudden movement, and I raised Nightmare, feinting left, then ducking the oncoming swipe of her knife. I somehow got beneath her guard, but her blade grazed my neck just enough to draw a sliver of blood.

Nightmare sung a tune that guided my hand right to the place it wanted to be. I rammed the dagger upwards, my arm juddering from the strength it took to see it through, and the blade sliced through skin and bone as if she was as human as me.

A look of horror crossed her face as she realised Nightmare was buried deep between her ribs. With a choked cry, her face crumbled, and her entire body began to shatter, bit by bit turning to dust and bursting into ash at my feet, even the blood which had splattered against my sheets fell to nothing but dirt in the face of her demise.

Her blade hit the floor with a heavy thunk and the sound echoed through my head with a finality that left me rooted to the spot. She was gone. Dead. Dust.

I had done that. I had killed an unkillable creature. And she had turned to nothing. Well, not quite nothing. But she was hardly coming back from a pile of soot.

"Holy shit," I breathed, turning Nightmare over in my hand in disbelief.

The blade purred like a cat with a fresh kill at its paws, and I did a mental sweep of my body, half expecting to find myself mortally wounded.

A line of blood trickled down my neck from where her blade had nicked me, but apart from some bruising to my back, I was miraculously okay.

I gazed down at the dark robes of the vampire which were covered in the debris of her crumbled body, my victory tempered by disbelief. If only Dad and Callie were here to see this…

My forearm flared with pain, and I spotted a red mark growing there in the shape of a blade. The words of my attacker echoed through my mind. She had called me slayer and declared Nightmare a slayer's blade, but if she was right, what did that mean for me?

Something swelled inside my chest, a mixture of triumph and strength creating a potent high. Nightmare seemed to praise my name, singing our victory, but just as a smile lifted the corner of my lips, I was delivered a sharp dose of reality.

"Rebel?!" Erik's booming voice carried from the hallway.

"Oh fuck," I gasped, staring from Nightmare to the crumbly vampire flakes on the floor.

Hide me. The blade's voice flared in my mind, and I knew it was a damn good idea to obey.

I had less than a second to act as I tossed Nightmare under the bed and threw myself down onto the shattered pieces of wood on the floor. I shut my eyes, pretending I'd been knocked out and shooting a silent prayer to whatever holy being might exist out there in the universe to give me a break.

The door hit the wall as it opened and Erik heaved me into his arms a moment later, laying me on the bed.

"Montana, wake up," he growled, running his finger near the cut on my neck. It hit me that this was the first time he'd called me by my name.

I blinked awake, fear rolling through me at how he was about to react.

"What happened?" he demanded, glancing at the remains of the vampire and the broken shards of wood from the window shutter.

I shook my head, not knowing how I was ever going to explain myself. But I had to get one thing straight at least.

"She attacked me," I breathed. "She chased me over there and I think she...impaled herself on the broken wood."

Shit, did that even sound plausible?

Erik's grey eyes flooded with confusion. He was shirtless, his muscles tense and his skin cool against mine where his hands gripped my arms. "She *attacked* you?"

"Yes," I confirmed. "I was sleeping. She came in and..."

I feigned a tremble as if I was oh so scared. But honestly, I felt invigorated. I'd just done the undoable, something I had dreamed of a thousand times over. My dad and I had invented a whole game dreaming up scenarios about killing the vampires, but never once had I considered it was possible for *me* to do it.

Erik moved to the vampire's robes, sifting through them as if looking for something. Giving up, he turned back to me and my gaze dipped to his bare chest.

Scars marred his arms and a crescent-shaped one was stamped on his midriff, the marks silvery and unlike any scars I had seen before. I dragged my eyes up from the hard lines of his abs and the way his sweatpants hung low on his hips to reveal a deep V of tapered muscle diving beneath them. The moment I met his furious gaze again, I knew trouble was coming my way like a dark storm.

"Who the fuck would do this?" he snarled, raking a hand through his hair, messing up his usually perfect look.

"I don't know," I whispered, dropping a hand to my forearm and covering the mark there. "Would Fabian send-" I started, but he cut me off abruptly.

"No. Why would he?" Erik snapped. "He doesn't know anything."

What would Erik think if he knew I'd killed that vampire? And with a *slayer's* blade no less. He might perceive me as a threat, one he would want to crush as swiftly as possible.

"Stay here," he muttered, and I nodded as he sped from the room.

Moments later, Erik returned with a strange hand-held machine with a tube at one end. He turned it on and it made a loud whirring sound that took me by surprise. Erik moved to the vampire's ashy remains, sucking them up with the object, the dust swirling around in a compartment at the top of it.

I gazed at him in alarm as he worked, cleaning up every scrap of the dead assassin just like that. When the dust was gone, he gathered the vampire's robes into a linen bag from my closet, holding them tight in his fist.

Turning to me with his jaw pulsing, he said, "Don't speak about this with anyone. I'll deal with it."

I nodded firmly, then pointed to the object in his hand. "What is that?"

He glanced down at it. "A vacuum cleaner." He cleared his throat, heading to the door as I tried to place the term, wondering if my father had ever mentioned it. "I'll be back soon."

He exited and I blew out a breath, my heart drumming against my ribcage and refusing to slow. I'd killed a vampire. A fucking vampire.

I ran my thumb over the mark on my arm, sensing it was important somehow, linked to that blade. It was definitely a bad idea to let Erik see it.

Heading to my closet, I grabbed out a sweater, tugging it on to hide the mark, but that wasn't going to be enough long term. I was going to be made to wear those fine dresses again, and then what would I do?

The vampire's voice filled my head again. *Slayer.*

The term was plain enough. Slayer meant killer.

My thoughts turned to General Wolfe, certain he had to be behind this. It was too much of a coincidence that he'd clearly been accusing me of that exact same thing. So he had…what? Sent that bitch to assassinate me?

I sensed Nightmare's presence in the room like another heart beating in my chest, and the air in my lungs thickened. I wanted to reach for it, to reunite with that warmth and let it whisper inside my mind. It should have frightened me, but it was excitement I felt. And a burning curiosity to learn of its origin, of why it felt so right to hold it in my hand.

Erik finally returned, and I prayed he wouldn't be able to sense the blade in the way I could, the heavy pulsing of its presence a dead giveaway.

Locking the door, he turned to me with an anxious look.

"What did she say to you?" he growled, his rage evident, and at least it seemed the blade wasn't drawing his focus.

"Nothing," I lied.

His jaw locked tight as he marched into the bathroom, returning with a damp washcloth. He dropped down onto the bed, reaching out to my neck.

"Here," he clipped, and just like he had done when I skinned my knee, he gently wiped the blood from my skin, frowning all the while. I couldn't even feel the pain, the adrenaline in my veins still keeping it at bay.

"I can do it." I reached for the cloth, but my hand only found his, the cold touch of his skin against my palm making my heartbeat stutter.

"I can do it," he said in a tone that told me he was in no mood to be tested, and for once, I didn't feel the urge to push back at him.

"This should never have happened," he muttered to himself. "I'll get to the bottom of it, I assure you. Someone in my household has betrayed us. No one else would be able to gain access to the castle. If only I'd seen the vampire's face... Do you remember what she looked like?"

"She had dark hair and was tall with hazel eyes," I said, trying to remember anything else about her.

He nodded stiffly, that information obviously not enlightening him. "Was she Elite?"

I thought about it, the way she had moved much slower than Wolfe, and certainly not as fast as a royal could move. "I don't think so."

"Alright. It is best if I stay with you tonight," Erik announced.

My throat tightened at the thought of trying to sleep with him so close by. "No."

"It almost sounded like you just said no to a prince of the New Empire. Try again." He bared his teeth at me, fangs glinting in a threat.

"Alright," I said, and his eyebrows arched. "No, thank you, prince of the New Empire."

His jaw ticked and he tossed the washcloth across the room where it landed in my clothes hamper. "I did not ask for permission, rebel. I will be staying to guard my property regardless of what my property thinks of that."

"Because I'm special?" I pushed, ignoring the shitty comments about me being his property and realising there might just be a link between my importance to him and the fact that I'd almost been killed. "Or my blood is?"

His eyes sharpened on me. "Nothing is more important than my sanity, and you are making quite the effort at cracking it. If you had come to my room like I'd asked, this wouldn't have happened."

"I didn't want to be manipulated anymore," I said coldly.

Erik frowned. "I wasn't trying to manipulate you."

"That's all you've been doing since I met you, Erik. I'm tired of it already, and I'm scared of what will happen when I choose Fabian at the ceremony when my part of the deal is done and you no longer have any interest in what happens to me. I don't want to be his wife, I don't want to end up in his bed. But that's what this leads to, isn't it?" I spat.

Erik's brows drew together. "I know this is difficult…"

I shoved his solid chest with a snarl. "You don't know. You have no idea what this is like. You're whoring me out to your brother and I can't stand it, and all I want from you is help for my family. But you're going to make me do the unspeakable to earn that priv-"

He pressed a hand to my mouth to halt me, his skin like ice against my lips.

"I *know*," he reiterated, his eyes boring into mine. "I didn't expect things to get this complicated."

I leaned away from his cool palm, my tongue heavy. "It's not complicated for you. You can dangle my father's freedom over my head, and you know I'll do anything to help him. What's complicated about that?"

His Adam's apple rose and fell, but he didn't answer.

Despite his cold skin, heat seemed to radiate from his body, and my eyes travelled over the faint silvery scars on his torso.

He turned away and I caught his arm. "What aren't you saying?"

He sighed. "I've become slightly, *minusculey*...attached to you, rebel."

I released a small, empty laugh. "How kind of you to care so little about me."

"I am a royal prince and I do not take wives or bed unwilling humans. So have some faith in me that I won't allow my brother to hurt you."

"That makes you trustworthy? That's a pretty low bar for decency," I hissed. "I have zero faith in you, because this is all *your* doing. So you can sit here and make pretty promises and try to convince me you have my best interests at heart, but it's all just bullshit to try and make me cooperate. And if you think I'm too stupid to see that, then maybe you need to wake up and look harder at the humans you've enslaved. We're not mindless fools and we never were."

I shoved him again and he caught my arm, tugging me closer so our mouths were barely an inch apart. "I'm covering up a vampire's death in your quarters, rebel. Is that not enough to make you trust me?"

"I'll never trust a bloodsucker." The words were my dad's. *Rule number one in this world: never trust a bloodsucker, little moon.*

"Then we're at a stalemate again." He stood, releasing me suddenly and moving to the chair before dropping onto it. "Go to sleep so I can be at peace," he commanded.

"If staying awake brings you torment, I will gladly go without sleep for days," I muttered.

Erik came at me like a flash of lightning, shoving me down onto the bed and rolling me away from him with so much strength I was little more than a stuffed toy being tossed around in a hurricane. He locked his arms around me, yanking me back against his chest and hooking a leg over both of mine to stop me from moving.

"Close your eyes," he ordered, a cruel humour lacing his voice. "And pray the gods take you swiftly into sleep before I get the urge to send you into a slumber you won't return from."

"Your death threats kind of fall flat after you risked your ass to cover for me," I bit at him, wriggling against his arms, but I was trapped good and tight. "Fine, I'll sleep. Just get your frosty paws off of me."

He didn't let go, if anything holding me tighter, and my body heated from how close we were to each other.

"You gave up the right to sleep soundly when you back-talked me," he said. "So you'll sleep like this, caged by me as the prisoner you are. That's how you prefer it, isn't it? Poor little rebel imprisoned by the monster."

"Fuck you," I hissed, jerking my shoulder back against his - for all the good it did me.

His muscles firmed as he fell quiet, letting me kick and fight and curse him until eventually I was forced to give up.

I released a slow breath and willed my heart rate to slow down, knowing the sound of it was bouncing its way to his bat ears. We lay like that with the silence thick and nothing but my frantic heartbeat and the hollow silence of his chest for company.

I closed my eyes and his arms softened around me just a little, allowing my body to relax.

As the minutes trickled into an hour, I hated myself for sinking back into the hard arc of his body. His dark presence followed me into my dreams, but there was something strangely comforting in it. And what should have been a horror show waiting for me in sleep became a twisted fantasy instead where his mouth raked against my burning hot skin and I gave myself to the power of this beast, tasting the sins on his flesh and wanting to know the reason for every one of them.

CALLIE

CHAPTER SIX

The horses' hooves clip-clopped loudly along the hard tarmac as we headed down an old highway into a small town. I could feel Magnar's unease coiling through his rigid posture where he was pressed against me on the stallion's back.

The tension between us was near a breaking point, the desire to murder him still wholly present in my mind though my body kept having other ideas while pressed against his. The tension between us was near breaking point, the desire to murder him still wholly present in my mind, though my body kept having other ideas while pressed against his. It was infuriating, sinful bastard that he was, but I wouldn't allow him the knowledge that he had any effect on me whatsoever.

Night was drawing in quickly and we still hadn't found a place to make camp. Though the horses had sped our journey south, we now had the added difficulty of finding a shelter big enough to house them as well as ourselves.

Although Magnar had wanted to avoid the town when we'd first spotted it, I'd convinced him otherwise. The area we'd been travelling through had held few houses, and the dilapidated town was the first real sign of anything from the old civilisation that we'd seen in a long time.

I had the feeling that it was our only chance to find a building large enough to house us for miles around, and Magnar had begrudgingly agreed. Besides, we needed supplies; food and water most of all. My growling stomach was a constant reminder of that.

This settlement was the largest group of buildings we'd come across so far that hadn't been destroyed by the bombs in the Final War. Dead leaves had gathered along the sidewalks, husks of rotting cars blocked the streets. The whole place screamed its unnatural silence at me. It should have been full of life but instead, it was abandoned and eerie.

A raven cawed from the top of a lamp post, and I flinched as I stared up at it with mistrust.

"Is that one of their creatures?" I asked in a whisper as the bird's gaze followed our progress along the street.

"No. Its soul is clean," Magnar replied, following my gaze, the rough scratch of his jaw brushing against my cheek with the movement. "When you've seen as many familiars as I have, you'll be able to recognise them easily. They don't move or react naturally, and their eyes shine silver in the light. You see how the vampires can make you mistrust everything though?"

I nodded. The more I learned about the vampires, the more reasons I found to fear them.

"They have used that kind of fear to control people for a long time, corralling or captivating them as they see fit. They are manipulative, devious things, born of death and seduction, with nothing but lies spilling from their lips," he said roughly, and I almost found myself glad of his arms banded around me, the powerful creature at my back likely the only man in existence capable of attempting to stand in defiance of them.

As the cluster of concrete boxes grew around us, a feeling of unease started to settle on me too. In such an enclosed space with so many buildings to hide within and between, it was hard not to imagine eyes peering at us from every darkened corner.

I placed a hand on Fury, but the blade was quiet, as though it was sleeping. That was the best reassurance I could get that no vampires lurked nearby, but I still felt on edge.

"How were such places created?" Magnar murmured behind me, and I twisted in his arms to get a look at him. His brow was furrowed with either concern or confusion, and I wasn't sure which worried me more.

"You mean the buildings?" I asked, following his gaze to an old sign which was shaped like a giant brown cowboy hat.

I tried to sound out the words splashed across it, but the swirling yellow text was illegible to me with my limited reading capabilities, and I couldn't make out anything after the big capital R.

"They're so…square." Magnar continued to frown at them like the buildings themselves offended him with their uniform angles alone, and I smiled.

"I think they used machines to make the bricks and stuff." I'd had little success in explaining much about anything mechanical to Magnar. My own understanding of electricity and machinery was limited as it was, and he'd had nothing like them in his own time to draw comparison to. It was easy to forget just how strange the world must have been to him. He'd found himself plucked from the reality he'd grown up in and dumped into the ruins of a civilisation beyond anything he ever could have imagined.

He didn't ask anything else, but I could sense his continued unease.

"What about that?" I asked, pointing to a huge building with heavy metal shutters barring the windows. The sign above the door was written in clearer script, and I frowned at it as I forced the letters to become words. "Su-per mar...market; I think that's a store where they sold food."

"This is where they held the market?" Magnar asked, grasping onto the word that made sense to him.

"I think so. Maybe we'll get lucky and find something they left behind before the Final War," I added hopefully. We'd eaten the last of our supplies that morning and my stomach was pitifully empty. Hunger was a feeling I was well used to, but it was one thing that I hadn't had to deal with since my escape from the Realm and I hadn't missed it.

Magnar guided the horses into the concrete space before the supermarket and dismounted in front of the glass doors, his warmth abandoning me as I was left balancing precariously where I was. He led the stallion to a metal post and tied the reins before turning back to help me.

"I've got it," I said firmly, though as I peered down at the ground, it seemed much further away than before.

"Alright then." Magnar folded his arms and leaned against the wall, watching as I tried to figure out how I was supposed to get down.

I pursed my lips, refusing to admit to this being any kind of mistake as I assessed the fall. It wasn't like I hadn't jumped from higher ledges while exploring the Realm. And I certainly wasn't going to be asking for help now that I'd refused it.

There was nothing for me to hold onto to help lower myself down aside from the stallion's mane, but I felt like pulling on the animal's hair might have been asking for more trouble than it was worth.

Shit.

I was just gonna have to rip the bandaid off and hope for the best.

I swung my leg over the horse's neck somewhat awkwardly, almost slipping from his sleek back as I did so, my heart jerking with fright as my balance wavered before I somehow righted myself and ended up sitting sideways on him, looking down at the drop below.

I was pretty sure Magnar had been facing the horse as he dismounted, but it was far too late for that now, so I drew in a breath and pushed myself off.

I stumbled as I hit the ground, staggering forward a few steps, my arms wheeling to try and save myself, and I cursed as the concrete loomed before me.

Magnar caught me before my face could hit the ground, his hands shifting the material of my coat up and brushing against the skin of my lower back as he set me on my feet again, a snort of amusement breaking from him.

"Graceful," he commented, a spark of energy dancing across my skin at the roughness of his touch, but he released me just as quickly.

"I had it," I grumbled, righting myself while refusing to thank him.

"Clearly," he agreed, the sarcasm in his voice thick.

I scowled at him and tucked a strand of my long, golden hair back behind my ear. I hadn't braided it since I'd washed it in the river, and I was enjoying the feeling of leaving it loose. In the Realm, I'd always been afraid of it attracting attention, but now that I was free, I could do what I liked with it.

Magnar pulled Tempest from his back and cautiously approached the glass doors to the building. I followed his lead and released Fury, but the blade slept on, unaware of any threat nearby. I wanted to ask Magnar if I could rely on the blade's assessment of the situation, but he was already pushing the door open.

I stayed several steps behind him as we entered the store and the massive space opened up around us. There were aisles and aisles of shelves lining what looked to be one huge, open area. Magnar moved away to check that the shop was clear, but my gaze fell on something which stopped me from following.

I moved forward with a smile pulling at my lips as I recognised the picture on the wrapper. *Chocolate.* A whole shelf was stacked full of it, just waiting to be devoured.

I grabbed a bar as long as my forearm and jogged after Magnar into the depths of the store.

I hurried down the aisle I thought he'd chosen and upped my pace in excitement to share my find with him, wanting him to know that I'd been the one to feed us and that I wasn't just some dumb asshole who knew nothing about horses.

Halfway along the aisle, I paused as a rack of lightbulbs and flashlights caught my eye. I knew Magnar had never seen electricity in action and my vague explanation of it couldn't compare to seeing it for himself. Besides, I may have had no experience in climbing off of horses, but he might just shit himself at the magic light stick when it appeared. Revenge called my name like a pretty little demon in my ear, and I wasn't strong enough to resist her call.

I shoved Fury back into its holster and grabbed a flashlight from the display, ripping off the cardboard packaging before starting after Magnar again.

But as I jogged out at the far end of the aisle, a huge body lurched from the darkness, tackling me and lifting me off of my feet before propelling me around and pressing me against the wall. A cry of fear escaped my lips, my finds falling from my grip as I lurched for Fury in a panic.

But before I could get near the blade, strong fingers banded around my wrist, pinning it in place beside my head, his other hand gripping my throat, the scent of oak and leather enveloping me.

"Have you forgotten everything you learned about stealth already?" Magnar growled as he held me still.

My heart pounded with a whole new set of emotions as I realised this was simply more of his bullshit and not an attack at all. It was almost pitch black this far from the doors and I could only make out the outline of his silhouette, so it was hard to tell precisely how pissed off he was, but as I aimed a knee for his balls, I was fairly certain I was about to find out.

Magnar blocked my strike with his own knee, forcing it between my thighs to stop me from doing it again, a breath of amusement escaping him as he leaned into me.

"Now what, drakaina hjarta?" he purred, an offer in those words which made my pulse riot.

I tried to force my heart rate to slow as I relaxed, knowing it was only him.

"You tell me," I replied, his grip flexing on my throat. "You're the one who keeps finding reasons to touch me like this."

"Were you hoping I might touch you differently? Are you used to tenderness and sweet declarations, Callie?"

My name on his lips was its own brand of unholy, but I simply swallowed, seeking out his eyes in the dark and shaking my head as best I could with the way he was holding me.

"I'm used to far worse than some bastard manhandling me whenever the mood strikes him. If there's some further point to this, then spit it out, if not, feel free to stop dry humping me at any point," I sneered.

Magnar breathed a laugh, his thigh pressing more firmly between my legs, making fire race through my core. The move was as intentional as the way his fingers flexed around my throat, but he released me all the same.

"So you simply forgot everything I told you about practicing stealth?" he pushed, making my hackles raise.

"No. But Fury doesn't think there are any vampires nearby and I found us food," I stated.

Magnar sighed like he was losing patience with a petulant child, and I folded my arms as I leaned back against the end of the aisle.

"You shouldn't rely on that blade entirely. Your own senses mustn't be ignored in favour of blind trust in that weapon. The runes help it to sense when a vampire is close, but they found ways around the runes in my time. When the Belvederes realise I'm back, I'm sure they will remember some of the tricks they used to use on us."

"Okay. Lesson learned." I didn't bother to point out the fact that if any powerful vampires were that close to me, then I didn't stand a hope in hell of escaping them anyway. It seemed like a moot point. "Are you going to thank me for the food or..."

I stooped down to retrieve my mega bar of chocolate, then ripped open the wrapper and broke off a square of it.

Magnar eyed the processed sugar like it was a turd on a rock, so I shrugged and pushed it between my own lips, perfectly content to eat the lot for myself if he would rather go hungry.

My stomach growled impatiently, and a moan rolled up the back of my throat as the heavenly taste consumed my attention. I let my eyes fall closed to appreciate it better, sighing with contentment and pushing another square between my lips.

"You must be very hungry to make such noises over whatever that is," Magnar grunted.

I opened my eyes, finding his heated gaze locked on me and wondering how he might like a taste of his own games.

"See for yourself," I offered, breaking off a small square for him – no need to offer up too much of my prize to the asshole after all.

I held it out, but Magnar still didn't move, so I sighed dramatically and stepped forward.

I lifted the square of sugary goodness to his mouth, and he arched an eyebrow at me in surprise as my fingers brushed against his lips.

"Don't tell me the big, bad warrior is afraid of trying something new," I taunted, a dare in my eyes.

He expelled a harsh breath and reluctantly accepted it, my fingers grazing against his lips for longer than was really necessary as I placed the square of chocolate on his tongue, smiling sweetly at him and making his eyes narrow in suspicion.

As he started chewing, his muscles relaxed and some of that heated tension loosened in his limbs.

"Are you going to moan for me now?" I teased.

"You'd have to do better than that, drakaina hjarta," he replied. "But I'll admit it's good. What is it?"

"Something they used to eat before the war. It's called chocolate. I couldn't have you thinking everything about this time is bad."

"It isn't *all* bad," he replied evenly, his eyes raking over me. "Not that I've ever been much opposed to bad anyway." A tingle ran along my spine at the implication. He looked away from me, towards the front of the store. "I should bring the horses inside and place the wards. It's nearly nightfall."

"There was something else," I added quickly before he could leave.

I grabbed the flashlight from the floor and flicked it on, shining the beam directly into his eyes.

Magnar stepped back suddenly, jerking away from the light.

"By the gods," he cursed, drawing a knife from his belt so fast that I barely had a moment to realise scaring him might have been a terrible fucking idea, especially if I ended up skewered for it.

I barked a laugh, then bit my lip, backing away from him as I swung the flashlight from side to side, the beam arching around us. "It's just an electric light. Like I told you, remember?"

"That is unholy," he growled, pointing at it with his blade like he still planned on stabbing the thing.

"This is the new world, old man. And you might want to get used to it before a vampire ends up defeating you simply by turning on the lights." I turned the flashlight off again and held it out to him, my revenge tasting even sweeter than the chocolate.

Magnar eyed it suspiciously, clenching his jaw before holding his hand out to accept it.

He turned the flashlight over in his hand and I leaned closer, placing my finger on the button. He watched as I pressed it and the light came on again. Only the faintest flicker in his gaze gave away how disconcerting he found the little device, but I didn't hate putting him on the back foot for once. He lifted it higher, shining it along the closest aisle before switching it off.

"I'm sure this will be useful," he said eventually, though his tone made me think he'd sooner throw it away than keep it.

A smile pulled at my lips, and I reached out and took it from him. "I can look after it if you're worried it might bite you in your ungodly ass or something."

Magnar caught my wrist before I could snatch it away from him and brushed his thumb across my slayer's mark. "If you're going to mock me, you might want to remember that I can put you on *your* ungodly ass in the blink of an eye," he warned.

"Not before I can flash my scary light at you," I replied, flicking the flashlight on and off, shining it in his face.

Magnar scowled at it for a moment, then released a low laugh, shaking his head. I stayed put as he released me and walked away.

Something about knowing that I was going to be leaving him soon made the tension between us feel stronger than it had before. Like there was a clock ticking down the seconds to our separation. It wasn't like I cared. But the more I told myself to keep my distance, the more I found myself seeking him out. None of that interaction had been necessary, and yet I'd stalked him through the dark to find him.

My stomach growled, reminding me that I hadn't eaten nearly enough, and I stuffed another lump of chocolate into my mouth, savouring the sweetness as I started to hunt the shelves for something more nourishing.

Magnar Elioson wouldn't be my problem for much longer, so I wasn't going to waste time on overthinking the time we had left stuck together like this.

It turned out that the store held more than we ever could have hoped for. Though a lot of the food left lying on the shelves had rotted away years ago, much of it hadn't. We'd enjoyed a meal made up of all the different things we'd found in more packets and tins than I could count.

Bags of oatmeal had made a meal for the horses too, and the large animals were now wandering the aisles contentedly, enjoying the time to rest.

Magnar had lit a fire in a huge metal bin to keep us warm, and the building was big enough that we didn't have to worry about the smoke.

We'd also found an aisle filled with bottles of water. There was so much of it that I'd stolen some so I could wash, finding a quiet corner of the store to do so. I'd even found some soap, and it wasn't like the scentless communal bars we'd been given in the Realm's bathhouse; it smelled good enough to eat. I'd taken a while to decide on a scent and had eventually settled for cherry. They even had some special shit for washing my hair. The picture of the woman on the bottle had told me what to do and I'd scrubbed half of the contents through my waist-length locks before using two bottles of water to rinse it back out again.

On my way back to the fire, I found an aisle filled with clothes. I grabbed armfuls of the different materials greedily before settling on a bottle green shirt which hugged my figure and felt as soft as butter. I added new underwear and a pair of black jeans to the ensemble, revelling in the feeling of being truly clean.

By the time I re-joined Magnar, I was grinning like a Cheshire Cat. He'd washed too and his long, half braided hair glistened with moisture as he sat shirtless beside the fire. The wounds he'd gained from the vampires were all healing incredibly quickly, apart from the two bites given to him by the Elite, and I eyed the inflamed skin with a flicker of anger rolling through me at the memory of that monster sinking her teeth into him.

I took a seat beside him and watched as he inspected the row of tooth marks on his right arm.

"You're not about to develop a taste for my blood, are you?" I teased, although a small part of me was afraid he might. There had been plenty of rumours in the Realm about how someone became a vampire and getting bitten was pretty high on the list. Though I guessed Magnar would have been more concerned about the bites if that were the case.

"It is rather more complicated than that to turn a mortal into a monster," Magnar replied, and I couldn't help but feel relieved. The idea of becoming one of them was about the worst thing I could imagine, and I was glad it couldn't happen easily. I'd rather die than be a vampire, cut my own throat, leap from the top of a building, drown myself in a lake – whatever the method, I'd take it a thousand times over becoming one of them.

"How does it work then?" I asked, a morbid fascination gripping me.

"A human has to drink their blood as well as being bitten," he replied with a sneer of disgust. "It's like being infected with a disease alongside suffering their venom."

"That's it?" I raised an eyebrow curiously.

"Then the mortal has to die. It doesn't matter how, so long as the heart is intact. Nothing else is fatal to them. They can fuse severed limbs back into place, even heads with some help. Only a direct blow to the heart will end them."

"That's...so gross," I said, not knowing what else I could say about a creature that could stick its own head back on.

"Indeed. Nothing about them is natural. They're an abomination, an insult to the living." He continued to inspect the row of tooth marks on his arm, and I shifted a little closer to see too.

"So why isn't your super-healing working on the bites then?" I asked.

"Just as my people developed ways to combat the vampires' power, *they* developed ways to resist us. Their fangs hold a venom which stops blood from clotting so they can drink freely from their victims. It also combats the innate ability in my blood to heal. While that venom remains present, my body can only hold the blood back but cannot force the wounds to mend. Now that I have flushed them with water, they should heal well. I'm just making sure no venom remains."

"You can see it?" I asked as I looked at the bite mark again curiously.

"It shines like moonlight. A mark of the curse which ties them to the hours of night – or at least out of full sunlight. Look; I missed some." He held his arm out to me and tilted it while pointing at one of the puncture wounds. The flickering light of the fire highlighted a glimmer of silver within the wound.

Magnar lifted a bottle of water and tipped it over the area, flushing the bite clean. When he inspected it again, all of the venom was gone, and I could have sworn the skin around the bite already looked less inflamed.

"Do you need help with the one on your neck?" I offered.

He clearly wouldn't be able to see it to check the venom was removed properly and despite my general disdain for him, he had gotten those bites by coming to save my sorry ass. So the least I could offer was my help in treating them

Magnar regarded me for a moment, and I got the feeling he wanted to refuse but he sighed, beckoning me closer.

"That would be helpful," he said finally.

I smiled sweetly as I shifted nearer, enjoying the moment where the brutal barbarian had to ask for help from little old me, and he tilted his chin up so that I could inspect the injury. I could instantly see that this bite was a lot deeper than the one on his arm. The flesh was torn around the holes the vampire had punched into his skin and despite his gifts fighting against it, some blood still trickled from the wound.

I couldn't believe he'd been suffering with the pain of it for over a day and hadn't said a word.

"Why didn't you ask me to help you with this before?" I asked. "Are you really that pig-headed that you couldn't bear to ask for assistance with this one thing?"

"We couldn't spare the water and I could take the pain," he replied dismissively.

"I would sooner have gone thirsty for a day to save you from suffering," I said irritably, and he glanced at me in surprise, the truth having fallen from my lips before I could consider it. I refused to take it back though. It *was* the truth, and it was ridiculous to put himself through such a thing.

"And I would sooner not see you go without food or water. Especially

144

as that is a burden you have had to bear before." His gaze flicked to my too-thin figure, and I shifted uncomfortably.

"It's something I'm more than used to. It wouldn't have been a problem," I replied dismissively.

"It would have been a problem for me." His gaze was unyielding, and I frowned at him, finding this side of him far harder to deal with than the brute who infuriated me to the point of tears.

I sighed in defeat as I turned my attention back to the job of tending his wound, deciding not to reply to that declaration and focus on the job at hand.

I moved to kneel before him and picked up the bottle of water. His gaze met mine for several long seconds before he turned to look at a point beyond my head.

I started to pour the water over the bite and his fist clenched tightly in his lap. I'd never seen him show a reaction to pain before, and the sight made my stomach twist uncomfortably.

"Sorry," I breathed.

"You weren't the one who tried to rip my throat out," he replied lightly, raising one huge shoulder like it was some kind of joke.

"Well, if you had just kept your swords in hand instead of offering her a fist fight..."

He laughed and the deep rumbling sound of it pulled a smile to my own lips.

I continued rinsing the wound clean and tried to ignore the tension in his body.

I was so close to him that his scent enveloped me entirely, my gaze drifting from the wound to the way the water tumbled over the carved muscles of his chest. I bit my tongue, forcing my gaze back to his neck. It might have helped if he'd had a fucking shirt on. Having his ridiculously ripped body inches from mine was making indecent thoughts flash through my mind.

Nope.

I bit my lip to stop myself from looking at his chest again and forced my eyes to stay fixed on the bite through pure force of will.

"You smell like cherries," he said, his voice rough with an emotion

I couldn't quite place.

"Is that a bad thing?" I asked.

"No."

I wasn't sure how to answer that, so I kept my attention on the bite instead of replying.

He tilted his head, blocking the light so that I couldn't see what I was doing. I reached up and caught his chin, lifting it slightly with my fingertips. The rough stubble lining his jaw scratched against my thumb as I shifted my grip, and I bit down harder on my lip to distract myself from it. The point where our skin touched sent sparks of energy racing right back to my thumping heart.

I felt his gaze shift to my face but didn't dare turn to meet it.

I continued to rinse the wound until all of the venom swirled out of it, leaving silver trails down his broad chest between the lines of his muscles. I realised I'd let my attention slip down to stare at his body again and quickly flipped my eyes up to meet his.

His golden eyes burned with molten fire and took me captive.

He didn't move an inch and I didn't release my hold on his jaw.

I tried to blink or turn my head or do anything to break the connection between us, but my treacherous body wouldn't let me. This thing between us was a storm cloud shot through with lightning, the sparks breaking free and lashing against our flesh whenever we got too close. It was heat and anger, regret and loss, a pair of paths which never should have crossed and yet had become entangled.

I wanted to lean in, my body ached with a desire which I rebelled against with what little willpower I held, and the two feelings immobilised me where I was.

"I have never met a man as arrogant as you," I said, the words falling from my lips like some feeble attempt at a shield, a challenge for him to pull away.

"And I have never met a woman as infuriating as you," he replied, his voice a growl which rolled down the back of my spine and forced a breath to expel from my lungs.

"So why stay with me?" I asked, because that was the crux of it, wasn't it? We both knew I followed along behind him for the sake of my family and nothing else. But his motivation had never been made clear to me. He'd claimed to have saved me when my family was captured but what about Dad and Montana? I'd seen him take on twenty vampires, including an Elite, and win since that day. I knew Wolfe could have called for reinforcements from the Realm, but everything I'd seen of Magnar made me think that risk wouldn't have stopped him. There was more to it, and I wanted the truth.

Magnar looked me over slowly, his attention dripping over my flesh and making every inch of it prickle with awareness.

He moved suddenly, gripping my waist and lifting me so easily that I sucked in a breath of surprise, finding myself in his lap a moment later, my thighs parted over his, the scent of him intoxicating.

I shifted my hand to balance myself, my fingers falling from his strong jaw, causing his stubble to graze against my skin. My palm fell heavily onto his chest, pressing down right above his heart, the solid thump of it matching with my own pounding pulse.

Magnar released a deep groan and the sound of it tied a knot in the pit of my stomach. He tightened his grip on my waist with his strong hands and dragged me forward with his strong hands so that the inch of space between us disappeared.

"What are you-" I began, but he cut me off.

"Bait," he said simply, his fingers moving to the side of my face, tangling in strands of golden hair as he tucked them behind my ear. "I'd been searching for any sign of my kind for days and had found nothing but a barren land and fences lit with lightning. I'd seen the blood bank, as you call it, and I wanted to strike at it. I'd already come to the conclusion that I would be doing so alone. My plan was simple enough; I was scouting your Realm so that I could take count of the vampires there. I wanted to lead them away from the humans they'd caged inside to minimise the casualties once we came to blows. I was already turning back to the blood bank when I heard the fighting which led me to you."

"So us fighting for our lives was just some curiosity to you?" I growled, trying to shift back, but he kept hold of me, his fingers tight around my hips.

"For a moment, I wondered if I'd found my people at last. But it was obvious your family were human the moment I saw them. But you… there was a ferocity to you which captured me the moment I saw you racing towards them, charging straight for death with no thought for your own life. I could see your intentions were fated to fail regardless, so I stopped you."

"Because you wanted to use me as bait?" I spat, giving up on trying to escape him and making myself listen instead. I'd wanted these answers after all, so I would force myself to endure the truth of them no matter how bitter it was.

"In that moment? No. I acted on impulse, the instinct to protect you rising in me the second I laid eyes on you," he replied, his fingers pushing into my hair, and I fought the urge to arch into the touch, batting his hand away instead.

"Why?" I demanded.

Magnar surveyed me, the corner of his mouth lifting in that arrogant way which made me want to smack him so often.

"I wanted you. Simple as that."

"Like a caveman claiming a rock?" I sneered, and he snorted.

"A vexing, provocative rock," he agreed, pushing his hand back into my hair and wrapping the length of it around his fist, tugging my head back so that I was forced to bare my throat to him.

"So when did the rock become bait?" I hissed, my fingernails biting into his chest above that pounding muscle.

"Once I had you, I had time to think my actions through. Time to assess why the gods had led me to you in that moment."

"Oh, so we're blaming the so-called gods, are we?" I replied scornfully, but he ignored my contempt as he went on.

"My plan was straightforward enough. I would attack the blood bank, killing the bloodsuckers who oversee the atrocities there, allowing one of them to 'escape' and run for help from your Realm. Then I would lie in wait for all who followed. But that came with too many pitfalls for my liking. I couldn't be certain there weren't other strongholds nearby. And though I am a man of legend, I am just one man."

"A self-proclaimed legend," I scoffed. "How humble you are."

"The truth is what it is, drakaina hjarta." Magnar tugged on my hair, the sudden jerk pulling a sound from my lips that was all too like a moan, and I dug my nails into his skin more forcefully.

"So you decided to use me as bait instead of relying on your first plan?" I demanded, refusing to let him turn me from the topic.

"They're hunting you. It makes for easy sport," he agreed, and I slapped him.

Magnar's head wheeled to the side, and he breathed a laugh, turning back to me with fire dancing in the gold of his eyes.

"You can be angry with me all you like," he replied in a level tone. "But I haven't lied to you. We *are* heading where I promised, and I *will* help you to retrieve your family just as I swore to. If in turn you help lure out the bloodsuckers and guide them to my sword, then all the better."

"So you're just using me?" I sneered.

"Aren't you using me too?" he tossed back, and fuck him because I was, and that smirk said he knew it.

"Fine. So I'm your bait and you're my...sword dude."

"What is a sword dude?" He frowned at me, and I rolled my eyes.

"An overly muscular asshole with an affinity for killing bloodsuckers and making it look easy."

"It is easy," he agreed, making my blood flare.

"You're infuriating."

"And you talk too much," he replied.

"Perhaps I'll stop talking altogether," I bit back.

"Good."

A noise escaped me which was an honest-to-shit growl, and he just fucking laughed.

"Maybe you'd feel better if you hit me again," Magnar taunted.

This time, I punched him.

"Motherfucker," I cursed, pain flaring through my knuckles as they connected with the solid curve of his jaw.

He ignored my cursing and my attack on him, tugging my hair tight in his fist and pressing his free hand to my spine to remove any lingering distance between us.

When his mouth claimed mine, a fire lit beneath my skin. My nails dug in deeper, drawing blood on his chest, my anger blazing into something far more dangerous as I parted for him, his tongue sweeping into my mouth, claiming it for his own and making me moan.

I wrapped my other arm around his neck, pulling him closer still, not sure if I wanted to kill him or kiss him but getting lost in the feeling of his lips against mine before I could decide.

That kiss was the first truly honest thing that had passed between us. No ulterior motives, no half-truths, no miscommunication. This was something both of us wanted without needing to spell it out. No matter how much bitterness, anger, or resentment there may have been hanging between us over his use of me or my rejection of his bloodline, *this* was real.

He rolled his hips beneath me, the thick ridge of his cock pressing into me through our clothes. I gave up on any pretence of rejecting this, any hesitation I had left melted at the feeling of his mouth against mine, his powerful body beneath me, giving in to him completely and letting the last of my resolve disappear.

Magnar's fist knotted in my hair, tightening to the point of pain as he pulled my head back and ran his mouth down my neck, arching my spine precisely how he wanted me.

My skin burned for him, and I moaned as I let any remaining walls between us come crashing down. My own hands ran down his chest, feeling the firm lines of his muscles beneath my palms, exploring the scars and the ink which I'd lusted over more than I cared to admit. I couldn't get enough of touching him; the feeling of his body against mine this intoxicating rush which I couldn't deny any longer.

Magnar's teeth raked against my throat, his stubble grazing the soft skin in a way that had me moaning before he bit down just hard enough to hurt, the jolt of pain racing straight down between my thighs. I rocked my hips against him, feeling the sinfully thick length of him against my core, my panties soaking at the thought of him filling me.

He fisted my shirt, twisting it in his grasp until the fabric tore, pulling a gasp from my lips as he tugged it off of me and revealed my bra.

His mouth dropped lower, and I lost myself in the feeling of his lips against my skin, the kisses interspersed with bites which verged on just the right side of pain. I tangled my fingers in his long hair, pushing him towards my aching nipple and moaning as he tugged the fabric of my bra down, sucking it into his mouth.

This was a mistake. A beautiful, fucked-up mistake which I wanted to keep making over and over again.

Magnar lifted me easily, pushing me down onto the floor beside the fire, his weight dropping over me instantly, his attention going to my other breast.

"I fucking hate you," I panted, my thighs locking around his hips, my clit grinding against the hard length of his cock.

"Say it again, maybe I'll believe you next time," Magnar taunted, his hand finding my fly and opening it with ease.

"I fucking-" I cut off with a moan as he pushed two thick fingers straight inside me, the heel of his hand rolling over my clit in a way that stole the breath from my damn lungs.

I arched against the cold ground, my nails biting into his scalp as I tugged him closer, needing his mouth on my nipple again.

Magnar fucking laughed against my skin as he complied, pleasure tumbling through me as he bit down on my nipple and thrust his fingers in deep at once.

The noise which escaped me wasn't one I'd ever made before. I'd fucked men in the Realm for an escape from my mundane reality, but it had always been a hurried, desperate collision of need, our clothes never fully leaving our bodies, the experience fast and to the point. Magnar was toying with me, teasing my flesh, and making me burn.

"Get on with it," I growled, my body writhing beneath him, the need in me building beyond the point that I could take.

He rose his head, meeting my eyes as he pushed his fingers in deeper, rode my clit harder.

"Is that what you're used to in your Realm, drakaina hjarta? A quick fuck to take the edge off that lasts a matter of minutes?"

"What else is there?" I hissed, the words faltering as he pushed his fingers in deeper still, my pussy pulsing around them, something building in me which I couldn't take any more of.

Magnar studied me for another moment and then laughed, his free hand leaving my fingers and curling around my throat instead.

"Oh, drakaina hjarta, I am going to enjoy educating you."

I frowned at him, but whatever I'd been going to say was lost as he drove his fingers into me again, deeper, faster, his grip tightening on my throat just enough to make a thrill dance through my veins.

I was utterly at his mercy, his powerful body dominating mine, his muscles flexing as he kept up that blissful movement between my thighs, tightening that knot inside me until I was melting beneath him, panting and cursing, unsure what I even wanted anymore until-

The pleasure that exploded through my body was unlike anything I'd ever felt before and yet somehow precisely what I'd been aching for at the same time. I cried out, my nails digging into his skin, spine arching beneath him, body blazing with a heat that was so exquisite my toes curled and my breath stalled in my lungs.

Magnar took my mouth with his, the smugness of his smile biting into my lips as he claimed them, the pleasure in my body so intense that I couldn't even summon the energy to be angry at him for it.

I had never felt anything like that before. And I needed more of it.

"By the gods, you're so wet for me," Magnar growled against my mouth, his hand still massaging the slickness between my thighs even though my legs felt like they'd turned to jelly.

He shifted back, kneeling over me as he tugged my pants down and I just lay there beneath him, staring up at the perfection of his body, letting him reveal every inch of my flesh.

"I don't care much for the modern clothing you wear in general," he said as he unlaced my boot and tossed it aside. "But the undergarments are…" he trailed off, drinking in the sight of me in my bra and panties while removing my other boot so that he could drag my jeans off too.

I bit my lip. Watching the heat in his golden eyes as he looked at me, fighting the urge to hide from that intensity. I'd never been so bare before any man, never had the time to even consider it. It wasn't like there was privacy to be had in my apartment or anyone else's. I'd stolen moments in alleys and half destroyed buildings in the ruins. Never anything like this.

Magnar moved his hands to the sides of my panties and dragged them down my thighs with such aching slowness that my body trembled from the anticipation he was building. I took his lead and stripped out of my bra, revealing all of myself to him, finding a rush of freedom in the act as the need in his expression deepened.

Magnar pushed my thighs apart, baring my pussy to him as he leaned down over me, his gaze intent and fixed between my legs.

"What are you doing?" I panted, my heart racing as he closed in on my core, his cock rigid in his pants, his body a coil of tension which he was clearly fighting to restrain.

"Educating you like I said, drakaina hjarta. And looking forward to hearing that sound from you again."

"But what-"

He dropped lower and spat on my clit, the strike of his saliva against it sending a bolt of shock and wicked pleasure straight through me and causing a moan to spill from my lips, his blazing eyes snapping to mine and holding there.

"Watch me," he commanded and for once, I had no objection to make against his bossy tone, simply nodding like a good, obedient girl and watching as he dropped his mouth to my core.

This was…hell I had no idea what it was or why he was doing it, but the moment his lips met with my pussy I couldn't find it in me to care anymore.

The noise that escaped me was pure carnal bliss, my thighs instantly locking around his head, muscles tensing, fingers biting into the hard floor either side of me.

"More," I gasped, his tongue lapping, caressing my clit and building that tension inside my body all over again.

His gaze remained locked with mine and I found myself unable to look away, captivated by the sight of him between my thighs, his broad shoulders tight with tension, his dark, part-braided hair soft against my skin.

This man was ruination given flesh, he was the devil built for sinning, an unholy creature created from all the darkest desires I'd never known I had, and everything about him drove me to desperate, furious insanity.

But I couldn't find it in me to care about any of that as he devoured me like a starving man, and I lost all sense of who I was or what I was or where I was…

I clenched my thighs as oblivion rose in me once more, and Magnar took hold of my ankles, pushing them over his shoulders, giving himself more room to do whatever godly thing he was doing with his tongue.

I did as he'd told me and kept watching him, the sight of his mouth on my pussy the filthiest, most intoxicating thing I'd ever seen. He had that look in his eyes again, that cocky arrogance which wound me up so tightly, but this time, he was offering the key to unlocking that tension, and I was giving in to it, desperate for it, pleading for it with every moan and curse that spilled from my lips.

He dropped one of his hands to his waistband, loosing the ties which secured his pants and unsheathing the huge length of his cock.

I bit my lip as I stared at it, wanting to feel the fullness of it inside me, aching for it in a way I never had for any of my previous lovers.

"Don't finish inside me," I gasped between moans, some lucid part of me knowing I had to protect myself against the consequences this act could bring.

"Don't worry, drakaina hjarta," Magnar growled against my core, vibrations rolling through me with his words and driving me closer to release. "You aren't ready for me to fuck you yet. I'm going to go easy on you this time."

Questions. So many questions sprung to my lips at his words but none of them made it free of my tongue because he chose that moment to thrust his fingers deep into my pussy once more, the combination of his hand and tongue making me cry out as I came for him like my body was utterly his to command.

The orgasm consumed me. I hadn't even realised what it was I'd been aching for when I'd been fucked before, but it was this perfect oblivion, this complete destruction. Magnar didn't slow his assault on my flesh, his other hand fisting his massive cock and gliding up and down it while he worked on me, taking his own pleasure too.

My heels drove into the ink which decorated his broad back, my fingers tangling in his dark hair as I rolled my hips against the movement of his mouth, fucking his face, his hand, everything but that perfect cock which I couldn't stop staring at.

I was on the verge of begging him for it, only the smallest thread of self-control keeping the words inside my mouth while he continued to punish me with pleasure. I could see it in his eyes, every harsh word, every curse, every bit of anger he held over the situation he'd found himself in after waking hundreds of years too late to fulfil his destiny. He was taking it out on me, and I was his willing victim, receiving all he would offer with stars flickering across my vision.

It was too much. My body couldn't process the level of pleasure he was offering me, my breathing rushed and shallow, my nipples tight and aching, my pussy slick and throbbing. I'd never felt so turned on, never needed sex like I needed it now, and I knew he wasn't going to give it to me. He was going to wait until I begged him for it, my pride the only thing standing between me and that perfect cock.

I came again so suddenly that darkness flashed across my vision, my spine arching against the cold floor, pussy thrusting so hard against his face that he was buried in it as my thighs clamped shut around him.

I lost sight of his eyes but could still feel them on me, devouring me even more devoutly than his tongue had.

He reared over me, pushing my thighs apart so that he could kneel between them, letting me watch as he fisted his cock, pumping it over the sight of me, the look of feral need on his face making me whimper with the desire for him to just drive it into me and take what he needed from my body.

I reached for him, wanting to feel him, and he let me take his cock in my hand, my thumb gliding through the precum which lined his tip as his fingers tangled with mine and he guided my movements.

I bit my lip as I watched him, his eyes darkening as he looked down at me, his hips pumping into our joined hands until he came with a growl, marking my flesh with his cum, a contented noise escaping me as I felt it splash hotly against my nipples.

Magnar leaned down to kiss me, his tongue sinking deep into my mouth, stealing the last of my breath as I wound my arms around his neck and drew him closer. His hand roamed over my breast, smearing cum across my nipple before shifting lower, seeking out my clit once more.

I was wound so tight, the feeling of his slick fingers massaging his cum against my core had me coming again within moments, our kiss deepening as he stole the last of my strength from me, and I let myself drown in the feeling of his mouth against mine.

I was lost in chaos and bliss, and I never wanted to resurface and face the punishing world beyond our bubble of stolen sin.

ERIK

CHAPTER SEVEN

1000 YEARS AGO

Nine times I almost broke and tried to force my way out of the cave I had trapped myself within. But the gods were mocking me. They had sealed it themselves; I was sure of it. It was no longer just rocks holding the wall in place, but a magic so ancient it slithered through the cavern like serpents come to witness my suffering.

No matter how much I battered the rocks, tearing at them with my bare hands, they did not shift. This had been my choice, but the hunger had quickly consumed me, and when the months had turned to years, my desperation had driven me to the brink of madness.

Andvari whispered to me sometimes and his laughter made my bones weak, like he was sucking out the marrow and making a meal of me.

I was a rabbit in a trap, but it was a trap of my making. And sometimes I remembered that I had to endure this hell if it would bring me salvation, though that clarity came and went as swiftly as two sides of a coin spinning on its axis.

The hunger grew maddening. Insufferable. And soon, I saw visions.

Shadows. Light dancing in my periphery.

Sometimes I saw a girl who looked like the moonlight given flesh. Other times the sun in ethereal form. But then I forgot I had seen them at all, and I could not recall the beautiful faces that looked upon me through the cracks in my mind.

Andvari was taunting me. I despised him and all of the gods along with him. Their omniscient cruelty. Their punishment for a crime I didn't commit.

I cursed my parents' names. There were times when I scratched and tore at my skin, trying to release my soul from this wretched body. Other times I lay still for days, weeks, months. Years perhaps.

Time was nothing and everything. Time was a trick of the mind. A plague that killed humans, brought mountains to their knees, dried up oceans and ravished stars themselves into oblivion, but never me. I would live on and starve and fall into insanity. That was my fate. The gods would not free me, the debt would never be paid.

Fabian visited less and less. Sometimes he called out to me, other times he only came near enough to listen for signs of life. There had been times where I had begged him to release me, but he had stuck to his word and kept me caged. Perhaps he had not come at all, and it was another illusion cast by the gods, mocking me, making me believe there was someone out there who cared for me, only to dash that hope to pieces.

Now, I lay on my back, feeling weightless, like I was floating in a limitless abyss. The hunger had hollowed out everything else inside me. I could barely remember why I had come here, but when I came too close to forgetting, Andvari would appear to remind me. Like he did now.

"Draugr, you are cursed for your parents' blasphemy against me. You are starving yourself in payment of the debt owed to me."

"Am I getting close to paying it?" I asked, my voice like the snap of dry bark.

"That depends," he purred, and I felt his holy presence fill up the space inside the cave, drowning me in his powerful ambiance. "Do you feel you have the answer to the prophecy?"

"I think on it sometimes," I admitted. "I try to find meaning, but I fear there is none. That the prophecy is just another way for you to torment me."

"There is meaning, Erik Larsen."

I closed my eyes, going over the prophecy in my mind. "Twins of sun and moon. Sometimes I see such things. Then I forget them."

"Yes…" Andvari whispered. "And what does it mean?"

I rubbed my face, having no answer. It was all too dark in here. Too dark to see or hear or speak or think.

"I cannot have children," I whispered. "It cannot be that."

"Oh, but you can, Draugr."

My brow creased and my heart thudded once in recognition of this news. The first gleam of hope in a void with no end. "Children?"

"A human mother could bear you a child," Andvari said, beginning to laugh. It was cold and vicious, his amusement in my torment another reason I despised him and his kind.

"And what animal would that child be?" I growled, thinking of the monster I would create.

Andvari's voice began to fade as he started chanting the first line of the prophecy. "Warrior born and monster made. Warrior born and monster made."

"Stop!" I clawed at my ears, willing him away.

Silence fell. And Andvari didn't speak to me again for a long time. Days and months and years dripping by. Falling one by one, until I was surely lost.

"A circle of gold," I whispered into the frozen air, though it was not nearly as cold as me. "Shall join two souls."

I repeated the line of the prophecy for a while, my tongue heavy and begging for blood instead of words.

The sun? Could that be the circle of gold?

"Two souls…twins…children," I repeated what little I knew from Andvari's ramblings.

A new torment had come to play havoc with me since the god had hinted at such an answer to the prophecy: the image of a fanged child with eyes the same shade as mine and blood spilling from its teeth. I saw it everywhere. Eyes closed, eyes open, there it sat and watched me. And I held onto one decision in the darkness of my cage in the face of that unholy creature. I would never birth a child with a human. It was just another trick of the gods. Another lie to drive me mad.

"The slayers are rising in numbers. Many are gathering now," Andvari's voice cut into my ears like a blade, slashing through the quiet and rousing me from my state of stasis.

Fabian hadn't visited for many weeks, but the last time, he had he'd spoken of the battles between the slayers and my family. Clarice and Miles had joined him in the fight. When he had visited, he had asked me to help them, but I had refused. The answer lay here, this payment surely still worth something to Andvari.

"Why are you telling me this?" I breathed.

"They will come for you if your brothers and sister are defeated," Andvari growled, seeming frustrated by that fact.

"And then you will have no one to torment," I said, realising why it bothered him so.

"All the answers you seek are in the prophecy."

"Am I on the right path? Is starving here helping at all?" I pleaded.

"A debt must be paid," Andvari whispered, but I didn't know if he was confirming or denying what I had asked.

"Is this the debt?" I demanded, my anger rising.

I stood and hunger gripped me in an unyielding fist. I dreamed of blood. It was all I had thought of when my mind began to fade, and I could hardly recall the words of the prophecy when it took hold of me. It was my truest captor now, the thirst so deep after all this time without blood that it was hard to think of anything else.

"Please," I demanded when Andvari didn't answer. "If I am wrong, then tell me so that I can find another way to pay the debt."

Andvari chuckled and began to recite the prophecy again. At some point, I snapped. The words broke me, or perhaps it was the lack of blood. Those words poured through my head in an endless circle, puncturing my skull and breaking me from the inside out.

I roared, punching stone, and tearing at the wall, but it didn't buckle, even with all my strength behind the blow.

"You're keeping me here!" I bellowed at Andvari. "You won't let me out! You will never let me out!"

"You chose to come," Andvari said sharply. "I am helping you keep your promise."

I sank down to my knees, my mouth burning and my throat so tight I was suffocated. "You are not helping me. If you were helping, you would tell me what to do."

"A riddle hides a secret in its words. It is there in plain sight if only you would pay attention."

I groaned, pressing my forehead to the icy floor. "The words are branded in my skull. I see them in the darkness bearing down on me like the great wolf Fenrir. And still I cannot find the answer!"

"Erik…" A warm presence floated around me, though I could not see Andvari in any fleshly way. "I admire how you try. I come here because you are the only one of the cursed who attempts to pay his debt."

"Then help me," I snarled. "Help me pay it."

"The answer lies between the moon and the sun, Draugr. You will find your answer there."

I laughed bitterly. "On earth you mean? Somewhere on earth is my answer, is that supposed to be helpful?" I spat.

"You see things too literally," Andvari sighed. "Look into the space between the words, what does that tell you?"

I closed my eyes, wishing he would leave me be.

"I do not know," I sighed. "*I do not know.*"

"A river can be water, but it can also be a life force. Do you see better now?"

"I see that your words hold more riddles. I see that you take pleasure in my pain. I see that the gods are cruel and unforgiving."

"That is where you are wrong, Erik. I can forgive. And I will forgive. But you must pay the debt…" He drifted away and silence found me once more, wrapping me in its lonely arms, never to let go.

MAGNAR

CHAPTER EIGHT

1000 YEARS AGO

A cold wind blew in from the north and my chestnut stallion, Baltian, whinnied in soft protest beneath me. I patted his neck absentmindedly as I continued to watch the road.

The sun was bright in the blue sky despite the time of year, and I was fairly certain it would keep the parasites out of sight until nightfall. Not that I'd be against killing a few if they showed up.

My small band of warriors waited anxiously behind me on their own horses. To have been given charge of the six of them, despite my sixteen years of age, was a great honour, and I was determined to prove myself.

Father had promised me a surprise if I managed to complete my first assignment to his satisfaction, and I was intent on not disappointing him.

As the day wore on, I pulled my furs closer around my neck. It wasn't like the Sacred Followers to deviate from their route. They believed their passage was assured safety by the false god they worshipped.

The evergreen trees were dense around us, concealing us from view where we waited for our prey, the heavy blanket of pine needles making for a soft surface under hoof. We were as inconspicuous as it was possible to be. Shadows wrapped in secrets. Waiting.

The landscape surrounding us was dominated by the dark green pines, making up a forest which was interspersed with lumps of grey rock where the ground was too barren for the trees to take hold. We were south of the mountains here, but the icy chill of the wind still reached us from their snow-crested peaks. Come winter, all of this would be dusted in snow, white for as far as the eye could see, and it would be far harder to hide our tracks in that weather. Harder still for those we hunted.

My lip pulled back in distaste as my mind wandered to the Revenant, Miles. He may have thought himself a god among men, but I was determined to burn every last altar to the ground.

I would have been tempted to release his Followers from this earth too if I didn't have to follow the sacred laws set out to govern the way of the slayers. *No human shall die by my blade lest my life itself is at risk.* I snorted in disgust. The Sacred Followers dreamed of becoming vampires. No doubt I'd be killing them in the end anyway. Why wait for them to gain immortality and become more difficult to dispatch?

Those were the rash and brazen thoughts of a child, according to my father, and as irritating as it was, I pushed them aside, trying to remember who I was and what our purpose was too. Miles was my target. Only him.

I sighed as I forced my mind away from the thoughts I'd had a hundred times before. I had tried voicing them to my father and his response had been clear. Our laws would be followed. Our personal opinions were not relevant. Taking the vow meant forfeiting my own thoughts or feelings on my actions. I was a weapon to be wielded now. And I would follow orders.

My brother was the only one who I could share my thoughts with on such subjects these days. Though my opinions never meant that I would deviate from my path, I needed an outlet for the injustices I saw in our work. So many of the slayers followed the path blindly. I was adamant that I would always keep my mind open, despite knowing I couldn't choose my actions. I would still own them. And I would still question them. I would be no one's blind pawn, not even the gods'.

A faint noise sounded around the corner as a wagon drew near.

I pointed to Casper and Eldred, indicating for them to head further up the hill and cover us with their crossbows. The two warriors followed my directions without complaint even though they were both over ten years my senior. No one questioned the word of my father, but I suspected it was more than that. They believed in me and I was determined to see that faith rewarded.

Bells sounded and the Sacred Followers began chanting, their voices becoming a single rhythmic cry that rose then lulled repeatedly. I beckoned for the remaining four warriors to follow me and nudged Baltian into motion beneath me.

The chestnut stallion had been a gift from my mother for my thirteenth birthday. He had been as wild as a storm; untameable by the three men who had tried before me.

The clan had laughed when he was presented to me, yanking against his lead rope and frothing at the mouth in his desperation to be free. No one had thought I would be able to saddle him. They believed my mother was playing a trick on me, making me look a fool. But I knew better. She was giving me the opportunity to show them my mettle. They were the fools to doubt me, and they soon learned it.

No one had questioned my grit since that day, and no other man could ride my horse. I smiled at the memory as we waited for the carriage to draw closer. I was about to prove myself again.

It had been a week since I'd taken my vow. No warrior younger than eighteen had done so before. But I'd known my own destiny since I was a boy, and when the leader of the Clan of Prophecies had visited us three moons ago, I'd asked her to show my father my future. She had foreseen my rise to greatness, my path as a leader of men and destroyer of vampires. My future was entwined with that of the bloodsucking Revenants so completely that even my father had had to agree I was ready. I was never going to be anything but a slayer, and there was no need for my vow to wait.

Despite the assurances of the prophet, I refused to leave my future up to fate. Each day I worked harder than the last. I would prove to all men that I deserved my place among our people. No doubt would ever follow my rise.

Miles was about to learn of me too. I'd spoken to my father of my hatred for the Sacred Followers, and he had given me permission to discourage their worship in any way I saw fit. So I might not have been able to take the life of a mortal, but I would happily take everything else from them.

The chanting and ringing of bells drew closer and the carriage appeared on the road. I eyed them, noting the flowing white robes they all wore, some of them riding in the back of the carriage which was drawn by a pair of tired looking mules. Others walked around it, ringing those bells and chanting, their ornamental weapons strapped to their waists. I doubted any of the silver swords would stand a blow from a slayer blade, they were pretty and pointless, unlikely to cause so much as a scratch, even by accident.

I silently drew my blade from the sheath on my back and my warriors followed suit. Tempest hummed with promise in my fist, my sword ever eager for a fight, though it seemed almost confused as it failed to sense any bloodsuckers nearby. Next time I drew it, perhaps I would offer it the tainted blood it thirsted for.

As the carriage passed our hiding place, I finalised my count. Twenty-four Sacred Followers to seven slayers. It almost didn't seem fair.

A savage smile pulled at my lips, and I indicated for my warriors to move into the road behind the carriage as I pulled Baltian around. I kicked the stallion into a canter, and we sped through the trees to the front of the group of Sacred Followers, their sounds of startled panic bringing a smile to the corners of my lips. They heard our approach and recognised the threat of the fate thundering closer to them.

The stallion leapt onto the dirt road and reared up, sending the two cart horses into a frenzy of panic, and making the man who held their reins squeal in alarm as he fought to get them back under control.

The road was narrow here. To one side, a steep rockface sloped up at an angle which was utterly impossible for the cart mules to even attempt, and the forest where we'd been hidden lay on the other, the trees too dense for any chance of the carts passage between them.

I'd selected this spot well. And with my men pouring onto the road at their backs, their only slight chance lay in getting past me. One boy on the verge of manhood perched atop the biggest warhorse any of them had likely ever laid eyes upon. And yet one look at me would be enough to tell them that I was far from the easiest of paths that now surrounded them.

I pointed Tempest at the man driving the cart and smiled the gods' smile; the one I was certain Loki offered to those he tricked, and Thor handed out while in the midst of battle.

"We'll be taking everything you have," I told him simply, begging him to challenge the authority of my words with that taunting look in my eyes. "I suggest you don't resist."

The Sacred Followers were recovering from their shock, all of them huddled close to the carriage, but some straightened their spines and drew their flimsy weapons.

My smile widened.

I may have offered them the option of surrendering quietly, but I was born of the Clan of War, my blood was heated in the fires of Brokkr's forge, and I was always hoping for a fight.

Shouts of alarm and confusion started up as the Sacred Followers fell into panic. A few of the braver men ran at me with their ridiculous swords raised while others made a dash for the forest.

I batted their strikes aside almost lazily, knocking the first sword from its owner's hands with a bark of laughter before striking another with enough strength to snap the blade in two. One of the motherfuckers got too close to me, gripping my ankle and trying to haul me from the saddle, but I yanked my leg free and kicked him squarely in the face, knocking him into the mud.

His white robes were splattered in brown filth, a cry of pure terror falling from his lips. I broke a laugh at him as he flailed around, scrambling to get up while trying to avoid Baltian's stamping hooves. No doubt the angry brute was aiming to break the man's legs and I didn't have it in me to try and curb his fun.

Baltian aimed a kick at another asshole who tried to circle around behind me. He was damn lucky the horse missed him; Baltian was a savage bastard and a solid kick from him could break a man's ribs, or worse.

I spun towards the man as he tried to stab Baltian's flank, aiming for my horse instead of me; a coward's tactic which only incurred my wrath. I bellowed a battle cry and swung my blade around, knocking his weapon from his hand, spilling blood as I cut into the meat of his arm. He ran from me, screaming in terror as he raced back towards the rest of his twisted congregation, those who had tried to flee already herded back into place by my warriors, all of them now cowering in or around the carriage.

I bared my teeth at him like a beast; no man would harm my horse and live to tell the tale. Laws be damned. If he had managed to strike Baltian, his head would have parted company with his shoulders. He should thank the gods he'd missed.

At a sharp whistle from me, my warriors surged in behind the carriage, blocking any of the Sacred Followers who tried to run, though it seemed as though the fight had already gone out of them, several of them sobbing now while others stared glassily on in some paltry display of defiance.

I whistled a signal and Casper and Eldred loosed arrows from their positions at the top of the huge rock to my left, striking the wooden carriage. The heavy arrowheads buried themselves deeply within the frame of the cart and several of the Sacred Followers screamed in fright. That was the last warning I'd be giving them. They were surrounded and staggeringly outmatched. This would only end when I decided it was over.

"Those who surrender won't be harmed!" I shouted loudly enough for all of them to hear me over their own panicked cries.

Despite my personal feelings about the pieces of shit who cowered before me, our laws were clear, and their deaths wouldn't come at the tip of my blade unless they ever succeeded in their quest for immortality and managed to become like the monster they worshipped. If that day ever came, I'd gladly show them how short-lived an immortal life could be.

The Sacred Followers hunkered together, many of them throwing glances at the man who sat at the reins of the cart. I assumed that meant he was the leader of this branch of devotees, their final, waning hope for help. The Sacred Father.

The man's eyes darted between my warriors fearfully, and I could tell he was wondering why I was the one addressing them, his gaze shifting from me to them, scouring the group, no doubt hunting for the one he thought might be the true leader among us. I wasn't insulted. I thrived on people underestimating me. It always made it all the sweeter when I proved myself to them beyond reproach.

"I may be younger than my warriors, cretin, but I assure you, I am more than a match for any one of them. You would do well not to disrespect me by looking to them for help," I growled.

This was my first mission against the Sacred Followers, and I couldn't expect them to know who I was yet. But they would. Soon they would all cower at the sound of my name and turn from their vile master rather than risk crossing me.

"Don't you know who we are?" the man asked incredulously. "Don't you know whose protection we are under? We follow the Immortal Creator, giver of eternal youth. He drinks the blood of those who deny him his offerings!"

"I should like to see him try," I taunted. Immortal Creator, was it now? The last I'd heard, Miles called himself the Benevolent Saviour. Perhaps one egotistical lie wasn't enough for him.

I signalled for my men to start stripping the Followers of everything they owned and watched the process unfold from Baltian's back while I oversaw their work.

As most of the Sacred Follower's belongings were already loaded on the cart, it didn't take my warriors long to gather the rest. They forced the men and women to place everything, including the clothes from their backs, onto the cart, then directed them to stand by the side of the road. I barked a command for the bells to be wrapped in some of the blankets, not wanting to have to listen to that incessant jangling for the entirety of our journey home. We'd melt them down and make good use of the gold eventually and silence would finally fall over them for good.

Holbard jumped up into the cart, inspecting the haul, making sure everything was loaded securely. His foot thumped down on the wooden floor of the cart and he paused, raising his head to meet my gaze, stamping his foot down once more, the hollow noise reaching me now too.

"You plan to leave us here, naked at the roadside?" the Sacred Father cried, the attempt to draw my attention away from Holbard's discovery not working in the least.

"Perhaps your shrivelled cock will freeze in the frigid air and fall off," I sneered at him, glancing at the flaccid, stumpy flesh which hung between his thighs, my upper lip curling back in distaste. "It would do the people who follow you a great favour, no doubt."

I'd heard plenty about the sexual aspect involved in the so-called worship these desperate fuckers performed, and I had to assume immortality was far more appealing to them than anything else in this world if the cost of it included spending time fucking that particular specimen.

I nodded for Holbard to continue his investigation, and he dropped down, ripping the hollow-sounding wood apart, easily lifting the loose boards away. I sidled closer, my interest piqued, and a muffled scream sounded as he dragged a young woman out of a hidden compartment by the scruff of her neck.

A swathe of dark hair covered her face as she struggled against Holbard's hold, but he simply tugged a gag from her mouth, allowing her to speak freely.

"Please, sir!" she panted desperately, her eyes seeking me out. "I am not a Sacred Follower. They took me from my village and hid me in there when I fought them. I don't know where I am or what you want with them, but please don't leave me with them."

"The girl is ours," the Sacred Father hissed. "Take the rest and be on your way, but she stays with us. Her father owes a debt, and she is the payment."

I eyed him coldly, then beckoned for Holbard to bring the girl to me. He briefly checked her for weapons, then tossed her over his shoulder, leaping down from the carriage and depositing her before me by Baltian's hooves.

The girl shrank back, clutching her white dress closer to her thin frame as she tried to avoid Baltian's restless stomping, and I sheathed Tempest.

"Speak," I instructed when she remained silent.

If she expected me to consider her request to take her away from the Sacred Followers, then I needed an explanation. Her long, brown hair hung over her face, but I could see that she was young enough to be unwed, pretty, probably several years older than me. The translucent white gown did little to hide her body, her nipples visible through it, though I was more interested in the red rims around her eyes and the terror which clung to her. I hadn't heard of the Sacred Followers growing their numbers by force before, but there was something wholly honest in her terror which made me pause to hear her out.

"I am not a Follower," she breathed. "They took me from my family to offer me up as a sacrifice. They plan to feed me to their master. The blood drinker; the demon said to lurk on the edges of the mountains…" Tears swam in her eyes, and I could see how desperately she wanted saving, her words nothing but pleading truth. She was willing to risk her chances with a band of wild warriors rather than stay with these people, and that spoke volumes of its own.

My attention whipped to the Sacred Father. "Is this true?" I demanded, grit coating my tone as I worked to keep my temper in check.

"Everyone knows that pure, virgin blood tastes the sweetest," he replied, raising his chin as if that were an explanation. "Such an offering may be the last pledge I need make before the Immortal Creator awards me the gift of eternal youth."

The man was already well into his sixties and didn't appear to be in the best of health, let alone particularly attractive. I knew for a fact that Miles would never sire someone so old. He favoured the young and the beautiful to add to his collection of immortal monsters. The girl he intended to sacrifice was more likely to be offered immortality by the false god than he was.

Holbard struck the Sacred Father across the face, and he fell into the mud with a cry.

"Come. We'll take you far from the reach of monsters like these."
I offered my hand to the stolen girl and hoisted her up onto Baltian
behind me. She wrapped her arms around my waist, and I could feel
her sobbing her relief into my battle leathers, my gut twisting with a
mixture of fury and unease.

Miles was changing the games he played. This was new. And I
didn't like anything new when it came to the Revenants.

I nudged Baltian forward so I could peer down at the Sacred
Followers where they clustered together, naked and pathetic in the
mud. None of them was either young or beautiful enough to be a likely
candidate for one of Miles's 'gifts', so I doubted I'd be facing any of
them as immortals in the future - though that simply meant they'd never
meet death at the end of my blade. It was freezing out here and miles
from any kind of shelter, let alone a town. Likely they'd all freeze to
death before they made it back to civilisation, though perhaps a passing
carriage would take pity on them. Either way, they weren't my problem
any longer.

"If you survive long enough to see your false god again, then you
can deliver a message to him for me," I spat. "Tell him that Magnar
Elioson did this to you. He does not know my name yet, but he will be
hearing it more and more often until the very sound of it fills him with
dread. And once I am finished with his Followers, I will be coming
for him and his brethren. I shall be a thorn in his side. An itch he can't
scratch. A voice promising death in his ear. And a knife through his
heart which will cast him and all he is to ash. So send him my warmest
greetings, and tell him I'll be seeing him very soon."

Holbard had gone ahead to take news of our success to our clan's camp,
and by the time we arrived with our haul, the drums were beating and a
feast had been prepared.

I tried not to smile at the treatment. No doubt my mother had
organised the celebration, and despite it being a little over the top, I
couldn't help but enjoy it.

The fire burned brightly in the centre of camp, and we made our way towards the rest of the clan with eagerness. Platters of food were laid out on a long table and the smell of it made my mouth water.

We handed the carriage off to some of the unsworn; younger members of the clan who had yet to take the vow and were in the process of proving themselves by serving those who had.

I dismounted a little way from the ring of clansmen who had gathered around the fire and held my arms up to catch the stolen girl as she followed. She stared around nervously, sticking close to me while observing the men and women who passed between the tents. I imagined we were almost as terrifying to her as the Sacred Followers had been. A travelling war camp wasn't the most familiar of surroundings for a village girl like her.

"We aren't as savage as we look," I teased. "Stay by my side tonight, and tomorrow I'll make arrangements to take you home. What's your name?"

"Astrid," she replied in a small voice, her wide eyes still taking in the strange surroundings mistrustfully.

"You shouldn't trust a word out of Magnar's mouth if you want to keep your virtue, sweet Astrid!"

I turned and grinned at my brother Julius, who was striding towards us, holding his hands out for Baltian's reins.

"Don't mind poor Julius," I said in a low voice which I knew would carry to him all the same. "He's just bitter because Father didn't let him take his vow with me."

"We can't all be the great and powerful Magnar Elioson," Julius sighed dramatically. "Some of us are only destined to be the forgotten younger brother. Thirteen full moons between our birthdays and you would think it was all the time in the world."

Unlike me, Julius chose to cut his dark hair short, but we were similar in most other ways. Our bronze skin and golden eyes were mirrors of our mother's, but we had our father's warrior build. Despite our young years, we both towered over men twice our age already, and we weren't finished growing yet.

"Julius is bitter because he has to clean up horse shit before he can join the feast." I pulled Astrid under my arm, and she didn't resist. Instead, she leaned into me, seeming grateful that I'd taken her under my protection.

Julius rolled his eyes and reached up to pat Baltian's neck. My brother was the only other person the horse would allow to handle him, but even so, Baltian snorted irritably, bobbing his head in a move which could only be interpreted as insistence for us to hurry this interaction along. No doubt he was hungering for his own meal.

"Well, if the great and powerful Magnar wants to head towards the fire and warm his great and powerful ass while I do all of the work, then who am I to complain?" Julius began to lead Baltian away from us, then paused to look back over his shoulder.

"Father's surprise has arrived for you," he said, his eyes sparkling with amusement. "Why don't you take sweet Astrid to see what it is?"

"Why don't you give me a clue?" I asked, sensing mischief in his teasing.

He knew something I didn't, but he shook his head as he led Baltian away between the tents.

"I wouldn't want to spoil the surprise," Julius called back to me, and that was that.

When I'd taken my vow early, a small part of me had worried that my relationship with Julius would change. I'd worried that my elevation might leave a bitter taste in his mouth. The unsworn had to serve the slayers and help with a lot of the menial work around the camp when they weren't training. Until last week, we had done so together, our easy camaraderie and competitive natures making the work fun, and I'd feared that might change when he was required to serve me instead. But when he continued to treat me exactly as he had before, my worries lifted. Nothing would break the ties between us. Especially nothing so petty as jealousy. No doubt he planned on taking his vow at the earliest moment possible and hoped to outdo me in every task I accomplished to prove his worth matched mine. I looked forward to the challenge he would present.

Feeling like I was on the back foot, I began to guide Astrid towards the fire. Her white gown trailed around her ankles, skimming her bare feet, the ends stained with mud. The light of the fire was making her body very visible through the sheer material, and I wasn't entirely sure she had realised it, so I took the cloak from my shoulders and slung it around her, offering her a semblance of the modesty I was sure she would prefer to hold onto.

She clung to me fearfully as we approached the laughter and shouting that carried from the men and women around the fire, but I didn't offer her the chance to head anywhere else. The safest place for her was right here by my side until I returned her to her village, so she would remain there while the night wore on.

Some of the warriors noticed our approach and began to call my name in greeting. I smiled at them, trying hard not to look as smug as I felt. The haul we had taken from the Sacred Followers was impressive, and the blow we had struck against Miles would be felt by him.

The crowd parted, leaving space for me to approach my mother and father who were sitting on the far side of the fire in chairs carved of solid oak, the tops decorated with antlers which cast shadowy crowns upon their brows. Many of the men and women we passed reached out to clap me on the back or offer words of praise for my first successful raid, and I kept my chin high, feeling my place in this world as perfectly as I could imagine any man might ever hope to.

"He's here!" I heard my mother cry excitedly, though I'd lost sight of her between the press of bodies after that initial glimpse. The clan were all eager to speak words of encouragement and congratulations to me – especially those who had been foolish enough to doubt my early ascension.

Astrid held onto me in a way that was a little indecent, but I didn't mind. I'd saved a maiden from the jaws of the vampires, and if she wanted to follow me around with her gaze full of wonder and gratitude, then I wasn't going to stop her. Perhaps it was a little crass of me, but I was enjoying the attention, enjoying this first taste of destiny as I stepped up to claim the place which had been foreseen for me.

Finally, I made it past the throng of clansmen and found Mother and Father standing together, waiting for me. My father was a fearsome warrior, his long hair and beard braided with rune-covered beads and his blade, Venom, was strapped across his back like always. The only time he took it off was for bed and even then, it was never further than an arm's length from him; he wasn't a man who would ever be caught unprepared for a fight.

He wasn't smiling; that wasn't his style, but his eyes shone with approval, at least until his gaze travelled to the indecently dressed girl on my arm. His jaw ticked in disgruntlement, and I wondered why for a moment – our people certainly weren't known for their chastity and decorum - but my attention was drawn away from whatever issue he had with it as my mother spoke.

"We hear you have had a great victory," she said loudly, a radiant smile filling her beautiful face.

It was said that my father fought fifty battles to win her hand in marriage. But she didn't accept his proposal until he had managed to defeat *her* too. The clan still told stories of the fight between them and of how he had barely won. Only his love for her had let him prevail. To this day, she still teased that she had let him win, wanting his hand as badly as he had wanted hers. I didn't believe that though; my mother was not the kind of woman to lose a fight willingly, even if it was for the man she loved.

"It was only a cart driven by mortals, Mother," I replied modestly.

Though I was proud of the way the day had gone, it certainly wasn't as if I'd fought a battle against the vampires and returned stained with the ash of victory.

"Exactly," my father rumbled. "The boy has done well, but there is no need to fuss, Freya."

My mother smiled lightly, but I could still see pride shining in her gaze and it filled my chest with satisfaction.

"I hear I'm to have a surprise of some sort?" I asked, unable to resist asking any longer.

"Indeed." My father gave me a penetrating stare, and I could feel the warning in his gaze. He didn't think I was going to like this, and I fought the frown which was summoned by that realisation. Why offer me a surprise I wouldn't like?

I squared my shoulders a little, relaxing my features into a mask of ease. The whole clan was watching us. I would have to keep my feelings in check if I was about to be disappointed. But I couldn't for the life of me think why he would give me something he didn't believe I'd want. And in front of the entire clan of all places.

"A prophet foresaw a chance for our clan to grow stronger," Mother said carefully, her hand brushing my arm for the briefest of moments, a warning in that touch which only heightened my unease.

Something twisted uncomfortably in my gut, and I pulled Astrid a little closer under my arm.

"There is to be a union between our blood," Father said loudly, his smile holding a hint of regret that only I could see. "Let me present to you your bride, my son. This is Valentina of the Clan of Storms." He stepped aside and a girl moved forward, a shy smile gracing her lips as she assessed me with obvious interest.

My heart grew cold in my chest as I stared back at her. I was sixteen. I'd taken my vow only eight moons ago and already the gods had decided on my *bride*?

I tried to ignore the fluttering of my heart which beat like a bird trapped in a cage, desperate to fly free. I'd known that this was a possibility when I'd taken the vow, but it rarely happened. Arranged marriages were for the purity of our bloodline, and no doubt some future child of ours had been foreseen doing great things. But all that I could see in that moment was a stranger who I was expected to share my life with. I was too startled to even note anything about her. My parents had married for love, their passion for one another was sung about over campfires, and I'd grown up watching their union with the greatest hope that I might one day find a match like theirs.

"It's an honour to meet you, husband," the girl said playfully, the glint in her eyes telling me this was no shock to her. Worse than that, she was excited, pleased, clearly more than happy with the assessment she had just made of me.

I clenched my jaw before I could say something that would embarrass our clan. I forced myself to look at her objectively. She was pretty in an obvious kind of way, her features fairly symmetrical, her eyes the same size as one another, lips in proportion to her nose. The cut of her dark blue gown was designed to draw my gaze to the swell of her breasts and the curve of her hips. She was tall enough not to be dwarfed by me, and her dark hair was braided artfully. I wondered if she usually dressed that way or if someone had forced her to come here looking like an offering. She certainly seemed far more civilised than I had ever claimed or wanted to be.

I wondered if she was just as unwilling as I was to follow through on this marriage. But as I met her gaze, I could see that she wasn't. She appraised me appreciatively and her eyes glimmered with excitement.

"It's an honour to meet you too, my lady. But I am not your husband yet." I forced myself to offer a teasing smile to take some of the sting out of my words, and I knew my father wouldn't be happy that I'd spoken them at all. But I couldn't help it. I wasn't hers, and despite this news landing in my lap a matter of moments ago, I felt a strong and thunderous certainty that I never wanted to be hers either.

Valentina's eyes fell on Astrid as if finally noticing I had a girl clinging to my side, and ice formed in them so suddenly that I arched a brow in surprise. It appeared she didn't appreciate my scantily clad companion. The knowledge made me tighten my hold on the stolen girl as I struggled to think of anything else to say.

"I presume you are some years older than me," I said, landing on the first thing that came to mind. "As you have already taken your vow."

"I am twenty-two," she replied with a small nod, and I could see that the information didn't bother her.

"Well, let's hope you can match the vigour of my youth."

My mother coughed loudly and stepped between us, placing a hand on my elbow. "Magnar, you must be famished after your day on the road. Let us find you some food and you can get to know your bride while you eat."

She led me away and I didn't resist, grateful for the momentary escape she was offering.

"Don't worry, my love," she breathed in my ear, her touch gentle on my arm as she sought to comfort me. "The gods may have seen your union in the stars, but they said nothing of a date. This betrothal could go on for years and years. Who knows what might happen in such a span of time."

She pressed a kiss to my cheek before leaving me to gaze down at a plate of food I had no appetite for anymore. But she had given me the one thing I needed. Hope.

MONTANA

CHAPTER NINE

I was in a moonlit field where I felt connected to everything around me, the bubbling of a stream close by, the caress of the wind. Everything was heightened, and the moon seemed to light the world as brightly as the sun.

Then a stranger was at my back, shifting the hair from my neck and winding powerful arms around me, pulling me tight against him. His mouth was on my skin, cool and demanding. I wanted more, my body arching back into his until the sharp scrape of fangs on my throat had my head spinning and the dream tumbled into chaos. I saw red brick walls, a flash of golden hair and a man with blades that shimmered like sunlight. Then I was in an iron cage, rattling the bars and screaming until my throat was raw. A man watched me from afar, a dark and twisted grin on his lips that awoke a deep horror in me. He moved closer, his hands curling around the bars as he glared in at me with a demonic glory in his eyes. "You will never be free of me."

I woke with a jolt, heart thundering as I bucked and kicked, still feeling that cage around me now. I clawed at the arms holding me, trapping me, my gaze locked on the window across the room where morning sunlight promised me salvation if only I could reach it.

"Calm," Erik growled, pushing me onto my back and gripping my chin in his hand.

He was rough as always, fingers biting into my skin and his leg locking mine down as he rolled onto his side.

My eyes found his and my breathing evened out, those ash grey irises blazing. My body relaxed, perhaps caught in some spell of his, though I didn't feel bewitched. The clawing fear of the dream reminded me of why it had felt so real. Because it was. This was my captor, bearing over me, in possession of so much power that he could break me the moment he decided it.

"Your heart is beating steadier now," he said, voice low, gruff, the deep tenor of it sending a wave of heat flooding through me.

His thumb dragged over my cheekbone and his eyes followed the movement, a hawk taking a moment to admire its catch.

My breaths were the only thing to fill the small space between our lips, his chest entirely still, void of life. So why did I feel the urge to reach out to this creature of darkness and draw him closer?

"Sometimes the gods send bad dreams to warn you," Erik said quietly, his brow lowering as if disturbing memories were tearing their way through his mind. It occurred to me that he had lived many lifetimes, had experienced things I couldn't even fathom, and had perhaps endured things that haunted him still. But that would assume a monster like him could feel, hurt and regret. Looking at him now, it was hard to deny that might be true. That he was not just evil incarnate, but a man trapped in death.

"What did you see?" Erik pushed when I didn't speak.

It felt as though there were few barriers between us right then, and perhaps it was because I missed my sister so much and needed to speak to her so urgently, that I let myself open up as if she was here now. "A moonlit field. A lover turned beast. A cage where I felt watched by a monster."

"A monster like me?"

"Yes," I breathed, though I didn't add that I wasn't sure if it was him specifically.

"What else?" he demanded.

I frowned, trying to recapture the dream that already seemed to be spiralling away from me like rainwater down a drain. I shook my head, unsure I wanted to give him any more details even if I could salvage some. If, like he said, the so-called gods had offered me the dream, then they were likely warning me of the very monster who held me now. I didn't exactly need the heads up on that one though.

He released his hold on my chin, but didn't get up, his hand moving to press against the pillow by my head. We were half tangled, his muscles tensing just enough to keep his weight from crushing me. His scent of cypress surrounded me, and with him this close, it was always too difficult to think straight. Like my body took over, heat and want making my skin prickle in a demand. It was his vampire allure, no doubt. But sometimes it felt like so much more than that.

"There is something I need to do. I shall return to you soon. Get dressed." He shoved to his feet and was gone in a flash, leaving me there with a curse on my lips.

I thought on all that had happened last night, pushing myself to sit up and looking at the spot where the vampire had turned to ash. Whoever wanted me dead surely wasn't going to give up so easily. Once they realised their assassin had failed, how long would it be before they sent another one after me?

Sunlight filtered through the broken window shutters, just a dreary, wintery glow. For some reason, the ordeal I'd been through didn't make me want to run. Instead, a strange feeling was stirring inside me. An intangible sensation like an anchor rooting my heart to this place, this room. Something was urging me to stay...

Moon child.

I sprang out of bed, my pulse pounding at the silky voice in my mind. Dropping down to my knees, I reached for the blade under the bed, certain it was the source of the voice. My fingers were drawn to its magnetic aura, and as I grasped the hilt, calm filled me like I'd been reunited with a vital piece of myself.

"What are you?" I breathed, turning the beautiful dagger over in my palm.

Nightmare. It warmed my skin and seemed to sing a quiet song just for me. Holy shit, was I talking to inanimate objects now? And was it talking back?

The shimmering gold blade was perfectly polished, reflecting my chestnut eyes back at me. I blinked as they momentarily appeared green, the colour of my sister's. I was either losing my mind or something strange was going on with me. The dreams, this blade and now the mark on my arm...

"Why can't you be here with me right now, Callie? Or better yet, why can't I be with you? I have so much to tell you."

I sighed, checking the clock on the wall, figuring I should probably wash and get dressed. I had to be ready to spend the day with Miles, and though another date with a vampire was the last thing I wanted, getting out of this room wasn't. I needed some fresh air and time away from Erik to just fucking *think*.

Reluctantly, I tucked the blade back under the bed and headed to the bathroom.

The heated water was a sweet gift. If there was one good thing about this place, it was this. I washed my hair, running my fingers through it and thinking over each and every detail of the fight I had won against the vampire who had come to kill me. How was it even possible that I was capable of such a thing? Capable of taking on the creatures who had kept me prisoner my whole life? Had I always been strong enough to do that? Were other humans able to kill them too? Could we make an army, rise up, actually have a chance at *winning*?

As I rubbed the soap against my skin, I scrubbed at the strange mark on my arm which seemed less red today than it had before. My fingers traced the image of a blade, and I wondered if it was possible that I *was* a slayer. Fabian had told me they'd been wiped from the earth, so what did this mean?

There were too many unanswerable questions, but there was one thing I knew for sure. General Wolfe had almost certainly sent that vampire to murder me because of the blade that was now hidden under my bed, so I was in serious danger. Would he tell the royals what he suspected? Or try to end me before they found out? I didn't know how the fuck I could prepare for any of those outcomes, but I would have to be on guard, ready for another attack to come at any moment.

Tension coiled in my stomach. The only thing that would make me feel safer was keeping Nightmare with me. Whatever strange power possessed that blade, it seemed to unveil a potential in me I'd never realised had been there. The ability to fight back. So I wasn't going anywhere without it.

I could keep it concealed, tether it to my thigh where it would remain hidden by the flowing dresses I was given to wear here.

The idea made my heart swell and bolstered my confidence, liking the idea of finally having some defence against the creatures who had captured me.

Stepping out of the shower, I wrapped myself in a fluffy white towel and walked into my room.

My heart lurched.

Erik had returned and was standing there in a white shirt and navy trousers, his hands stuffed in his pockets.

"Could you ever knock?" I hissed, hugging the towel tighter around me.

His eyes travelled over me. "I'll add knocking to the long list of ways I so wish to please you," he said hollowly.

"Back to the dickhead behaviour today then," I said lightly, moving to the closet and opening the door so it concealed me before I dropped my towel.

"I tend to become rude when I am bored," he said.

"So it's my fault you're an asshole?" I scoffed. "I think that's all on you, Erik."

"There's no need to get riled up."

"I'm not," I growled.

"She says, whilst riled up."

"Stop saying riled up," I said irritably.

"I think I preferred you when you were sleeping, actually. Much less lip."

"I prefer you when I'm sleeping too. It's like you don't exist," I said, tugging on some underwear, followed by a flowing grey dress with a tight bodice. I pulled on a cardigan, the sleeves hiding the mark on my arm.

"Except when you dream of me," he taunted. "You moaned my name at least three times last night. It's sad how obsessed you are really."

I shut the closet door sharply, finding Erik watching me with wicked amusement gleaming in his eyes. I had a moment of doubt, a terrible fear that he wasn't lying about that, and heat flashed through my cheeks. He noticed it, head cocking to one side and a dark laugh rising in his throat.

"I didn't moan your name," I hissed. "I would sooner choke on it."

"It sounded like that wasn't the only thing you were dream-choking on."

A snarl left me and I strode toward him with intent, unsure exactly what I planned but wanting to tear that mocking look off his face. His eyebrows arched, waiting to see what I might do with complete intrigue, like this was all some game for his entertainment. And I realised that was exactly what this was. The bored prince playing games and hoping it might be enough to fill the void in him.

I slowed my charge, giving him a sweeping look up and down. "You know what's really sad?"

"What?" he mused.

"For however many years you've walked this earth, you have never found anything to make you feel even close to human again. Because that's the thing, isn't it? You want to feel something, find anything worth making this endless existence worthwhile. But you can't find it, Erik, can you? You're trapped in a perpetual, unchanging body. You've reaped all you can from the barren fields of your soul, and now there's nothing left that grows. Your torment of me is a small distraction from the colossal abyss that lives in you, but when it's quiet and there are no distractions left to keep your mind from that truth, it haunts you, doesn't it?"

His throat bobbed, eyes hardening, and victory surged through me at knowing I had finally cut him deep enough to wound.

Maybe I should have held my tongue, seeing as he had covered for my ass after killing a vampire and I needed him on my side. But I was tired of his cruelty, of his baiting and mocking. And the more I thought about him admitting his 'miniscule attachment' to me, the more insulting I found it.

"You're angry with me," he stated.

"No shit," I muttered, moving to the dressing table and snatching up a hairbrush.

There was no sign of Nancy today, so I guessed Erik agreed I didn't need to look my absolute best for Miles.

"Well…" His lips pressed together as I watched him in the mirror. For a moment, I glimpsed that humanity in him again, glimmering just beneath the surface of his eyes. But it couldn't have been real. This was the illusion my father had warned me of, their ability to lure us in, mimicking human behaviour. It wasn't genuine.

He cleared his throat. "Your assessment of me isn't so far from the truth, I'll admit. And yes, I do enjoy finding out how deep I can delve under your skin, rebel. But you are wrong too. There was a time in the early days of my curse that I tried to reclaim humanity, but I have long since accepted the truth of what I am. I tried to make payment to restore my soul, I tried to abstain from drinking human blood. I tried. Once. But that was very long ago, and somewhere along the way, I embraced this power in me and decided to wield it instead of fear it. I have the strength of a god in my veins, so why shouldn't I use it to rise? To make a mark on this land. But do you know why we call ourselves princes and princesses instead of kings and queens?"

I shook my head, shocked that he was opening up to me at all.

"Because the only true rulers of this world are the gods. I know what it is to scorn them, to have their wrath lay on my shoulders. So I became one with their wrath. And there is power in that, if nothing else."

He gave me a bleak look, no longer distracted but laid bare, and I hated how it made me almost empathise with him. But he had said it himself, he chose power over fighting his apparent curse, so this was on him. Honestly, I didn't know if I believed anything that came out of his mouth anyway.

"These gods…" I said, returning to brushing my hair. "You speak about them as if they're real. Like you're certain they are. But my father only ever spoke of things like that in terms of myths and legends."

"Is my kind not proof enough of their existence?" he questioned a little sharply.

"Forget it," I muttered

A beat of silence passed, then he spoke again. "There are many gods and goddesses, but all are divided into two kinds. The Aesir gods are those of war, bravery, courage and society. They reside in Asgard, a celestial palace in the sky."

I turned to him, intrigued. He examined my expression as if checking to see if I was going to scoff at him, then decided to go on.

"The Vanir gods are one with nature, they wield magic and pursue peace far more readily than the Aesir. They are gods of fertility, wisdom and harvest, and they reside in a lush land known as Vanaheim. Right here, where we are. This is Midgard. The land of man."

"And women," I added, and he twitched a smile.

"Yes, and draugr now too."

"Does that mean…vampires?"

"Smart little pet, aren't you?"

I gave him a dry look.

"That is enough learning for today. I think any more might strain that tiny human brain of yours."

I pursed my lips. "Does pretending humans are stupid make you feel better about imprisoning us?"

"If you really think I need to tell myself lies to ease the guilt of my actions, then you are not grasping how little I care for your kind."

"But you did. Once."

His eyes sparked with anger. "*Once*. In a time long before the now. There is only so much blood one can spill before caring becomes irrelevant. What use is it to care? It does not wash their deaths from my hands. I will not pity any who fall because of me now. In fact, there is much to envy from those who die at our hands, for their souls remain intact, welcomed into the Hall of Valhalla in the heart of Asgard, or into the underworld of Helheim. If I am ever to die, my soul will either be too fractured to make it into the afterlife, or if not, the pieces of it which remain will be so tainted it shall be sent to the region of Helheim called Náströnd, where sinners are sent to suffer, and the great beast Níðhöggr will feast on what is left of me for all of time." He spoke with force, but I could see the fear lying beneath those words that he would truly face that fate one day.

"Why not release the humans, make up for all you've done?" I demanded.

"I cannot undo my sins," he hissed, stepping closer to me. "And I do not intend to make up for them either. I am set on a path of malevolence, and you are my latest misdeed. I suggest you start praying to the gods I speak of, for they are far more likely to favour you than me, but they are also the ones who gifted me this power. So go ahead and pray, rebel, let us put it to the test to see if my will is greater than the gods'. Because I do not believe even they could tear you from me now."

My throat constricted, the tension wrapping around my neck like a tether that led straight back to the hand of my captor. "And what of *my* will?"

A flicker of surprise crossed his face. "Yours?" he laughed, and anger flooded my chest.

"You're a fool to discount me."

"Then I am a fool." He shrugged, then changed lanes, speaking casually again as if we hadn't been on the verge of a full-blown argument, "I will continue my pretence of courting the other women today."

"Pretence?" I echoed. "You seemed pretty captivated by Brianna yesterday."

He dropped his head beside mine, gazing at my reflection in the mirror. "There is only one thing I am interested in pursuing in this world." He trailed his fingers up my neck, then curled them around my throat, his touch light yet threatening. The closeness of him made me burn, and it wasn't just in the bad ways, but the wickedly good ways too. "And it is not a woman."

"Then what?" I growled, reaching up to pull at his hand, but he didn't seem to notice.

He didn't answer, his gaze tracking over me in the mirror with a hard and penetrating scrutiny. His thumb caressed the pulse point on my neck and a look of hunger glimmered in his gaze that made my hackles rise.

"By the way, I've sent General Wolfe to the west coast to release your father," he revealed in a casual tone, dropping his hand from my neck just like that.

I turned to face him fast, grabbing his shirt in my hands and fisting it tight. "You *what?*"

"I believe you heard me." He scraped my hands from his shirt, keeping my fingers trapped in his.

"Thank you," I gasped in utter relief, tears searing the backs of my eyes at the thought of Dad walking free from that place.

"I told you I would," he murmured.

"Will you bring him here once he's released?" I asked.

"Like I said before, it will be more complicated." He frowned as my heart fell. "But," he added, and my heart lifted again. "Perhaps I can arrange it. If that's what you'd like?"

"Yes," I said firmly.

He couldn't go back to the Realm, it was unthinkable. And I wanted to see him with my own two eyes, to prove he was really safe. This wasn't exactly freedom, and I'd be damned if I submitted to this way of life, but at least here, Dad would have regular meals. We'd have each other too, and we could make a plan to escape and find Callie. The thought of it filled me with so much hope that it brought an actual smile to my lips.

"Then it's done," he promised. "As soon as Wolfe has finished questioning him about the location of your sister, he will be freed."

"Wolfe won't hurt him, will he?" I asked in fear, certain my father wouldn't give up a scrap of information about Callie even if he did know where she was.

"I've told him not to be violent," Erik said.

I had to believe him, unable to see a reason for him to lie. He needed me to cooperate, and this was the key to getting that from me. I knew I still had to pay the price for this, but in the face of Dad being safe and free, no cost seemed too great. Even if ultimately, it came down to letting Fabian claim me as his wife. For family, I'd do anything.

"Miles will be here soon to collect you." Erik drew me a little closer, his cold hands still tight around mine. "He will treat you as if you are equal to him, it tends to be his way. He has a fondness for humans, but do not make the mistake of thinking he is your friend."

I nodded, only half listening as I was still wrapped up in the news of my father's release.

"Rebel," Erik growled, and the warning in his voice made me focus. "Miles likes his ego stroked. He plays god whenever he can, and I would hazard a guess that he has sired more vampires than any of us. He wears his curse like a medal of honour, a gift from the gods which he hands out to his favoured followers, but it is a fragile delusion. I doubt he would ever admit it, but his bravado is a guise put in place to fool those around him, himself most of all."

"What's your point?" I asked, unsure why he was telling me this.

"Do not question his boasting. He will treat you kindly if you go along with his delusions of greatness, but prod at him too much and you might rouse the beast in him."

"Are you trying to protect me, oh valiant prince?" I goaded him, and he gave me a flat look.

"I am trying to protect my asset, yes."

"Fine, I won't point out that Miles is a bloodsucking monster with no redeeming qualities."

"I mean it, rebel," Erik snarled, his fingers digging into mine.

"Alright," I breathed, his ferocity making my heart rattle in the cage of my ribs. "I'll watch what I say."

"Good," he exhaled, eyes searching mine before he finally released me, and it felt like the air in the room was at once more breathable.

He gave me a sweeping look, a line of tension on his brow that made me sure he was frustrated by something, but I couldn't tell what.

"You look…passable." There was a tightness to his voice, like he had planned to say something else but settled on that.

"I guess the plainness of humans is just another thing to bore the timeless prince. I'm sure you can't wait to go and look at someone flawless. Perhaps your own reflection."

He didn't rise to my baiting, instead frowning, his grey eyes still picking over my features. "Perfection isn't beauty. Looking at faces that never change, never age, never bronze in the sun, it grows tiresome fast. Everyone starts looking the same." He flattened out a crease in his shirt, then dropped his hand as if noticing the action and rebelling against it. "I found an old snow globe once in the ruins at the edge of the city. It was sat there on a shelf, a miniature model of New York trapped inside the glass orb. It must have been there for years, untouched, collecting dust, just waiting for someone to come along and shake it."

"What happens when you shake it?" I asked, trying to picture the thing he described.

"A snowstorm swirls inside it. Chaos. Change…" He eyed me a moment longer, then bowed his head in a polite sort of goodbye, moving to the door. He seemed confused by the action, his brow furrowing as he exited, and I was pretty damn confused by it myself.

I thought on the story about the snow globe, seeing how clearly Erik wanted his own life shaken up. But I supposed when you lived forever, eventually all the novelties of the world ran out.

I headed to the bed, bending down to retrieve Nightmare, keen to reunite with it. My hand curled around the warm hilt, and I stood, carrying it to the closet and taking out a silk scarf. I lifted up the skirt of my dress, holding the blade against my thigh and tying it there with the scarf. When I was sure it was secure, I dropped the skirt and eyed myself in the mirror. No one would be able to tell I was carrying it. And its presence built a wall of strength around my heart.

A rhythmic knocking came at the door. "Get your ass out here. You're officially mine for the day, Montana," Miles called, an eagerness to his tone.

I opened the door, finding him there in an open collared blue shirt, sleek golden hair pushed back and a roguish, friendly smile on his too-handsome face.

He gave me an appraising look, flicking a lock of hair from his deep blue eyes. "Fuck me, no wonder my brothers are warring over you."

"They aren't warring over me," I scoffed. *Erik is using me as goddamn bait.*

"Yeah, yeah, play it modest. They'll eat that up." He grinned, then snatched my hand, tugging me into the corridor.

I spotted a burly guard standing behind him in a black uniform, his skin dark and eyes softest brown. His raven hair was shaved short, and his jaw was sharp and square, everything about him speaking of strength and composure.

"This is my bodyguard, Warren," Miles explained. "Don't worry about him, he'll just follow us around and scare off a crowd. There's a lot of people in the city who are kind of obsessed with me." He chuckled in a way that said he wasn't really joking, then pulled me along and Warren fell into step beside us. I recalled what Fabian had said about Miles and wondered if Warren really was his partner.

"So what do I call you?" Miles asked. "Montana is a mouthful. Do you go by something else? Tana? Ana? Mo? Monty?"

"Not Monty," I said quickly. The only people allowed to call me that were Dad and Callie, and even then, I didn't like it so much. Though to be fair if they stopped, I'd be upset, but I wasn't going to let them know that. "And please god not Mo."

"God*sss*." He emphasised the s. "Plural. Clarice said you probably didn't know about them. There's twelve you should definitely be aware of. Thirteen if you include Loki – he's a trickster. Never trust him if he comes offering you riches and glory. He'll likely turn you into a goat for it. An ugly goat at that. Anyway, the others you should be shooting prayers to are Odin – the all-father, king of gods, a fucking badass warrior too. Then there's his wife, Frigg – she's the hottest thing to walk the realms, queen of Asgard, goddess of all things love, and fate; then there's their son, Thor, god of storms and the fiercest warrior ever-"

"Hang on, slow down," I said, my head rattling from the information he was hurling at me a mile a minute.

"I'll get you a book on it instead, how about that?" he suggested, and I shrugged, not sure if I believed in all this gods stuff or not. But I guessed it wouldn't do any harm to learn about them.

"I have a surprise for you this morning. But first-" Miles reached into his pocket and produced an apple. "Breakfast."

I took it eagerly, my empty stomach coming to life at the sight of food.

Miles made endless small talk as we walked downstairs and I devoured my apple, the golden-haired prince seeming able to hold an entire conversation without me having to do much but nod my head at the right moments. We walked out to the front of the castle where the wind was cold and the clouds were thick above. A gleaming white car awaited us, and a guard handed the keys to Warren as we approached it.

I held the apple core in my hand, fully picked clean, swallowing the last of the sweet fruit. Miles plucked it from my fingers and tossed it into the trees with such strength that it flew through the air in a blur and slammed into an oak so hard it dented the bark.

"In you get." He opened the back door for me, and I dropped inside before he followed. "So here's the deal, Snow White."

I frowned at the name. "What?"

"You know, dark hair, pale cheeks, blood-red lips. Like the story? You need a nickname, so there it is."

"That's not shorter than Montana," I pointed out.

"Sure it is." He waved a hand, clearly set on calling me that, though I didn't recognise the story he'd mentioned.

"It really isn't," I said.

"Anyway, you may have heard through the grapevine that I'm with Warren."

My brows lifted in surprise at his honesty.

"If you pick me, I'm gonna be more like a friend than a husband, alright? I'd like to get that clear, in case you fall for my excruciatingly good looks and top tier personality today. Warren is mine and I'm his."

Warren glanced at us in the rear-view mirror, looking wary. "Are you sure you should be telling her that? You didn't tell the others."

"Well, that's because Fabian went and told her already, didn't he?" Miles rounded on me accusingly, and I saw a glint of that beast Erik had warned me about. Not that I needed to be warned about the threat a vampire posed, though I could see he had a point about Miles's easy demeanour. It wouldn't have been too difficult to forget he was a vicious creature if I only focused on his smiles and apparent warmth.

"Yeah, he did," I admitted, not seeing any point in trying to lie. "But why do you have to hide it?"

"I only hide it from the humans I'm courting," Miles said with a frown. "I don't think they would want to pick me if they knew they couldn't actually have me."

Super arrogant, but okay.

"So the public know?" I asked.

"Kind of. They know Warren is part of my harem, but they also think my human wives are true wives. Like, they believe I love them and we have real relationships."

"But why lie? Don't you and the other royals make the rules?"

"It's politics," Miles sighed. "This whole ritual garners a lot of interest from the public, and it can sway people's opinion on us. I have a court of Elite who I sired, and they will always be loyal to me first and foremost, as is the same for those my brothers and sister sired. But there are generations of vampires spanning many years. Those we sire, sire others, and then they sire others, and on and on the chain goes until the waters of allegiance get a little murky. We have to make conscious efforts to win the support of those vampires so there is never reason for insurgence. There are already rebel groups on the rise-"

"Miles," Warren growled as I hung on the prince's words.

"It's fine. Who's she going to tell?" Miles said, then thankfully continued on, giving me more information than I had ever gotten from Erik. "The polls show that this ritual gains us favour. Everyone loves the intrigue of it. Vampires marrying humans is complete insanity on paper, right? So I realised I had to commit to it, let them think I was fully invested, be out there courting the humans alongside my family. It gains me new followers every year."

"So that's what this is all for? Aiding your political campaigns?" I asked, not disguising the bitterness on my face and my disgust over the charade.

"No, not just that," he murmured darkly.

"Miles," Warren said again. "That's enough, you'll frighten her."

"I don't care. Tell me the truth," I insisted, but Miles shook his head, giving me an apologetic look that set my heart racing.

"Anyway, Warren came up with this idea. I didn't want to do it like this, but he was right. It works. If you choose me, I won't be a true husband. And you won't ever win my heart, no matter how much you try to claim it. Warren has held it for many, many years, and there'll be no changing that."

He looked to Warren, their eyes catching in the mirror and tension passed between them that charged the air. Confusion ran through me as I took in their heated look, unable to deny the love that they seemed to hold for each other. But were vampires truly capable of emotions like that? It went against the way I had perceived them all my life and challenged everything I thought of them. Love was tender, warm, pure. But those weren't things I had ever associated with these monsters.

"You do know I have absolutely no interest in winning anything from you or your-" I bit my tongue on the words 'bloodsucking siblings' and tried to curb my tone, considering Erik's warning. "Brothers."

Miles laughed like I was joking, and Nightmare flared with heat on my thigh, as if it was angry with my present company. *Strike true, strike deep.*

The words urged me to take action, the blade desiring the death of the vampires around me, but that sounded like a suicide mission right there.

Warren drove us into the city, and we took streets left and right, sailing between towering skyscrapers that blocked out any glimpse of the sunlight beyond the clouds.

The further we drove, the more relaxed I felt about putting some distance between me and the castle. I felt less like a prisoner beyond those walls, but I wondered if I'd ever escape them fully. If Dad was brought here, would we be able to come up with a path to freedom together? Or was I fooling myself into believing there was really a chance for us?

He just has to get here, then we'll figure it out.

Warren parked outside a glass building nestled between two tower-blocks. We exited onto the street and Miles took my hand, keeping me close. Warren opened the trunk of the car, taking out two duffel bags, then followed without a word as Miles led me up to the building and pushed through the door.

A sharp scent reached me in the damp, heated air and I glanced at Miles with curiosity.

"Good morning, your highness," said a female vampire behind a white desk. "We've had everything organised for the courtier."

"All warmed up?" Miles asked, and she nodded, gesturing to a wooden door across the room. "The changing rooms are just through there."

I frowned as I followed Miles past her, and we emerged in a short corridor. Two doors stood ahead of us, one marked with the symbol of a man and the other with a woman.

"Here." Miles took one of the bags from Warren and thrust it at me.

"What do you want me to do?" I asked, eyeing the bag.

"Get changed into the bikini and meet us back here," Miles announced before heading through the male door, followed closely by Warren, before I could ask either of them what the hell a bikini was.

I was left feeling a little lost as I headed through the other door and emerged in a blue room with a row of small cupboards on the wall with a bench in the middle.

I unzipped the bag, finding the item Miles had called a 'bikini' which looked like underwear to me. The only difference was it was bright red and had a strangely smooth texture.

I hesitated a couple of minutes, not liking the idea of walking around in next to nothing, especially with the mark on my arm.

Someone banged on the door. "You ready, Snow?"

"Fuck," I breathed. "Yeah, just a sec," I called then stripped out of my clothes and eyed the golden blade strapped to my thigh with anxiety in my chest. Shit, maybe bringing it was a bad idea, but how was I supposed to know he was going to bring me somewhere I had to take my clothes off?

I exhaled a sharp breath, making my decision – not that I really had much choice. I loosened Nightmare from my leg and wrapped it in the scarf before tucking it at the bottom of the bag. Stuffing my clothes around it, I pulled on the bikini and looked down at myself.

This was...so weird. What the hell did Miles have in mind for us to do?

Spotting a white robe in the bag, I tugged it out and relaxed a little. The sleeves were long, and would cover the mark fine, but this wasn't looking good.

I took the bag and headed back out into the hall, finding Warren and

Miles there in nothing but shorts. Both of their bodies looked cut from glass, their abs firm and shining, not a single blemish on their gleaming skin.

My mouth opened in surprise.

"You don't need that." Miles strode toward me, snatching the bag from my hand, and my heart jolted.

Shit.

He headed into the women's changing room, and I gazed at Warren with an awkward expression.

"He's a little extroverted," Warren commented. "You get used to it."

I nodded, forcing a smile and looking to the women's changing room, anxious for Miles to return. If I followed him, it would draw suspicion, so I forced myself to stand there and wait.

"So... doesn't it bother you that Miles has to take wives?" I asked, slightly concerned I might offend him. But surely this was maddening for him? Why would any of the royals take wives if they didn't want them? Erik didn't, so why did Miles?

"I can handle it," Warren muttered. "For the greater benefit."

"Which is?" My eyes narrowed and my heart thumped frantically.

I wanted to know this truth that was being kept from me, but equally, I feared knowing it too, certain it was going to be nothing good.

"It's not my place to say." He looked away, ending the conversation abruptly.

I frowned, sensing I wasn't going to get anything more out of him on the matter, and when the quiet became unbearable, I asked, "Why are we all wearing this underwear?"

"Because we're having a spa day." Miles reappeared at last, grabbing my arm and pulling me along.

"A what?" I asked, glancing up at him and sensing no threat in his expression, so I guessed Nightmare remained hidden.

"Pampering," he explained, but I was still confused.

I soon learned the entire building was designed to indulge in various things, and I picked out a couple from Miles's explanation that didn't sound like I'd have to take my robe off.

When my nails were painted red and my face had been scrubbed and moisturised, Miles led me along another corridor. He and Warren looked like plastic dolls since they'd been oiled up during something they called a 'Swedish massage'.

"Are we done now?" I asked, wanting to get my clothes back on and stow Nightmare back on my thigh.

"No, now we have pool time," Miles announced before leading the way through a set of double doors.

We emerged in a massive glass room with a bright blue expanse of water at the heart of it. A fake arrangement of rocks sat at one end where a waterfall ran into it, causing the surface to bubble and foam.

"Is that a...lake?" I regretted the words as Miles barked a laugh.

"Kinda. Like an indoor, warm lake, I guess," he said. "It's called a swimming pool."

"Oh," I exhaled, taking a step back. Swimming? Absolutely not.

Miles ran toward the edge of the pool, diving into the water and swimming under it in a graceful arc. Warren followed, coming up for air beside Miles before they both turned their eyes on me. Though as neither of them actually required air for their survival, I supposed that wasn't so impressive. I, on the other hand, very much enjoyed the pleasure of breathing.

My stomach twisted. My throat tightened.

I'd never been near water like this, and I wasn't able to swim. Even more importantly, taking my robe off would expose the mark on my forearm. So all in all, this was a hard pass from me.

"Come on, Snow!" Miles urged. "Jump in."

I shook my head, backing up further from the edge of the pool. "I'll just watch."

"Don't be ridiculous. Shed that robe and get in here," Miles demanded, an edge to his voice that spoke of how little he was ever told no.

I shook my head, but he swam forward, clearly intending to come after me.

"No," I growled more forcefully.

"Come on, you'll like it," he insisted.

"Leave it. She doesn't want to," Warren called, floating lazily on

201

his back.

"But I want her to," Miles said. "She'll like it once she's in."

"I don't want t-" I started but Miles leapt out of the water with a burst of speed, rushing behind me and tearing my robe off.

"No!" I yelled as he picked me up with a wild laugh, like this was all some game.

I screamed as he jumped into the pool with a whoop leaving his mouth and the moment we slammed into the pool, he let me go.

My scream poured out into the water in a stream of bubbles and I kicked, flailed, thrashed, trying to fight my way back to air.

Somehow, I made it up, but only for a second before I went under again, my feet kicking out and not finding purchase.

An arm looped around me and Miles yanked me above water with wide blue eyes fixed on me.

"I can't swim, asshole!" I shouted, shoving his shoulders, but he only held me tighter.

"Oh shit, sorry Snow."

Warren moved closer, giving Miles a look that said 'I told you so', and Miles gave him an innocent expression in return.

Miles roughly pushed some wet strands of hair out of my face, practically poking me in the eye.

"Ow, watch it," I snarled.

"Woah, chill. I've got you. I won't let you drown. And if you do, I'll just turn you into a vampire," he laughed, and I glowered.

"Miles, you're doing that thing again," Warren said.

"What thing?" Miles muttered.

"That thing where you think everyone wants to play your games and dance to your tune."

"But my games and tunes are the best," Miles insisted.

"You just threw a fragile human who can't swim into deep water," Warren pointed out.

"I'm not fragile," I insisted, but they weren't listening.

"Yeah, but I've got hold of her now, and I'll play nice this time," Miles said.

"Maybe ask her what she wants," Warren suggested, and Miles

turned his gaze back on me.

"I get overexcited sometimes," he admitted. "I can teach you to swim."

"That wasn't asking," Warren said, but Miles continued on.

"I've got you. Just do what I say, and you'll be fine." He smiled, and I could see I had no choice here.

I'd have to try and keep my arm underwater, and just hope for the best.

"Alright, show me," I relented.

"Okay, I'll hold your waist and you just kick your legs and spin your arms in a kind of cartwheel."

"What?" I blurted but he flipped me over, laying me face down in the water and keeping me afloat by holding onto my waist.

I kicked like mad and water went up my nose, some chemical in it stinging the back of my throat.

"Just stop jerking like a finless dolphin and you'll have it," Miles said.

Warren roared a laugh, then started swimming on his back, moving his arms over his head as he went, cutting a path through the water. He made it look damn easy.

"C'mere. We'll do it where you can put your feet down." Miles guided me over to the shallower side of the pool, and I immediately relaxed as my toes touched the floor. With the water up to my shoulders, I could still keep my arm concealed too.

Miles demonstrated how to move in the pool, swimming in a style he called breaststroke. Thankfully, it allowed me to keep my arms under the surface, and I practised for a while in the shallower depths until I actually started to get the hang of it. The movements grew more fluid as my body adjusted quicker than I'd expected. There was a strange feeling in my limbs, like they knew what to do, like they were made for this.

"Shit, you're a natural," Miles commented. "Wanna swim to the waterfall?" He pointed across the pool and I nodded quickly, feeling more confident in my movements.

As we arrived at the fall, Warren appeared from underneath it, the water streaming over his glossy skin. "There's a cave back here, want to see?" he asked.

"Go on in," Miles encouraged, and Warren gestured for me to follow him.

Holding my breath, I swam under the flow of water, emerging in a plastic cave lit by blue lights.

Warren sat up on a ledge that was cut into the fake rocks, and I drifted closer, keeping my arms under the water.

"This is pretty cool, I guess," I said, looking around.

"Yeah," Warren agreed. "Hey, don't let Miles's eagerness put you off him. He means well. He just needs to be reminded he can't always do what he wants."

"And you remind him of that?"

"Yeah." He smiled. "When we met, he was the most arrogant, world-dominating insufferable bastard."

"You sure he's changed?" I asked lightly, and Warren actually laughed.

"Yes, more than you know. I keep him grounded, and he reminds me to enjoy life. I was so damn regimented before. We were polar opposites. But now..." He shrugged, light gleaming in his eyes. "We balance each other. That's how love is, I think. A push and pull finding harmony in the middle."

I sensed no lie in his words, his love so brutally clear, I found my opinion shifting on vampires just a little. And if they could love, didn't that mean they were capable of good things too? Didn't that mean they, in fact, did have souls and feelings and desires that went beyond power, greed, and blood?

Warren suddenly caught my arm, pulling me out of the water with inhuman strength, and making me curse in surprise as he placed me down beside him. His gaze fell on the mark on my arm and horror jolted my heart as his expression turned to alarm.

"Wait," I hissed. "Let go."

I tried to pull away from his vice-like grip, but his hold was unrelenting.

His eyes whipped up to mine. "Holy shit," he breathed.

My gut spiralled and panic bloomed.

"Don't tell Miles," I gasped just as the prince appeared under the falls, and Warren let go of me.

"Don't tell me what?" he growled, his eyes flicking between us and a threat dancing in the air.

I shook my head at Warren, begging him not to say anything, but he beckoned Miles closer.

"You need to see this," Warren said, and I tried to scramble away across the rocks.

Warren caught my ankle, yanking me back to him before grabbing my forearm and presenting the mark to Miles.

Fear thrummed through my bones as Miles's expression darkened and the atmosphere thickened with danger.

Miles looked to Warren, then back to me. "You've got five seconds to explain yourself," he demanded, his light tone thoroughly abandoned.

"I don't know what it is," I admitted, my heart rioting with fear. All I had was the truth, and I prayed it would be enough. "It appeared yesterday."

"Miles," Warren said urgently. "We have to inform the others."

"No, please don't," I begged, certain that would be the end of me.

"She has slayer blood, like all of them do," Miles replied to Warren, acting like I wasn't there. "Hers must be far stronger."

I took in that information with a shaky breath. "You knew about this?"

"This is not normal, Miles," Warren pressed. "They are never *this* strong. The others could turn on her. Kill her."

"Tell me what you're talking about," I demanded, knowing it might be my only chance to get answers, the reality Warren's words painted making my chest crush with terror.

Miles gave me an assessing look, his expression growing more intense as he thought about something, then he turned to Warren again. "What if this is worth a shot? The others might not risk keeping her alive, but I'm willing to. Because if she's a true slayer, maybe that's what we need, maybe she's the one."

"The one what?" I pushed, fury blazing a path through my chest.

"Miles..." Warren shook his head. "Don't you dare say what you're thinking."

Miles's expression became calculated as he turned my way, and the monster that lived in him peered through his eyes, locking its sights on me.

"I won't tell anyone, Montana. I'll keep you safe," he promised. "But on one condition."

"What?" I whispered.

"You *must* pick me at the ceremony."

My pulse thumped loudly in my ears and my skin tingled all over with dread. That would mean breaking my promise to follow Erik's orders and pick Fabian. It could jeopardise my father's safety.

"Promise me." Miles's hand gripped mine, his desperation obvious.

I didn't have a choice. I had to agree for now or he'd tell the others. A vampire had already tried to kill me because she thought I was a slayer, and they clearly thought the other royals might do the same. But if I truly made this choice at the ceremony, Erik would go back on his word. He'd send my father straight back to the blood bank, or worse.

"Okay," I breathed at last, securing myself more time, if nothing else.

But the clock was already ticking.

CALLiE

CHAPTER TEN

It took the entire next day for us to travel the remaining distance to the blood bank, and with the short hours of daylight due to the harsh winter, the sun was already beginning to sink towards the horizon by the time we spotted it through the trees.

Magnar had been quiet once again, though the silence had felt different today, less tense, more...comfortable? No, I wouldn't have gone that far, but there was a line that had been struck out between us now. I didn't fight against the feeling of his arms surrounding me where we sat together on the horse, not after having his mouth between my thighs and his fingers inside me. That seemed pretty pointless after what we'd done. There was still tension between us, but it had shifted. Or perhaps it was simply my take on where it would lead that had shifted. Hard to say. Especially when his grip around me tightened and his hands rested on my thighs where he held the reigns.

I stirred uncomfortably as night began to fall around us. I doubted I'd ever be able to feel truly at ease after dark even with Magnar by my side. It was like it was built into my psyche to head inside and stay there once the sunlight faded.

My skin prickled uneasily, and I leaned back against Magnar, stealing some heat from his huge body and fighting off the thoughts of his mouth on my skin, his voice rough with command and my utter complicity with his every order for once.

We hadn't said a word about what we'd done together since waking this morning, but Magnar was less than subtle in his own smugness. I wanted to call him out on that shit, but honestly, I was just glad my legs had remembered how to move when we'd gotten up to leave at dawn and had chosen to cling to what pride remained to me. Besides, we'd both taken what we wanted from one another, so I wasn't going to start worrying about it after the fact.

None of that even seemed to matter now anyway.

My breath stalled in my lungs the second I spotted the blood bank through a parting in the trees, my heart thumping harder with every breath as the foul sense of the place crept over me. It was like the air was tainted here, the silence so thick within the forest that I had to assume even the wildlife had decided to vacate this place, wanting nothing to do with the shadows cast by that imposing building.

"You really think we can get my family out of there?" I asked quietly, a mixture of excitement and terror filling me as we found ourselves at our journey's end. They were so close now, all I loved and cherished in this world. The only things that mattered to me at all.

The stallion's chest rose and fell steadily beneath us as he cooled off after the long ride, the mare further back carrying our bags, secured to us with a long line of rope.

Magnar had stopped the horse within the trees, keeping us out of sight from any guards who might be on watch outside the menacing building. The mare sidled closer, nuzzling her companion affectionately, the two of them quieter than they had been all day, as though they sensed the darkness here too.

The blood bank was solidly built with red bricks that had faded and stained over time. It spread away from us out of sight over one level, the windows high and unreachable, no door visible from our position. Dad said it used to be a factory before the Final War. Hundreds of humans would have worked within those walls. Now it was a place where all mortals dreaded ending up. It was the final destination on our way to the stomachs of the vampires. The place they took you when the only reason to keep you breathing at all was the blood running through your veins. I doubted any human who had entered it since the vampires' rule began had made it out alive.

Tall, white chimneys stood at either end of the menacing building, the one on the right belching black smoke into the darkening sky. An acrid stench filled the air, and I tried not to think about what they were burning, fighting against the bile that rose in my throat. Everything about the place made me want to turn and flee in the opposite direction, but I steeled my resolve, pushing those fears back with all I had. I couldn't waste time on pointless emotions. My family needed me, and I'd do whatever it took to help them.

I swallowed a thick lump in my throat as the reality of what we were planning pressed down on me, the imposing building seeming to mock every plan we'd made and scorn every thought I'd let myself believe in over the way this reunion would go. How the fuck were we supposed to get my family out of there?

"Are you sure we can do this?" I breathed, not out of fear for myself, simply out of the knowledge that if we failed, then that was their only chance gone. It was all or nothing.

"I will get them out or die trying," Magnar swore.

"Less of the talk about dying," I grunted, trying not to take his words seriously.

I knew what we were about to attempt was all kinds of insane and death was only one of many terrible possible outcomes. But if there was the smallest chance of getting my dad and Montana out of that hell hole, then I had to try.

Magnar twisted his fingers around a lock of my hair that had fallen forward to hang near my eyes, tugging it back over my shoulder so he could lean in and speak straight into my ear.

"Death doesn't frighten me, drakaina hjarta," he rumbled, his stubble grazing my skin, rough words sending a shiver through to my core. "Valhalla waits beyond this plane of flesh and fury. But I will dance with violence this night and deliver you what I promised."

He bit my neck, and I sucked in a sharp breath, my fingers knotting in the stallion's mane. My skin came alive beneath his touch and my heartbeat stammered with surprise as my blood heated. A blush crawled across my cheeks at the casual intimacy of the gesture. Magnar didn't seem to have any reservations about touching me. He simply acted on whatever impulse took him, claiming what he wanted without apology for it.

I probably would have growled something at him in any other circumstance, warning him back, maintaining the distance I'd always kept so clearly around myself. But I leaned into him instead, letting my eyes fall closed for the briefest moment as I enjoyed the roughness of his mouth on my skin and took the opportunity to stamp on my fear for good. It wouldn't help me. And I needed to stay focused.

My mind travelled back to all we'd done last night, and I bit my lip to stop myself from turning to face him, from taking more from him and stealing another of his lawless kisses.

But he wasn't mine and I certainly wasn't his. One night of surrendering my flesh to his command didn't change what we were to one another. A means to an end.

With the cold light of dawn had come the truth we'd both been closing in on from the second we'd met. Each moment we spent together was bringing us closer to the time when we would part. Every brush of his skin against mine since then was filled with the promise of goodbye, no matter how sinfully perfect some of those touches might be.

His hand travelled to my throat, his grip tightening until it grew hard to draw breath and I stiffened in his hold.

"There is nothing to fear in death," Magnar breathed, his grip flexing and my blood heating. "It is the natural way of things. In death, we are reunited with those we have loved and lost. I have many people waiting for me there. I am not afraid to join them when my time comes."

He released me, as though trying to prove just how closely we walked the line between life and death at all times, but I raised my chin in defiance of that statement.

"Well, I'm not ready to face it yet," I replied.

We'd reached the final intersection of our differing paths, and if everything went to plan, we would go our separate ways before the sun rose tomorrow. Death could let us pass until then.

Magnar released my hair, letting it fall against my neck again as he shifted back, moving out of my personal space and letting me breathe without the intoxication of him filling my lungs. Apparently, he hadn't forgotten either. And he hadn't changed his mind.

"I will do my best to stay alive then," he agreed, before dismounting and holding his hands up to help me down.

I gave in for once, allowing my pride to take the hit as I slid from the stallion's back and let Magnar catch me, his powerful arms taking my weight easily, my body pressing to his as he placed me on my feet. The setting sun made the ink on his bronze skin darken with hidden meaning, that power which always surrounded him thickening until I considered whether he was right about the gods watching over him, wondering if they were paying attention now.

"I never thanked you," I forced myself to say. I held his gaze, wanting to speak these words to him even if they cut my pride to shreds and made the anger inside of me flare up once more. But it wasn't really aimed at him. It was the injustice of all my family had endured every damn day because of those fucking bloodsuckers. "For saving me the day the vampires took my family captive. At the time, I was so angry that I couldn't see what you'd done for me. Regardless of your reasoning, despite only being your bait. If you hadn't stopped me from running to them, then I'd be stuck inside that building now too. And we'd have no hope at all. Whatever happens tonight, I need you to know how much I appreciate it. If anything goes wrong, then I just want you to know-"

Magnar stopped my rambling with a kiss that set my skin on fire. He crushed me against him, his fingers tangling in my hair, and I lost myself in his strong arms.

The kiss was all heat, passion that raged beyond the flames that had ignited between us last night and spoke of a truth far more potent than simple lust. He claimed me with the rake of his tongue against mine, the press of his mouth and the bite of his teeth as he drew my bottom lip between them and tugged almost hard enough to hurt. That kiss was air in my lungs and the scent of freedom on the wind, it was a thousand possibilities that had never been mine before and a defiance of the fate life had dealt me. But it was goodbye too.

I stood on my tiptoes and pushed my body against his, feeling the firm press of his muscles as his hands fisted in my hair. And I let myself steal that small moment just for my own.

All too soon, we broke apart and Magnar trailed a hand down the side of my face, brushing his thumb across my lower lip.

"I was alone before I found you," he said roughly, his fingers tracing the mark on my arm, and a knot formed in my stomach at his words. "And no matter what happens tonight or tomorrow, no matter where our journeys take us now, I am not alone in this world anymore. The slayers will rise again. My destiny can be rewritten."

My lips parted to reply, but I didn't know how to form the roiling storm of emotion zipping through my body into words. I slid my hand from his neck down to his chest, laying it over his heart which pounded beneath his fighting leathers.

"I was alone too," I said eventually. "I was like a butterfly in a jar, staring out at a world which should have been mine to claim, unable to fill that longing for freedom in my chest. There were only ever two people who made it into the jar with me. I locked it up tight against everyone else, and I thought that meant I was strong, but really, it just meant I was isolated. So I was alone too. I just didn't realise it until now."

Magnar leaned in once more, pressing his lips to mine in the barest brush of a kiss before stepping away.

My skin grew cold without him, and I watched as he moved to gather supplies from the bags on the mare's back, readying for our next move, the culmination of all we'd done until now.

I turned away from him and walked towards the tree line, keeping my footsteps silent as I looked out at the blood bank again.

I needed to focus my mind on what we'd come here to do. Dad and Montana were in there and it would take everything I had to get them out. Perhaps more than I had. Either way, I would give it up willingly for even a chance at success.

Goosebumps swept over my skin which had nothing to do with the freezing wind. I didn't need to put a hand on Fury to know there were vampires nearby. I could feel their presence like a breath on the back of my neck, like eyes gleaming in the darkness.

Despite the undeniable fear that coursed through my veins, I was also filled with hope. Montana and Dad were *so* close. I'd never gone a day without seeing them before, and it had been so long. My whole world had changed in every imaginable way since we'd last been together. But now we were finally here, and if by some miracle this plan worked, then I might truly be able to live my life in freedom. Such a thing had been nothing more than an impossible dream such a short time ago and now it was almost within reach. We only had to take it.

"They have familiars watching the area," Magnar said softly behind me. "We need to remove them before we can approach."

"How do we do that?" I asked as my gut plummeted.

The last familiar I'd tried to destroy had easily gotten past me. If these were anywhere near as slippery as that rat had been, then I didn't rate my chances against them.

"We can't head out into the open with them watching, so we'll have to draw them to us," he said, the challenge rousing something in his tone that reminded me he'd been born for this, the thrill of the fight lighting him up before it had even begun.

"Won't the vampires notice us killing them?" I questioned, my unease growing as I looked up at the branches overhead, hunting for any sign of the ungodly creations.

"Likely not. The connection the vampires maintain with the familiars isn't constant. The vampires set them tasks, then leave them to it. If the animal sees or hears something the vampire would want to know about, then they use the connection between their minds to send a message. We will need to kill the creatures without being seen. Sudden and swift. In all likelihood, the vampires controlling them won't know anything about it until it's too late. Unless we get unlucky and they choose to contact the creatures themselves at the precise moment when we strike, we should be safe." He gave the building one more sweeping glance, then beckoned me further back into the trees.

I turned away from the view and followed him, making sure to keep my footsteps silent. I didn't want to take any chances this close to our enemies, and I begrudgingly accepted the fact that Magnar's insistence on me practicing this had been worthwhile.

Magnar led me to a small clearing and handed me the flashlight we'd taken from the store. I waited while he moved around the area, inspecting the trees and vegetation until he'd found what he was looking for.

"I want you to hide here and point the light back towards the building. Once I'm in position, start flashing it on and off. That should draw them to us, and I'll take care of it from there."

I nodded in understanding as I looked down at the little flashlight in my hand. I knew the plan made sense, but the idea of drawing those creatures towards us felt more than a little insane.

I ducked down into the bushes and waited while he took cover behind a towering trunk opposite my hiding place. Magnar pulled Venom into his grasp and held it ready, falling still. In the diminishing light, he was little more than a silhouette to me, and I knew where to look for him. Hopefully that meant the creatures we hunted wouldn't stand a chance.

I took a deep breath and flicked the flashlight on and off again.

I waited a few moments then repeated the process. Seconds dragged into minutes as I continued to flick the light on and off and we waited, and waited...

Soft snuffling reached my ears as something approached, and I flicked the light off, leaving us in total darkness once more.

I held my breath, the faintest padding of paws drawing closer through the undergrowth.

A large, grey rabbit hopped into the clearing, looking about curiously. I almost doubted that evil could lay inside such an innocent looking creature, but Fury burned at my hip in recognition of what resided within the animal, any doubts banished by the blade's certainty.

The rabbit hopped closer, ears back, nose twitching-

Magnar appeared like little more than a shadow at its back, his movements so swift that he delivered a fatal blow before the familiar could so much as turn, cleaving through its small body and striking its heart with a precision that made my pulse leap.

The vampire's slave dissolved into dust before my eyes, and Magnar quickly moved back into the cover of the trees.

The second familiar arrived a moment later in the shape of a rat. I glared at the creature, noting the little white mark down the centre of its nose. It wasn't the same familiar that had eluded me in the tree days ago, but it still made my stomach twist with irritation. Magnar dispatched it as quickly as the first, and I started flashing the light again.

It took a few minutes before the third familiar approached. I almost didn't notice the huge bird as it swept through the trees. The owl landed silently on a low branch not far from my hiding place, then twisted its head back and forth, searching for the source of the light.

Luckily it had landed in such a way that the trunk of a tree blocked Magnar from its sight, but there was also no way for him to approach the owl without it spotting him.

I bit my lip as I tried to decide if I should take it on. I was the only one able to reach it without being seen first, but after my failed attempt with the rat, I was terrified of missing again. If the creature got a warning about us back to its master, then any chance we had of making it into the blood bank and saving my family was gone.

I had a clear shot though. And as the seconds ticked on, I could almost sense Magnar's frustration, trying to work out the best way to handle this.

I was the answer, I just had to trust myself. So, I held my breath and eased myself upright, taking my first, tentative step towards the bird.

It ruffled its feathers as it scoured the clearing again and I took the opportunity to close in on it from behind. The branch it had chosen for a perch was low enough for me to reach from the ground, and I silently unsheathed Fury.

The blade hummed excitedly as I closed in on my quarry. *Strike fast and true,* it urged eagerly, and I let its excitement guide my arm as I swung the blade.

The owl began to turn and I leapt at it, driving the knife straight into its back, the strike dissolving it into dust before its eyes could find me.

I allowed myself a wide smile as I took cover again to wait for the final creature to come and investigate our trap.

Minutes dragged on but nothing arrived. I willed Fury to use its gift to search for any signs of another familiar approaching, but it couldn't sense a thing.

Eventually, Magnar stood and beckoned me to join him. I left my hiding place and made my way over to him in the clearing as he placed Venom over his shoulder.

"Nicely done."

My lips twitched at the touch of praise, but I just shrugged, letting him go on.

"The final creature has moved away, but I am confident it remains unaware of us. We'll have to risk it returning while we're exposed, but there is little more we can do to draw it out without raising too much suspicion and bringing the vampires to us too," he said, his brow low with irritation, but he was right, we couldn't wait here any longer in hopes of it heading back this way.

"Okay, so what now?" I asked.

"Now?" Magnar asked, and the way his mouth lifted with amusement let me know that whatever his plan was, I was going to hate it. "Now it's time for the Belvederes to learn of my return," he growled, the threat and promise in his eyes telling me the prospect of that excited him far more than it terrified him. "Let's make sure they know I'm coming for them."

A fierce smile lit his features, and I stole a little of his courage as he led the way through the trees back towards the blood bank.

I already knew what my role would be once we made it inside. While he fought and killed the vampires we found, I had to release any humans they held captive. We'd stay together so that he could protect me and clear a path to my family. Fury would help me when I needed it, and I trusted Magnar to keep me safe after all we'd been through together. I might have been his bait, but I didn't expect him to leave me in the trap once it had sprung around his real prey.

We made it to the edge of the trees and hesitated in the safety of their shadows.

The sun was sinking beneath the horizon and darkness loomed in earnest. This was it. The time the vampires held dear. We were attacking their stronghold during the hours when they held the most power. I didn't question Magnar's decision to go in at night, but what I would have given for a blazing summer's day to aid us.

The moon had appeared in the sky, low and fat, a shining silver ball to take the place of the sun. Mom had always called me her sun and Monty her moon, so I tried to take the sight of it as a sign that Montana was close, waiting for me within those walls, ready for me to come for her at last.

Not long now, Monty. I smiled as I pictured her face pinched in irritation at the nickname, and I hoped to be seeing it for real very soon.

"Draw your blade. Keep close to me," Magnar instructed, and I pulled Fury into my grasp again. His bossy bullshit might not fly with me most of the time, but in this situation, I was willing to nod and obey every note of instruction he offered.

Yesss, Fury sighed in anticipation. *So many. So close.*

I swallowed a lump in my throat as I drew on the blade's enthusiasm to try and banish some of my own fear. Of course my little pocket psycho was thrilled to find a whole army of vampires waiting for it. Mortality really did take the edge off of the excitement for me though.

"Fear is a weapon you can wield," Magnar said, catching my eye with his golden gaze which blazed with a mixture of determination and anticipation. "It is nothing more than your own desire to survive. The very essence of mortality. The things you'll be fighting in that place are already dead. They know nothing of what it is to live anymore. And they know nothing of love. The power you hold simply through the intensity of your feelings towards your family is far greater than their desire to cling to a life which was lost to them long ago. Use that power against them and they will fall before it."

My heart skittered at his words, my resolve building.

"You fight for the freedom of your family," he continued. "And you will succeed at all costs."

"I will succeed," I echoed, needing the power of the words to get me through this.

What we were about to do wasn't about me. It was about *them*. The vampires had taken my family from me once, but I would die before I let them keep them from me.

I felt the power of that determination rise through my blood like a tide and the slayer's mark on my arm tingled in anticipation.

I wasn't afraid. I was ready. And heaven help any bloodsucker who stood in my path.

MAGNAR

CHAPTER ELEVEN

1000 YEARS AGO

I lay beneath the thick canvas of my tent with my arms behind my head, frowning as the wind battered the material. Usually, I loved the sound of a storm when I was tucked within the confines of my tent. Knowing the wind and rain were thwarted in trying to reach me always made me feel like I was somehow outsmarting the gods themselves.

I wished that were true today more than ever. Because if ever I'd needed a way around the will of the gods, it was now.

"Idun?" I murmured, careful not to wake Astrid where she slept soundly beside me.

The lost girl hadn't wanted to leave my side in this camp of heathens, and I couldn't say I blamed her entirely, so I'd obliged, allowing her to sleep in my tent with me. I knew a small, petty part of me had agreed as a sneer to my betrothal too, but I had needed that small act of rebellion to help quiet the thrashing of my heart. Still, it wasn't enough.

I'd tried to forget my worries in the comfort of her company, had even stolen a kiss from her sweet lips between stories of the lives we'd led. But once she'd fallen into an exhausted slumber, the reality of my situation had drawn close again.

When the sun rose, I had to pledge myself to Valentina and make our betrothal official. Today, I had to give up any hope I had of finding love. Or happiness. I would tie myself to a stranger and forfeit the dreams I'd had of a life holding something *more*.

"Idun?" I muttered again a little louder, hoping the goddess might heed my call.

If only she'd listen, I'd offer her anything she asked of me. Anything but this. I only wished for one thing in this life and that was to find a woman who was my equal in every way and to love her for everything she was. I would sacrifice everything else in the pursuit of my destiny, I would fight any battle, take on any challenge, but this I wanted for my own. And I knew in my heart that Valentina wasn't that woman.

"I will give you anything if you'd just free me from making this promise," I vowed.

The tent began to buckle and sway under the pressure of the storm, and I pushed myself upright. I sensed something powerful drawing closer, my pulse quickening as the power of the gods folded itself around me. Had she answered my call?

I stood and placed a hand against the thick canvas of my tent, a chill creeping across my palm from the pounding rain outside.

I pulled on my trousers and fastened my boots, my skin prickling from the electricity in the air. Thunder crashed overhead, the eye of the storm rolling in, the chaos of nature bowing to the whims of the gods.

I took hold of Tempest and moved towards the exit, unfastening the toggles so I could lift the flap and peer out into the storm.

Rain fell in torrents, skimming over the tents and pooling in the mud. Lightning forked through the sky, momentarily illuminating the camp around me. No one else was foolish enough to be outside in such weather, but something about it called to me, the power of it stirring the blood in my veins.

I looked up at the sky, wondering if I might spy Thor himself riding on his chariot pulled by the goats Tanngnjóstr and Tanngrisnir. Lightning flashed in the distance as he threw his hammer, and I took it as a sign that the true powers of this world had heard my call and might just be willing to listen.

The wind shifted, driving water into my face, and Astrid mumbled something from the bed behind me as the cold air found her skin.

I stepped outside, dropping the tent flap. The freezing rain cascaded over me, plastering my long hair to my scalp and raising goosebumps along the exposed skin on my arms and chest.

Tempest purred with expectant energy, but I didn't get the sense that a vampire drew close. This was something else.

I welcomed the thrashing power of the storm when it slammed into me, calling out a greeting to Thor as I looked between the tents of my people.

Darkness pressed in thickly, the deep storm clouds blotting out the moon and stars. It was hard to see anything of the camp around me, and I squinted at the space to my right where I knew my parents' tent lay. I wondered if I should wake them, but something stopped me. Whatever was coming wasn't meant for them. It was here for me.

Shimmering golden light caught my eye, and I turned to find a tiny hummingbird, blazing with a gold that just couldn't be natural, flitting back and forth above the mud beside me. The water pooling beneath it sparkled with golden light like the rays of the sun.

I frowned as the creature circled me once, flashing out of existence before appearing again further away.

I adjusted my grip on Tempest and followed the tiny bird through the pounding rain.

I passed by my parents' tent and my brother's. The trail it led me along wound its way further through the camp, beyond the horses who huddled together beneath their canopy to try and escape the worst of the storm where the rain blew in. Baltian lifted his head and whinnied hopefully as he spotted me, but I couldn't spare him any attention beyond a wave of my hand as I followed on after the path that had been set for me.

The hummingbird drew me further into the night, away from the camp, towards a sheer cliff lined with pale rock. Further and further I walked, until the camp was far behind me and the cliff towered overhead.

Lightning flared, blinding me for a moment, and a figure appeared at the base of the cliff. She sat on a throne which seemed to have grown from the ground itself, the tiny bird coming to perch on it, its job done.

Each time I tried to look at her directly, my gaze fell upon the throne instead. It called to me, offering me everything and promising nothing at once.

Its legs were roots which twisted into a thick trunk lined with glimmering golden bark. The back of the throne rose up behind the figure who sat on it, splaying into branches which rippled in a faint breeze, much more gently than the raging storm which buffeted me. Along the branches, pale blossoms budded then bloomed before my eyes, golden apples growing to their fullness as the petals spilled to the floor, the fruit sparkling so appetisingly that my mouth watered just looking at them. I was filled with a longing I couldn't understand. Those apples summoned me, whispering promises of dreams fulfilled and life never ending.

I took a step towards them, my hand raising as if to pluck one from the closest branch, but then I fell still.

With a growl of irritation, I dropped my hand and forced my eyes away from the temptation of the fruit. Those thoughts had not been my own, and I wouldn't let my fate fall on the bite of some magic-ridden apple.

Finally, I managed to look upon the face of the goddess who sat on the throne. I didn't need to have seen her before to recognise her. I knew who she was in the pit of my stomach.

Idun smiled as my gaze met hers. Her face was beauty beyond words, my chest aching as I looked upon her, unable to take the sheer perfection of her, my heart stumbling in my chest as I took in her full lips and shimmering skin. Her hair was the same bright gold as the apples which adorned her throne and it trailed down the full length of her body, pooling around her bare feet in swathes as soft as silk.

The rain didn't touch her. She sat in an impossible bubble of calm amidst the raging storm which fell on me. Had she asked Thor to assist her with the storm or stolen some of his power for her own?

"I'm impressed," Idun purred, and her voice was deep and seductive, echoing through to the depths of my soul. "Not many men can resist the temptation of my immortal fruit. But you are no ordinary man, are you, Magnar Elioson?"

"I do not compare myself to other men," I replied fiercely. An ache of longing filled me, and I was struck with the urge to throw myself at her feet, begging for a moment in her arms. "Your tricks won't work on me."

I pushed aside the desire to worship her without end and stepped closer, entering the pool of warmth which surrounded her. The pounding rain withdrew and only the water dripping down my body and through my hair remained.

Idun observed me through narrowed eyes, a small smile pulling at her lips. Her dress was a living carpet of vines and flowers which twisted its way around her figure, blossoming before my very eyes.

"No, there's nothing ordinary about you at all," she concluded, though her tone gave away nothing of her thoughts on that.

"I wish to be free of the promise I am to make today. Don't ask me to take Valentina as a bride; the only thing I've ever wanted for myself is love. I will give you anything else. Everything else. But please don't take that from me."

I gazed at her imploringly, hoping to find some humanity in her glassy eyes, but there wasn't so much as a flicker of reaction to my words.

"And what of that which has been taken from me?" she asked, a hint of rage lacing her tone. "Who will set that right for me?"

"*I* will," I replied instantly. "Only tell me what it was, and I will return it to you."

She laughed and the sound was a dark, poisonous thing which mixed with a rumble of thunder from the sky above us.

"The thing they stole was their immortality," she spat. "Your people have tried to right that wrong for two hundred years already, and to no avail. I created your kind to do just that, but I have been sorely disappointed. I saved a pregnant girl from the Revenants' village when they were in the first throes of their bloodlust. I gave her much more than I should have and created a village of warriors strong enough to protect her unborn twins and save her bloodline from the vampires. In return, all of them swore to destroy those creatures, but none of them succeeded. What makes you think you will be able to do what they have not?"

"I do not understand." I knew that she had created our people to fight the vampires and end their curse, but I had never heard of them stealing anything from her before now. If all she wanted was their deaths, then I was already committed to delivering that.

Idun stood and approached me. The urge to drop to my knees flooded me once more as she exerted her will, but I did no such thing, and she smiled, reaching out to touch my chest. The vines which created her dress shifted, exposing much of her flesh and luring my eyes to roam over her. My body shuddered with desire as her hand skimmed across my skin and she circled behind me, but I didn't move, didn't act on what she was trying to tempt me with in any way.

"Of course you don't understand. You mortals never do," Idun sneered, her fingers trailing over my bare flesh as she circled me, gooseflesh rising in their wake, her touch like liquid glass, soft and sharp at once, burning with untold power. "What I desire is the return of my reputation. *I* am the keeper of immortality, and I never offered that gift to the Revenants. While they continue to live, I continue to suffer the shame of their creation. If you want my help, then finish what your ancestors started."

She moved back in front of me, and I shivered as she removed her hand from my skin.

"My life is devoted to destroying the Revenants already; I took my vow two years early. If you need further proof of my dedication-"

"Your dedication doesn't interest me," she hissed. "You are all *so* dedicated to the task and yet you are no closer to achieving it than you were when I created your kind. All four Revenants still roam this earth, mocking me with their very existence."

"Tell me what you do want then." Desperation clawed at me. I needed to be free of this betrothal.

Idun sat back in her throne and plucked an apple from its branches. She took a bite, her eyes staying on me as juice poured over her bottom lip and her dress blossomed with white flowers, covering her exposed skin once more.

"Prove your dedication," she said quietly. "If you wish for true love, then you shall find it...eventually. Once you've proven yourself to me."

She snapped her fingers and my heart thumped solidly in my chest as her power washed over me. I buckled forward as something flowed through my body, rocking my soul so that it felt like it wanted to burst free of my skin. The power which rolled through me rattled my bones, my lungs spasming with the need to draw breath, muscles lurching from the onslaught of raw energy.

I gasped, plunging Tempest into the ground as I used it to hold myself upright, feeling like that was the only thing tethering me to this earth while her power caressed me until the wave of energy slowly faded away again.

"So that's it?" I asked. "I don't have to go through with my betrothal to Valentina?"

Idun laughed again and the storm roared beyond our cocoon of warmth. "Oh, you'll have to go through with it alright. You shall seal your betrothal when the sun rises this very day. You want to prove yourself, don't you?"

"But I thought-"

She waved a hand, silencing me. "Many challenges will come your way now Magnar Elioson," she promised. "And if you manage to pass every test, then your reward will come to you. *True love.*" She sighed like the idea appealed to her on some level, though I doubted she was capable of any such desire. "But you cannot falter. You cannot fail. You will end the vampire curse and remove the gift of immortality from those who should never have been offered it. Or you will die trying."

I opened my mouth to respond as lightning flared so brightly that I was forced to close my eyes. The pool of warmth that surrounded me disappeared and the freezing rain slammed down on me once again.

I opened my eyes, and the goddess was gone. I was alone in the rain with nothing but the hope that she would keep to her promise. I had to follow my vow and end the Revenants. And perhaps one day, I'd be able to find my own happiness in return.

By the time I made it back to camp, the storm had blown itself out, Thor finishing his ride through the skies, and all that remained of his passage was the deep puddles and thick mud between the tents. A sliver of sunlight had crested the horizon, and I could finally see clearly in the growing light.

I didn't know if my interaction with the goddess had helped me or not. My position hadn't improved, but she'd given me hope that it might. I only had to pass whatever tests she lay before me and destroy the Revenants. The fact that our people had been trying to do so without success for hundreds of years didn't deter me. I had always been dedicated to finding and eradicating them.

She had said all four of them still remained, and that knowledge stirred a feeling of unease within my chest. There had been no sign nor report on the whereabouts of Erik Larsen in over a hundred years, and my people had begun to believe him dead, hoping one of ours might have finished him before perishing themselves from the fight. If he'd managed to remain hidden for so long, then finding him now could prove to be very difficult indeed. But I would rise to the challenge. Perhaps the deaths of his supposed siblings would draw him out of hiding.

People were waking and leaving the shelter of their tents as the sun began to climb into the sky. I doubted sleep had come easily to many while the storm raged.

As I closed in on my tent, someone stepped into my path, and I blinked heavily as my gaze landed on Valentina. She was dressed immaculately in a deep green gown which was cut low, exposing much of her chest and leaving her stomach bare. I let my eyes trail over her, trying to appreciate her beauty. It wasn't as though I couldn't see any way to desire her as I might any beautiful woman. I just didn't feel any inclination to do so. Besides, I didn't know her at all. And she did not seem the warrior type. The type that usually set my blood pumping.

"I came looking for you in your tent. I thought we might have breakfast together," she said, her eyes searching my face for something I doubted she would find. "I thought maybe we could get to know each other a little, but your brother wouldn't allow me to enter. He told me you weren't there."

I blinked at her, taking in her words while my mind remained full of the goddess. Julius had covered for me, though some part of me wished he hadn't bothered. Had let her see Astrid in my bed, and... I sighed. That was a petty hope and a cruel thought. I doubted Valentina would have called off the betrothal over the slight anyway, and it probably would have just compounded my problems.

"Where have you been?" Valentina pressed when I didn't reply, a frown barely concealed on her face.

I glanced down at myself. I was half-dressed and soaking wet. It was clear I'd been out in the storm and no doubt she was wondering if I was insane.

"I needed to clear my head. Breakfast sounds appealing though." I offered her a faint smile and her eyes lit up. Perhaps I was being too harsh on her. I assumed she hadn't asked for this fate any more than I had, she simply seemed more willing to accept it. Perhaps I'd had one too many fantasies of what I thought love would be for me. The push and pull of a wild, chaotic kind of romance that spoke to my soul. One I felt thrashing within my blood the very moment we met. It was how Father had described his feelings upon first meeting my mother, and I supposed I had hoped my own love would declare itself just as fast.

Julius appeared behind Valentina, and I turned my attention to my brother who was looking seven shades of amused.

"Been walking in the storm, Magnar?" he asked with a knowing smirk, and I suppressed a sigh. "No doubt you were tossing and turning in your bed *all night* with the excitement of today and could hardly sleep."

"Something like that," I replied flatly, refusing to let him bait me.

"I got quite the surprise when I came looking for you at dawn. To find your bed...*abandoned* like that." He raised an eyebrow suggestively, and I knew he'd found Astrid precisely where I'd left her. Perhaps allowing the stolen girl to sleep in my tent the night before my betrothal became official hadn't been the best idea I'd ever had. I guessed I owed Julius for covering for me.

"Thank you for your concern, brother. I was just about to have breakfast with my bride to be. Perhaps you could make sure my tent is tidied before I return?" I asked, and I knew he would understand the request to see to it that Astrid was removed from my bed and given something to eat.

"No doubt you'll reward me well for such service. Save me some breakfast." He smiled widely at Valentina and turned away, heading towards my tent. I knew he'd arrange for someone to return Astrid to her village, and she'd be long gone before Valentina even remembered her existence.

"Your brother is still unsworn?" she asked me as she watched him leave.

"For now. We plan to have his prophecy told after his sixteenth birthday so that he might also take his vow early." I turned away from Julius and led her through the tents towards the campfire which was being built up again after the rain.

"You must be so proud to have taken your vow early," she breathed, grabbing hold of that topic of conversation and laying a hand on my arm. "No one has ever done so before."

I wondered why she was telling me something I already knew, but I murmured some response in agreement.

"Do you often go walking in the rain?" she asked, and I was reminded that she belonged to the Clan of Storms. Perhaps walking in such weather was normal for her people.

"I was searching for...answers I suppose. But the goddess wasn't very forthcoming."

"The gods often speak in riddles," she agreed. "Did you find any clarity?"

I half considered telling her about my encounter with Idun, but I doubted she'd appreciate the fact that I'd gone to beg to be released from the promise I had to make her.

"I suppose I did find clarity," I agreed eventually. I knew now that I had to prove my dedication to the goddess.

I had to do this and anything else she asked of me if I ever hoped to find love for myself. So, I would lock myself into this betrothal, but I intended to follow my mother's advice too. I wouldn't go through with the wedding unless my hand was forced by another prophecy or if by some miracle I fell in love with the girl walking beside me. I knew that would be the simplest answer to my problem, but as I looked at Valentina, I just couldn't see it. She was all poise and perfection, ice and stone, where I desired a wildfire which would keep me ever chasing.

I took a seat on one of the huge logs that sat around the campfire, choosing a spot away from the unsworn as they worked on preparing breakfast so that we could have some privacy. Valentina dropped down beside me, angling herself towards me and arranging herself just so. It was all very staged, and I got the strange impression that she might have practiced the way she was sitting, her legs crossed towards me, encouraging the slit in her dress to part just a little, her spine straight but shoulders positioned to allow a glimpse of her cleavage, her braided hair carefully drawn over one shoulder. She tilted her head up at what looked like a slightly uncomfortable angle to allow that view of her breasts too.

Guilt stirred in my gut. Was she just a puppet who had been placed here by her own elders? Had someone trained her in the art of whatever it was she was attempting now?

"Is this betrothal truly what you want?" I asked her quietly.

"Of course it is," she replied, her dark eyes finding mine, nothing but truth in her gaze which drew a sigh to my lips that I had to fight back. "Don't you want it too?"

I couldn't force my tongue to bend around a lie, so I offered her something else instead. The bullshit I had given out a time or two when I was hoping to gain company in my bed for the night. "What man wouldn't desire a woman like you?" I reached out to brush her braid back over her shoulder, and she smiled. She *was* objectively appealing, if nothing else.

"I know I'll make you so happy, Magnar," Valentina breathed.

Before my mind could conjure up a response, she leaned forward and pressed her mouth to mine. Her lips were warm and firm against my own, but the heat of them didn't ignite anything within my soul. She slid her hands across my chest as she deepened the kiss and I kissed her back, fighting against the urge to pull away. Perhaps I wasn't being fair to her. Maybe I was so sure I wouldn't feel anything for this stranger that I was blocking off the possibility of it. But nothing about the two of us felt right to me. The kiss was stale on my lips, my cock resolutely uninterested. I wasn't even drawn to her in the way I had been to other women before her. The desire to fuck her wasn't even there. She just wasn't the right fit for me.

My father cleared his throat from somewhere close by and I glanced at him, realising that my eyes weren't even fucking closed, which only made this kiss all the more awkward, and I took the opportunity to release myself from Valentina.

"I'm glad to see the two of you are getting along." His gaze met mine and I was sure he could see the reluctance in my eyes, his brows tightening just a little, an apology in his expression which wouldn't equal my release from this decision. He reached out and clapped a hand on my shoulder. "The sun has risen. It's time to make this betrothal official."

Valentina jumped to her feet and hurried past the fire to join my mother who was waiting for us, an eagerness to her movements which I was utterly incapable of matching. My father held me back as I moved to follow.

"I know it doesn't feel like this is the right thing now," he murmured. "But I hope that in time you will come to see that following the path laid out by the gods will always work out for the best. Your sacrifice will be rewarded."

"I know," I replied. Idun had told me so herself. I had to face this challenge and any more that came after it. In the end, I had to have faith that it would be worth it. That didn't help remove the sourness from my tongue though. "But I wish you would have asked anything other than this of me," I added, unable to conceal the truth of how I felt from him. "The only thing in this life that I wished to choose for myself was a wife. The single thing that I had hoped to claim for my own has been denied me now."

Father sighed, looking across the fire to Valentina, his gaze straying to my mother, his great love. I knew he understood what he was denying me, that he wished it wasn't so.

"I'm proud of the way you are dealing with this," he said slowly. "It is a lot to take on at such a young age, and I understand the sacrifice is a difficult one. You need to seal the betrothal today, but your mother suggested we hold off on the wedding until after your training is completed."

"She did?" I looked across the fire to my mother, who gave me a knowing smile. There was no set time for how long a warrior's training would take, but I'd only bonded to my father a week ago. At the very least this would buy me a year. Likely more.

"Would you prefer that? As Earl, it is up to me to decide, if I say your training must take priority, then none can go against me."

"I would." I practically sagged with relief, and I reached out to grasp his arm. "My training is the only thing I want to focus on at the moment. I haven't learned enough of myself to consider marrying and having children yet-"

"I wouldn't mention grandchildren to your mother if you want to keep her on your side with this. If she thinks the situation will bring babies for her to fawn over, then she'll be all for pushing you into it as soon as possible," he chuckled. "I also want it noted that I fully realise she is steering my hand in postponing this union."

I released a breath and smiled with a little embarrassment. Perhaps allowing my mother to fight this battle for me wasn't becoming of a sworn slayer, but I didn't care. I would take whatever help I was offered in this matter.

Father laughed, placing an arm around my shoulders and drawing me after Valentina to a clearing beyond the fire. I'd knelt in that dirt just nine moons ago and taken my vow. My father had agreed to train me and the skin on the back of my right hand had been marked with a crescent, binding us together. I brushed my fingers over the mark now. It had felt like freedom at the time, now it felt like a trap.

The rest of the clan gathered around us, and I caught sight of Julius watching me with pity in his eyes. For all his teasing, I knew he was probably the only one here who fully appreciated what this was costing me. We had dreams, he and I. Of the lives we wished for once we vanquished the Revenants. Too many of our people seemed happy to accept that their lives might come and go without them ever finding out if we won this war, but not us. My brother and I would see it done and revel in our victory for years after it, enjoying all the bounties life might offer.

I took my position in the centre of the circle created by my people and Valentina stood opposite me. The rising sun shone down on us, and I felt the air humming with a touch of the power I'd felt last night. The goddess was watching, making sure I kept to my word. I wouldn't disappoint her.

My father moved to stand beside us, lifting my hand and placing it over Valentina's heart. It beat solidly beneath my palm, a smile lifting her lips as her eyes shone with anticipation. He lifted her hand next, placing it on my chest too. My heart rate picked up, but it wasn't through excitement. It wished to be free, a wild beast fighting to break the chains it could see coming for it.

"Those gathered here will bear witness to the binding of your souls. Speak the words and let your lives be tied together from now until death divides you. This promise will lead to your union and the birth of blessed children. Do you understand the oath you are making?" my father asked loudly enough for everyone gathered to hear him.

"Yes," Valentina replied firmly, and I nodded.

I knew what I was about to do, and my heart was heavy with it.

"Valentina of the Clan of Storms, do you claim this man?" my father asked, the first of the chains clasping tight around my thrashing heart with her reply.

"I claim Magnar Elioson of the Clan of War to be my betrothed. My heart is his. My life is his. We will be one." Her eyes danced with excitement, and for a moment, I thought I saw lightning flashing within them, the power of her people stirring beneath her skin.

"Magnar of the Clan of War, do you claim this woman?" my father asked.

A long beat of silence passed before I forced the promise from my mouth, my tongue fighting against me, rebelling until the last moment, unwilling to bend to the words. "I claim Valentina Torbrook of the Clan of Storms to be my betrothed. We will be one."

If anyone noticed that I didn't pledge my heart and life to her, then they didn't speak of it. Valentina's lips lifted into a full smile and the weight of the goddess's power moved closer to us. I could feel Idun's will wrapping its way around us like a rope biding our souls together.

Pain blossomed beneath Valentina's palm on my skin, and I sucked in a sharp breath. Valentina gasped too as runes began to appear on the flesh above her heart, marking her, marking *us*.

The power finally faded, and I retrieved my hand, glancing down at my skin. Valentina drew back as well and looked at the new tattoo which curled beneath my heart. The runes spoke of love and my bond to the stranger standing opposite me, binding me to her in a physical, immovable way, making sure none could question where my destiny lay. It was a mark all betrothed slayers bore, one that would be completed upon our marriage, and one I had never wanted to claim without choosing for myself.

The desire to burn the thing from my skin gripped me, my eyes darting to the fire and a flaming brand that lay at the centre of it. I clenched my jaw as I forced myself to look away from it.

"It is done!" my father announced. "Let the feast begin!"

A cheer went up from the people surrounding us and they surged forward, slapping my back and calling out their congratulations. I forced a smile onto my face which made my jaw ache and let them sweep me away from my bride-to-be as subtly as I could manage, allowing them to guide me closer to the ale so that I might drown my emotions in drunkenness. It seemed like the obvious thing to do.

I hoped Idun understood the weight of the sacrifice I'd just made to her. And I hoped she intended to keep her word. Because her promise was the only thing that was keeping me going in that moment, and if she didn't hold to her side of our bargain, then I might just end up breaking my vow to a god.

MONTANA

CHAPTER TWELVE

I'd remained in my room all afternoon, having made my excuses once Miles had taken me back to the castle. He had returned to his pleasant tone during the journey, but I'd barely said another word to him when I'd realised he wasn't going to tell me more about the mark or what would happen beyond the choosing ceremony. I didn't like the way he and Warren had kept sharing looks, whispering words I couldn't catch. This was bad. Really fucking bad.

I hugged my knees to my chest, thinking about Nightmare, which was now tucked under the pillow behind me. If Miles had found it, would he have been so lenient with me? If he had presumed I'd planned on killing him with that blade, would I have been at the mercy of the four royals now, torn to pieces by their rage?

I considered showing Erik my mark and hoping he might be reasonable, but I didn't like my odds. And if I was killed, nothing was going to keep Dad out of the blood bank.

I warred with myself, reaching for Nightmare and gripping the hilt. I wondered if it could steer me in any particular direction. Insane as it was, I felt in the deepest regions of my bones that I could trust the blade's judgement.

Have faith, Moon Child.

"Have faith in what?" I whispered, feeling foolish the moment I openly replied to the object.

Trust your heart.

I guessed that was as good of an answer as I was going to get, and I sighed, settling on a decision.

I hid Nightmare again and waited for Erik to come to my room like he usually did, but the hours ticked by, and he never came. As evening arrived, I decided to seek him out myself and make a request of him that would hopefully be enough to protect Dad.

Creeping into the hallway, I hurried along it, searching for the red door to his room. I soon found it and lifted my hand, readying to knock and trying to get my words straight in my head.

"Impressive, rebel, nearly a full minute without knocking. Should I be flattered?"

I turned in alarm, finding Erik standing there in the hallway as silent as ever, dressed in a navy suit with the crest of the royals on his breast pocket.

I dropped my hand, my mouth growing dry. Whatever expression was on my face suddenly morphed his amusement into concern.

"What's going on?"

"I need to talk to you," I said.

"Well, would you like to do it at a party? We're all going out. Everyone's waiting downstairs, I figured Miles had told you."

"What? No, I can't. I really need to tell you something."

He stopped half a foot from me, his brow furrowed. "Go on."

"Is my father free?" I asked hopefully.

He folded his arms. "Not yet. Wolfe has assured me he will be released by tomorrow."

"I changed my mind," I said suddenly. "I want you to let him go. Once he's free, release him outside the Realms."

Maybe this way I could keep my secret and still give my father a chance at freedom.

"That is a big ask," he growled.

"Please," I breathed. "Don't bring him here, he'll hate it. I just want him to be free, where he always wanted to be." *And maybe he'll find Callie and they'll evade the vampires together.*

He shook his head. "Rebel, it's not that simple. There are laws I must follow. We cannot just free humans."

I reached for him, gripping his arm tightly. "Please," I begged, desperation drowning me.

He stepped closer. "Your heart is pounding. Take a breath."

"Don't tell me to take a breath," I growled, shoving his chest as anger tore through me. "What do I have to do to make you give me this?"

He stared down at me, an ominous aura spilling from him. "You're asking me to go against my brothers and sister, to break our own laws."

My shoulders fell as I realised he wouldn't do this.

"The price of such a thing would be great indeed," he said darkly, and I glanced up at him, my hope rekindling.

"Anything," I breathed. "Whatever you want."

My stomach knotted as I waited for him to make his ask of me, for the axe to fall upon my neck. But any sacrifice was worth it to see my father free, to know that he was far away from the vampires with a chance at finding Callie and securing a life together.

"I will think on the debt," he said. "And if I can come up with something worth what you ask of me, then when your father is brought here, I will steal him away in the night, fake his escape and take him to the wilds myself."

A sharp lump rose in my throat, and I nodded, moving into his personal space, driven on by what I needed from him, sliding my hand up his arm and gripping the back of his neck.

"You will find a price high enough," I commanded. "You will think on it every minute you have spare in your eternal hours."

"Montana..." he said in a dry voice, his fingers gripping my hips and drawing me closer.

"Say it," I hissed.

"I will," he said fiercely, his ashen eyes blazing with those words. "But understand this, any price I may come up with will likely cost you everything. Are you willing to lay your soul on the line for the sake of your father?"

"Yes," I said, emotion coating my voice.

"Then I will make my ask of you soon," he said, pulling me closer possessively.

I pressed my forehead to his chest, trying to make myself believe this deal would truly protect Dad.

I was so afraid. Afraid of what he would ask of me, afraid of this mark and what it meant. I was afraid for my own life and of what would happen if I chose wrongly at the ceremony. But most of all, I was afraid for the only people I cared about most in the world. Callie and Dad had to be safe, that was all that mattered.

Erik tracked his thumb down the rivets of my spine, causing a shiver to ripple through my body. Fire followed the line of his touch, and part of me wanted to move closer, to escape into that feeling and let it tame the wild fears of my heart. Even though he was the very one who stoked them.

I pulled away, unsure what had just passed between us, but it felt like some unearthly power had trickled into our veins, binding us with unbreakable tethers.

"You will accompany me to the party," he said, his voice falling into that casually rude tone he preferred.

"I don't want to go to some party," I said in frustration.

After this day, all I wanted was to be alone.

"I cannot arrive without my courtier," he growled. "This is part of the tradition. The press will be there, and if they report me going without you, they will make assumptions about your absence. They will say you are not invested in the ritual, that you do not wish to choose a husband at the ceremony."

"Which would be correct assessments," I pointed out but I sensed I was going to have to go along with this.

Erik opened his mouth to retort, but a deep, male voice carried from his room, the tenor of it making my bones quake. "A circle of gold shall join two souls…"

Erik stiffened at the voice, and I turned to the door, a strange and haunting presence creeping over me.

"Who's in there?" I asked, my skin chilling all over.

Something drew me toward the room, and though I knew I should turn away and retreat from that eerie voice, I found myself opening the door instead.

Erik followed me as I stepped into his room as if guided forward by the same lure.

Dark walls stared back at me. The space was vast with a huge four-poster bed at the heart of it, draped with blood-red curtains. Beyond the bed was a large desk piled with books, scrolls, odd artefacts, and a heap of neatly stacked journals.

I glanced over my shoulder and Erik watched me intently as I approached the desk, but he didn't stop me. My heart drew me to something on its surface, and I scoured the names of the books, unsure what I was looking for. *Odin's True Path. The Prophets of the Norse Lands. The Wrathful Gods of Asgard.*

As I searched for the source of the strange pull in my chest, my eyes fell on a silver hand mirror. The handle was engraved with flowers, running up and around the oval glass. It was captivating, more than just beautiful. Something about it called to me, almost like Nightmare did.

I picked it up and Erik darted to my side in a flash of movement.

"Don't," he warned, his hand falling on my wrist, but I didn't know why.

"It's just a mirror," I whispered, though the energy tingling against my fingertips told me I was wrong.

Erik took it from me, his face etched with some unreadable emotion. "It is far more than that."

His grip tightened on the handle and his eyes searched his mirrored gaze. As I watched, his reflection smiled, but when I looked up, Erik's face was still, making my stomach lurch.

"What just happened?" I gasped, hoping for an answer, but he gave me none.

Erik placed the mirror face-down on the desk, his eyes hardening. "Forget you saw this."

"How can I?" I asked in disbelief, the back of my neck prickling.

"I shouldn't have let you come in," he said tightly. "But their power can be undeniable…"

"Whose power?" I frowned, hugging my arms around myself as the room seemed to grow colder. "I heard a voice, Erik, who was that?"

He sighed, and I sensed a heaviness weighing on him, which I was sure had to do with that mirror.

"I have lived for over a thousand years, Montana," he said, and shock rolled through me.

That long? It was impossible to imagine living so many lifetimes, seeing the world change through all that time. I had assumed a few hundred years perhaps, but this…it was inconceivable.

"The mirror is almost as old. Sometimes it speaks to me….in riddles."

"What do you mean?" I asked, thinking of Nightmare. Did this mirror speak to Erik the same way the blade spoke to me? I knew I couldn't ask too many questions without revealing my possession of the blade. It was too risky. But I longed for answers.

"Forget the mirror," Erik said, capturing my arm and squeezing. "There are things in this world best left untouched."

"But-"

"It is dangerous, do you not understand?" he said cuttingly. "I am trying to protect you."

"You're trying to keep me ignorant," I countered, and his jaw pulsed in annoyance.

"Go to your room. Get changed. I will not ask twice." He gave me a push towards the door, and I shot him a glare over my shoulder. But I could see this conversation was done.

I headed out of his room, throwing the door wide so it hit the wall and not bothering to turn back to shut it. I was offered an immediate relief as I left that mirror behind, its presence cold, unlike Nightmare's warmth.

A feeling of eyes on my back made me glance over my shoulder again, and I found Erik stalking after me like a predator on the hunt. I refused to let him intimidate me, not quickening my stride even a little as I walked to my room. He moved to lean against the wall beside it, folding his arms and giving me an impatient look.

"Two minutes," he said, holding his arm out to look at his glitzy watch.

I gave him a cool look, heading into my room and kicking the door shut behind me.

It felt like much more than a door parted us. An entire sea of secrets, and a fortress of enigmas.

It was tempting to cut holes in a dress, put it on, then smear lipstick all over my face, but I knew Erik would tie me to a chair and fetch Nancy if he had to. So I changed into a pale blue gown of soft silk, put on the lowest heels, and did my make-up as best I could, feeling more like I was donning war paint for my ongoing battle with my captor. My hair had curled a little from my time in the pool but it looked fine, and I didn't really care either way. I was making the minimum effort possible for a night I was not going to get out of either way and was simply saving myself the harassment of being forced into dressing up like a doll.

"That's more than two minutes, rebel," Erik called.

I shoved the door open, stepping out and offering him an obviously false smile. "Oh, but I needed a few extra moments to make myself dazzling for you, my prince."

He gave me a look up and down, biting down on the inside of his cheek like he was holding back a smile at my sarcasm. "Well you have done very poorly."

"Gosh, whatever will I do? You'll have to send one of your servants to whip me for my failure."

"I think I could handle the whipping myself," he said, his gruff tone setting my pulse hammering, and suddenly the game wasn't so funny.

He caught my arm, tugging me tight against him and guiding me down the corridor.

Nightmare was strapped to my thigh once more, and it seemed to growl in response to Erik. It was a strange sensation, but I was definitely in agreement with the angry vibes it was giving out. Though it was weird that the blade seemed to emit feelings at all.

"Fabian will be there tonight," Erik said, dragging me back to reality. "You will listen in on his conversations if you get the chance. Which you will, because you will make sure of it."

I realised he was agitated, which was only apparent because of the way he kept pushing his hand into his hair.

"Alright," I agreed. "You look like something's on your mind, Erik. I really hope it's not giving you crushing anxiety you can't escape from."

"Hm," he grunted at my jibing instead of giving it back, letting me know there really was something keeping him distracted.

Clarice waited in the hall below us, dressed in an incredible black gown that hugged her narrow waist and pushed her tits up to high heaven. Beside her was Joshua with his huge muscles straining against the suit he'd been dressed up in, his copper beard trimmed and styled neatly, the man looking far more relaxed than when I'd first met him. He stood beside Clarice, his eyes skipping to her regularly like he was enamoured with her, though she didn't pay him much attention in return.

"I sent the others ahead," Clarice announced, tossing a golden curl over her shoulder. Her eyes snapped to Erik. "Miles took Brianna with him, she looked a bit disappointed."

"She'll get over it," Erik growled, gripping my arm tighter. "Montana would have missed the party if I hadn't fetched her."

Clarice shot me a look, then arched an eyebrow at Erik. "Well we wouldn't want that, would we?"

Erik pursed his lips and said nothing more.

"Erik and I actually went for a walk together, that's why we're late," I said, and Erik frowned at me in confusion. "He took me all around the grounds of your fancy castle. And we would have made it back on time, only…" I bit my lip, glancing at Erik as if I shouldn't go on, and he gave me a gesture to continue like he was curious to see where this lie was going.

"What happened?" Clarice asked.

"Well, I don't like to say. But Erik stepped in a huge racoon shit. It splattered everywhere. The splashback even got him on the face, right on his mouth." I shook my head sadly as Clarice burst out laughing, and I glanced at Erik, who was not scowling like I expected but grinning in amusement. Joshua seemed unsure how to react, chuckling along with Clarice, then quieting when he glanced Erik's way.

"I was only trying to point it out to you because collecting little animal turds in jars was your favourite hobby back in your Realm, wasn't it?" Erik nudged me and a laugh caught in my throat. *Motherfucker.*

"Wow, well...that's an interesting pastime, Montana." Clarice straightened, smiling at me like she had actually believed that. "Come on, the car's waiting."

She took Joshua's arm, and we followed them toward the entrance hall.

"Bitch," Erik murmured into my ear.

"Prick," I muttered back, suppressing a smile.

Clarice led the way out of the castle, and we were swallowed by darkness as we followed, moving down the steps.

Two black cars awaited us on the road and Erik promptly steered me toward one of them, opening the door and sliding in beside me. Clarice and Joshua headed off in the other vehicle, and our driver sped after them across the grounds.

I understood the concept of a party from what Dad had told me, but attending one was something else. I had no idea what to expect as we carved a path through the flood-lit streets of New York, gazing out of the window in search of our destination.

We arrived on a brightly lit street, and I spotted a crowd of vampires on the sidewalk behind a red rope. A row of guards kept them back, large swords strapped to their bodies as if they expected trouble. The crowd's faces were skewed with anger, and they held signs in their hands which highlighted the cause of their protest. The words written on them made my stomach churn.

We have the right to bite!

Let us chase the human race.

We won't abstain from the vein!

"Who are they?" I asked, turning to Erik in horror.

He scowled out at them. "Rebels. They don't want human blood provided to them. They want to hunt for it."

My stomach dropped. Since Fabian had mentioned the rebels, I'd assumed their cause was just anti-authority. But the reason for their rebellion made me sick. They wanted to *hunt* us? It struck me that the laws the royals had decreed protected our kind from that fate, but I wasn't going to start thanking them for it when their alternative was

247

caging us and keeping us in squalor. Still...

My breathing hitched and Erik reached out, resting a hand on my wrist "It's just a bunch of fanatics. My family and I would never allow it to happen. Well...most of us anyway."

"Fabian?" I guessed as nausea gripped me. "He supports them?"

"Not openly. But I have my suspicions. They have been more organised lately. My guess is that someone more powerful is leading them."

He didn't say more, but I was left with a sense of deepening dread over the fact that I was to be handed to Fabian like a rabbit on a platter. What if he wanted to feed from me directly?

The car rolled up opposite the crowd beside a grand building on the corner of the street. It was a gigantic square tower of cream stone with an impressive entryway. Flags of red, white and blue hung from a balcony over the doorway, fluttering in the breeze.

A guard hurried forward to open the car door and Erik stepped out, pulling me after him by the hand.

The crowd started shouting as they spotted the prince, chanting, "We have the right to bite!" over and over until the words were drilled into my head and left me feeling sick. They were staring right at me, hungry eyes burrowing into my skin like they saw me as nothing but food waiting to be devoured.

Erik ignored them, pulling me toward the building, but I glanced over my shoulder to look back. Some bared their fangs at me, openly salivating, and one pointed at me, then carved her finger across her neck in a vicious threat.

"Erik, give the humans to us! Their blood belongs to everyone!" that same female vampire cried, looking desperate to move past the armed guards.

Erik drew me over to a savage looking guard, murmuring something in her ear that I couldn't catch. The guard bowed her head, then prowled out into the crowd of rebels, grabbing the one who had addressed Erik and pulling her away by force until I lost sight of her.

"What did you do?" I whispered, but he didn't answer.

Erik's jaw ticked as he led me up the steps, but I couldn't look away from the baying rebels. A shadowy figure caught my eye among the crowd, standing rigidly with no picket in hand. He was huge, built with muscle, and something about him screamed familiarity. Though his hood was pulled up and his face was shrouded, I was certain I recognised him as memories crawled into my mind. The night I had seen that beast of a vampire kill one of their own kind on the grounds of the castle. It was him. I was sure of it.

I pulled away from Erik, but the crowd surged forward, hands reaching my way, jeers pouring from their mouths. The figure was lost among them, and I looked left and right, trying to spot him again, but it was like he had never been there at all.

Erik caught my hand, pulling me back to him. "What are you doing?" he hissed.

"I…"

"Rebel?" he questioned.

"Nothing," I said.

If there was a monstrous vampire out there hunting his own people, it was none of my damn business.

"Come on then." Erik guided me up the steps, and I tried to shake the anxious feeling crawling up my spine.

As we approached the door, I spied a name above it written in golden lettering on the frosted glass. *The Plaza.*

"What is this place?" I asked, thankful for the distraction.

Erik slid his arm around my waist, drawing me flush to his hip. "It's a hotel, a place people stay when they're visiting from elsewhere."

"Are we staying here?" I frowned.

We hadn't exactly come far from the castle. What was the point in it?

"No, we're using some of the rooms for the party, that's all."

"Right."

We stepped into the entrance hall, and my thoughts abandoned me. An ornate floor sprawled out before us, decorated with painted red roses on swirling golden vines. A huge table at the heart of the room was topped by an elaborate arrangement of white flowers that screamed opulence.

Vampires milled about the space in elegant clothing; the women wore sparkling dresses and high heels which they walked in with impossible ease, and the men were dressed as finely as Erik with long-tailed coats and bright waistcoats glinting beneath them.

Erik dropped his mouth to my ear. "Feel free to interrupt if any of these ass-kissers try to inflate my ego too much."

"If your ego gets any bigger, Erik, it will need a castle of its own to live in," I said under my breath.

"I rather like that about you, rebel. Zero ass-kissing. When you say things, you mean them."

I hunted for the insult in the compliment but came up short.

I could sense people's eyes on us, taking me in with curious looks, the first courtier Erik had ever chosen for himself. If only they knew I was just a new pawn on his chessboard.

He led me through the room with purpose and vampires turned to him, bowing low or offering comments of praise on his royal attire. He nodded and replied politely, playing a part he had clearly played many times before. He seemed at ease, welcoming, friendly. Everything he wasn't behind closed doors. I played along, smiling when necessary but most of the vampires didn't speak to me directly, like I was just a pet to be cooed at.

I spotted Clarice surrounded by a group of male vampires, all keen to get closer to her, but she didn't seem to be entertaining any of it. She shot me a small smile as we passed her by and Erik guided me up a beautiful white marble staircase, following the line of a golden railing as it led us to the balcony above the room.

We trailed along side by side, and I whispered, "I counted eight ass-kissers back there. How's your ego doing?"

"It's reached its maximum, I think," he murmured, leaning in so close his cool breath skated over my cheek. "Are you planning on behaving this evening?"

"I'm still debating it. Or are you planning on blackmailing me into behaving?"

"I believe you're the one who tried to play the blackmail card," he whispered. "I'm surprised it didn't come out again this evening during your request. Though I have to say, I quite enjoyed seeing you beg."

I bit my tongue on a stream of insults, remaining silent instead. I hadn't threatened to expose his plan to Fabian for the sake of what I needed, because I couldn't risk Erik calling my bluff. And if I exposed myself as Erik's spy, who was really likely to take the fall? I doubted it was the hot, dead son of a bitch walking beside me. More like the blood bag who could be easily disposed of.

Erik's hand pressed into my spine as he offered two female vampires a polite smile, but I didn't copy him. I felt like I was in a snake pit, so many piercing eyes turning my way, the glint of fangs within those hungry smiles.

"Don't you have anything to say to that?" Erik pushed.

"I have plenty to say, but it involves a lot of cursing and would be best delivered with a punch to your smug face, so I'll save it for after the party."

"Sounds like foreplay."

I shot him a glare.

"Ah, Prince Erik," a squat man in a rich brown suit came over, puffing out his chest before bowing low.

"Roger," Erik said, giving him a curt nod.

"I wanted to congratulate you on your fine selection." Roger took me in with appraising eyes and I had the urge to take a step back. "Such a delightful specimen indeed. Have you sampled her yet?"

"No," Erik said, and my skin crawled all over as I realised what he meant.

"You haven't given your prince a donation?" Roger balked, looking to me in astonishment. "It is the least you could offer him in gratitude for the envied position of a place in the royal ritual."

My throat became too tight, and I had no answer to give him that wasn't full of fury, so I had to swallow my tongue, sure I was going to choke on it. I'd given blood donations all my life, but hearing it spoken about directly from the mouth of one of the monsters who would happily drink it was something else entirely.

"We're saving it for the wedding day," Erik said, pulling me closer, like he sensed I was a flight risk.

Roger laughed. "You're confident she's going to choose you then?"

"How could she not?" Erik said, then bid him goodbye and towed me along.

I glanced around for the nearest exit, wanting to run and never stop running. A door to my right beckoned and I lurched away from Erik, making a dash for it and finding myself stepping into a grand office with no exit.

"Fuck," I breathed.

The door clicked shut behind me and I wheeled around, finding Erik there with his brow drawn low.

"I can't do this," I blurted. "I hate it here. I hate the way they look at me. I hate that fucking asshole who thinks I should give you my blood. I never felt it belonged to me, Erik, but here it's worse than that. It's like I'm in an oven, slowly cooking while hungry eyes watch me from the outside."

"Roger is a cunt," he said frankly, and my lips parted in surprise. "I hate these events. I hate the rich bastards who squabble over which of them I like best, when in reality I would not spend a single minute more in their company if I could get away with it. I will not ask for your blood, rebel. I have an endless supply of it – which I am sure makes you feel disgusted at the thought. But that is the way of the world now. It was the best-case scenario in the long term."

"What do you mean?" I asked.

"We had sired too many vampires, and when the war broke out among men, it quickly descended towards the end of the fucking world. The vampires saw no need to hide anymore, and with so much blood being spilled daily, there were too many frenzies happening. The humans were annihilating one another, and the vampires were picking off the last of them, to the point where we could see there would be no humans left. No blood. And that would lead to something too horrifying to imagine. An eternal life in starvation. So between my brothers and sister, we made a plan. We reclaimed control of our kind, and we turned them into soldiers of our own, commanding them to corral the last of the humans and keep them alive. We crowned ourselves rulers of the land and protected the most vital resource that had come so close to being extinguished." He stepped towards me. "You hold value untold. The vampires are weak without the humans. We are only kept sane by your blood, but if you could see us starved…" He shook his head, horrors crossing his eyes that told me he had lived that reality. "If the people out there aren't kept fed, then the glamour, the civility, the etiquette-" He snapped his fingers. "It vanishes just like that, and our base nature returns." He plucked at his suit jacket. "This bullshit is for them, but it's for us too. I have painted myself as a royal and I play that part every day, every moment committed to the act. Because I have seen what I become without laws and restriction to guide me. So I occupy myself with the quest for power, dominance, total control in this tumultuous world. But we are all one slip away from falling into anarchy and bloodlust."

"Why are you telling me this?" I asked, my heart hammering from all he'd said, and I hated that I could see the logic in it. At least from their point of view.

He glanced at a clock on the wall, gazing at the second hand ticking on and on incessantly.

"I don't know," he murmured. "Perhaps because you are the only one I can say it to. Perhaps because it is refreshing to speak to someone who despises this world as deeply as I do. My siblings seek the best in it, though I fear we are all lying to ourselves, afraid of each other pointing out the cracks in our perfect façade. So I don't, I sell the lie as well as they do and hope it buys them peace of mind."

"Even Fabian?"

"Yes, even him," he said quietly. "But that does not change our power struggle. I'm not sure where it ends, but I am on this path now and don't intend to turn from it."

I nodded, my attention moving to the desk beside me as I grazed my thumb over the grain of the wood. My thoughts fell on the Realm, how hunger had turned people feral, desperate. Sometimes fights would break out over the rations and blood would spill. Other times, the savagery was quieter. A thin woman slumped in the street, coughing and wheezing, the life trickling from her until one day she'd be found dead with half the clothes stripped from her body. We were animals too when it came down to survival, but the difference was, the vampires had placed us into that nightmare. We had never caused them to starve, but they had caused us to. But then I thought of Realm A and the pretty lie most of them probably believed about how we lived. Perhaps it wouldn't have been so bad if that was the truth of it. It stopped the vampires hunting us, like those rebels wanted to. And that kind of world didn't bear thinking about.

"What are you thinking?" he asked.

"I think your solutions are imperfect and you should look closer at them," I said. "You say the Realms aren't your responsibility, but if humans are so valuable to you and your kind, then I suggest you make them your responsibility."

His brow creased and I could see he was actually listening to me for once, but I didn't want to push him too far in case he dismissed me again. "Perhaps we can work together on that. But I cannot step on Fabian's toes without him lashing back at me, so I will need some leverage on him."

"The kind a spy could get," I said, lifting my head to look him in the eye.

"Exactly," he said, then offered me his arm. "Come back to the party with me."

"Alright," I agreed, stepping forward and taking his arm, feeling like a fragile alliance was forming between us.

We exited the office and Erik guided me into an elevator further down the hall, the two of us moving to the back of it as a group of vampires filed in behind us. Some of them tried to catch Erik's attention, but he ignored them, angling himself towards me.

Nightmare warmed against my thigh, pulsing angrily like it could sense the group of vampires around me.

Erik and I were pressed close to one another in the small space, and I found my eyes locking with his, unable to tear my gaze away. There was such a sharp energy between us that it raked at the inside of my chest. I wanted to dismiss it as hatred, but my mind shifted to the kiss we'd shared in my room at the castle, the explosive heat that had passed between us which should never have existed. I didn't want it to. Because the truth of that lust cut me raw. If it was just his allure, then why was it only him? Why didn't the rest of the royals make me feel this way, like his touch alone could set me alight.

The doors opened and the vampires stepped out, chattering in low voices about Erik and I but their words were drowned by the music pounding through the room.

We followed them into a low-lit bar with glinting crystal chandeliers hanging above the space. Several vampires were dancing, grinding up against one another, kissing and pawing at each other without care. It was primal, like all their politeness had been left at the door and they were giving in to the call of the music and their want for those around them.

Erik led me through the crowd, keeping me close as he forged a path between the vampires. He took my hand as we emerged in a seating area with black sofas and chairs surrounding small tables. I spotted Fabian chatting with a group of men in suits; Paige and Brianna were sat across from him, talking in low voices.

Fabian's gaze fell on us and his easy smile slipped from his face, a flash of menace in his eyes before he smothered it. My pulse picked up at witnessing the small crack in his facade, his hatred for his brother clearer than ever.

Erik leaned down, his mouth grazing my cheek as he muttered, "I'll fetch us drinks," before disappearing into the crowd and leaving the feel of his mouth on my skin.

I dropped down beside Paige with an impossibly wide smile, and she immediately gripped my arm.

"Isn't it beautiful here?" she cooed, her blue eyes widening.

I nodded, taking in her silver dress which sparkled like moonlight. She seemed...happy. Ecstatic actually, and one glance at Brianna told me she was feeling pretty relaxed too. What the hell had changed?

"How was your day with Miles?" Brianna leaned forward, brushing down the folds of her crimson gown. "I think he's my favourite. He's so easy to talk to."

My heart sank a little as I recalled my time with Miles. "Yeah...it was okay."

"Just okay? The man is a delight," Brianna said.

"I thought you hated it here?" I said in confusion, and her smile faltered.

She shifted closer to me on her seat, glancing around like she was worried someone had heard. "I did," she whispered. "But this life is better than anything I've ever known, Montana. I was hesitant at first, but surely you're enjoying all the food, the lifestyle?"

"It's like a dream," Paige agreed. "And we can bring our family here once we're married."

"At what cost?" I hissed. "They're going to turn us into *them*."

Brianna winced a little but looked to the sea of dancing vampires, then back to me with a guilty look. "It scares me, but…just look at them. They have everything. Anyone in my Realm would jump at the chance to seize this life from me if they could."

"It's not right," I growled. "You wanna drink blood? The blood of your own people?"

Paige grimaced, shaking her head violently. "I don't want to think about that part."

"We'll want it once we're like them," Brianna said darkly. "It won't matter."

"Won't matter?" I snapped. "How can you say that?"

"You can judge me all you like, but we don't have much choice here," Brianna whispered, taking my hand and squeezing. "Your morals aren't going to save you from reality. It's this or return to being a blood bag who doesn't know when its next meal is coming. I'd rather be the predator than the prey."

Paige nodded sadly. "She's right, Montana. Fighting it doesn't change it. We've gotta see the good in this."

I sat back in my seat, falling quiet, and the two of them shared a look of concern.

"Who are you going to choose?" Paige asked to change the subject, her fingers knotting in her skirt.

I glanced over at Fabian who had returned to his conversation. His hair was neatly tied back by a coil of black silk as dark as the suit he wore and there were plenty of female vampires close by trying to draw his attention.

"I'm not sure," I answered honestly, exhausted by the situation I was in.

Miles would keep my secret, but choosing Fabian ensured Erik kept his promise. So what the hell was I supposed to do? If Erik didn't make his request of me soon, and make sure Dad was released before the ceremony, I was pretty much fucked.

"Imagine if we all picked the same brother! We'd all be sharing a husband," Brianna said, seeming sort of excited by that idea. "Who do you like best, Paige?"

"Erik's nice." Paige threw a glance over her shoulder and my stomach knotted as I followed her gaze, spotting Erik by the shiny black bar. At his side, clad in a glimmering green gown, was Valentina. Her hand was curled around his arm, and they looked intimately close as she spoke to him. My gut clenched further. He spoke with casual familiarity, the two of them clearly used to being that close to one another.

"Nice?" I scoffed. "I wouldn't call him that."

"I don't know…" Paige trailed off, biting her lip. "There's something about him."

"So you're really okay with this? Both of you?" I looked between them. "Because we're talking about vampires here. Marrying them, fucking them." I was getting angry, and I couldn't hold it back.

Paige flinched and Brianna sighed.

"It's not the worst fate," Brianna said. "Just look at them. And I don't think they're as bad as the ones from my Realm. They're not interested in hurting us."

"We're their captives," I said in disbelief. "And you're falling for their lies."

"My eyes are wide open," Brianna growled. "And I still choose this."

Paige leaned between us, patting Brianna's knee and giving me an imploring look. "Let's just agree to disagree."

"Are you going to choose Erik?" I asked Paige, keeping my expression neutral, trying to ignore my twisted stomach.

"No," Paige sighed, leaning in closer. "He told me not to."

My lips parted in confusion. "What, why?"

"He told me the same thing," Brianna announced with a shrug.

Paige observed me closely. "I think he has his eye on *you*, Montana."

A hollow laugh rolled from my throat, but I said nothing of the truth which only I was privy to. Especially as Fabian was right there, able to turn his attention to our conversation any time he liked. I was Erik's little puppet, and he was the last vampire I'd be choosing at the ceremony.

"He's always looking at you," Brianna agreed. "But Miles is the only one I even slightly trust in this place."

I frowned, knowing Miles's secret, that he was lying to her about his real intentions, but I didn't open my mouth to tell her that truth. That his heart belonged to someone else, and he wouldn't be any kind of real husband when they got married. Maybe that would be better for her anyway.

"I wouldn't trust a word out of his mouth," I said icily.

Paige glanced around at the vampires, waving her hands to hush me. "Don't say that."

"Why? What are they gonna do? Drain me?" I glowered, though she probably had a point. Talking openly about my dislike for the vampires probably wasn't the best idea in a place full of them, but Erik had said himself I was valuable. What could they really do to me?

"So who's your choice then, Montana?" Paige pressed.

"I don't know," I insisted. "Are you going with Miles too?"

She pursed her lips then her eyes drifted to Fabian. "Well, Erik was my first choice, but *he* isn't a bad second."

"Do you actually like him?" Brianna interjected before I could, and Paige blushed.

Picking him was an awful idea and Brianna obviously sensed that too. But I wondered why, considering I was probably the only one privy to the knowledge that he ran the Realms. If I hadn't known that, Fabian wouldn't have frightened me the way he did.

Erik reappeared, planting a glass in my hand, and I gazed down at the pink substance swimming in a glass that was shaped like a Y.

"What is it?" I asked him, sniffing the pink stuff suspiciously.

"It's a raspberry martini," he said.

"Oh, is that a ducktail?" I asked, excited by witnessing something my dad had told me about in his stories.

A cruel grin grew on Erik's face. "What did you say?"

"A ducktail," I repeatedly confidently. "My dad told me about them."

Yeah, Erik, I'm not totally ignorant to the world.

"It's called a *cock*tail," he said.

"What?" I snorted. "No, it isn't."

"Are you sure about that, little human?" he asked, sniggering.

"You're trying to make me look stupid. Why would it be called a cocktail?" I argued, looking to Paige and Brianna for backup, but they seemed clueless.

"Why would it be called a ducktail?" Erik shot back.

"I dunno, because it's wet and colourful like a duck's tail?" I guessed thinking of the ducks I'd seen on the lake in the castle grounds. "How is it anything like a cock?"

Erik barked a laugh, and our little argument caused eyes to turn our way, including Fabian's.

"Is he bothering you, love?" Fabian called.

"He's just being an ass," I said.

Paige sucked in a sharp breath and Brianna sat up straight like she expected danger to descend at any moment.

"No change there then," Fabian said, then beckoned me with two fingers. "There's always a seat for you over here."

Erik stepped in front of my chair, blocking any passage to him even though it seemed like a decent opportunity to spend some time listening in on his conversation.

"Try your ducktail then, tell me if you like it." He brought the glass to my lips, my mouth fully in line with his crotch as his hand slid into my hair and gripped tight. He tugged to make me tip my head back and my heart stuttered as our eyes met and he tipped the drink between my lips. I felt stares on us from every direction, but I couldn't look away as the sweet, fruity drink spilled over my tongue, making my tastebuds crackle. I swallowed, a sharp burn following the drink as it spilled down my throat, and Erik's gaze bored into me as he watched.

"Well?" he asked in a low voice. "How does it taste?"

"Sweet at first, then it burns," I said a little huskily.

His hand was still tight in my hair, and the way he controlled my movements made heat pour through my core. I couldn't focus on anything else in the room but him, the way my pulse was thrumming, and the heat of Nightmare against my thigh.

"Good, that's how it should be," he said. "The fruit hides the alcohol. Don't drink too much of it or it'll make you forget yourself."

I was pretty sure I had already forgotten myself because I had just let him pull my hair and pour a drink down my throat in front of a whole audience.

He released my hair then placed the drink in my hand, catching my wrist and yanking me out of my seat. In a flash of movement, he took my place in my chair, then tugged the back of my dress sharply, so I dropped down onto his knees. He steadied me, making sure not a single drop of the drink spilled, and I found myself looking at Paige and Brianna who weren't even trying to hide their shock at what they'd just witnessed. Fuck, this was not exactly helping my case. I'd been arguing two seconds ago about my horror over picking a vampire to marry, and now here I was in the lap of one like a good little whore.

Erik's hand pressed to my knee, his other capturing my chin and turning me to look at him. "Try mine." He swiped a glass from the table beside my chair where he had apparently left his own drink, the glass the same strange shape as mine, but the liquid inside was clear with a strange green vegetable floating in it.

"What the fuck is that thing?" I pointed at it.

"An olive," he said. "It's just for presentation."

"I don't like the look of it. How can you even drink this? It's not blood," I asked, confounded.

"We can drink other things, we just don't need to for sustenance," he explained.

I spied the array of chalices and glasses in the hands of the other vampires in the room, realising he was right. They weren't all drinking blood, though some of the ducktails looked like they might be mixed with it. Which was somehow a whole other level of gross.

I took a tentative sip of his drink, then promptly spat it back into the glass. "That tastes like shit."

"Oh my God," Brianna gasped at what I'd done, but there was no undoing it now.

Erik looked down at the drink I'd ruined in amusement, his fingers tightening on my knee, his touch sending an electric charge up my thigh. "You spoiled my drink."

"If I slit my veins and let my blood fill up your glass, you'd drink it readily. Surely you don't care about a little spit," I goaded him, and his eyes flared with the challenge I was presenting.

"You want me to drink it?" he asked gruffly, then tugged me close to whisper in my ear. "Will it give you a kick, rebel?"

"Seems like a punishment too small for what you deserve. But yeah, I think it would brighten my mood," I murmured, my head turning towards his so the glass was squashed between us and our lips were all too close.

He let me lean back, shrugging his shoulders. "So make me. If you dare."

I shot a glance at Brianna and Paige who were giving me looks of warning that I didn't plan to heed. I pushed my hand into Erik's perfectly styled hair, scrunching my fist up and pulling tight. He pressed his tongue into his cheek, watching me and spreading his arms over the back of the seat.

I brought the glass to his lips the way he had done to me, and he let me pour it between his lips, swallowing every last drop of it. His gaze was full of a dark want that crept into me and tainted my soul, because I felt it too. This pull between us which, if surrendered to, could destroy me. He was the worst kind of bad, a living drug that was made to make addicts out of human souls, and I was letting him ensnare me.

I took the olive from the glass, balancing it on his head and grinning. "For presentation."

"Montana, would you like to dance?" Fabian's voice made me jump, and I turned to look at him, catching a deep growl rumbling through Erik's throat, the olive tumbling to the floor as he sat up straighter. But he didn't try to keep me, in fact, his palm pressed to my spine in encouragement to go with his brother, and I suddenly realised that entire show had been for this very purpose. He had played this whole game to capture Fabian's attention, and shame crept over me at how readily I'd fallen for it.

I slapped a big ass smile on my face, shoving down the embarrassment I felt at not realising sooner that this had been Erik's plan.

"Sure," I said, taking Fabian's hand and Nightmare burned hotter. *Kill him, strike true.*

I ignored the blade's demand for death and let Fabian pull me off of Erik's lap and guide me away. I didn't look back, steeling myself and preparing to do what needed to be done.

Fabian gently slid an arm around my waist, starting to sway me to a slow song that warbled through the room.

"Listen, love, Erik won't offer you what I will," Fabian said in a low tone. "I know he seems charming now, but when the ceremony is over, he will use you and discard you. That's how he is." His upper lip curled back slightly, and I caught sight of his fangs.

My throat dried up as I nodded, moving closer into the arc of his body. Erik was using me already and Fabian had no idea.

"You don't like him," I stated, and Fabian's eyes darkened.

"It isn't about like or dislike. We have different visions for what the New Empire should be. He doesn't agree with me, and I don't agree with him."

"What do you have in mind?" I asked, curious for myself as much as I was for Erik. He was technically my ruler after all. And if he gained full power, would things get even worse for humans?

Fabian's eyes lit up as he answered. "This world needs a single leader. The four of us are too different to rule together eternally. I wish to take on that responsibility and steer our country toward greatness."

"How?" I whispered, a prickling feeling crawling up my spine.

"We need to colonise more of the world. More vampires, more strength. That is my sentiment."

A male vampire suddenly grabbed Fabian's arm, his eyes darting left and right, and I recognised Roger, the one who had questioned whether Erik had drunk my blood yet. "Your highness, a word please."

"Not here, Roger," Fabian snarled at him. "I told you to keep your distance."

Roger muttered an apology but didn't leave. "It's important."

Fabian schooled his frustrated expression, turning to me. "Sorry Montana, I'll find you later."

He released me, pushing the man ahead of him as they moved toward the bar, tension lining Fabian's shoulders.

I stood stock still, unsure what to do, but my legs urged me after him. Whatever it was Roger wanted to say was clearly important, and if I was going to keep my promise to Erik, I had to try and listen to their conversation.

The throng of bodies kept me concealed as I moved after them, and I positioned myself a few of feet from Fabian at the bar, behind a woman in a hat so enormous it was arguably an umbrella.

"-is everything under control?" Fabian hissed.

"Yes, sir. But..." The vampire glanced around nervously again, and I shrank back into the shadow of the hat.

"Come, let's talk about this in private," Fabian said, and they started moving through the room again.

My heartbeat stuttered as Nightmare grew hotter on my leg, seeming to whisper *follow.*

CALLIE

CHAPTER THIRTEEN

We crossed the open field toward the blood bank, my movements a lot closer to silent than they would have been without Magnar's lessons. He may have had a point about that, not that I'd be thanking him for the advice. He needed to work on his delivery in my opinion.

The grass shone silver in the moonlight, the tips of the brown stalks sparkling with a new frost as the temperature plummeted, winter clawing at me, a shiver building in my flesh. My breath rose before me in a cloud of vapour, reminding me of the warm blood that pumped through my veins. I was mortal. I was a slayer. And I was *alive*. No vampire could claim such things. And it was time they remembered that they were dead.

Fury pulsed with anticipation in my palm. The blade was working itself up into a frenzy as we drew closer to the danger. I was starting to feel its revelry too, leaning into the anticipation and using it to stave off any fear that might try to creep in. Now wasn't the time to let fear guide me. We were about to find my family, and I was going to get them back. No doubts, no exceptions.

The thought alone made my chest swell with hope and banished the fear from my body.

Magnar led the way straight up to the wall of the blood bank before turning right, using its shadow to conceal us from prying eyes as he hugged the stone and moved more silently than the wind.

The building's windows had all been bricked over, presumably to keep all traces of sunlight out. The newer mortar and brickwork stood out like ugly scars against the rest of the old factory, but I guessed the vampires hadn't cared about the way it appeared. This place wasn't supposed to look pretty, it was a death sentence, pure and simple.

We moved quickly, and I was almost at a jog, hurrying to keep up with Magnar's long stride, my pulse picking up as I worked to contain my own jitteriness. The chilling silence kept us company. Even the wild animals knew this place was evil. Nothing dared approach it.

A piercing scream sounded from within the building, and we both froze as the echoes of it reverberated into the valley beyond. I knew my old Realm lay somewhere in that direction, though no lights shone to show me where. I wondered if anyone had heard the screams carried on the wind tonight.

My gut clenched with terror, but I hardened myself against it. I was no longer a helpless human hiding in my apartment after dark while the pain-filled howling on the wind sent nightmares to my slumber. I was going to see this place destroyed. Tonight would be the last time the Realm was terrorised by these screams. The constant threat of the blood bank was about to be removed from the humans' lives for good.

Magnar started moving again and I followed in his shadow, his presence enough to help me keep faith in our plan.

He made it to the corner of the building and stopped abruptly, holding out a hand to halt me too.

Fury growled a warning across my flesh and a shiver rolled down my spine in reply. There was a vampire somewhere close in the dark, though no sound gave it away, only the heat of the blade in my fist.

I bit my lip as Magnar slowly released Tempest from the sheath on his back before sinking into a crouch. His hand swept through the bristly stalks by his feet for a moment until he located a stone which filled his palm.

As he stood again, he tossed the stone ahead of him and it thumped into the grass a few feet away, making it rustle unnaturally.

Magnar's grip tightened on his blade, and my breath halted in my lungs as a vampire stepped into view.

She looked at the rock, then whirled around, some supernatural instinct or maybe just guesswork putting her on alert, but it didn't matter. Magner struck like a cobra from the long grass, his blade slicing through the air with unavoidable brutality, carving through her chest and obliterating her heart with a single strike before she could so much as scream.

The vampire fell to ash and was carried away on the gusting wind in less than five seconds. Here then gone, her eternal life ended as simply as that. Magnar tossed the small pile of her clothes into the shadows behind me, and I kicked them into the cover offered by a patch of brambles, the only evidence of our presence concealed.

"The lesser vampires won't cause us much issue," Magnar explained in a whisper. "But I can feel the presence of more than one Elite inside, and they could prove more difficult to dispatch. If at any point I tell you to run, then run."

"I won't just turn and flee at the first sign of trouble," I hissed.

"You will do as I say," he replied in a low growl, his eyes burning with dominance. "Or I'll tie you to a tree and make you wait outside. If you're going to follow me into this mess, then you'll do so at my command or not at all."

"You forget that I haven't taken any vow Magnar," I replied icily. "So I don't follow your commands unless I *want* to."

"What if I said that I won't go any further until you swear to do as I say? What would you do then, drakaina hjarta?"

"Then I'll go in alone," I replied simply, and I meant it too. "Because my dad and Montana need me, and I won't abandon them any more than I would abandon you if you needed me. I owe you a life debt, Magnar, don't go thinking I'll forget that until we're even."

Magnar blew out a breath which was part amusement, part frustration. "You really would, wouldn't you?"

"Try me," I growled.

He glared at me for several long seconds before shaking his head and turning away, moving around the corner. I jogged after him, at least a little smug that he hadn't forced a promise from my lips which I wouldn't have been able to keep. No matter what he told me to do, I knew I could never save myself at the cost of his life, and if I told him otherwise, it would be a lie. He'd come for me when I'd been captured and, bait or not, we were bonded because of that.

A heavy wooden door stood ajar ahead of us, and Magnar made a beeline for it. I stayed close, relying on Fury's senses to reassure myself no vampires were about to strike.

Magnar stepped through the doorway, and I slipped in behind him. He hesitated as he looked up at the long fluorescent lights which illuminated the wide corridor.

"What magic is this?" he breathed in astonishment, seemingly unable to tear his gaze from the flickering bulb above his head.

"It's just electricity," I reminded him, laying a hand on his arm in case he decided to attack a lightbulb and fuck this whole thing up before it had even started. "Like the flashlight but bigger."

I felt the tension ease out of his muscles at my words, but his gaze remained fixed on the lights for several more seconds before he forced himself to look down.

He frowned at the floor as he processed what he'd seen and convinced himself to accept it before moving on. My gut twisted uncomfortably at the pain which flashed in his gaze. Every time he was reminded of the changes which had happened to the world in the thousand years he'd spent sleeping, it seemed to bring up what he'd left behind, the weight of that loss pressing down on him more firmly. There was nothing I could do to ease that pain, and I ignored the knot of sorrow which tangled inside me as we continued on our hunt for my family.

A set of double doors lay directly in front of us. They were made of heavy metal and the handle on the right-hand side was drooping in a way that suggested it was broken.

Magnar squared his shoulders and began walking quickly, closing the distance to the doors in several long strides. I glanced nervously down the corridors to my left and right before scurrying after him.

His eye caught mine as he placed a hand on the broken handle and eased the door open.

A wave of warm air washed over us, and a cloud of pungent smoke caught in my throat. I slapped a hand over my mouth as my lungs filled with pressure and I fought back the urge to cough.

Magnar headed inside and I followed him into a wide room lit by an orange glow which came from a furnace to the back of the space.

The hot air was dry and made my tongue thicken with distaste. The smoke filled my nostrils and a sickly stench accompanied it. I had to fight the desire to cover my face entirely. I really didn't want to know what they were burning in here, but I got the feeling I was about to find out.

I began to cross the open space and head towards the furnace, but Magnar caught my arm, yanking me to a halt. I stumbled, glancing up at him in confusion, and he pointed to the floor before my feet. I squinted in the dim light and could just make out a hatch.

Magnar released me and dropped down to pull the hatch wide. Soot spiralled out of the area below as the air was disturbed, and I blinked down at the dark space in confusion.

I fumbled in my pocket and pulled the flashlight out, glancing at Magnar for confirmation before flicking it on, the small beam of light illuminating a shaft beneath us.

I leaned closer, peering down at a drop of around twenty feet to the basement below. All I could see was piles of ash and soot. I swept the beam from my flashlight to and fro and gasped as the light fell on a skull.

I almost dropped the flashlight as I stumbled back, and Magnar let out a low curse before swinging the wooden door closed over the hatch.

"They're burning people," I whispered in horror, my gaze shooting to the furnace which continued to blaze beneath the giant chimney. "Do you think they're alive when-"

"It is very unlikely. They would want to remove all the blood first," Magnar growled.

A fluttering of relief passed through my chest. Death was bad enough, but the idea of being burned alive filled me with a special kind of horror.

"We should move on," Magnar said in a low voice. "There isn't anyone alive in here."

I nodded my agreement, more than happy to turn my back on that room and its disgusting stench. I flicked the flashlight off and jammed it into my pocket before following him back out, the cold air in the corridor beyond a sweet balm to my senses.

Magnar hesitated for a moment, running his thumb across the runes on Tempest's hilt before choosing to follow the corridor to the right. My connection to Fury made me feel sure that this was where most of the vampires were assembled, and I let out a long breath as we made our way towards them.

"You didn't want to pick the safer direction then?" I hissed, but Magnar's only reply was the feral grin he threw back over his shoulder at me.

Magnar stopped at the first door we came to and eased it open. I peered over his shoulder as icy air washed out of the room and kissed the exposed skin on my face. A shiver ran down my spine and I realised it was a giant refrigerator. Magnar shifted aside, revealing metal trolleys holding row upon row filled with bottles of gleaming red liquid.

"They take human blood as if they were milking cattle," Magnar growled angrily as he stepped inside.

"We were required to *donate* two pints of blood every few months in the Realm," I explained as I eyed the bottles with disgust. "They claimed it was for our own protection – no chance of accidental death from a vampire who was a little too thirsty. The whole thing was supposed to be *civilised*."

A sound like the growl of a feral beast escaped Magnar's lips, and I barely managed to jump aside before he pushed one of the huge racks over. The sound of the metal trolley hitting the floor alongside a hundred bottles smashing was more than enough to tell every vampire in the building that we were here, and I cursed in alarm, my grip on Fury tightening.

I leapt out of the way, pressing my back against the cold wall as he lunged towards the next trolley.

My shock turned to glee as I watched the way the blood splattered against the walls and mixed with every speck of dirt and grime on the floor. What he was doing was utterly insane, and yet the satisfaction it built in me was endless, because fuck them. Fuck their thirst and their realms and their fucking barbaric idea of civilisation.

It was already too late to try and hide. The vampires had to have heard the crashing and shattering of glass, so instead of wasting my time on terror or calling Magnar out on his utter lack of subtly, I took several running steps towards the closest trolley and hurled it against the wall with as much strength as I could muster.

A bark of laughter fell from my lips, a hint of mania lacing the sound because I knew this was it; the vampires were racing towards us right now, their anger at what they would find immeasurable. Yet something about destroying this stock of stolen blood was so utterly freeing.

I grabbed a bottle which hadn't smashed as it rolled against the side of my boot and hurled the thing at the far wall, red splattering the ceiling, glass cascading down into the ever-growing puddle on the floor.

Magnar picked up another trolley and hurled it overhead, aiming it towards the door, and I watched in terrified glee as the contents shattered everywhere.

Between us, the other three racks quickly followed suit and the ground was littered with smashed glass and ruined *donations*. A tide of spilled blood washed over the toes of my boots before flowing out of the refrigerator into the corridor beyond, staining the filthy floor with the evidence of the crimes those bloodsuckers had been committing against humankind for too fucking long.

"The vampires," I breathed, barely able to believe what we'd just done. "They'll know exactly where we are-"

"Let them come," Magnar growled, pulling Venom from his back to join Tempest in his other hand and moving to the centre of the refrigerator. "Stay behind me."

That order was simple enough to follow, and I backed away from him, pressing my spine to the rear wall as the sound of the vampires approaching reached my ears. The fact that they weren't silent was enough to tell me just how many of them were coming our way, and my pulse skittered in reply.

Fury burned red-hot in my palm but rather than hurting me, the heat seemed to find its way into my veins, pricking at my senses and dialling them up. My vision seemed sharper and more focused, every sound was clearer in my ears. Even the metallic scent of the blood pooling by our feet smelled stronger in my nostrils, the taste of it racing along my tongue.

Instead of cowering against the wall, I stood ready to defend myself, Fury in hand. If it came to a fight, I would face it.

Magnar rolled his shoulders, casually rotating the two huge blades as he awaited the vampires' arrival. I could tell he held no fear, only rage at what they'd done to us while he slept. Rage at what the last thousand years had brought upon the mortals. And he was about to collect payment for that debt.

The first of the vampires made it to the door, and he cut through them before I could even count how many he killed. Dust swirled behind his blades as he swung at them again, using the door as a bottleneck, carving into any who tried to find their way through.

The clash of metal on metal rang out as the next row of vampires realised they were under attack and drew their own weapons. Adrenaline spiked through my veins like wildfire, but I wasn't cowering like a rabbit caught in a bright light, I was waiting like a snake in the grass, letting Magnar do what he did best and preparing for the moment when they forced their way past him so I could have his back.

He held them at the doorway, using the narrow space to stop them from overwhelming him, spinning and kicking, striking with furious, feral blows which were met with screams and explosions of ash. He swung his swords and mercilessly hacked his way through all who came at him, a wildness to his movements which spoke of the warrior who had been destined to defeat these monsters hundreds of years ago.

The vampires rallied themselves, barks of command and urgent calls forcing them into line before they surged forward as one and Magnar was forced to step back, allowing them to spill into the room. He roared a challenge as they tried to make it past the fury of his mighty blades, spreading out and coming at him from both sides, trying to overwhelm him, but none could get close.

I watched in utter awe, my heart pounding a frantic rhythm as time and again, he parried blows and delivered death, his movements unearthly, his instincts seeming to guide his blade to the perfect position time and again.

Magnar swung to the left and a vampire leapt around him, aiming straight for me, forcing my attention back to survival instead of staring at the slayer from legends.

The vampire's eyes glittered with malice, and my pulse hammered in my ears as he swung his sword straight for my head.

Somehow, I managed to get Fury between us to take the blow, the blade pushing memories into me which weren't my own, offering me just enough to wield the weapon effectively. I cringed back as the strength of the vampire's attack resonated right down to my bones and he swung at me again.

My feet moved quickly, and I danced aside, half feeling like I knew what I was doing as Fury poured information into me like I was an empty vessel just waiting to be filled. Whatever the blade was doing, it was working, so I didn't question it as I ducked beneath a third swipe of the vampire's blade, my hair flicking around me as I spun aside.

Strike now!

I did as Fury commanded and the golden blade sliced across the backs of the vampire's legs, cutting through muscle and tendons, spilling blood that was too bright a red to be human.

The vampire hissed as he fell backwards, his legs unable to hold him upright anymore. I scrambled away from his blade as he thrust it at me from his position on the floor, ducking to my right and coming close to the raging tornado which was Magnar.

I tightened my grip on Fury, lunging toward the vampire I'd brought to the ground, meaning to finish him, but Magnar's sword made it before I could, carving him in two, finding his heart and leaving a heap of clothes and ash where he'd been.

"That was my kill," I growled, whirling on Magnar, but in the moment he'd given to help me, a female vampire had leapt onto his back, wrapping her arms around his neck.

Magnar bellowed a challenge as he tried to throw her off, his fingers ripping a great chunk of hair from her scalp, but she held on tight, snarling as she attempted to find his flesh with her teeth.

He swung around again, forcing me to leap aside but leaving his back to me in the movement. I lunged at the grappling pair, driving Fury straight at the vampire's back where it found a space between her ribs and made it to her heart with a sigh of pleasure.

Magnar didn't spare me a glance as he was released from the vampire's grip in her death, simply charging to take on our final two enemies, a battle cry spilling from his lips.

He cut down the first with a single strike and the last one turned and fled.

I pushed away from the wall, breaking into a run, expecting us to take chase, but Magnar slapped a hand against my chest to stop me, pushing me back firmly.

"Let her tell her masters what she found here. We'll be elsewhere by the time they get back."

"You're enjoying this," I accused, my chest rising and falling heavily, blood and ash staining my skin, adrenaline making my limbs tremble.

"So are you," he shot back.

"Of course I'm not," I snarled. "What kind of psychopath would enjoy fighting for their life in a bloodbath?"

Magnar took a step closer to me, sheathing Venom over his shoulder before taking hold of my jaw in his bloody fingers and tilting my face up to his.

"You can lie to yourself all you want, drakaina hjarta, but not to me. I see the way your eyes blaze with the hunger for their deaths. I feel the way your pulse is thundering with the thrill of the fight, and if I kissed that pretty mouth of yours, I'd taste the bloodlust on your tongue. You are born of my blood, and our kind wasn't meant to bow down to the rule of the fucking vampires. This rebellion has been locked away inside your heart for a long, long time. I'm simply the key you needed to unlock it."

He leaned closer, the sin of his mouth drawing me in, the sweetness of his breath brushing over my lips and the feral freedom in his golden eyes promising me so much more of that rebellion if only I decided to claim it.

Then he was gone. His grip left me and he turned away, leaving my heart to jolt back into rhythm, the tension in my limbs falling to nothing.

I glared at him as he stalked towards the door. Fuck him, because deep down beneath the utter terror and complete disbelief over what we'd just done, he was right. This was something I'd never even dared dream of being possible, to have hit back at the vampires so ferociously, to have killed so many of their kind after enduring a lifetime in servitude to them as little more than livestock…

Magnar headed out of the room, taking the other corridor and heading away from the fleeing vampire.

I didn't question him as I followed, the truth that was being revealed within me too potent to put words to.

We trailed bloody footprints along the corridor as we went, not making any attempt at subtlety or stealth now. It wouldn't be difficult for the Elite to locate us, and I just hoped Magnar would be ready for them when they arrived. It was one thing for him to fight a group of lesser vampires, but I'd seen how much more of a challenge the last Elite had been. I wasn't sure what would happen if he had to go up against more than one of them at once.

We moved quickly, and Fury didn't seem to think any more vampires were close to us yet, so I allowed myself a moment to catch my breath.

The corridor we were in held no doors and we continued along it at speed, searching for a way on, hunting for the humans they kept here, my need to reunite with my family stoking my moves with urgency.

Finally, we made it to another door and Magnar pushed it wide. I stepped through behind him, squinting as we were plunged into darkness. The light from the corridor illuminated a switch on the wall, and I flicked it on just as Magnar slammed the door behind us.

Light flooded the huge space as bulb after bulb illuminated above us and Magnar flinched in surprise. A smirk pulled at my lips as I glanced at him. The warrior who didn't bat an eyelash at enraging a group of vampires flinched at the flick of a light switch.

Magnar noticed the look and rolled his eyes at me. "Fuck you."

"Fuck you," I replied in kind.

"Be careful what you wish for, drakaina hjarta," he warned, sending a lick of fire right through my core.

I turned away from him dismissively, refusing to allow him to see the effect he had on me when his voice got all rough like that. The door we'd passed through was made of heavy metal and held large bolts, which I quickly slid across to secure it.

"Will that keep the Elite out?" I asked.

I knew they were strong, but I was doubtful that they could punch through solid iron.

"It looks like it might," Magnar agreed, placing Venom back into its sheath.

I returned my attention to the cavernous room we'd found ourselves in. It was filled with two long rows of coffin-sized boxes, a narrow walkway passing down the centre of them. The space was cool, the vaulted ceiling strung with pipes and wires which ran down to the coffins.

"I didn't think vampires really slept in coffins," I said as I took a step towards the closest row.

"They don't," Magnar replied darkly. "This is something else."

I bit my lip as I approached the first box. There was a glass lid over the top of it and two tubes ran into it from the ceiling. One was filled with clear liquid. The other was filled with blood.

I peered over the edge of the box and sucked in a sharp breath as I came face to face with someone I knew.

Thomas lay completely naked and perfectly still beneath the glass. His chest rose and fell steadily, though he showed no other signs of life. The last time I'd seen him, he'd punched me in the face for following him out of the Realm.

I guessed this meant the vampires had figured out that he'd been leaving too. Perhaps I should have felt guilty about that, but as I remembered the way he'd loomed over me, death flashing in his merciless gaze, I found it hard to be particularly remorseful. My family had needed the supplies which were available beyond the fences, and

I wasn't going to feel bad about exploiting the secret he'd found in an attempt to help them.

The clear tube delivered a drip directly into a vein in his left arm while the red tube took blood from a vein on his right.

"It's like intensive farming for people," I said in disgust. "They're keeping them alive so they can drain them." This was what we'd always known went on here, and in a way, it was a relief to see him lying there the way he was. He didn't know what was happening. It wasn't like he'd been strung up or was even conscious, he was simply asleep, unaware. It was practically humane. If you ignored the fact that he was there against his will and having his bodily fluids stolen to be used as food for monsters.

I looked around for some way to release him from the coffin, but there was nothing. The whole thing was sealed shut, no catch or lock that I could find, no buttons or levers either. I shoved at the glass lid, then pounded on it with Fury's hilt, but nothing happened. It was shut tight and impenetrable.

Magnar moved to stand beside me, throwing his shoulder against the lid, his muscles straining as he tried to force it open to no avail. The thing was rock solid.

"How are we supposed to get them out?" I asked desperately, my heart thumping to a painful rhythm as I looked around, wondering which of these boxes might hold Dad and Montana.

"We should locate your family. We can figure out how to release these people once we know where they are. I'll check one row while you check the other. I saw your father when he was taken but didn't get a clear look at your sister. Her hair was dark, wasn't it?" he asked.

"Yeah, her hair's as dark as mine is light, but we're twins so we still look a lot alike. Probably enough for you to recognise her. Mom used to call us her sun and moon. Dad too." Magnar's brows pulled together as I said that, but I didn't have time to question why. My family was close, I just knew it. They had to be.

"Just call me over if you see anyone you're unsure of," I told him, then hurried across the room and started moving along the other row of coffins.

There were many faces I didn't recognise but some that I did. Most were people who had been taken from the Realm for breaking rules. And a few were elderly people who had just disappeared in the night.

"Callie?" Magnar called.

I ran back to look into the coffin he'd found with my heart in my throat. A girl around my age lay in there, her hair was as dark as Montana's, but the similarities ended there. I shook my head as disappointment ran through me and I returned to my search.

Box after box, face after face, and none of them were them.

As we approached the far end of the room, my heart plummeted. There was no sign of them. If my family weren't here, then I didn't know what we would do. I had no idea where else they might have been taken. No idea what the vampires might have done to them. The terror of not knowing, the fear of them being lost was rising up in me until I felt like I might choke on it.

Tears pricked my eyes, but I forced them away, blinking hard and refusing the urge to fall to panic. We would rip this place apart before I'd give up on them. If they weren't in this room, then I just had to presume they were in another.

I reached the end of the row, and my soul fractured a little when I didn't find them. I turned to Magnar, and he shook his head sadly, confirming he hadn't located them either.

I moved past him and began to check his row for myself. He didn't know them. He couldn't be sure like I could be. I had to check again.

As I closed in on Thomas's coffin, a huge crash sounded from the door we'd bolted, and my heart hammered in terror, my feet stalling before moving faster as I continued my search, needing to be certain, determined to check thoroughly.

"We hear a human has dressed themselves up like a slayer of old!" a voice called from the other side of the iron door just as I made it back to Thomas's coffin, my heart sinking with the certainty that my family weren't in here.

I began to back away, and my slayer's mark tingled in warning, Fury burning hot as I drew it once more.

"Why not come and see if you can face a real opponent or two," the voice jeered.

The door rattled again, and Magnar caught my arm, pulling me behind him. I could tell he wanted to take the vampire up on the offer of a fight, but we kept retreating until we made it to the far end of the room again, and I turned around to find a way out.

A small door was tucked into one corner, and I ran for it, trusting Fury's assessment before pulling it wide.

I found myself in a control room filled with CCTV screens. I recognised it from the Realm. They'd had one just like it in the Emporium and I'd seen the little cameras that recorded us in all of the communal spaces. Even the bathhouse. My skin crawled as I thought about the invasion to our privacy. They wouldn't even allow us that much dignity.

Magnar froze as he looked at the screens, his eyes flicking from one to the next as he tried to process what he was seeing.

"Think of it as looking at lots of different places at once," I said quickly. "It just shows us what's happening elsewhere."

He stared at them in fascination and slowly raised a hand to point at one of the screens. "Isn't that your father?" he asked.

I spun to stare at the man he'd pointed out, and the bottom fell out of my stomach.

"Dad," I breathed, a tear spilling down my cheek.

He was in a small room, his arms were suspended by chains at his wrists, his body marked with signs of torture. They'd removed his shirt and he shivered in just a pair of torn jeans. Blood trickled across his skin from bite wounds on his neck and wrists. Bile rose in my throat as I took in the fact that he'd been here, enduring this the entire time we'd been searching for him.

I flinched as someone else moved into the view of the camera, and I realised he wasn't alone.

General Wolfe stalked towards him, his finger raised as he pointed it directly into my dad's face. It looked like he was asking him a question, but there was no audio to go with the footage, so I had no idea what it could be.

Dad shook his head firmly, though I could see something horribly like fear in his gaze as he did so.

The General shouted angrily, striking a blow to my father's face which sent him staggering back. He only remained upright because of the chains holding him so. Before he could recover, the General lunged, biting his neck.

My own scream met the one I could see falling from my father's lips, and I rushed towards the screen, wishing I could get to him.

"We have to find him! We have to help him!" I demanded as Magnar caught me in his arms, dragging me back against him.

"We will. He must be here. We'll find that room." He pulled me against his chest for a brief moment, then released me, holding me at arm's length. "Is your sister on one of these boxes?" He pointed at the screens, and I got the distinct impression he didn't like them.

I forced myself to look at the CCTV again, searching frantically for any sign of Montana, but she wasn't there. I shook my head, unable to say it out loud. Where else could she be? It didn't make sense. I could see the room where Thomas was contained on two of the screens but there wasn't another one like it, nowhere else that she might be unless it was somewhere without a camera.

My thoughts snagged on that skull I'd seen in the basement beneath the furnace. Maybe she hadn't been unconscious when they took her away. What if the General had struck her too hard? What if she'd never woken up?

"What if she's...I mean what if they..." I couldn't say it out loud.

If she was dead, I'd die too. I just knew it. There couldn't be a world where one of us existed without the other.

"What does your heart tell you?" Magnar demanded, forcing me to stand still and placing his palm above my racing heart.

I took a steadying breath, banishing the panic as I looked into his eyes and stole a measure of strength from him.

"She's alive," I said firmly, refusing any other answer to pass my lips.

Magnar nodded, his golden eyes hard and full of determination. "Then we will find her."

MONTANA

CHAPTER FOURTEEN

I watched as Fabian headed through a door at the end of the room, intending to follow him, but I was intercepted by Valentina.

Her full lips curved up into a bright smile. "Good evening, Montana."

"Valentina," I acknowledged her with a small nod, glancing over her shoulder as I tried to get by.

"Have you made your choice for the ceremony?" she asked, fluttering her long lashes.

"Um...not yet." I tried to step around her again, but she took hold of my arm to keep me there. Tension rippled through me as I gave her my full attention.

She gave me a concerned frown, then lowered her tone. "I'm sorry you have to go through this."

I gazed up at her in suspicion, her heels giving her an extra few inches on me. "Why do you care?"

She shifted closer, glancing cautiously around the room. "I don't want to see you getting hurt."

"I can handle myself," I said firmly.

I glanced longingly at the door Fabian had exited through. I needed to hurry the fuck up.

Nightmare hummed frantically on my thigh. *Follow, Moon Child.*

I gave her a brief smile. "I just need the bathroom…"

I tried to step away, but she took hold of the back of my neck, pulling me close so her mouth was by my ear. "When Erik finds out what you are, he'll kill you. I'm trying to protect you. You're the last of our kind. Please, listen to me."

I tugged away from her in shock, and her eyes flashed like there was a storm brewing in them.

"What do you know?" I whispered, acting casual so no one looked our way.

She stepped closer so she could talk into my ear again. "I know that I have many regrets, and being sired is one of them. If there are slayers being born again, I want to help them. You don't understand the power you possess, but I can help you."

Nightmare buzzed angrily on my thigh, urging me to hurry after Fabian.

Doubts trickled through me as I remained there, caught in limbo. I didn't know if I could trust her. She was just another vampire, another monster, even if she had been something else once. And beyond that, she had been the one who told Erik to get rid of me.

"I don't know what you're talking about," I said, playing dumb.

She pursed her lips, eyeing my right arm like she suspected what lay beneath the sleeve of my dress, and I took a wary step back.

"Maybe I'm wrong but…" She shook her head, seeming confused.

"I've really got to go." I darted away into the crowd, glancing over my shoulder to make sure Valentina wasn't following me. She floated toward the bar seeming deep in thought, clearly having no intention of chasing after me.

This was not good. If there was one thing I didn't need right now, it was more shit in my shit show. How could she possibly know about the mark? Could slayers sense their own kind? I certainly hadn't sensed anything when it came to her except danger, but that was how it always was around the vampires. What if she was telling the truth? What if she could help me, could get me out of here?

There wasn't much I could do about it at the moment, I'd just have to add it to the list of headfucks I'd be debating late into the night when I got to my bed later. Right now, I needed to track down Fabian.

Taking a breath and angling my thoughts back on the task at hand, I moved toward the door Fabian had exited by.

When I was sure no one was watching, I slipped through it and quietly shut it behind me.

A dark hallway lined with doors greeted me. I listened, trying to work out which room Fabian occupied. Moving as quietly as I could along the cream carpet, the sound of voices finally reached me.

Creeping closer, I approached the door I was sure Fabian was behind, my breaths coming a little quicker and Nightmare encouraging me on.

Seek. Find. Kill.

The blade was getting carried away with itself, but I felt more confident knowing it was close. Because if I was caught, I was not getting off lightly. Fabian might attack, and I had to be ready.

I willed the fear away, stepping up to the nearest door and pressing my ear to it.

"-if anyone realises I'm involved in this, I'm in deep shit," Fabian snarled. "I must end this tonight. Promise me it will be handled quietly."

"It will, your highness, I assure you," Roger answered, his voice quavering.

"Then pull yourself together!" Fabian snapped, and the sound of a smack rang through the air.

Hide. Nightmare's voice flared in my mind.

Certain I should obey, I darted toward the door across the hall and turned the handle. It swung open into a pitch-black room and I fled inside, pushing it closed with a quiet click.

I rested my ear to the door, willing my heartbeat to slow as Fabian's voice carried into the corridor. "I want him dealt with before the night is out. I won't have him causing us any more issues."

I pressed myself to the wood, desperate to hear them leaving, but they moved as silently as the wind, so I couldn't be sure if they were gone or not.

Their voices sounded further down the hallway, and I relaxed a little, pressing my forehead to the door. I couldn't believe how close I'd come to being caught. Without Nightmare, I would have been fucked.

I ran my hand over the blade where it was strapped to my thigh, its quiet presence reassuring me.

Nightmare started to hum with a different kind of energy, and I wondered what it meant, but I had no idea how to decipher the strange feelings it gave off.

When I'd waited several minutes, I gripped the door handle and opened it. Stepping into the corridor, I was suddenly crushed face-first to the opposite wall, a strong hand clamped to the back of my neck.

Cold fingers held my wrists behind my back, and I cried out, terrified Fabian had caught me. I tried to get free, wanting to reach for Nightmare as the blade buzzed frantically on my thigh.

Fight, Moon Child.

My captor released me, then flipped me around, and I came face to face with Erik.

A breath staggered from my lungs, but I didn't know if my relief was justified because he looked fucking furious.

"You motherfucker." I threw a fist at his chest which thumped hard yet uselessly against it.

"Is he in there?" he snapped, pointing at the room across the hall.

"Who?" I gasped, my heart rioting.

He spat a snarl, then shot away from me into the room I'd just been in. A beat later, he came stalking back to me, his shoulders tight and his eyes a sea of pitch.

"What is your problem?" I demanded.

He boxed me in against the wall, and I sucked in a breath as he pushed a knee between my thighs to hold me in place, then rested his forearm above me, leaning in and devouring the space between us.

"Where's Fabian?" he growled threateningly. "One minute you're on the dance floor, the next, you're sneaking away into dark rooms with him."

"Are you fucking serious?" I balked. "You're the one who told me to spy on him."

"I never told you to fuck him," he spat, eyes wild, the beast in him unleashed.

"What are you talking about?" I slammed my hands against his chest to try and force him back, but he didn't move an inch. "He came down here with that Roger asshole. I followed him and listened in on their conversation, then I hid in that room so he didn't catch me."

Erik stilled, taking in those words, and the monster in him slowly receded, his jaw locking tight.

"Have you lost your fucking mind?" I hissed, fury darting through my skin. How dare he attack me? This was all his idea, and now he was punishing me for it?

"I am starting to think so, yes," he gritted out.

"You have no right to be angry with me, even if I had fucked Fabian – which I would never do – what difference does it make to you? One minute you're demanding I do anything it takes to get close to him, the next you're throwing me against a wall and shouting at me for the possibility that I used my body to get the answers *you* want. So what is your goddamn problem?"

The music thumped loudly in the distance, but nothing seemed louder than my pulse, the wild tune of it thrashing in my ears.

"What did you overhear?" he asked, ignoring everything I'd said.

I shook my head at him in disbelief. "It sounds like he wants you gone, and I can't say I'm surprised," I said cuttingly.

Though I couldn't see his expression well in the dark hallway, I could tell he wasn't distressed. "That's not news to me."

"He said he wants you dealt with *tonight*," I added. "Or someone else, if not you."

He barely seemed to be listening, and I stilled as he lifted his hand, skating his thumb across my cheekbone.

"I think the gods are toying with me again," he rasped. "You torment me like they do. Only this torment is new. It's deeper than my mind, it's in my blood, my very veins. I cannot carve you out, and yet that is what I must do if I am ever to be rid of this madness." He gripped my face tighter, glaring at me. "They designed you for this purpose, I am sure of it."

"Erik, you're scaring me," I whispered, his grey eyes gleaming in the dark, full of untold demons.

"You should be scared," he said fiercely. "The terror of it should wake you in the night and haunt you deeper than any nightmare ever has. Because if the gods have crafted this desire in me for a creature such as you, then there will be no escaping it. No future in which I do not exist in your waking life."

"Erik," I pleaded, grasping his arm and trying to pull his hand from my face. "Stop. I'm not what you think I am. You've got it wrong."

"They have cursed you as they cursed me," he growled. "If they wish for me to want you like this, to inspire jealousy in me at the thought of my brother's hands on you, then you are the unluckiest creature on this earth. I am already your captor, but I will become your bane too."

"Jealousy," I whispered the word, unable to believe what he was admitting to me.

"I want you," he said darkly. "Not to love and adore, but to own and possess. I want every piece of you, and I have denied it to myself too long. The thought of you with him tonight has cracked my resolve. I resent you for that, despise you for it even, for awakening this insanity in me and destroying the plans I have laid. But it does not change the fact that I must have you."

He took my hand, holding it to my heart where it pounded violently beneath my palm, like it wanted to break free.

"I don't want this," I said, breathless from his proximity, his declaration.

I could see his desire as clear as day, even if he hadn't spoken the words, but the worst part of it was how I desired him too. Between the hate and the bitterness I felt towards him, that forbidden, carnal need crawled from the shadows of my heart and demanded I bow to it.

"Liar," he accused, pressing his knee deeper between my thighs, and I swallowed back a whimper. "You think I don't see the way you look at me or hear every drum of your heartbeat when I get near?"

"I fear you, that's all," I insisted, denial all I had left, but my resolve was crumbling before my eyes. I wanted to break, just for a moment, to let chaos reign and forget the consequences of this choice.

"I would believe it if you hadn't kissed me back," he said, the truth cutting and impossible to refute.

I gripped him by the collar, fingers knotting, choking him with the material despite him not needing air. Before I knew what I was doing, I was drawing him closer, breaking, shattering, letting the madness take over.

His mouth clashed with mine and he growled, crushing me to the wall and sinking his tongue between my lips. His kiss was rough and wicked as I wrapped my hands around his neck, then clawed at his hair. The rougher he was, the more I bit back, the more I took out my anger on him for the way I felt. For allowing this and revelling in every second.

"Finally," he sighed against my mouth, his fangs raking over my lower lip and drawing a moan from me. I shouldn't have liked that. This was so fucking wrong, but I couldn't stop now I'd given myself to this feeling. It was lust and heat and everything, and I needed him to release it from my body in the most sinful way possible. But the truth was, I had never let any man near me like this. I'd avoided the opportunities I'd had to claim pleasure from men, never wanting to get that close in case I got attached. Or worse, we had sex and I fell pregnant. But there was no risk of that here.

Erik hooked my dress up and I cursed, feeling Nightmare hum louder but he didn't come near it as I parted my thighs for him, and he sank his hand into my panties. His fingers were cold and I gasped, my back arching as I held onto his neck for support, our mouths parting long enough for him to look me in the eye and watch as he slicked his fingers between the hot wetness he found waiting for him. There was no denying my lust for him now, and I didn't want him to stop.

He growled his approval, then kept his gaze on mine as he sank two fingers deep inside me, inching them in like he was enjoying every second of his victory over me.

I cried out at the new sensation, my head tipping back as he ground the heel of his palm down on my clit, and my cry turned to a moan. He showed me no mercy as he pumped his fingers in and out of me in hard, firm strokes, and I adjusted to the feel of it, liking it more and more.

"Is this what you want from me?" he asked roughly.

"Yes," I sighed, the perfection of his touch unlike anything I'd experienced before. "I want to take and take from you and give nothing back."

He snarled in anger, then used his free hand to yank my head sideways by my hair and expose my neck to him, grazing his fangs over my pulse point.

"And how would you stop me?" he breathed, making my heart judder.

For a second, I feared he was going to bite me, and alarm rang through me, my shoulders tightening. But then he moved on, tugging my earlobe between his teeth and sending a line of fire down my spine. I'd never been touched like this before, with a skill that had me shivering, bowing to the power of his body over mine.

He drew his fingers out of me, sliding them over my clit instead, circling and rubbing that tight, sensitive spot and making me cry out in pleasure. I gripped his arms, furious at how easily he was bringing me to the edge of bliss, yet wanting it more than anything. It was wrong, so goddamn wrong that I was allowing this monster to lay his hands on me before any other had, but I couldn't pull away, lost to the pleasure he was feeding me and aching for more.

"You're the Devil," I snarled, my fingernails tearing at his shirt, but he slicked his fingers over my clit again in a motion that made me moan louder. He laughed coldly at me, forcing my legs wider with his knee.

"In the flesh, but you're still going to come for me," he growled.

I ground against his fingers as they worked me so damn perfectly that I knew he was right. The first wave of my orgasm crashed over me, and Erik pinned me to the wall with his body to keep me up, his fingers rolling over my clit, drawing out the ecstasy. His fingers slid into me again, two at first then three, stretching me and feeling my pussy pulse around his hand.

"If you let another man between your thighs, I'll kill them and make you watch," he warned, leaning back to glare at me.

"You're insane," I panted.

"Fucking deranged," he agreed, then pulled his fingers out of me sharply, making me curse.

He ripped my panties, tearing them off me and rubbing them between my thighs to wipe away my arousal, then pushed them into his pocket. I shoved my skirt down as he gave me more space, and Nightmare thrummed angrily against my leg, but it thankfully hadn't drawn his attention.

I stared up at the vampire who I had just let do the unthinkable to me and tried not to hate myself as deeply as I hated him.

"What now?" I demanded, and he smirked, looking me up and down.

"Now we go back to the party." He strode away from me, and I stared after him in disbelief.

"Erik," I snapped, but he didn't turn back. "What about the plan? Fabian? All of it?"

He said nothing and I marched after him in fury, finding my legs unsteady from all he'd done to me.

He shoved through the door back into the party and I was forced to chase him, finding a throng of people looking our way. Their eyes scraped over us, over the lipstick on Erik's mouth that was no doubt smeared across mine too. I rubbed at my lips to get it off, but that only drew more attention, and I swore beneath my breath, picking up my pace.

He didn't glance back once, his long stride outpacing me back to the seating area where Paige smiled dreamily up at me.

"Hey, where have you been?" Her eyes scraped over my hair, my ruffled dress. "And what have you been doing?" She gave me a knowing look, and heat blazed along my cheeks.

Erik released an obnoxious laugh, then swept on over to join Miles and Warren, who had taken the seats that Fabian's associates had vacated.

"Nothing," I insisted, snatching my drink from the table, taking a long swig to get the taste of Erik off my tongue.

"Where's Brianna?" I asked, and Paige pointed into the crowd. She was dancing with her arms in the air, grinding her hips against a male vampire, her eyes hooded and a lucid smile on her lips.

"Oh shit," I breathed. "What's she doing?"

"I dunno. I think it's those drinks...that make you feel all *swimmy*." Paige smiled lazily, and I quickly put my drink back on the table. The last thing I needed was my head to feel more messed up tonight.

"Paige, I've done something stupid," I whispered, leaning closer to her.

"No shit," she laughed. "You look like you had a good time doing it though. I knew he was into you."

"It's not like that." I pressed my fingers into my eyes, regret ripping through me. When I looked up again, my gaze fell on Erik, who was manspreading in his chair, his ankle resting on his knee. A waitress handed him a fresh drink and he took a swig, watching me over the rim of the glass, the asshole exuding smugness. He hadn't even bothered to wipe away the lipstick that was smeared over his mouth and cheek, wearing it like a goddamn trophy.

I despised him more than ever before as I realised all those words he'd spewed at me had been bullshit. He didn't think I was some temptation from the gods, and he had no intention of making me forget the plan with Fabian at all, or he would have said it there and then. It wasn't like he'd gotten much out of it himself, but maybe the triumph over me was enough.

Shame washed over me, and I had a mind to go snatch that drink from his hand and throw it in his fucking face.

Shit, Callie would kill me if she knew what I'd done. How stupid I'd been.

My eyes slid back to Paige, who was bouncing in her seat, clapping along to the music, and I envied her of her carefree night.

Erik suddenly lurched from his seat, making a beeline for Brianna through the crowd, roughly pushing people aside before snatching her arm.

"Hey!" she shouted at him, but he didn't let go even when she shoved at his arms.

He guided her toward the sofas and planted her down in a seat, looking furious.

Joshua stumbled out of the crowd with a bemused look, and Clarice came bounding after him.

"Just rest for a minute," she urged, pushing him toward the sofas.

"*Miles*," Erik snapped, and his brother looked up. "The humans are getting drunk."

"So what? They're having fun," Miles said with a shrug.

"The press are watching, that's what." Erik's jaw ticked as he turned to Paige, seeming to assess if she was affected like the others. "What about you?"

"I only had one," she insisted, pointing at her empty glass on the table as evidence.

Erik shifted his gaze to Brianna and Joshua on the sofa, now leaning against one another for support. "Right, they'll go back to the castle." He snapped his fingers at the nearest waiter to get his attention. "Have my car brought out front."

"Yes, your highness." The waiter scurried away.

"Oh, leave them be, you're such a buzzkill," Miles complained, throwing an arm over Warren's shoulders.

"No, Erik's right," Clarice said anxiously. "They can't stay here like this. People are beginning to stare."

Erik leaned down, pulling Brianna to her feet, and Joshua stood, wrapping an arm around her waist.

"Can you walk straight?" Erik asked them.

Joshua nodded and Brianna started hiccoughing her ABCs.

"Fucking hell. Just follow me," Erik ordered, turning on his heel.

He caught my arm as he passed by, tugging me from my seat. "That includes you, rebel."

I shrugged him off, giving him a cold look, but followed all the same. I was done with this place and craved the silence of my room to process the bullshit of this night.

I glanced at Paige. "Do you want to come?"

"Stay!" Miles called from behind us, patting his seat. "Come on, Paige, we'll have fun without these boring motherfuckers. I'll teach you to do the bachata."

"You can't do the bachata for shit," Warren laughed.

"I could bachata the fuck out of you and you know it," Miles challenged.

Paige broke a smile, tucking a lock of hair behind her ear. "I'll stay," she said to me, squeezing my hand. "See you tomorrow?"

I nodded, saying goodbye and heading after Joshua and Brianna. Erik took the lead, moving at a steady pace as we guided the others downstairs, him holding Joshua up while I helped Brianna.

"Q, R, S," Brianna hiccoughed. "T, U – damn, what comes after U again?"

"V," I offered, and she burst out laughing, slapping me on the arm.

"Oh my lord, how did I forget that one? V for vampire. V for vein, V for...vaginaaa."

Joshua snorted loudly, looking back at Brianna, then losing his footing on the grand staircase, nearly slamming onto his ass, but Erik caught him by the shirt and shoved him back upright.

We soon arrived in the entrance hall and exited onto the street where the temperature had plummeted, causing me to shiver in the frosty air. Thankfully, the rebels had moved on and a guard was removing the cordon on the other side of the street, whistling softly as he did so.

A car was waiting for us, and as Joshua and Brianna got into it, Erik took my arm to stop me following. "You'll come to my room when we get back to the castle."

"No chance," I hissed, trying to tug my arm free.

"Just to talk," he growled.

He held me tighter, and his ashen eyes turned to liquid silver in the moonlight. I shivered harder, and he shed his jacket, putting it around my shoulders before I could refuse. He gripped its lapels, keeping me trapped as Brianna tugged the car door closed.

We were bathed in the golden light of the porch as the sound of the engine filled my ears, and I feared we were going to be left behind.

"There's nothing to say," I whispered angrily, my breath fogging before me. "You made me come, good job. Do you want a medal?"

The guard's eyes slid our way, looking awkward as he clearly overheard what I'd said.

Erik's eyes blazed, fury gripping his features. "Montana, I-"

Fire flared and a loud blast tore through the air, ripping the world apart. Something collided with me and I hit the concrete hard. Pain exploded through the back of my head and all I could see was black hair as the weight of Erik crushed me down.

He forced me onto the stone floor, and a roar of noise told me something terrible had happened.

I pushed my head out from beneath him and ash sailed down over my face from the blazing fire. Shrapnel lay around us on the ground, the back of Erik's shirt torn to shreds from pieces that must have hit him, bright red blood wetting his back. Smoke billowed into the sky, and I stared at the car which had been reduced to a burning husk, shock jarring through me. Two figures lay still in the back seats; Brianna and Joshua, their corpses ablaze and the scent of death spilling into the air. The driver stumbled out of the front seat, rolling on the ground and crying out in fright as he worked to put the flames out.

My ears rang so hard, it swallowed every other sound but the thumping of my heart.

Erik was saying something, but I couldn't hear him as I tried to decipher the movements of his lips.

He cupped my cheek, and I felt hot blood trickling down the back of my neck. He held the wound I couldn't feel, cradling my head, and his shirt sleeve turned red. His lips moved in a bellow for help, his face swimming in and out of focus.

Nightmare thrummed fearfully against my thigh, and just before the darkness claimed me, it spoke words in my head I didn't understand, the mystery of them chasing me into oblivion.

A warrior born but monster made, changes fates of souls enslaved.

CALLIE

CHAPTER FIFTEEN

"Wait here. I'll deal with the Elite," Magnar commanded as I tried to follow him out of the control room. "But-"

"I'll fight better if I don't have to worry about you. You should find a way to free those humans from the coffins. We need to focus on moving fast and getting to your father. The best way to do that is through those vampires. I can carve us the path we require." He gazed into my eyes and my resolve wavered. He was right. We needed to get to Dad and find Montana. This room was filled with controls, and there was a map pinned to the wall too. If I could study it, maybe I could make sense of where we were and where Dad was too.

"Okay," I answered in acceptance. Magnar turned away, but I caught his arm and pulled him to me. "But promise me you're coming back."

His mouth quirked up at the side. "I'm coming back."

He placed his palm against my heart for an impossibly brief moment, then winked as he turned and left me alone, closing the door between us.

That fucking man was going to give me a heart attack before we parted, I just knew it.

My chest ached as he headed into danger, but there was nothing I could do about it. I had to trust in his strength and believe his promise.

He'll come back to me. He won't die.

I wanted to convince myself that I only cared because I needed his help to rescue my family, but a nagging feeling in the pit of my stomach had me worrying about him beyond simply that, defying every oath I'd ever made about letting myself care for anyone beyond my family. I didn't want him to die.

I blew out a harsh breath, ignoring that thought as I focused and tried to forget about what Magnar was doing beyond that door.

I moved to look at the screen which showed the warehouse where Magnar stalked towards the exit, swords in hand. I bit my lip anxiously as he approached the door the vampires were trying to break through. I didn't know if I wanted to watch, but I didn't think I could tear my gaze away either.

My heart leapt as the bolts securing the door gave way, but I couldn't waste time watching him fight those monsters while I hid away in here. I squeezed my eyes shut. He was born to take down the creatures of the night and I could only trust in his ability to do just that.

I opened my eyes and turned my attention to the screen which showed my dad hanging forward, slumped in his restraints. At first, I thought he'd passed out, but then he lifted his head, seeming to look right at me through the camera. It only lasted a second, but my resolve hardened. I was going to get him out, alongside everyone else stuck in this hellhole.

I searched the screen for some sign of the general, but I couldn't see him. It took me several seconds of scouring the other screens before I spotted him striding down a long corridor. It was impossible for me to tell where he was heading, but I had the immovable feeling that it was straight towards us. *Shit.*

My heart fluttered like a bird in a cage as I watched him moving a little too swiftly for it to be entirely natural. Though I was afraid of all vampires, General Wolfe awakened a special kind of terror in me. This was the monster who had taken everything from me as if it were nothing. His teeth had pierced my father's skin. He was responsible for whatever had happened to my sister. I longed to end his immortal life more than anything else. I wanted his presence struck from this world and his soul banished to the deepest pits of hell where it belonged.

Fury sang in my palm, wishing the same fate on him, the blade aching to feel the final beat of his black heart and curse him into death.

Take your vow, Sun child, and we can end them all.

I blinked in surprise as the voice swirled through my mind from the blade. I hadn't given the vow any more thought since Magnar had told me about it. Though the idea of having the strength to take on General Wolfe was seriously tempting, I still didn't want to relinquish my freedom in exchange for that power.

The sound of swords colliding carried from beyond the door, and my gaze snapped straight back to the screen showing the warehouse. Magnar was locked in battle with three of the Elite at the farthest end of the room. It was hard for me to make out much of what was happening between the four tiny figures on the screen, and I nervously chewed the inside of my cheek.

He threw one of the vampires away from him and she collided heavily with a coffin, reminding me of the task he'd set, snapping my mind back into focus.

I forced my gaze from the screens and started to scour the room for some way to release the humans.

On the opposite wall were various power cables, several switches, and levers.

I moved towards them and flicked the closest switch. The light above my head instantly went out and I cursed myself as I fumbled my hand along the wall to find the switch again then turned it back on.

I decided to leave the other switches for now and grabbed a handset instead. It stayed connected to the wall via a cord and I frowned at the buttons covering it. The numbers one to nine ran in sequence, waiting expectantly for me to do something.

I stared at it for several seconds then pressed number one. I glanced hopefully over my shoulder at the screen showing the coffins, but nothing happened.

"Hello?"

My heart leapt in surprise. The fucking handset was talking to me. Or I'd gone insane. I stared at it mutely, wondering what I should do.

"Hello?" the voice repeated.

"Yes?" I held it at arm's length and frowned at it in complete confusion.

"We had a report that you were having some trouble over there? Did you still want us to send a team?" the tinny voice asked.

I moved the handset a little closer to my ear so I could hear it better. Somehow, I seemed to be talking to a vampire somewhere else. My mind whirled with memories of the old world, the things my dad had described to me, and I realised the thing must have been a phone, though it didn't look like the mobile devices I'd seen the vampires in the realm with.

My fingers bit into the plastic as I tried to figure out what to say.

"Um no... false alarm," I replied a beat too late for it to come off naturally.

"Is there something wrong with the line?" the voice asked.

I wondered what line he was talking about and answered the only way I could. "The line?"

"Yes, the line – the line!"

"The line's fine. It's a perfect line. Straight as straight can be," I said, looking around in desperation for the line he was referring to.

"What?" the voice balked. "Wait, is that you again Jenny? I told you to stop this. It was a one-time thing. If the general knew we were mixing work and pleasure, he'd get rid of us both. And I like this job, Jenny. I get to be on corpse duty, and you know how much I love corpses. You just want to take that away from me, don't you?"

"Well that's the problem, isn't it?" I hissed, going full Jenny.

"You said you loved that about me! You called me Dr Death."

"Well I lied," I snapped. "It's creepy, and you're not Dr Death, you're Dr Dick."

I quickly placed the handset back where I'd found it and hoped the vampire wouldn't question that conversation.

I gave the screens another sweeping glance, but my dad hadn't moved, and it was too difficult to make out much that was going on with Magnar. He was still fighting though, so he was alive. That was enough for now.

A few of the levers had signs beside them, labelling their uses, and I cursed myself for my nearly non-existent literacy.

"Bee-oh, un-it... bi-oo unit?" I cursed again and begged my brain to cooperate as the letters seemed to dance around to avoid me reading them. "Bio unit!" *Okay, next word.* "Rel-ee-aa-ssss. Release!" I grinned at my find and quickly yanked the heavy lever down.

I looked up at the screen showing the warehouse and sighed in satisfaction as the coffins all slid open. But my mood shifted from elated to terrified as one of the Elite started running at full speed towards the room I was hiding in.

Magnar tried to cut him off, but two more Elite leapt into his path, forcing him back.

I stumbled away from the door, raising Fury, which burned in my palm. I was dead. I knew it. The vampire knew it. Hell, Fury even seemed to know it too. The blade felt sluggish in my grip, like it had already accepted our defeat.

The door was thrown wide, and I gasped as General Wolfe stalked into the room, his cold blue eyes gleaming with triumph as he pushed a hand into his silver hair, slicking it back away from his face.

"Callie Ford. How I have hunted for you," he hissed excitedly, then stalked towards me.

I balked as he said my name, hating that he knew it, hating that fear was gripping me so tightly at the mere sight of him. "Why? What's so special about me?"

If I kept him talking, then I had the faint hope that Magnar might be able to get to me. Fury was back to its usual self, urging me to attack, and I shifted my grip on its hilt, willing it to be quiet. I might have gotten lucky with a few lesser vampires, but I wasn't foolish enough to rate my chances against an Elite. Especially *this* Elite who might just have been the most evil, terrifying creature on the planet.

I swallowed a thick lump in my throat as I backed up, putting a small office chair between us. It was a pretty pathetic line of defence, but I felt better with there being something to separate us.

"Nothing," he spat. "You're just a worthless human. You're all just as irrelevant as the next. At least to me. But my master wants you for your blood."

"My blood?" I recoiled. That was nothing new; we were just food to them. But why would some important vampire want *my* blood specifically?

"Yes." He licked his lips, and I caught sight of his fangs.

A shudder ran down my spine.

"Your master?" I'd backed up as far as I could go and bumped against the wall.

"Erik Belvedere has something in mind for you and your sister. I'm going to take you to join her in New York." He smiled at me like he wanted to eat me, and my stomach swooped. But one thing he'd said gave me reason to hope. Montana was still alive, and he was here to capture me not kill me. Not that I'd be going anywhere with him if I had any say in it.

"Erik Belvedere?" I asked, trying to feign ignorance, but I remembered that name. The vampire who had murdered Magnar's father and turned him into a vampire. Killer of a Thousand Souls. If Montana was with him, then I had no idea how I would rescue her, but she was *alive,* so I'd figure it out. Assuming I survived this.

The general kicked the office chair aside as he continued his lazy advance. It spun away on rickety wheels before bumping into the desk and coming to a halt.

"Don't worry, there will be plenty of you left for him to toy with when I'm finished. But I think I'll have my fun with you first." He leapt at me, and I cursed as I tried to twist aside.

Fury blazed commands into my mind, but I couldn't react quickly enough to even try and utilise them.

The general grabbed a fistful of my hair, wrenching my head back and exposing my throat. His other hand caught my wrist and he twisted viciously, forcing me to release my hold on Fury. My metal companion clattered to the ground, the sound filling me with dread. As the blade left me, the warmth of its presence fled too, and I found myself hopelessly alone.

Wolfe forced me back, slamming me against the cold wall, his free hand splaying across my stomach as he pinned me in place. I was a fly caught by a spider, unable to do anything but watch as it came for me.

General Wolfe increased the pressure on my hair, forcing me to bare my neck to him.

I gritted my teeth against the whimper of pain which tried to escape me. I wouldn't let him see my fear. I'd never let him know he was hurting me.

He leaned in, his horrifyingly beautiful face closing in on mine as if he might kiss me. But it wasn't desire for my body that heated his gaze, it was lust for my blood.

My heart thundered wildly as he shifted closer, and panic tried to take hold of me. He released a deep growl in the back of his throat as he pressed his cold lips against the skin of my neck, inhaling deeply.

I recoiled, my stomach roiling with disgust as I tried to squirm out of his grasp, but his unbreakable strength held me paralysed.

He inhaled again and ran his cool tongue along the length of my neck. Bile built in my mouth, and I was pretty sure I was about to vomit all over his polished boots.

"Get the fuck off of me," I hissed, straining against his hold.

Wolfe sighed, almost sounding disappointed, and moved back an inch. His icy blue eyes met mine, and I swallowed back the bile, letting every ounce of hatred I felt for him boil in my gaze. His eyes glimmered with amusement like my anger pleased him, like he wanted it almost as desperately as he wanted my blood.

"I may not be allowed to sample the goods yet," he purred. "But I'm sure my master will share you with me once he's finished."

I stared into his eyes, wondering how on Earth I'd just escaped the call of his bloodlust. I could still see it swimming beneath the surface of his barely maintained composure. He longed to taste my blood. But his fear of his master held him back. And if this monster was that afraid of Erik Belvedere, then I knew without doubt that I had to escape before he delivered me to him.

Any creature horrifying enough to strike fear into General Wolfe's dark heart had to be beyond evil.

And that's who has Montana.

The blood drained from my face as I considered that. She was facing a worse fate than I'd imagined. I *had* to save her, no matter what it took.

Wolfe released my hair and shoved me towards the door with such force that I slammed down onto my knees.

Fury called to me from inches away and I lunged for it, reaching desperately for the blade.

General Wolf laughed as he kicked Fury, sending it skittering out into the warehouse.

"Tell me, Callie Ford, how did that slayer awaken your mark?"

I started crawling after Fury, my heart pounding as the general's footsteps slowly followed.

Magnar was still locked in battle with the two Elite at the far end of the room, the sound of clashing blades and cries of rage filling the cavernous space.

"Did you have to do something? Maybe he made you recite an ancient chant or do a savage dance to the moon? Or did you fuck him? Did spreading your legs awaken the power of it?" he chuckled, but there was no joy in the sound, only malice.

I was getting close to Fury again, so close, but Wolfe kicked me in the stomach, sending me rolling away from it. I gasped as the air was forced from my lungs and pain blossomed through my body. I glared up at him as I scrambled back into a crouch. He was a cat playing with a mouse. But mice had teeth too, and he'd find that out if I got the opportunity to show him.

"Fuck you," I spat.

I might not have been much of a slayer, but the blood of my ancestors flowed through my veins, and I refused to cower in fear before him.

The general smirked, his gaze drifting from me to look at the rows of coffins which now stood open. "You know, this batch of stock hasn't been producing the best quality of blood lately. We've been meaning to have a clear out." He strode towards the wall and reached over to open a panel filled with controls and switches.

I got to my feet shakily, my gaze flicking between the general and the door at the far end of the room. I knew it would be useless to try and run but adrenaline flooded my limbs, urging me to do just that.

General Wolfe hit several buttons on a keypad and turned to smile at me as he yanked on a big lever. He had dimples. How could something so cruel have such a beautiful face? But I could see through the visage to the darkness beneath it, and nothing in his beauty beckoned me closer.

A mechanical whirring started up, and I looked around at the room in confusion. Bright green fluid began to slide down the tubes which had been delivering the drips to the unconscious humans. I wheeled around, looking down into the coffin beside me where a middle-aged woman with greying hair lay sleeping. I stared in horror as the green fluid made contact with the woman's blood and she began jerking violently.

A gasp of alarm escaped my lips, and I raced around the coffin, yanking the drip from her arm before it could deliver any more poison. She didn't stop fitting though, and all around me, the humans contained in the boxes were jerking and flailing as the poison flooded into them too.

Wolfe released a soft laugh as he stalked towards me.

I forgot about the pointlessness of it and fled. My boots pounded through the warehouse, and I tried to ignore the dying humans all around me as their bodies fitted and fell still, the horror of it scoring through my brain.

I raced towards Magnar, and my approach made one of the Elite hesitate just long enough to give him an in. Tempest plunged through the vampire's heart and the Elite fell apart like a million scattered grains of sand.

I'd almost made it to Magnar when Wolfe caught me. He lifted me clean off of my feet and hurled me straight past Magnar and the last Elite. I crashed to the ground, pain tearing through my body as I tumbled over and over before slamming into the heavy metal door.

I coughed weakly as I tried to push myself upright, my head spinning from the collision as Magnar let out a roar of pure rage.

"Callie!" he bellowed, and I blinked up at him, trying to align my thoughts while my vision swam.

Before I could get up, Wolfe caught my arm and dragged me out into the corridor, my boots kicking uselessly at the floor as he hauled me along.

I lost sight of Magnar, but I could still hear the clash of steel as the last Elite stopped him from following us, the gap between us widening with every passing breath.

Wolf broke into a run, racing down the corridor, dragging me behind him so quickly that I could only kick my heels against the floor in an attempt to stop him from wrenching my arm from its socket while I swore at him at the top of my lungs.

As we approached the refrigerator where we'd destroyed the stock of human blood, I threw myself aside, twisting my arm in his grasp and tumbling free of his hold.

I scrambled to my feet as Wolfe whirled on me, throwing a punch to his jaw which damn near broke my knuckles. Wolfe grinned, barely even reacting to the strike before slapping me squarely across the face, the hit so powerful that I was thrown against the wall.

He grabbed hold of me and yanked me into motion again, pain tearing through my arm as he came close to ripping the fucking limb off, but I'd achieved my goal. My boots were coated in blood, leaving a trail of it as he dragged me further into the building, marking a path for a slayer set on murder.

MONTANA

CHAPTER SIXTEEN

"**H**ave any idea how close I was to *turning* her?" Erik's sharp voice made my head ache. And fuck, did it ache. My left shoulder hurt too, more of a slicing pinch than the throbbing in my brain. I didn't know which was worse.

I groaned, reaching out and finding soft sheets beneath me, disoriented as I tried to place where I was. Memories stirred from the darkness of my mind, of my hand finding my sister's in the night, reaching over to her bed which was parted from mine by a small gap. No matter what nightmares had found me in the quiet hours of early morning, she had always been there. But now as my hand reached blindly for my twin, I found nothing but empty space.

"Well thank the gods you didn't," Miles's voice filled the air. "She still has to choose one of us at the ceremony."

"Is that all you fucking care about?" Erik barked at him.

"She wouldn't be much use to us if she wasn't human anymore, would she?" Miles retorted.

My chest tightened in horror as I realised Erik had actually considered turning me into a vampire. Were my injuries that bad? And why the fuck was it so important that I was still human for the ceremony?

I shuddered, reaching for the back of my head which was throbbing like a bitch. A bandage was wrapped around it, and the spot I'd hit on the pavement was tender, but there was no blood soaking through, so that had to be a good sign. I was still wearing the dress from the party, and the steady purr of Nightmare against my thigh said the blade was with me.

"Shut up, Miles. Just leave him with her," Clarice hissed, and the sound of a door shutting sent another dagger through my skull.

I blinked, groggy as I took in the room. My room. I was back in the castle, the shutters open and moonlight spilling through them. How long had I been out cold?

Erik paced toward me, his pants covered in dust and his shirt ripped, stained with blood.

"What happened?" I murmured, my heart rate picking up at his ferocious expression.

"Fabian," he snarled. "He rigged my car. That should have been us in there."

Panic spilled through me as the whole explosion came back to me in a flood of clarity. "Brianna…Joshua?"

"Dead," he confirmed in a cold tone.

I sucked in a breath as that truth burrowed into my heart. I hadn't known them well, but their loss still cut into me like a knife.

Oh fuck…what if it had *been us in that car?*

My stomach roiled as nausea gripped me, and I shut my eyes, seeking out a space of calm within me. The safe space inside my mind where nothing bad could ever happen. When I'd grounded myself, I let the fantasy slip away and faced reality again, knowing there was no escaping it.

"Did you catch Fabian?" I asked, desperate to know he'd been dealt with. That he was no longer a threat.

Erik shook his head. "He has an alibi."

"But you know it was him," I cried. "I heard him making the plan."

"No one will believe you," Erik said in a low tone. "No one but me."

"So tell them you overheard him," I growled. "You're as powerful as him, aren't you? Surely you can stand against him."

"I have no proof, Montana," he spat. "It's our word against his, and he'll have a hundred chancellors backing him to the bitter end. Besides..."

"What?" I clipped.

Erik frowned deeply. "It doesn't make sense that he would set a bomb to kill me. I'm immortal. It would take a lot more than that. It was either a failure by whoever he ordered to set it, or..."

"Or?" I pressed.

He shook his head. "I don't know."

I wanted to push him for answers, but my head throbbed again and pain bloomed along my left shoulder, distracting me. "Fuck," I hissed, grinding my teeth through it.

"You should be dead," he said. "You hit your head really fucking hard. It's a miracle you're still breathing. I..." He paced back and forth, stalking around the bed like a caged animal. "I knocked you over, it was my fault. I used too much force. I was trying to put myself between you and the blast."

I remembered laying on the pavement, his body arced over mine, taking the brunt of the shrapnel from the explosion, and I realised with a jolt what he'd done.

"You protected me," I whispered, and he stopped pacing, eyes snapping my way.

"Don't speak those words like I'm some hero," he snarled. "You are mine to safeguard. You think I would let some rogue assassin take you from me? You think I would give them the pleasure of that?"

"Oh, I get it now," I said bitterly. "Your little possession got damaged. Scratched up by your brother, or some other enemy of yours. And you can't stand to take the ego hit."

His jaw pulsed furiously as he stared at me, taking in the bandage around my head, my shoulder.

"Who tended to me?" I asked, touching the bandages, worrying that whichever vampire had done it might not even know how to look after a human.

"I had a vampire brought here who used to be a human doctor. A piece of shrapnel hit your shoulder, but it didn't go too deep, though that's where most of the blood came from. The injury to the back of your head was the most concern to her, but somehow you pulled through regardless."

I nodded slowly, absorbing that information. "Are you hurt?" I asked, remembering the lacerations I had seen along his back from the shrapnel.

Erik shook his head. "I heal, unlike you. My wounds are long gone already."

His eyes drifted to the blood on his tattered shirt, and he suddenly took it off completely, tossing it aside. I noticed the faded scars marring his flesh and wondered how it was possible they were there if his body could heal itself. He moved closer to the bed, sitting on the edge of it, angled toward me.

"How did you get that?" I pointed to the crescent-shaped scar on his midriff that looked like it had once been very deep.

He glanced down at it with a frown, and my fingers itched with the quiet urge to touch the silvery mark.

"A slayer. Their blades are designed to hurt us. They're the only weapon which can leave a scar like this. It takes a lot longer for us to heal from a cut delivered by their blades."

My heart pounded faster at the mention of the slayers and their weapons. "Fabian told me about them. He said they're all dead now?" I questioned, wondering how much more Erik might reveal.

He nodded. "Yes, they are long gone. We defeated them many years ago. But there were a few who presented more of a challenge."

I reached out, unable to help myself as I brushed the tips of my fingers over the scar on his stomach. His skin was silken and not quite as icy as I'd expected, more like glass cooled by the rain.

"Does it hurt?" I breathed, tracing the half-moon.

"Not anymore," he said, his tone rough. "A slayer called Magnar Elioson gave me this. He was gifted by the gods, as all slayers are, but he was far more powerful than most. He called himself a Blessed Crusader."

"So the gods cursed you, made you into a vampire, then offered the slayers power so they could-"

"Destroy us," Erik finished grimly.

I frowned, not sure I believed it. If it was true, and the mark on my arm really meant I was a slayer, I was made to destroy his kind. But after all I had witnessed of the vampires' cruel dominion, feeling utterly powerless to their rule, it was difficult to believe anyone could fight back against them and win. Then again, hadn't I proved it possible by destroying that vampire who had come to kill me in this very room?

The gods chose this path for you, Moon Child.

Nightmare's voice crept into my mind, the blade warming against my thigh and reminding me of its presence. My eyes lifted to the dangerous creature in the room, considering what all this meant if I could accept the possibility of it. I was his sworn enemy, gifted by the gods to cast him from this world, and this very night I had let him lay his hands on me. I had taken a taste of the carnal heat between us and damned myself in his arms. The vampires had hunted the slayers to extinction, and if Erik knew one sat in this bed, I doubted he would hesitate to end me. But then again, Miles had spoken of some importance I held. That the other humans had slayer blood too. And even if mine was stronger than most, maybe Erik would see the value in me his brother had seen. Not that I planned on putting that theory to the test.

Erik's eyes drifted to the shirt he'd discarded on the floor, a mix of my blood and his staining it.

"Does it make you hungry?" I asked, my skin prickling at the thought.

"Yes. It has been a little while since I had a drink, I will seek one out soon. But I am no animal. It would take some time before I succumbed to the thirst."

"How long?" I questioned, my voice a little dry.

"Some time," he repeated, apparently in no mood to elaborate.

Quiet fell again and I wasn't sure why he remained here, but some fucked-up part of me wanted him to. Perhaps what I really wanted was the company of my sister and Dad. Whenever any of us had been injured or sick, the other two would be their rock. Now, I was alone for the first time in my life, and I found myself wounded in the face of a vampire prince. He wasn't likely to tell me stories, cook me up soup, or make me tea, but he was bringing *something* to the situation. A distraction maybe.

"Dad will be here tomorrow, right? In the morning?"

"Yes," he confirmed, and I blew out a breath of relief, my anticipation for the moment I saw him again making my heart squeeze.

Erik's eyes drifted to my dress. "You should change."

I glanced down at the blue dress which was dirtied with ash. There was blood around my collar too, and my left sleeve had been cut away so the bandage could be secured around my neck and shoulder. Thank fuck it hadn't been the right sleeve, or the slayer mark would have been found.

I pushed myself upright, figuring he had a point, and when he offered me a hand to get up, I took it. He guided me to my feet, and I felt immediately dizzy, my feet stumbling forward. Erik shot into my path, and I crashed into his chest as he caught my arms to steady me. "The doctor gave you some painkillers for your injuries, she said it might make you feel dizzy."

"I'm fine," I said, but my feet went stumbling sideways of their own accord and Erik caught me by the waist. Okay, maybe I wasn't so fine.

He unzipped the back of my dress and I sighed, letting him.

In truth, I needed the help. And even though it was asshole prince offering it, I would have let him continue had it not been for the slayer blade strapped to my thigh.

"I need to pee," I said quickly, then staggered into the bathroom, pushing the door shut behind me.

I rested one hand on the sink, blinking back the swimmy feeling in my mind and reaching beneath my dress, unwrapping the scarf that held Nightmare in place. I bundled it up in the scarf, then shoved it into a space between the basin and the wall, concealing it from view. That was gonna have to be enough, because my head was spinning.

I flushed the toilet and ran the sink before opening the door, the room tilting a little as I stepped out of it.

"I don't want any more of those things," I said. "Don't let that doctor woman give them to me again."

"Alright, but the pain will be much sharper by tomorrow. You may change your mind," Erik said, watching me as I staggered past him towards the closet, clutching my dress to my chest so it didn't fall down.

I grabbed a pair of silken pyjamas, gritting my teeth with determination and shuffling my way to the bed to place them down. Now all I had to do was take my dress off and put those clothes on.

"Turn around." I wafted a hand at Erik, and he gave me a dry look before complying.

Getting out of the dress was the easy part, simply letting it drop to the floor to pool around my feet. I had no underwear on beneath, thanks to Erik stealing the pair of panties I'd been wearing, and the bodice of the dress had required no bra. I picked up the silk shirt which was a button-down style with long sleeves that would cover my mark. I slid my arms into it, then stepped out of the dress, but instead of placing my foot down, I somehow started tilting backwards instead. Gravity was my newest nemesis as my ass hit the floor, and I cursed in pain as I threw my arm back to catch myself, jarring my injuries. And painkillers or not, it still hurt like a bitch.

Erik was suddenly there, scooping me into his arms like a baby and sitting me on the edge of the bed. The pyjama shirt hung open, exposing my body to him, but he looked at nothing but the pyjama pants, grabbing them and stooping down to put them on me. He caught my ankle in a tight grip, pushing it into the left leg and I offered up my right, giving in to the inevitable.

He slid them up my legs and I lifted my ass as he tugged them all the way on then he caught hold of the shirt and started buttoning it down from the top with deft fingers.

My gaze flicked up, watching his face, a stern concentration lining his features. He was so deep in my personal space, there was no escaping him.

Words of thanks got stuck on my tongue, too heavy to take flight.

We were so close, his hand resting on the bed beside me, his eyes on mine, my breaths fluttering against his mouth. The world made so little sense when we were this near to one another, like the laws of the universe no longer applied.

Erik's phone rang in his pocket, and he stood up straight, snatching it out.

He lifted it to his ear and pressed the screen. "Straight to the point Wolfe, what is it?"

My thoughts sharpened at the name.

"What?!" Erik roared, his sudden anger making me flinch in alarm. "How is that possible?"

He fell silent as Wolfe answered and my heart thumped harder as I tried to hear his answer, but it was too quiet to catch.

"Who said that?" Erik hissed, grinding his teeth whilst Wolfe replied. "Good, bring her here immediately. And don't you dare play your usual games with her. She is the sister of my courtier, do you understand? That makes her life more valuable than yours."

"Callie's there?" I gasped, shoving to my feet and reaching for the phone in his hand, a lifeline that suddenly connected me to my twin. "Let me talk to her!"

Erik caught my wrist to hold me back, listening to something Wolfe was saying.

Terror clawed up my throat at knowing Callie was with that monster of a general. That she hadn't outrun him. She'd been caught after all.

I reached for the phone with my other hand, but Erik twisted away to stop me getting close. Desperation filled me and I could almost sense my sister on the other end of that phone call, so close and yet untouchable.

"Callie!" I yelled, needing to speak to her, to hear her voice.

"That's not possible." Shock poured through Erik's eyes at something Wolfe said. "Describe him," he growled and a moment later he ground his jaw so hard I was sure he was going to break some teeth. "Get his fucking name, Wolfe." He hung up a second later and his gaze drifted down to me.

"You didn't let me speak to her," I snarled, my eyes scorching with unshed tears.

"She's fine, rebel. Relax. Wolfe will bring her here."

A jagged lump rose in my throat, and I looked away, my heart sinking at knowing she had been captured. This wasn't how it was supposed to go. She was meant to remain free, and Dad was meant to join her.

"Get out," I said quietly, rage and fear tangling together to make my hands shake.

"Montana-"

"Get out!" I screamed.

He glared at me with frustration in his eyes before turning his back on me, marching from the room, and slamming the door behind him.

I sank down on the bed with my thoughts in turmoil. Callie was safe, but she was also with Wolfe, and he'd already threatened to hurt her. Would he keep his word to Erik and bring her here in one piece?

I scrambled off the bed, moving into the bathroom and gripping the sink as I got hold of Nightmare, gripping the golden hilt.

Its essence was dark, and its stony silence didn't bode well, but a little warmth trickled from the metal into my palm. I glanced at the mirror, liking the way the blade looked in my hand, like it had always been meant to find me.

Callie was alive at least, and that was what I had to hold on to. She would be brought here with Dad, and perhaps I could bargain for her freedom too. Though the way Erik had spoken of her value stuck a needle of dread in my heart.

I couldn't bear for her to come here and get wrapped up in the twisted company of the royals, to befall the same fate as me. The ritual was almost over, so perhaps she would avoid the bullshit I'd been put through. I just didn't know.

Fuck, she was going to be so angry if she learned of what had happened between Erik and me.

I recalled the feeling of his fingers inside me, the press of his powerful body crushing me to the wall. I'd wanted it, that was the worst part of it, or perhaps it was how much I'd enjoyed it that was most shameful. It was pointless denying the lust between us now, the hatred that sparked into flames until they roared, demanding more. Until eventually, I gave in to the want that lay beneath my vitriol, seizing a moment in the arms of a monster and ending up appalled with myself because of it.

I drew in a deep breath, trying to unwind my web of thoughts to no avail. Nightmare pulsed against my palm, and I gritted my jaw, resilience carving a passage through my chest.

I gazed at my reflection and a warrior stared back, willing to go to war for those she loved. Tomorrow would be a day of reckoning. Both the day of the choosing ceremony, and the day my family were returned to me.

I only had hours left to decide which promise I was going to keep, and who I would select because of it.

All I knew for sure, was that when midnight came again, I'd be betrothed to a beast.

CALLIE

CHAPTER SEVENTEEN

Wolfe dragged me to the end of the corridor where a row of doors were clustered together on both walls. He tore open the final door on the left and pulled me inside. I kicked out at the wall as he yanked on my arm, smearing blood from the side of my boot along the grey brickwork for Magnar to see.

Please be alright. Please come for me again.

I was making a habit of relying on him to rescue me, but I couldn't summon a fuck to give about it. He was the only hope I had of escaping this fate, of surviving whatever Wolfe and the Belvederes had planned for me, so I could only hope he was on his way already.

Wolfe slammed the door behind us and tossed me away from him, sending me flying into the rear wall, my head colliding with the brickwork. I crashed to the ground, spitting blood from my mouth where I'd bitten my tongue.

I used the wall to claw my way upright again, glaring at Wolfe while looking for some way out of this, keeping my back pressed to the freezing stone.

The small room was empty save for some chains hanging from the ceiling. It was cold and dank, a dirty puddle which I had no interest in identifying staining the floor. It looked just like the room my father was being held in, though he was nowhere to be seen. I wondered if he was trapped nearby.

My gaze skimmed past the evil creature standing before me and fell on the wooden door. Escape beckoned, but with that monster blocking my way to it, it might as well have been a mile away.

"What do you want me for?" I demanded, my voice sounding braver than I felt.

I straightened my spine in defiance, hoping that my slayer blood would help me to hold my own, though I missed the defiant warmth of Fury in my hand.

Wolfe's gaze flicked to me without any real interest, and he pulled a cellphone from his pocket, dialling a number before turning away from me to talk.

"Good evening, sir, I'm sorry to interrupt your-" He cut off abruptly, and I caught sight of a scowl on his face which didn't match the simpering tone he was using with whoever he was talking to. "It's just that a situation has occurred here. I'm afraid we had to destroy the current batch of humans being held in the blood bank."

He winced as the person on the phone started yelling at him, their outraged voice reaching me. I couldn't hear the words behind the tone, but I could tell they were pissed. I wondered if he was speaking to Erik Belvedere, if the answer to my sister's whereabouts was within reach.

"We had a security issue. The bio-units were all compromised and there was a chance of contamination to the product. The decision had to be made in the interest of public safety. I'm sure we can make up the loss by upping donations within Realm G for the next few months. We might lose a few of the weaker specimens, but it never hurts to cut the wheat from the chaff."

I glared at him angrily as I realised what he was saying. The people in the Realm would suffer because he'd murdered the prisoners here.

"I'm going to fucking kill you," I growled, moving towards him with my fists clenched. "I'm going to carve you up while you scream for mercy before I cast you to ash like the rest of your bloodsucker friends. You psychotic piece of-" Wolfe took a step towards me and backhanded me hard enough to split my lip and knock me into the wall again. I stumbled back as the iron tang of blood filled my mouth, my eyes flicking to the door as he left more space open before it.

"Sorry, sir. That was the other reason for my call," Wolfe went on, smoothing a hand over his silver hair, his contemptuous gaze roaming over me. "The Ford girl we've been hunting is the one who broke in here. I have her contained."

He paused to listen while the vampire on the other end of the phone spoke. I glared at him and he eyed me hungrily in return, his gaze snagging on the blood marking my mouth. Fear licked down my spine as he took half a step towards me, his intent clear.

"Of course. I understand but...she wasn't alone. There is a man here with her. A slayer. And I don't mean someone who has trained themselves to hunt us; this mortal is like a slayer of old. If I hadn't seen him with my own eyes, I wouldn't have believed it. He was taller than any man I've ever met and built like a bear. He fights with two slayer blades the likes of which I've never seen, and he has killed almost all of us who were here tonight. The last I saw he was still fighting Helga, but I am not confident she will win. Of course, I only refrained from killing him myself to be sure of bringing you the Ford girl, as I know she is your highest priority right now and-"

"More like you were afraid, you cowardly sack of shit," I shouted, loud enough for whoever was on that phone to hear me.

Wolfe bared his fangs at me as he listened again.

"Tall, like I said. Long, dark hair. Thick with muscle and full of rage. There are tattoos and scars on what little of his skin I could see, but he is wearing fighting leathers, so I couldn't see much."

He fell silent for a few seconds, then looked down at the cell phone like it had done something surprising.

"Oh, I'll get you that name," he growled as he pushed the phone into his pocket and advanced on me.

I backed up, hitting the cold brick wall behind me as my heart rate spiked with fear.

"Prince Erik wants to know the name of the slayer who brought you here," he said.

I took a deep breath to buy myself a moment before I answered. If *Prince Erik* wanted to know who Magnar was, then I wasn't about to tell him shit.

"Why not ask him yourself? Or does he frighten you?" I taunted, waiting for his anger to fall on me. There was no way I would give him Magnar's name.

I forced my own fear aside as I prepared to take what was coming for my silence on the matter. It was a small rebellion but an important one. He might be stronger and more powerful than me, but my defiance ran to the marrow of my bones, and if I held information he needed, then there was no fucking way I'd be giving it up.

"I don't even remember what fear is," Wolfe mused, taking a step closer to me, leaving the door further behind. Not that I could see myself making it that far. "But I'm sure *you* know it well."

His eyes dropped to my mouth and the blood which I could feel on my lip and chin.

"That'll be why you ran from that slayer like a frightened little bitch then," I replied with a smile which I knew would earn me another smack.

Wolfe punched me in the gut, and I doubled over as the breath was knocked from my lungs. Before I could recover, he hauled me upright again, pinning me against the wall, his fingernails biting into my shoulders.

"Tell me his name!" he roared, and his anger sent terror coursing along my spine, but I wouldn't let it rule me.

I gathered every inch of resolve I had left and spat in his face.

Wolfe snarled like a feral beast, seizing me around the throat and raising me up above his head, my feet scrambling against the wall and my fingernails biting into the flesh of his hand as I fought to get him off me.

"I will have his name from you, whore. Or I will have your head," Wolfe barked, his fangs flashing in the light.

The door burst open at his back, slamming against the wall hard enough to break one set of hinges and leaving it hanging half out of the frame.

Wolfe dropped me as he spun away from it. I crashed onto the concrete floor, pain flaring along my side while I smiled widely at the living legend who had just broken down the motherfucking door.

Wolfe stared up in horror, recoiling from the huge man who stood in the doorway, swords held ready and smeared with the ash of his kills.

"My name is Magnar Elioson, and I was put on this earth to wipe your kind from it. Tell your master I have returned for him. I hope he has made the most of the extra years he was gifted in my absence, because his time is up."

My heart thumped furiously as I scrambled towards Magnar, but Wolfe was quicker; he lunged at me, catching my arm and heaving me upright against his chest.

I tried to kick and claw my way free of Wolfe, but his hold was unwavering as he pulled out a dagger and pressed it to my throat. I stilled as the sharp blade scratched against my skin and a warm trickle of blood trailed down my neck.

"What's it to be, slayer? My life or hers?" Wolfe hissed.

"You fear me that much? What will your master say when he learns you didn't even attempt to stop me from coming for him?" Magnar asked icily.

"He hasn't asked me to kill you. He just wants me to bring *her*." He pushed me forward a step, but Magnar didn't move aside.

"And which Belvedere's day am I ruining by stopping you from taking her?" Magnar asked in a tone that suggested they were discussing the weather, not a flicker on his face to hint that he was the least bit concerned about me.

"Prince Erik has requested Miss Ford's presence, and I will be delivering her along with your name. Do you think you can stand against he who has killed a thousand slayers?"

Before Magnar could reply, Wolfe shoved me towards him and leapt into an attack.

I stumbled into Magnar's chest, and he twisted, delivering me into the safety of the corridor whilst trying to block the thrust from Wolfe's dagger. He grunted in pain as Wolfe managed to drive the small blade into his bicep before he could deflect it, and a gasp escaped my lips.

Magnar slammed his fist into Wolfe's face, throwing him back into the small room where he crashed against the rear wall. While he righted himself, Magnar wrenched the dagger from his arm and tossed it at my feet.

"Find your father," he commanded. "I'll catch up with you."

Wolfe was on him again before I could respond, and I quickly grabbed the dagger from the floor, wiping Magnar's blood off of it on my pants. It was a cold, soulless thing, nothing like a slayer blade; just a hunk of sharpened metal. It did little to reassure me as I held it close, and I desperately wished I hadn't lost Fury.

I hesitated for half a heartbeat as Magnar slammed into Wolfe again, driving him back into the small room. He still hadn't drawn his blades and I got the feeling that was because Wolfe was unarmed, his honour or just masculine stupidity urging him into a fist fight. I willed him to simply draw Tempest and end it. If any monster deserved a certain, inescapable death, then it was Wolfe.

A pain-filled groan drew my attention away from their battle, and I recognised my father's voice. I spun around and ran to the door behind me, wrenching it open and finding him still hanging by the chains on his wrists, just like I'd seen on the CCTV screen.

"Dad!" I gasped, racing into the room and throwing my arms around his neck as the reality of finding him slammed into me.

"Callie?" he frowned in confusion, his voice sounding fuzzy. "Am I dreaming again?"

"It's me, Dad." Tears slipped from my eyes as I squeezed him tighter, and he groaned in pain. "I came for you. I'm here. We're going to escape. We'll find Monty and-"

Another pained sound fell from his lips, and I released him guiltily, making myself look at what they'd done to him. He seemed thinner than he had the last time I'd seen him, his ribs poking out harshly through his skin making me wonder if they'd even fed him in all this time.

His bare chest was marked with bruises in colours ranging from yellow to blue, purple and red, telling me he'd been beaten repeatedly over a period of time. But the cuts on his arms and neck were the worst of his injuries. I counted more than ten bites, all of which continued to ooze blood. It was hard to be sure of exactly how many there were because they overlapped so many times.

"I'm going to get you out of here," I promised, stomping down the panic rising in my throat and focusing on what I needed to do. "You're going to be okay."

I stood on my tiptoes to inspect the chains holding his wrists suspended and was relieved to find they were only secured by thick iron pins. I yanked the first pin free, and his arm fell heavily as his weight swung him towards the other side.

I grabbed his arm and pulled it over my shoulders so I could take his weight before releasing his other wrist. It didn't seem like he'd be able to do it himself, and I was afraid he'd fall if I didn't help him.

"Where's your sister?" he muttered.

"We'll get her back too," I promised. "Let's just get you out of here first."

I pulled the other pin free, and he fell against me. I stumbled as I struggled to hold his weight, and he groaned weakly.

"Can you walk?" I asked anxiously.

"I'll walk for you, little sun," he mumbled.

He leaned against me, and I half dragged him towards the door. I hesitated as we reached it, the sound of Magnar and Wolfe's continued struggle making me unsure of the best course of action.

"Wait! Your mother's wedding ring." He pointed to a small table beside the door. On top of it lay my mom's golden wedding ring hanging from a silver chain. Dad had worn it around his neck ever since she'd died.

"Here." I grabbed it and handed it to him, causing a faint smile to lift his lips.

"She'd never let me live it down if I lost it. It's been in her family for generations," he muttered as he placed the chain over his neck.

I nodded vaguely; a piece of missing jewellery was the least of my concerns at the moment. And seeing as Mom was dead, I highly doubted she cared either way.

I set my jaw and dragged Dad out into the corridor. He shuffled along as quickly as he could manage, and I pulled to make him move even faster.

Magnar roared in anger behind me, and I chanced a look over my shoulder just as he and Wolfe fell out of the room where I'd been held.

My breath caught as Wolfe landed on top of Magnar and lunged towards his throat, teeth bared, but Magnar slammed a powerful fist into the side of his head before his fangs could make contact.

"Who the fuck is-" Dad began, but I cut him off.

"Vampire Slayer. It's a whole thing. I'll tell you when it's less likely we'll die at any moment," I panted, urging him to move faster, and he nodded in agreement as he hobbled on.

I gave all of my attention to helping my dad, wrapping my arm more firmly around his back. We needed to get out of this place before their fight followed us along the narrow corridor and crushed us with its ferocity.

We finally made it to the heavy wooden door which led outside, and I flinched aside as General Wolfe went flying over our heads, crashing into the wall.

Magnar came running after him with a challenging cry, and I watched with wide eyes as they collided again, their fight moving them towards the room with the furnace.

I forced my attention back to getting my dad out of there and shouldered my way through the door. Dad's teeth started chattering as the winter air hit his exposed skin. I moved him towards the wall, resting him against it, then quickly shrugging off my thick coat.

He tried to protest, but I forced his arm into the padded material and he relented. It wasn't big enough to fasten over his broader frame, but he stopped shivering as he huddled into it.

A heavy crash sounded from inside the building and my heart leapt. Magnar hadn't taken this long to finish an opponent before now, and I was beginning to worry that he'd met his match in the psychotic general.

I wished I hadn't lost Fury.

As my mind drifted to the blade, I could feel my connection to it calling me back inside. I guessed it was still where I'd last seen it, laying in the room of coffins which was now filled with the dead. I wanted to run and retrieve it, but my dad was too vulnerable to leave alone.

He'd closed his eyes and was leaning against the wall so heavily that I wasn't sure I'd be able to get him moving again. The horses were so close to us, hidden within the trees, but retrieving them would mean leaving him.

Indecision froze me, but every second I wasted was precious.

An almighty crash sounded from within the building, and I flinched, fear clawing at me as I waited to see what happened.

The door flew open, and I spun to place myself in front of my father, holding the pathetic metal dagger before me as Wolfe paced out.

Magnar didn't follow him, and my heart twisted painfully as I stared in horror at the beautiful demon stalking towards us.

"Don't cry, little slayer," Wolfe purred as he closed in on me, paying no attention whatsoever to the blade I held ready. "I'm sure you'll be joining that one in death before long. Prince Erik has such plans for your family, and I can't wait to-" He stumbled forward, a cough falling from his lips and bringing up blood which trickled down his chin.

I recoiled as he staggered towards us, grasping at something behind him. He turned, his hand closing on the hilt of the blade which hung from his back. With a grunt of pain, he ripped it free, but bright scarlet blood continued to spill from the wound.

Wolfe hissed in pain as smoke rose from his fingers, and he flung the golden blade aside. It embedded itself in the ground by my feet, and I snatched it into my grasp, relief flooding me as I recognised my violent companion.

So close. Fury sighed in disappointment, but relief filled me at reuniting with it.

Magnar shoved the door aside as he exited the building. Blood ran down his face from a wound hidden in his hairline, and he was coated from head to toe in grey soot.

"That fall should have killed you," Wolfe spat angrily. "Next time I'll make certain you're dead."

"You're not looking so capable of following through on that threat," Magnar replied with a challenging grin as Wolfe's wound continued to bleed. "I wonder what your master will say when he finds out I set his blood bank on fire?"

The stench of smoke filled the air, and I noticed flames rising from the building behind Magnar, silhouetting him in a golden halo.

Wolfe glanced between Magnar and me, seeming to see that his odds of survival were dwindling by the second, something flashing through his cold eyes which looked all too like that fear he had claimed not to feel.

"If you're thinking of running, you have to know I'll catch you in your present state," Magnar threatened as he continued to close the distance between them. "Why not let your eternal torment end? I can give you a warrior's death. What more can any man ask for in the end?"

"You forget, *mortal,* that I am no man. And I have no plans to die." Wolfe leapt into motion but instead of heading for Magnar, he turned his murderous gaze on me.

I cursed as Fury tried in vain to guide my muscles into action so I could defend myself, but he was moving so quickly that I could do little more than brace for the attack and pray the blade would help me strike true. The moonlight glinted on Wolfe's sharpened fangs and his dark eyes glittered with malice as he came for me.

But a second before Wolfe could collide with me, my dad threw his weight into me instead. I crashed to the frozen ground and Dad cried out as Wolfe's attack fell on him in my place.

I shoved myself upright again, screaming in terror, but Wolfe had already leapt off of my father and was tearing away towards the trees, a heavy limp in his stride slowing him down as he went.

Dad clutched his neck where blood pulsed between his fingers, and I threw myself towards him with a sob catching in my throat, my own hand closing over his, willing the wound away with all I had.

Magnar moved to take chase after Wolfe while I prised my dad's hands away from the wound to try and assess the damage, and the cry which parted my lips made him still. The bite was unlike the others he had suffered, Wolfe had ripped into the skin, tearing it jaggedly so it bled endlessly, something vital torn open within.

"It's okay, baby girl," Dad rasped, reaching out to cup my cheek.

"No," I breathed as the blood continued to pulse from the wound, my hand closing over it again, pressing down hard. "No, *no.*"

I used Fury to slice a long strip from the base of my shirt and wadded it up to press against the bite. It was saturated instantly, but I kept pressing down, willing the blood to stay in his body even as he dropped to his knees.

"Why did you do that?" I breathed, holding my dad's eye as his gaze flickered, his hand closing over mine and a look in his eyes which spoke a word I refused to hear.

That blow had been meant for me.

"I'd never let anything happen to you girls," Dad replied, his voice hoarse, the words difficult for him to speak.

I flinched as Magnar's hand landed on my shoulder. "Keep pressing on the wound," he said. "We need to flush the venom out."

I looked up at him in confusion as he bent low to lift my father over his shoulder. My dad wasn't a small man, and even with the extra weight he'd lost, he would have been almost impossible for me to move like that alone.

Shock rattled through me as I realised Magnar had let Wolfe escape to help me save him.

"Thank you," I said, another sob catching in my throat as more blood pulsed from the bite.

I stayed close, pressing on the wound while Magnar started a quick pace, moving into a run as we raced back towards the horses. Blood soon coated my hands and began to drip between my fingers onto the frozen grass at my feet despite my best efforts to hold it back, terror consuming me while I fought to hold on, begging my father to stay with me. His eyes had closed, and his breathing was shallow, but he was still here, still fighting.

A freezing wind gusted around us, and I shivered as it kissed the skin exposed by tearing my shirt.

The air was thick with smoke, and I looked over my shoulder to find the blood bank engulfed in flames. Golden light lit up the night's sky, the fire consuming the building which had been the source of my nightmares for so long.

We'd won. And yet somehow, we'd lost too.

We made it to the horses and Magnar lowered my dad to the ground before hurrying to retrieve some bottled water.

He'd passed out and I leaned down, pressing my forehead to his and willing him to stay with me as tears poured from my eyes and ran over his cheeks.

Magnar returned quickly and pulled my hands away from the bite. I couldn't bear to watch as he flushed it clean but kept my cheek pressed to my dad's chest, listening to the slow thump of his heartbeat to reassure myself that he was still alive.

"There is nothing more I can do," Magnar said quietly. "The rest is up to him."

I pushed myself upright and looked down at the thick bandage Magnar had made from his own shirt and tied around the wound. His fighting leathers lay on the ground beside him, and his bronze skin was illuminated in the moonlight that made it through the trees, showing several new wounds which bled freely, not that he seemed to have noticed any of them.

"Is he going to be okay?" I asked, and I didn't miss the pleading tone my own voice had taken on.

We'd come so far and gotten so close. I couldn't bear to lose Dad after we'd risked so much to make it here. And Montana. How was I ever going to find my way back to her now?

Magnar hesitated before replying.

"Callie," he said softly, my name sounding like a prayer on his lips as he dropped a hand to my shoulder, his fingers brushing against me in a far softer touch than any he'd offered before. "He's lost a lot of blood, and he's been used for food many times this past week..."

I felt a pain like nothing I'd ever experienced carving its way through my chest at his words, and I descended into sobbing again as I wrapped my arms around my dad, refusing that implication with all I had. This wasn't the end for him. It wasn't.

Magnar touched my cheek, but I shrugged him off aggressively. I didn't want his fucking pity. I just wanted my family to be okay.

"If he is as strong as his daughter, then perhaps he can fight his way back from this," Magnar added carefully, and though I could hear the doubt in his voice, I clung to those words like a life raft. They gave me the only thing I needed in the haze of fear and loss that was threatening to engulf me. A chance. And I wouldn't let it go until my father took his very last breath.

I didn't remember much about our journey during the early hours of the morning. Only holding my dad's hand as I walked beside the stallion where Magnar had tied him in place to stop him from falling.

We'd taken shelter in an old barn, and I'd made a somewhat comfortable bed for my dad to lay on among the old hay bales. The stacked bales also served to block the drafts which found their way into the building, making our shelter relatively warm. I wished we could have found somewhere suitable to build a fire, but we'd had to settle for the first place we came across. Travelling on horseback was only making Dad's situation worse.

I hadn't wanted to move him at all, but with what we'd done to the blood bank, it was only a matter of time before more vampires came to investigate, and we were in no state to take on another fight.

I sat on the floor beside the bale I'd made into a bed for my father and clung to his cold hand. He hadn't woken since our escape, and I was trying not to focus on the blue colouring around his fingertips. I squeezed tightly, hoping to lend him some warmth. Not that I had much to spare. He still wore my coat, and I shivered in my ruined shirt despite my best attempts to make our shelter draft-proof.

Magnar had been gone for hours. He'd taken the stallion and headed off in hunt of supplies, despite him protesting against the idea. But I'd insisted he go. It was daylight and for once, the sun was shining outside, lighting the earth in golden tones, and hopefully keeping any nearby vampires at bay. If my dad was going to have any chance at all, then we needed bandages and warm clothes. Antibiotics, ideally.

I knew Magnar didn't want us to stay here for long. Wolfe would have reported back to the Belvederes about Magnar's return by now, and they would no doubt be sending an army of Elite to hunt him down. But Dad was in no state to travel. I knew a day on horseback in the freezing cold would take what little strength he had left from him.

He'd lost too much blood. If I could have cut open a vein and given him some of my own, I would have done it in a heartbeat. I'd have given him all of it if that was what it took. I'd sooner die than face the rising tide of pain I could feel coming for me.

I'd seen it in Magnar's eyes when he'd carried my father into the barn. He wasn't going to survive this.

Not wanting to listen to the truth in his gaze, I'd sent him away from me. But now all I needed was for him to return and hold me in his arms because I was struck with the terrible fear of knowing that I was going to have to endure this alone.

Dad groaned weakly and I squeezed his fingers.

"I'm here, Dad. We're safe," I said soothingly.

It wasn't the first time he'd made such a sound, and I could tell that his moments of rising consciousness were filled with pain.

His fingers momentarily tightened around mine, then relaxed as he passed out again. It was impossible to know if he really understood what was happening. If he knew that we'd gotten him out of that place. I hoped he did though. I hoped that somewhere deep down he knew he was finally free and that I was with him.

I wished Montana was here too. She deserved to have the chance to say goodbye, if nothing else. My heart swelled with worry for her and whatever plan the vampires had in mind. It seemed like whatever it was included me too, and I hoped that by staying out of their hands I might be buying her some time.

The sound of hooves clip-clopping on the concrete outside the barn made me freeze. I removed one of my hands from my father's and rested my palm against Fury's hilt. The blade remained peaceful, a feeling of easy companionship resonating from it in response to Magnar's swords approaching. I let out a relieved breath and turned towards the barn door as Magnar pulled it open and led the stallion in. The mare whinnied in greeting as she reunited with her friend, trotting over to nuzzle him, the two horses seeming at peace when they were together.

Magnar pressed the door closed behind them to keep the freezing wind out and took the supplies he'd gathered from the horse's back.

He approached me, his arms filled with a pile of blankets, and I swallowed a lump in my throat as gratitude flooded me. I didn't know what I would have done if he'd never found me. Even if by some miracle I hadn't been taken alongside my family that first day, then I'd never have been able to get Dad out of the blood bank on my own. And even now, Magnar was still with me. He'd let Wolfe go in favour of helping my father. He was going to hunt down the vampire who had Montana too. Despite everything he'd said, and I'd said, despite understanding that we were simply making use of one another until the time came for our paths to separate, he was still here. I wanted to ask him why, but I feared pointing it out might send him on his way, and despite all I wanted to believe about myself and my own capabilities, I needed him.

That need wasn't something I admitted to easily, my fear over relying on anyone beyond my own flesh and blood warning me against it, but I had no other choice. Montana was trapped in the hands of a monster I had no hope of facing alone, and Magnar was the only faint glimmer of hope that I might be able to retrieve her.

He'd done nothing but help me from the first moment we'd met, even if his methods had left a lot to be desired, and I doubted I'd ever be able to repay that debt.

"How is he?" Magnar asked solemnly, and I could tell he was half surprised to find my father still breathing.

"Good. Better," I said a little defensively as I took the blankets and quickly piled them on top of my dad. I tucked his cold hands inside them too and stood watching him for a moment, hoping that he might feel warmer already.

I chewed on my thumbnail, wondering if there was any chance that the blankets would be enough to warm him. Maybe even save him.

He can't die. I don't know how to live without him.

"Better?" Magnar asked gently, and I could tell that his observations meant he didn't agree.

"He squeezed my hand. He almost woke again," I said, desperation seeping into my tone. "That's a good sign, right?"

Magnar looked down at me sadly and reached out to tuck my hair behind my ear. His touch sent an ache of longing through me, and I had to fight the urge to throw myself into his arms. If I gave in to the feelings of despair that were growing in my chest, then I knew I wouldn't be able to hold back the tears, and crying meant accepting this fate, meant giving up.

"Would you like me to check his wounds?" he offered gently. "I found clean bandages."

"Yes. Please." I had no idea how to dress a wound or anything like that, but Magnar seemed well trained in such things. I only wished that didn't mean he was so sure of what was to come. It was obvious he'd seen these kinds of injuries before and his prognosis was based on more than guesswork. But Dad was strong. He'd never leave me and Montana. He'd fight with all he had to stay with us.

Magnar headed back to the stallion and returned with a new coat for me as well as the bandages. He held out the thick jacket and I slid my arms into it gratefully. I hadn't realised that I'd been shivering until I stopped, far more concerned with my father's health than my own.

Magnar fastened the toggles and tugged me closer to him, pressing a kiss to my forehead, and I buried my face against his chest. The gesture was so at odds with his usual, brutish behaviour and the thickness in my throat told me why that was, even while I fought against the burning in the backs of my eyes. I leaned into him for a single second, grabbing onto some of the strength he radiated and taking it for myself.

I blew out a long breath and stepped back so he could tend to my father, my chin high and determination renewed. This wasn't it. Dad was a fighter. He'd been fighting before I was born and hadn't stopped for a single moment since. He wouldn't give up now.

I backed away as Magnar knelt down beside my dad and pulled his arm out from beneath the blankets.

My stomach knotted as Magnar removed the strips of black fabric he'd used to bandage the bites earlier that morning, and I realised they were still weeping blood, not scabbing over, not healing at all.

Magnar began rinsing the wounds with bottled water again, his shoulders taut as he concentrated on his work. I fought the urge to pace while he worked, simply standing there and counting each breath my father took, noting every flicker of his expression and begging him to come back to me.

Magnar moved from wound to wound, cleaning and dressing them all, finishing with the jagged rip to Dad's neck, the sight of torn flesh and bright blood making my stomach knot.

He finally finished, wrapping more white bandages tightly around the laceration, lifting him so he could secure it around his chest, creating pressure against the padding he'd used to try and stem the blood loss. I bit my lip as I looked between the bandages on his arms and legs, blood seeping through them all, slowly staining them red despite everything Magnar had done.

"Why is he still bleeding?" I asked desperately. "I thought all the venom was out?"

"He is not slayer born. Your bloodline is obviously your mother's," Magnar replied softly. "A human can only stand so much of the vampires' vile secretions before their body is overwhelmed. The venom has made it into his bloodstream. It flows within his blood, stopping it from clotting. Slayer blood doesn't do that. It will not merge with the venom but instead tries to force it from our bodies, keeping it near the surface so we are able to wash it out. It is possible for a human to survive one or two bites, for their system to eventually flush the venom out, but this..." He didn't finish his sentence, but his meaning was clear.

He wasn't healing, his body *couldn't* heal what was flowing through it fast enough.

Pain caught in my chest, and I suddenly couldn't breathe. I sank down onto one of the hay bales and started shaking my head. This couldn't be happening. I refused to believe it was happening. After all we'd done, everything we'd gone through, how could it end so unfairly? How could freedom have been so close, only to have been snatched away like this?

The bale shifted beside me, and Magnar pulled me into his arms. I resisted for a moment, then gave in to his embrace with a shuddering sob as the tears finally came. I held on to Magnar, the scent of oak and leather enveloping me. He wrapped me in the strength of his arms and embraced me so tightly it felt like he was the only thing stopping me from shattering entirely, falling into a million pieces never to reform again. I cried against his chest about all the injustices my family had suffered, about the life we should have had and everything that had been stolen from us.

We'd come so close to freedom. My dad was finally out from under the vampires' control, and it didn't even matter.

It had all been for nothing.

MONTANA

CHAPTER EIGHTEEN

I was walking through a dark fog, my sister's hand holding tight to mine, pulling me along through the gloom. I ran faster, trying to keep up, crying her name and hearing it echo back to me from every direction.

She yanked my hand firmly and I went stumbling forward, losing my grip on her, and suddenly I was on the precipice of a cavernous hole so deep I couldn't see anything at the bottom. My arms cartwheeled, terror locked a scream in my throat, then someone caught me by the shoulder, drawing me away from the edge.

I glanced back, finding myself eye to eye with Erik, a cruel and sinister sneer on his lips. He stepped closer, banding an arm around my waist and forcing me to look back over the edge.

I wanted to demand he let go, but no words would escape my lips.

"The fear is in the falling," he growled. "It only ends when you hit the ground."

He shoved me, and my scream made it free of my lips as I went sailing over the edge, spiralling down into the depths of darkness. I lost sight of everything, falling deeper and deeper into nothingness, and only one sound found me among it all. Callie was crying, shattering *somewhere without me, but before I could even try and find her, the ground rushed up to meet me.*

I bolted upright in bed, fingers knotting in the sheets and heavy breaths heaving in and out of my lungs.

"Callie," I panted, feeling her so near yet so impossibly far away.

My sister felt somehow closer when I was asleep and waking always felt like her fingers slipping through mine. But this time had been worse than that. I'd heard her, I'd sensed her anguish over something I couldn't perceive.

As I caught my breath, I tried to remind myself it was just a dream, no matter how vivid. It wasn't real. The only thing that was solid and true was the bitter reality staring back at me. A heaviness clung to me from that dream though, like a weight was attached to my heart. I didn't know why but Nightmare seemed to feel it too, giving off a strange, morbid vibe.

I slid my hand under the pillow, trailing my thumb over its warm hilt, and it relaxed at my touch - if a blade *could* relax.

The door opened and I jerked my arm away from the blade, causing a stabbing pain in my injured shoulder.

I stifled a groan, but Erik clearly heard it, walking toward me dressed for the day in his royal attire. Though he looked perhaps even more regal than usual, his navy jacket trimmed with gold and the tree symbol stitched onto his breast pocket more decorative than those I had seen before.

"The doctor left more painkillers for you." He pointed to the nightstand where a little white bottle sat.

"I don't want them," I said firmly. "I'd rather feel steady on my feet and have a sharp mind around a bunch of bloodsuckers. Besides, Callie and Dad will be here soon, right?"

"I am awaiting an update from General Wolfe. But yes, I assume their arrival is imminent," Erik said, and my skin prickled as I wondered if he had decided on what he was going to ask me for in exchange for Dad's freedom.

"Have you found out anything more about the bombing? Do you

have any evidence it was Fabian?" I asked.

"My people are looking into it," he said, a single line forming on his brow.

"Right...but...nothing has changed?" I asked, meaning with the plan for me to choose Fabian. Erik blinked, his ashen gaze trailing over me.

He hesitated, and a beat of silence passed between us that spoke of what we'd done at the party last night. I thought of the words he'd spoken to me, declaring his jealousy at seeing me with his brother. But it had all been some twisted game of his, none of it was real.

"Do you think anything has changed, rebel?" he asked, his tone low, his eyes piercing, and I knew we weren't talking about the plan.

I thought of everything that had happened since the moment I met him. How he had trapped me, tormented me, used me. Then of last night, how he had made my body bow to his, and how it all just felt like another way to assert power over me in hindsight. Even him protecting me from the blast had been for a selfish motive. I was a doll in his fist, and dolls were made for playing other people's games. They didn't get a choice of their own.

"No," I said coldly. "Nothing."

"Well then, let us get on with our day, shall we?" he sniped, like I was wasting his time. "Get dressed. We will be leaving shortly. It's customary for us all to attend an opera before the choosing ceremony."

"What?" I gasped in horror, sure that was the word Dad had mentioned when describing what human doctors used to be capable of. "You mean we have to watch someone get cut open?"

Erik's eyebrows raised then, a wicked look gleamed in his eyes. "Yes, we do. So hurry along. We don't want to miss the first splash of blood."

"Fuck no," I said in disgust. "You think I'm going to come with you to watch some innocent human get tortured?"

Erik barked a laugh, then grabbed my comforter, ripping it off me and throwing it across the room.

"Get up," he commanded. "I said an opera, not an operation. It is a kind of singing. Now get moving."

"You asshole," I hissed.

"It's past noon already," Erik said. "And I'm growing bored of this interaction. I want this day over and done with so I can head home at last."

"You don't live here?" I asked in surprise, though I was still pissed at him for the shitty joke as I shoved out of bed and headed to the closet.

"My family take this time off specifically for the ritual. We will return to our own houses and our duties once it's over. The castle is equally ours but living on top of each other is a little suffocating for all of us."

The door flew open and Clarice stormed into the room with her blonde hair streaming out behind her. "Erik! You're not supposed to spend time with the courtiers on the day of the choosing. Get out."

"The circumstances are a little different today considering my courtier almost died," he snarled as she shoved him, but he didn't move an inch.

Clarice's eyes whipped to me, then widened. "She's not even dressed! Where's your stylist? Get her in here this second."

"Gladly." Erik dragged his sister out of the room.

Nancy soon appeared holding a large bag, looking flustered as someone shoved her through the doorway. I didn't need to guess who.

"Take your shirt off, Montana, the doctor advised me how to clean the wound," she said gently.

I folded my arms, shaking my head in refusal. Not because I was embarrassed but because of the mark on my forearm. I couldn't take the risk of it being seen again.

"Don't be silly, I'm not going to look at you." She released a laugh, but I didn't join in.

After a moment, she headed to the bathroom to fetch a towel, then held it out to me.

Having no real choice, I turned my back on her and tugged my pyjama top off, wrapping the towel around me so only my left arm was poking out. I looked like a dumb bitch, but Nancy didn't question me as she opened her bag and took out a bottle of clear liquid and some fresh bandages.

She patted the stool before the dressing table, encouraging me over. I sat on it, and she shifted my hair aside, unwinding the bandage from my neck and shoulder. I took in the wound, frowning in surprise, the injury not half as bad as it had seemed last night. A little blood stained the jagged edge of the slice into my skin, but there was no fresh blood leaking from it this morning.

Nancy took the cap off of the bottle in her hand and poured it over the wound.

Fire flared inside my arm, and I bit down on a cry. "What the fuck was that?"

She gave me an apologetic look. "I'm just following instructions."

I sucked air through my teeth and the pain finally subsided. Nancy started binding the wound with a new bandage, being more gentle with her movements.

When it was done, she picked up my pyjama top and passed it back to me. "The doctor will check on you again tomorrow."

I nodded, and she turned her back while I pulled my shirt on.

We set into our usual routine as she brushed my hair and painted my face. Would I be considered attractive without all this? I wasn't really sure. I'd received attention from men back in the Realm, but I'd never taken an interest in preening for them. I'd never really valued looks because they didn't save you from starvation or make you any warmer at night during a hard winter. It felt wrong to be sitting here, letting Nancy make me into a creature of temptation when so many humans were out in the world suffering, not knowing when their next meal might come. I couldn't do anything for them, but going along with this bullshit did something for my family. And I would buy their protection in whatever way I could.

My stomach clenched as I thought of the dilemma I was faced with today. Choosing Fabian secured Erik's promise, and choosing Miles secured my secret. I chewed anxiously on the inside of my cheek, still torn between the fates I was faced with.

I found myself lost in my own eyes, wondering if I even recognised the woman staring back at me. Something told me I needed to trust this new woman, that I needed to have faith in my instincts, wherever they might lead me.

Nancy finally stepped back, leaving me looking polished to perfection with half my hair pulled up into a delicate bun and the rest of my dark curls hanging loose down my back. I had to admit, this was Nancy's best work so far, and she admired me a moment longer before heading to the closet.

"Erik already chose a dress for you. He sent it here yesterday." She took out the item hidden within a large white bag before unzipping it.

I stood, curious as she pulled out a gown that seemed to embody the night sky.

The deep, navy material was speckled with tiny diamonds which glittered like starlight. It was long sleeved - thankfully – with lace arms and a satin corset. At the bust was a glittering broach as bright and as round as the moon.

"It's..." I shook my head, not finding the words.

"It's fit for a princess." Nancy smiled, and her final word ricocheted through my mind, driving a sliver of dread deep into my heart.

The choosing ceremony wasn't a distant fear anymore. It was here. Today. And I wasn't getting out of it.

Whoever I chose, I'd have to marry. A human bride for a bloodsucking monster.

I stood in a royal box beside Paige, my hand locked around hers as we gazed down into an incredible room that one of the guards had called a theatre. Golden pillars reached up from an enormous stage and luxurious red velvet adorned the many hundreds of seats angled towards it, all occupied by a finely dressed vampire. Our eyes were on the dark wooden stage where a woman sang her heart out in a luxurious cream dress that trailed behind her in a swathe of satin.

The sound was nothing like anything I'd ever heard before, and it evoked an ache in me over what had happened since I'd left the Realm. To me, to dad, to Callie. Something about the music spoke of that pain, their absence. Though the vampire didn't sing in any language I knew,

I understood her song in a way that didn't need words to be conveyed.

Behind us sat Clarice's remaining two courtiers, Hank and Luke. They were dressed in suits almost as fine as the royal brothers'. The family sat on the other side of the theatre in a box of their own, the gilded lettering on the front of it blazing with the name Belvedere.

I closed my eyes to avoid looking at them, drinking in the final notes of the song as fear gathered in my heart. We'd been told that the moment the opera ended, we'd be taken to the choosing ceremony, and I could sense the conclusion drawing in.

I wasn't ready. I hadn't made my choice, still in turmoil over which path to take. It wasn't as simple as choosing Fabian to protect my family, because even if I took that path, Miles would out me as a slayer. And if that truth was discovered, it surely didn't just implicate me, but Callie too. She was my twin, we were one and the same. If this blood ran in my veins, then it surely ran in hers too. So what then? Miles would expose her as well, and she would face whatever dark fate was coming my way. But if I selected Miles, then what if Erik sent Dad back to the blood bank? What if he punished Callie for my disobedience?

I grappled with the crisis, not knowing what to do, fearing whatever path I picked would lead me to deeply regret it.

My forearm prickled, and I released Paige's hand to rest my palm over the material hiding the mark. Nightmare was strapped to my thigh again, humming a tune as beautiful as the woman's song. The emotions in my body seemed like someone else's. Like another soul was reaching into mine and telling me I should be sad. But why?

Paige wiped a tear from under her eye as the song ended and the silence in the room turned to roaring applause. The red curtain fell, and the crowd started filing out of the theatre, heading along the aisles toward the exit.

I spotted the royals moving too, and watched as Erik took hold of Fabian's arm, tugging him to a halt before he vacated the box. Erik snarled something in his ear and Fabian shook his head at him with a look that said he was equally furious.

Paige prodded me and I turned, finding two guards with swords on their backs gesturing for us to leave the box. I ducked past them, but they followed closely, guiding us down the corridor with crimson carpet and cream walls.

We were prisoners walking to the hangman's noose, only the noose was a wedding ring and the gallows the altar.

Nightmare hummed angrily on my thigh, and the nagging feeling it emitted told me something was deeply wrong, I just didn't know what.

This life was casting a curse over me, and I vowed to break it. Whatever my fate was today, I wouldn't bow to it willingly. Marrying a monster was one thing, but if they expected to turn me into a vampire too, I'd die trying to resist that fate before I ever succumbed to it. I had to fight, had to find a crack of light in this bleakest of fates and step into it.

The other courtiers and I were led downstairs and out of a door onto a dark street. A shout filled my ears, and something whipped past my head, smashing against the wall, and making my heart leap in fright. I gasped as I took in the broken bottle and the blood splattered all over the brickwork.

"We have the right to bite!" a protestor called, and I spotted a crowd running toward us under the orange glow of a streetlamp, their eyes flaring with anger.

My pulse rioted as the guards grabbed us, tugging us toward a large black vehicle and pushing us into the back of it with firm hands.

Paige pressed up against me on the back seat, huddling close while Hank and Luke were squashed in beside her.

"Oh my god, what's going on?" Paige whispered frantically.

A crash sounded as another bottle hit the car, blood splattering across the window beside us, and I swore, adrenaline surging through me as our driver sped off down the road.

"Nothing to worry about," she called to us, accelerating faster away from the mayhem. "The rebels always get agitated during the choosing ceremony. It's under control."

"It doesn't seem under control," Hank muttered, and I had to agree.

My heart wouldn't settle even when we rounded another corner and put more distance between us and the rebels. Knowing what those creeps wanted from us made me sick to my stomach. They'd hunt us, sink their teeth into us, and feed directly from the vein. It didn't bear thinking about.

We approached a tall building with an arching glass window at the front of it, the bright light within beckoning us closer. A red carpet ran all the way up to the street out front, and I caught sight of the Elite stepping out of cars and moving along it in beautiful dresses and suits. A group at the far end of the carpet seemed to be recording the event with large cameras. Armed guards stood with swords on their backs, lining the pavement in droves, and I hoped that meant the rebels would be kept away.

Instead of driving up to the carpet, our car veered to the left and passed down a narrow street beside the building. We turned down a steep ramp and arrived in a huge area beneath the building full of other stationary cars. A couple of guards hurried to open the doors for us, and Paige caught my hand again as we followed them, keeping close to me as if I could somehow offer her protection. But she was a fool to think I could do any such thing. Still, it felt nice to have the company in our moment of reckoning.

We moved across the echoing, concrete space and approached the steel doors of an elevator.

"Where are we going?" Luke asked one of the guards as she punched her finger on a button beside the doors and they slid open.

"Floor two, an official will be waiting for you," she said, gesturing for us to head inside without them. I eyed the sharp looking blade at her hip with unease and stepped past her into the space.

The doors slid closed, and I glanced at the others, wondering if they were as nervous as me.

"Are you ready?" Hank asked us, and I shook my head.

"Ready as I'll ever be," Luke replied, pushing a hand into his dark hair.

I looked to Paige who dabbed at her eyes, her low lip trembling a little.

"Are you alright?" I breathed.

"It's Brianna and Joshua...what happened to them was so awful. And then those rebels, I don't know, they just gave me a fright."

I nodded, leaning closer to her, feeling a bond growing between all of us humans. I'd never let myself care for other people, or at least tried not to. But I couldn't deny how shaken I'd been by the loss of Brianna and Joshua, and the thought of anything bad happening to the others made me worried as hell.

"Paige, listen to me," I said as the elevator rose upward, figuring we might not get another chance to talk tonight. Her bright blue eyes turned my way. "Don't pick Fabian. I can't tell you why, but Miles is the better option. Just don't pick Fabian...promise me."

Her mouth parted, but she didn't answer.

"I think Montana's right, there's something off about Fabian," Hank said, giving me an anxious look.

Paige nodded weakly and I hoped that meant she agreed.

The doors opened and a bright hallway with marble flooring opened up before us. Two guards stood on either side of the elevator and a male vampire with jet-black hair and a silver ring in his ear stood waiting for us. He had a clipboard in his hand and immediately ushered us out of the elevator. "Come on, come on, we don't have all day."

He looked us up and down, then put a large tick on his clipboard. "You're all looking fabulous, now you're going to step through this door up here and I want big smiles for the cameras, okay? The whole of the New Empire is watching tonight!"

We nodded vaguely as he escorted us to a set of red double doors at the end of the corridor and my heart took a dive. We were so close now. Moments away from making the decision that would bind us in chains for good.

I glanced at the vampire for instructions, but he seemed to be listening to something as he pressed a finger into his ear.

"One minute," he announced, and my pulse drummed faster.

I still had my fingers locked with Paige's and Hank suddenly took my other hand. Luke took hold of Paige, and we shared a fierce look that united us as one.

At least I'm not alone.

"Okay, go, go, go," the vampire called, and the doors opened wide in front of us.

A hundred flashes of light blinded me as we walked onto a huge stage. Before us was a grand ballroom with a polished floor glimmering under the light of an enormous chandelier. A series of steps scattered with rose petals led down from the stage deeper into the room. The place was packed with Elite, all gazing up at us with golden chalices in their hands, standing around the wide hall below.

The crowd applauded at the sight of us, and I spotted a camera crew filming us at the bottom of the stairs, recording every second of this nightmare.

A huge screen at the back of the hall showed a live feed of us all standing in line. We didn't look afraid as I'd expected, but strong, a band of humans standing in a united front. And I took pride in the sight, lifting my chin as I gazed down at the sea of vampires, vowing that no matter what they claimed from me this night, they would never break me.

My dress sparkled like stars, winking as the tiny gemstones caught the flash of the cameras.

Our attention was grabbed by a woman to the right of the stage dressed in a silken purple gown. Felicia looked as beautiful as the first day I'd met her when we'd been presented to the royals. Her flowing dark hair was braided with a white ribbon and her stunning features lifted in a wide smile. "Ladies and gentlemen of the New Empire, welcome to the twenty-first annual choosing ceremony! Our royals have selected the finest humans of the Realms, but today, they will make their own choice and pick a prince or princess to unite with."

Doors opened at the far end of the hall and the royals appeared, walking into the room and dominating the air. Erik's brow was drawn low, and Fabian took the first opportunity to break away from him, a smile hitched onto his lips but his eyes as dark as sin.

As Erik's attention turned to the stage, his gaze locked with mine. Time seemed to slow, and oxygen stopped travelling in and out of my lungs. His mouth pulled up at one corner and I mirrored him, achingly drawn to him in that eternal moment, like for one second in time he was on my side, offering me a slice of encouragement. Then it was gone, his eyes still on me, but there was no kindness in this look. Now, he looked fierce, possessive, like the raging creature I had met in the dark corridor at the party last night.

Felicia gestured for us to descend the stairs, and I guessed that was our cue to join the masses. I finally dragged my eyes from Erik and moved down the staircase, immediately more at ease out of the spotlight. Eyes still turned our way, but the Elite parted, allowing us through as they talked among each other, excited chatter filling the room.

We found a space within the crowd and huddled close, sharing nervous looks and waiting for someone to tell us what to do next.

Felicia raised her arms, calling out to the room again, "I present to you the wives of the royal brothers!"

I turned to look back up the stairs to the red door we had entered through, finding it opening once more. A group of female vampires arrived in flowing white gowns, followed closely by children of varying ages, and I frowned, unsure what I was witnessing. I'd never seen a single child since I'd been here. Not one. Because vampires didn't breed, right?

Clarice let out a cry of excitement, running up the steps to greet the children and falling to her knees as she gathered a couple of dark-haired kids into her arms. "Aunt Clarice!" many of them called to her, running forward and squeezing her affectionately.

Miles was hot on her heels, placing kisses on some of the women's cheeks before kneeling to embrace a few fair-haired girls.

I stopped moving. Stopped breathing as Felicia's words resounded through my head. The wives of the royal brothers. These women, these vampires…they had been like us once. Humans from previous years, now changed into immortal, lifeless vampires. And that meant these children were…

I took a step back, horror crashing through me and echoing through every cell in my body.

My gaze fell on Erik across the room, and his ominous expression confirmed what I suspected. My fear turned into a penetrating certainty. This was why they wanted human wives. This was what they wanted from us.

Children.

Nightmare was buzzing furiously on my thigh, trembling with rage, as if the sight of the children upset it as much as it upset me.

Fabian moved to greet his wives, kissing the backs of their hands like he was the perfect gentlemen, and I gazed at the youngsters gathering around him, narrowing my eyes. Their skin was glossy like a vampire's but something about them screamed life. Like they were half dead, half living. Half human, half vampire.

I backed up again, knocking into Paige, and she gave me a fearful look that told me she'd figured it out too.

"I can't – I won't," I gasped, unable to draw breath. Panic was washing over me, rushing in too fast for me to escape it.

Paige opened her mouth as if to warn me to be quiet, but I pushed past her, desperate to get away. To find some breathable air.

I ran through the crowd, finding a side door and darting through it into an empty corridor. I sprinted down it, searching for an exit, some way forward, but every other door I found was locked tight. I found myself at a dead end, shaking and bracing my hands against the wall, revulsion carving down the middle of me.

No. Not this. I don't want this. I won't do it.

Nightmare whispered soothing words. *Be still, Moon child. You mustn't allow this fate.*

"How can I avoid it?" I rasped.

A hand caught my arm, twisting me around, and I grimaced, finding Erik there with a sombre look on his face.

"Montana," he said in a low voice. "Listen to me."

"*No*," I snarled. "I don't want to hear it. You're not going to convince me to do that. To have children with your brother. I won't. I'll die first." Nausea gripped me. I'd never wanted human children, let alone *this*.

It wasn't natural. It was twisted. What even were they? Did they drink blood? Were they as monstrous as their immortal sires?

He slowly closed the distance between us like I was a rabid dog about to bite. "It can be insemination if you prefer, you do not have to-"

"Fuck you!" I roared, and Erik came at me, clapping his hand over my mouth and forcing me back against the wall.

"Quiet," he hissed. "Whisper or I will not let you speak at all."

I nodded, grinding my teeth as he peeled his palm off of my mouth.

"You can't do this to me," I said, voice cracking.

"This is what the ritual is in aid of," he said darkly. "We don't tell you sooner because of this very fear I see in your eyes."

"Is this what you want from me? To marry Fabian and let him-" I couldn't get the words out, choking on them. "Is this the price I have to pay? Are you going to dangle my family over my head forever? Keep me compliant with a threat against their lives? Did you ever intend to free my father at all?"

"I do not care for the ritual or its outcome. I only want eyes on my brother," Erik hissed. "But you are causing me a confliction that I cannot escape. And I do not remember the last time I felt any such thing."

A sneer lifted my lips. "I'm a puppet on your stage, my strings tethered to your hand. You move me in any direction you want, so what confliction can I possibly cause you?"

I didn't know why I was bothering to argue, only that the burning rage inside me needed to escape. The truth had struck me like an axe, and now I was bleeding in the aftermath of that knowledge. Vampires expanded their numbers by turning humans, not by breeding with them. I'd never even considered this possible.

"Montana," Erik said roughly, caught in hesitation. "You told me I could make an ask of you to secure your father's freedom. To walk him beyond the city and take him somewhere safe once he arrives."

"I did," I whispered, fear trickling through my chest.

"Well, I have a request of you now, one that I believe will quiet this madness in me."

A lump rose in my throat as I took in the beast before me who seemed barely restrained. His muscles were taut, his eyes two forbidding wells of darkness that were full of threat.

"You have been a poor spy who has reaped little to nothing in your time with Fabian," he said cuttingly.

"I hardly had much time," I said in anger.

"And you will have no more of it either," he snapped, making my heart stumble. "You have frustrated me to no end. Argued with me, provoked me, jeered and scoffed at me."

I pressed harder against the wall as he moved closer, a demon in a fine suit, ready to flay the flesh from my bones. There was no escaping him, and I feared his request was going to involve punishment for all the things I'd done to insult him.

"But you have amused me too," his tone softened, and my brows lowered in suspicion. "You have made me laugh when I thought there was no laughter left in me, and you have made me question things I had long forgotten to question. You, rebel, have made me feel more than I have in a thousand years, and now I find myself making a decision this night, while you stand on the cusp of a destiny I chose for you. But I am rewriting that destiny here and now."

"I don't understand," I rasped.

He gripped my jaw, hand rough and firm as he held me so our gazes couldn't break. "You will be mine. That is my request of you. You will choose me at the ceremony, and you will marry me. Do this, and I will promise you infinite protection. I will be your keeper, even when I am your monster too. But understand that there will be no reneging on this vow if you make it to me this night. You will belong to me in every way imaginable. You will never run from me, and if you dare escape, I will hunt you to the ends of the earth and make you pay for every day we were apart. That is my offer. Speak my name at the ceremony, and the deal will be done."

My rampant breaths wouldn't slow, and Nightmare burned with furious intent, begging me to take the blade into my hand and drive it deep into his chest. But even if I attempted such a thing, I'd seen Erik's strength firsthand and had no doubt I would fail.

"I have two caveats to this deal, however," he said before I could form the words to speak. "The first is that I will never sire you. You will remain human, and even if you decide to become one of my kind, I will deny you of the opportunity. And secondly, I will never demand children of you. I have never partaken in this ritual, and I do not intend to start now. That will never be a request I make of you, do you understand?"

I nodded mutely, trying to process everything he was saying. He was asking me to become his prisoner for good, one he would declare his wife.

"Why not just force me to do this, why give me the choice at all?" I asked bitterly.

"Because I want you willing."

"Willing," I scoffed, shaking my head to free my chin from his grip and feeling a tear slip from my eye, rolling down my cheek.

"The choice is yours, rebel," he said, then turned from me, shooting away down the corridor and disappearing back into the ballroom.

I stared after him, a new path laid out beneath my feet, but walking it would lead me to a future in the clutches of a callous prince. None of the options were what I truly wanted. Freedom alongside my family was the only future I wished to claim, but it looked like I was going to be forced to pick a cage instead.

CALLIE

CHAPTER NINETEEN

I couldn't remember when I'd started pacing, but the nervous energy filling my veins had needed an outlet and I guessed my feet had come up with the solution.

The day had been the longest I could ever remember enduring, and yet it had gone by too quickly as well.

Dad was still breathing but it was becoming more laboured, and I was finally beginning to accept the fact that he wasn't going to pull through. The inevitability of the situation was what made it impossible to bear. I knew he was dying, but he was still with me as well. A part of me just wanted it to be over, but I hated that part of me too because if it was over, then he would be dead, gone, lost to me forever.

"You're exhausted," Magnar rumbled. Not for the first time. "Come and sit with me. I'll watch him while you get some rest."

I hesitated as he held a hand out to me. If I didn't sit, I was at risk of falling down anyway, but I was afraid to let a single moment slip by while each of them seemed so precious. His hand enveloped mine and I let him guide me closer, the pain in his eyes reminding me that he had faced the death of his own father too, that he knew this agony all too well.

Magnar pulled me down so I could lay with my head in his lap, and I tried to force myself to relax, the tension spiralling so tight within me that the thought alone made me want to pace once more.

"I promise to wake you if anything happens," Magnar said as he started to run his fingers through my hair, the small comfort drawing more tears from me, and despite the worry churning through me, I let my eyes fall shut.

Magnar began to hum a tune which somehow felt familiar despite my certainty that I'd never heard it before. The deep tenor of his rough voice rumbled through me where my body lay across his, and the gentle touch of his fingers twisting through my hair helped uncoil the tightness in my chest just enough to let me breathe again.

My hand drifted to Fury which was strapped to my belt, the blade calling to me as exhaustion pressed down on me. Its calming presence made me feel more secure with just that simple touch.

Come, Dream-Walker, it seemed to sigh.

I didn't expect to actually sleep, but before long, my exhaustion forced me to let go and I drifted off into the dark.

I was walking down a street, the likes of which I'd never seen before. Everything was clean and bright, shining in the light of a blazing sun. There were people everywhere. Some were laughing or talking to each other as they walked by. Others were moving quickly, sighing in irritation as the ramblers got in their way.

All of them were human.

I stared around in awe, realising this was what the world had been like before the Final War. Before the vampires.

A woman came jogging towards me, her hair loose and golden like the rays of the sun.

"I know, I know," she called as she approached, a smile dancing on her lips. "I'm late again. But I promise I'll make it up to you."

Her gaze was on someone right behind me, and I turned to see who she was talking to.

"Dad?" I asked in surprise as my eyes landed on him.

He was younger than the man who lay dying in the barn. His hair was thicker and darker, less lines marked his skin. He looked happy.

The huge smile he had plastered across his face slipped as his gaze moved from the woman to me. "Callie?"

I spun back to look at the woman again, suddenly realising who she was. My mom stood before me, her features clearer than they ever were in my own memories. I reached out to touch her, but she dissolved before my eyes, swirling away alongside everything else that surrounded us.

I quickly turned back to Dad, wondering what the hell was happening. He was the only thing that remained with me as everything else disappeared. Slowly, he began to change, lines formed beside his eyes and his hair thinned too. It started to turn silver at the sides, far more grey appearing than was there in real life. I wondered if that was how he saw himself or if it was simply a reflection of the future which should have come.

"What is this?" I asked in confusion.

"I was just visiting the best parts of my life," he replied, lifting a hand to my cheek.

His touch felt as solid and real as if he were truly standing before me. A tear slid down my cheek and I leaned into that touch, savouring it, my hand landing over his as if I could keep him there simply by wanting it enough.

"Does it hurt?" I asked. "Are you in pain?"

"No, baby girl. I only wish Montana were here too." At his words, the scene around us changed and shivered until we were standing in our old apartment in the Realm.

Montana stood between us. Her eyes were full of more life than I remembered, and her smile was wider than it had often been. I realised I was seeing her the way that he did. I'd always noticed the sadness in her eyes, but he'd always seen the light. Perhaps my life under the rule of the vampires had left me so jaded that even my memories held a touch of misery. My only happiness had ever been them.

Though Montana had joined us, it wasn't in the same way that we were both here. She smiled and blinked and looked almost normal, but it wasn't really her. This was Dad's dream, and we were the only ones who were really present for it. He just wanted Montana with us, so it *appeared as if she was.*

"Are you really here, Callie? Is it truly you?" Dad asked as he frowned at me. "Something tells me it's really you standing there inside this dream with me."

I didn't know how it was possible, but I knew this was real, that somehow I'd stepped straight into his dreams with him, that we were really together, even though we were both sleeping.

"It is me. Do you remember what happened?" I stepped closer and tightened my grip on his hand where he still cupped my cheek. It felt so firm, I could have sworn we were truly together and the world beyond was the nightmare.

"Are we free?" A smile lit his face as he thought back on what had happened. "Did you come and rescue your old Dad?"

"I did but..." My gaze travelled to Montana. I didn't know how much he knew about what had happened to her, and I wasn't sure I should tell him now, not when there was nothing he could do for her.

"The vampires took her somewhere else," he said, and I could hear the pain of being separated from her in his voice. "The one who held me said a vampire calling himself Prince Erik took her and that he wants you too. That's all I know, Callie. You have to keep away from that-"

My dad stumbled forward and sank to his knees as the dream world around us flickered in and out of focus. Montana fizzled out of existence, and I moved to grasp his arm in the darkness, trying to draw him upright again.

"Callie?" He frowned up at me in confusion, and I helped to pull him back to his feet.

"I'm still here," I assured him, though the pain in my chest was tightening again. I felt that quake rolling over us, this place trembling as his time ticked down. "I'm not going anywhere. I'll be right here with you for as long as you need me."

Dad ran a hand over his face and the darkness around us began to lift until we found ourselves standing in a park filled with lush green grass. Dad looked at something over my shoulder and I turned to find Mom and Montana lying on a red and white blanket. The sun warmed my skin and birdsong filled the air.

This wasn't a memory. Montana and I had never been to a place like that. And our mom had died long before we'd grown up. I looked down and found myself wearing a thin blue dress with daisies around the hem. It was perfect for the rolling heat that surrounded us, but I'd never worn anything like it in real life. I guessed this was how Dad wished our lives had been. Lazy days in the sunshine with all of us together, not a vampire to be seen.

Dad moved to sit beside Mom, and she took his hand, gazing at him lovingly.

"Sit down, Callie," Montana pleaded. "You're blocking the sun."

I noticed the shadow I was casting over all of them and smiled as I sat too. This was too strange, but it was too good to miss out on, the imagined reality something I wished had been true. Tears pricked the backs of my eyes as I gazed around at my family, longing for this to be real with all my heart. I wanted it more desperately than I'd ever wanted anything in my life. The four of us together, happy, free.

They all made small talk and joked together, and I just watched, basking in the glorious almost-reality.

"Have you forgotten why you're here?" Dad asked me suddenly, and I looked up at him in confusion. For a second, I couldn't work out why he wanted to ruin such a perfect moment. And then I couldn't remember why I had come at all. There was something dark waiting for me outside of this perfect illusion. Something I didn't want to face. But it was so tempting to lose myself in the dream. To let it become mine as well as Dad's and simply soak it in for as long as it lasted.

I glanced at Montana but instead of laughing in the sunshine, I found her terrified and struggling against the hold of a man whose face was obscured in shadow. I tried to reach for her but found her further away than she'd been a moment ago, her screams cutting into me as I fought to reach for her outstretched hand.

Each time I tried to close the distance between us, it grew instead of shrinking, the darkness deepening all around her.

"You need to get to her," Dad said urgently, and I turned back to him.

Mom and the picnic blanket were gone. The park was no longer bathed in sunshine, and a full moon had risen into the dark sky.

"But I don't know how. I need to get to the Belvederes. Wolfe said they're in New York, but I don't know where that is." The enormity of the task before me was enough to drown me. I didn't even know where to begin, only that I had to do it somehow, that I had to find my sister and rescue her from the clutches of that dark beast.

The heavy wooden table which had sat in our old apartment materialised beside him and Dad laid a big piece of paper over it. I bent closer to see it and recognised the battered map he'd scavenged from the ruins when we were children. He'd spent some time trying to teach us about the states and cities from the world before the Final War, but it had never meant much to me. Our world was confined to the Realm and anything beyond that had been impossible to imagine until recently.

"We're here, in northern Washington." Dad pointed at a place on the left of the map. "If Montana is being held in New York, then you're going to have to cross the whole country. It's not a short trip." He traced his finger all the way over to the right-hand side of the map and tapped on a spot near the coast, the image burning itself into my mind.

"How long will it take?" I asked anxiously. If Montana could just hold out for a few more days, then maybe I could get her out-

"On foot? Weeks. Months, actually. Too long. But if the vampires already have her there, then there must be another route available. Over the years, I've heard them talking about supply trains coming from the east once or twice. That might be your best bet."

"What's a train?" I asked in confusion. The term was vaguely familiar to me, but I couldn't remember what he'd told me about them.

The ground beneath my feet started to vibrate and a deep rumbling echoed all around us. Wooden tracks appeared beside us, marking a trail through the darkness.

"The tracks will lead you to them," Dad said.

The sound continued to grow as something huge closed in on us, my heart pounding at the enormity of that noise, my hair shifting in an unnatural breeze. I turned as the gust of wind pulled at my hair more forcefully, and I found myself looking at a monstrous metal vehicle as it sped towards me along the tracks. The train shot past us, sending my long hair flying as it raced by. Carriage after carriage loaded with all kinds of things from people, to stacks of lumber, to vehicles. I stared after it with my mouth hanging open. My dad's stories had never been able to give me a clear visual of things like that, and I was starting to think I had massively under-imagined a lot of what he'd told us about. The images my brain had conjured were not in any way like the reality.

Before I could think of anything to say in response to what I'd just seen, a roar started in the sky, and I twisted to look up at a gigantic metal bird soaring overhead. I blinked rapidly, realising it was an aeroplane, the object's wings entirely stationary, the engine bellowing far louder than any bird.

"The other option would be to fly," Dad explained as he stepped closer to me. "But it would be a lot harder to find a way to board a plane secretly than a train."

"What if I can't do it?" I breathed, uttering my deepest fear. What if there was no way I could free Montana from the Belvederes? I may have had Magnar on my side, but we were still only two people. And they were the leaders of this new and fucked-up world. A thousand vampires could be standing between us and them.

"I believe in you, Callie. The two of you are born of one light, sun and moon, destined to be together. I know you'll find your way back to each other." He smiled at me encouragingly, but I still wasn't convinced.

Everything around us flickered in and out of focus, and my dad disappeared too.

My heart leapt in panic, and I twisted around, trying to locate him in the darkness.

He appeared again behind me and sank down to sit on a soft, brown armchair.

"I'm afraid I'm going to have to leave you soon, little sun," he sighed, and I could tell he was struggling to form the words.

"Not yet," I begged as I hurried to him and grabbed his hand. "Please stay with me a bit longer." The rising tide of grief was growing closer, but I pushed it back, wanting to enjoy what time I had left with him.

"I wish I could. I wish that I'd gotten us out of the Realm before

*now. I wish I could have given you girls a real life. A free life. I wish...
so many things. More than I ever got to give you. Most of all, I just want
you to be together. Free and happy. Promise me you'll find happiness."*

"How can I be happy without you?" Pain was constricting my
chest, and my grip on his fingers began to feel like it was the only thing
keeping him there at all

"You will be. I know you can be. Take this." He removed Mom's
wedding ring from the chain around his neck and handed it to me. "Your
mom wanted you girls to have it, but as there were two of you, I never
knew which one of you to give it to. Then I just got used to wearing it.
Maybe you can take turns once you get back to Montana." He smiled
knowingly; the two of us had never been able to share well as children
and 'take turns' had become Dad's catchphrase when he was constantly
reminding us to attempt it. The thought that I'd never hear him say it
again nearly tore me in two.

"I'll find her, Dad. I promise," I said, knowing he needed to hear it.

He let out a deep sigh, and our surroundings began to shimmer
unsteadily. When they solidified again, he'd moved away from me and
the chair was gone.

My hand closed on nothing where his fingers had just been. My
mom reappeared standing further away still, a serene smile on her face.

Someone took my hand, and I found Montana standing beside me,
smiling bravely. It still wasn't truly her though, just a reflection of what
I needed to see.

Dad walked away from us, pulling Mom close and pressing a kiss
to her lips. I wanted to follow him, but a gulf of space had opened up
between us and I was forced to remain where I was or fall into the
ravine.

"I love you girls," Dad said sadly as he turned to face us one last
time. "Never forget it."

I tried to reach for him, to cry out and beg him to stay with me, but
everything faded away faster than I could comprehend. The last thing
that remained was the golden ring in my fist, its imprint forcing its way
onto my palm as I gripped it tightly, but then that faded too.

And I was left entirely alone.

Magnar was shaking me as I came back to my own body, and a sob escaped my lips as I woke in his arms.

"I'm so sorry Callie," he breathed.

I pushed myself upright and buried myself against his chest as tears poured from my eyes in a steady torrent. I didn't need to hear why he was sorry. I already knew. Pain flourished through my chest more sharply than I'd ever felt it before, and he held me tightly as sobs racked my body and the grief came crashing in.

Dad was gone.

MONTANA

CHAPTER TWENTY

I'd returned to the ballroom, keeping my distance from the surrounding vampires while Nightmare thrummed furiously against my leg. The other humans were caught in conversation with many of the Elite, but I avoided every eye that came my way.

Erik had given me the option I needed to save Dad, but it still left me with two serious problems. The mark. And Callie.

Miles would tell Erik if I betrayed him, so I had to tell him first. Frustratingly, Erik was currently surrounded by vampires. Every time he seemed to break away and I shifted toward him, someone else would snare his attention.

Anxiety seized me. I needed to discuss this now in private before I was forced to choose a prince in front of the whole crowd.

Music started up and the guests parted to make a dance floor at the centre of the room. Clarice pulled Hank into a slow dance as the soft strumming of a string instrument trilled through the air. Fabian approached Paige, offering her his arm, and she quickly joined him in a dance. Miles and Erik started searching the crowd and I knew there was only one person they were looking for. Me.

This was my chance.

I made a path for Erik, but Miles approached faster, gripping my wrist, and pulling me onto the dance floor.

Shit.

I watched as Erik stood at the edge of the crowd, looking like he was about to walk out here and take me from Miles's arms, and I hoped he would do just that.

Miles pulled me against him, and I rested one hand on the shoulder of his dark green jacket, having no choice but to comply.

He tugged me along, his bright eyes darkening. "All set for today?"

I couldn't risk him talking to Erik before I did, so I smiled and nodded. "Of course."

"I'll move you into an apartment that overlooks the Brooklyn bridge. You can have anything you want Montana; you just have to name it."

"And in return you want children?" I said through gritted teeth, ice washing through my veins.

He cleared his throat as he led me faster around the dance floor. "Yeah...but it's the only thing I'll ask of you, I promise. And it'll be through insemination."

I shook my head in anger. "I don't want to."

"I know," Miles said in a low tone, moving his mouth to my ear. "I don't want this either, but it's the only way. And the children are worth it, I promise you'll love them."

"The only way for what?" I whispered, ignoring his final comment. I wouldn't be having children with him. Ever.

His sparkling blue eyes dimmed further. "Not here, Montana. I'll tell you after the ceremony."

I was about to push him for answers when Erik snared my waist, cutting into the dance. Miles bowed his head to him, not seeming bothered by the act as he backed up into the crowd and re-joined Warren.

Erik guided me in the moves, his eyes pinned somewhere over my head as we danced a simple dance that was easy to follow. I tried not to falter but didn't really care what the crowd thought of my dancing abilities. There was only one thing that mattered now.

"So?" Erik muttered. "Have you made your choice?"

"You told me to pick your brother," I said in a whisper, unsure how much I should say while we had witnesses, but Fabian looked engrossed in a conversation with Paige. Between the music and the chatter in the room, I doubted we could be overheard.

"Yes, and now I'm telling you otherwise, rebel. Keep up." His mouth lifted in a smirk, but I was in no mood for his games.

I gathered my courage, wishing we could have had a more private place for me to reveal the truth. But I'd run out of time.

"I want to make new terms as part of this deal," I said in a low voice. "You listed plenty of demands from me, so I get to make more from you."

Erik's jaw ticked. "State your demands then."

"Callie goes free with Dad. When they arrive, you'll take them both out of the city."

Erik pressed his tongue into his cheek as he avoided my eye. "We'll talk about it after the ceremony. Besides, don't you want her here? She will be company for you."

"She'll be a prisoner, Erik," I spat. *And I can't risk her getting caught up in this.*

My eyes strayed to the children who were beginning to dance and integrate with the crowd. That was what they'd ask of Callie too. And offering myself up to Erik wasn't going to change that unless I could force him to agree to her freedom.

Erik followed my gaze, tugging me closer by the waist. "You will not be a prisoner if you choose me, rebel. Once this is over, we will leave the city together. You can have as much freedom as you wish."

"Just so long as I remain as your obedient little wife?" I hissed.

"I don't recall mentioning obedience," he muttered. "Simply that you cannot run."

The song was coming to an end, and I started to fear what would happen if I didn't tell Erik the truth about the mark right now, but without assurances about my sister's safety, I couldn't move on. "Erik, promise me you'll set Callie free, no matter what happens."

"What's going on?" Erik stopped dancing, holding me firmly by the waist. "What aren't you saying?"

"Just promise me," I begged.

He skated his thumb across my cheek, his voice lowering. "Tell me what's wrong."

I reached for my right arm, my fingers brushing the place the mark was hidden. "Erik, I-"

"Master, a word please!" General Wolfe burst through the crowd; his silver hair dishevelled as he marched toward us straight across the dance floor. He awkwardly clutched his back as he moved, his expression stretched with discomfort as if something ailed him.

"Wolfe, what are you doing here?" Erik demanded, releasing me as he took in the fiendish general.

Nightmare flared with hunger as if it longed to drive itself into the heart of the beast before us, and I had a mind to give it what it wanted. My heart beat harder as I searched the space beyond Wolfe, suddenly terrified I might see Callie and Dad there. But there was no sign of them.

"I got the first flight back – I lost my phone and none of the lessers I encountered along the way had the clearance to be able to contact you. It's very important I speak with you." Wolfe bowed low, and I noticed many of the vampires behind him were beginning to mutter.

"Where's my family?" I demanded, the heat in my blood rising.

Wolfe's eyes snapped to me, his upper lip curling back. He looked ready to berate me but managed to return his gaze to Erik.

"This is the second time you've interrupted the ritual, General," Erik snarled at him. "You had better have a good explanation."

Wolfe nodded, bowing his head again. "Please, let's speak in private, your highness."

Erik muttered an apology to me before taking Wolfe's arm and pushing him roughly through the crowd. I watched as they slipped behind a curtain, heading into a concealed passage beyond it.

Nightmare urged me to follow, but before I could, Fabian caught my arm and forced me to dance.

"Good evening, Montana," he said lightly. "You're looking beautiful tonight."

Rage spewed through me at being captured by this monster when so much was at stake. But I couldn't let my fury be known to him.

"Are you well?" he asked. "I heard about what happened last night.

You must have been terrified. There are more and more rebels in the city these days, it's quite dangerous for humans beyond the castle grounds." There was an edge to his tone that made my blood chill.

I tried to compose my face into something that resembled calm. "Thank you. Yes, I'm fine. It was lucky Erik was standing in front of me at the time or I don't think I would have survived."

"Absolutely," he said with a nod, his eyes bright with concern. He was a damn good liar, which made him a formidable kind of enemy.

"So, have you decided who you'll pick tonight?" Fabian asked with a slanted smile.

"Um..." I chewed on my lip, unsure what to say. What I really needed to do was talk to Erik about this mark, but I wasn't sure how much time I had left to do so. "I don't know."

"You're cutting it quite close." Fabian arched a brow. "Surely there's someone more appealing to you?"

I shrugged, glancing over at Paige who was now dancing with Miles. I hoped she'd heed my warning and pick him over Fabian.

The song finally changed to a merry tune and the rest of the vampires joined in with the dancing, filling up the surrounding space. I took the moment to break free of Fabian and dart into the crowd.

With my eyes set on the curtain Erik and Wolfe had disappeared behind, I started walking at a fierce pace.

Where's my family, you twisted piece of shit?

I reached the curtain and slowed to a walk as eyes turned my way. Feigning interest in the beautiful surroundings, I inched along, listening hard to try and pick up their voices.

"-the slayer is alive, it's true." Wolfe's voice.

"How is that possible?" Erik snarled. "He is supposed to be dead. And even if he somehow survived, no mortal can live a thousand years."

"I don't know how, but he lives, sire."

Nightmare reached out to me, hissing a warning to move away, but I needed to hear what Wolfe had to say about my family.

"You let him escape?" Erik barked at him, and a heavy thump followed.

When Wolfe spoke, he did so with a murmur of pain. "I tried my hardest, sire. But he was powerful and had already killed many of the Elite. My back still isn't fully healed from the slayer blade he drove into me."

"Do you think I give a shit about your injuries? What's the point in having a general who cannot kill a slayer? What use are you to me?" Erik snarled followed by another thump.

My gut knotted. *Will Erik want me dead too when he finds out what I am?*

My breathing quickened as I listened, pressing myself to the wall. A flare of pain shot through my shoulder, and I released a gasp before I could suppress it.

Silence fell beyond the curtain.

I turned to run, but an arm shot out and dragged me behind it into the concealed passage.

Erik's eyes flared as they narrowed on me. "Spying, rebel?"

I gathered my wits, figuring I had every right to know what Wolfe had to say.

"You can hardly be surprised." My eyes adjusted to the darker space, and I spotted Wolfe against one wall with a trickle of bright red blood flowing down his brow.

The general's eyes narrowed on me, venom pouring through his gaze.

"She's one of them," he spat. "Look at her arm. She's the same as her sister. I saw the Ford girl with a slayer's blade. She may have been weak, but there was fight in her like no normal human."

Fear made my heart pound as Erik's gaze locked with mine, seeming to hunt for the answer in my eyes. Nightmare hummed so loud, I feared it would give itself away, and I stepped back, ready to grab hold of the blade and fight for my life if I had to.

"Wait-" I started in alarm, but Erik snatched my right arm, ripping up my sleeve.

Time stuttered to a halt as his eyes fell on the mark. A noose seemed to tighten around my throat. I had no words, no explanation. I'd wanted to do this on my own terms, but Wolfe had taken that from me.

"Rebel," Erik growled in a deadly voice that dared me not to test him. "Are you a *slayer*?"

"I don't know – maybe." I glanced at Wolfe over Erik's shoulder, my heart beating at a frighteningly fast pace.

"But if Callie's one, then I must be too. She's my twin." I gazed up at him, praying the repercussions of this weren't going to be brutal. But I had no choice now.

"Twin?" Erik breathed, his grey eyes melting like solder. "You're *twins*?"

I nodded, unsure why that was important, but his intense expression told me it was.

"Fuck." Erik scraped a hand through his hair, his brows knitting sharply together. "Why didn't you mention this before?!"

"Why does it matter?" I asked, confounded at his fury.

Felicia's voice rang out from the ballroom.

"The choosing is about to begin! Courtiers, please make your way to the stage immediately!"

Erik gazed at me, but he didn't seem to see me at all, his eyes glazed in thought and tension lining his posture.

"Go," he barked, pushing me toward the curtain and sending my heart into a riot.

"No." I fixed my glare on Wolfe. "Where's Callie? Where's my dad?"

Wolfe's lips twitched, but he said nothing, looking to Erik for direction.

"You will go now," Erik said threateningly. "Make your choice. And for your sake, you'd best make the right one."

I backed up, my mouth dry as I returned to the ballroom, and the crowd nudged me in the direction of the other humans at the top of the steps.

My heart crushed with every stair I climbed, because I didn't know where my family was or when I would see them again. Had Wolfe brought them to the castle? Would they be waiting for me the second I got back there?

I moved to Paige's side, and she gave me a frown as she noticed my rattled expression. As the cameras were pointed our way, my rage and fear was reflected back at me on the large screen opposite us, ferocity blazing in my eyes.

Nightmare hummed furiously, sending a tremor through my body that felt like a warning. But I didn't know how to heed it. I was on the precipice of my own hell, and the only way to protect my family was to dive headfirst into it. But if Erik kept his word, at least the wretched path that lay before me was mine and mine alone. Though he still hadn't made any promises when it came to Callie, I would insist she was freed before I ever married him.

My gut dropped at the thought, dread washing over me as an image brightened the inside of my mind. Me walking up an aisle dressed in white, just as my father had described his marriage to Mom. But instead of walking into wedded bliss, I would be a shackled prisoner chained to a beast.

Felicia drifted closer with a bright grin as the crowd gathered and gave us their full attention. An electric tension pulsed through the room as the vampires fell quiet.

Fabian, Miles, and Clarice stood at the bottom of the stairs, gazing up at us with anxious look,s and Erik pushed through the crowd, his expression chaotic as he joined the royal line-up. His gaze swung my way, a command in them that told me to choose him and no other. It was my choice, yet it was really no choice at all.

Hank moved to stand beside me and Luke stood beyond him, seeming agitated.

"Hank, make your selection," Felicia asked, and a spotlight fell on him. The rest of the room darkened, and a hushed silence fell.

Hank visibly swallowed, gazing down at the vampires. "I choose to join Clarice's harem."

A tumult of applause broke out, and Hank moved down the steps, taking hold of Clarice's waist and placing a kiss on her cheek. She smiled brightly, then turned her attention to us once more, seeming keen for the ceremony to continue, though a tension in her shoulders told me perhaps she wasn't as excited as she was pretending to be about all of this.

"Luke, it's your turn," Felicia said, and the spotlight fell over him.

Luke shifted from foot to foot and a bead of sweat sailed down his brow as he gazed from Clarice to the camera crew. "I want to go to Realm A."

A jolt went through me, unsure if I'd heard correctly.

"Clarice told me I had a choice," Luke went on, looking to the princess.

She smiled, not seeming too bothered by his choice. "I did. And if that's what you want, you can have it. Your family will be moved there too."

Luke's shoulders sagged as he jogged down the stairs and Clarice embraced him to a smattering of applause. A moment later, a couple of guards strode to his side, escorting him away.

My throat constricted as I shared a confused look with Paige. This had been the offer Clarice had given the men? How was it fair that they were allowed a way out and we weren't?

"Paige." Felicia gestured for her to make a choice, and my heart galloped into top gear.

She gazed across the three brothers, knotting her fingers together. "I choose..." She took a breath, glancing at me before saying, "I choose Prince Miles."

I reached for her, and she squeezed my hand before darting down the steps. Miles seized her in his arms, placing a brief kiss on her cheek, and horror washed over me at what he was going to demand of her. She may have escaped Fabian's clutches, but she would still have to provide Miles with a child.

The crowd applauded, crying out to them, and my gaze turned to Fabian who was fighting hard to not look pissed off. For once, the mask he wore had slipped and anger shone in his brown eyes. A second later, he turned to me expectantly, jaw pulsing.

Felicia turned back to the stage, and the spotlight fell over me, the heat of it like the full rays of the sun. My answer was obvious yet would place me in a snare I would never escape. It would declare me a bride to a vampire, the bored prince who had made a plaything out of me from the moment we'd met.

"I choose Prince Erik," I announced, my voice ringing around the room, praying this choice would cast a shield of protection over my loved ones. Nightmare screamed in protest, but the blade couldn't save me now.

Erik smiled the darkest of smiles as I bound myself to him with those words, and Miles's mouth fell open in shock.

It was done. My choice was made. And my soul had been served to Erik Belvedere.

CALLIE

CHAPTER TWENTY ONE

I'd cried until my eyes were raw and aching and no more tears could find their way from my body. After everything we'd done to bring down the blood bank. Everything we'd risked to save him, my dad was lost. A hopeless kind of despair filled me as I stared at the cairn we'd created around his body, my grief so sharp it cut deeper than any blade could.

Magnar had carried him to the top of the hill for me. It was the highest point for miles around, and we'd lain him to rest looking down on all of it. He was finally free.

It had taken hours to collect the stones required to cover him. My fingers were numb from the cold and coated with dirt from digging the rocks out of the soil. My fingernails were broken and bloody, but I couldn't feel any pain from my injuries. The pain in my heart was too much to allow room for anything else.

The sun began to set as I looked at the monument we had created for my dad's final resting place. The clear sky was streaked with lines of pink and orange, and the full moon had already risen too. It was as if the heavens had brought the sun and the moon together to say goodbye.

I clutched Mom's wedding ring which now hung on the chain

around my neck. The metal felt warm, its presence making me feel closer to my parents somehow. Like carrying it with me kept their souls close to mine.

My mind drifted to Montana, trapped with the murderers who had done this. She didn't even know Dad was dead. It wasn't right that she didn't know.

I gritted my teeth as my grief began to give way to rage. Who did the vampires think they were to do this to us? How could they rip my whole world apart and feel no remorse?

The pain clawing at my soul needed an outlet, a bloodlust rising in me to rival the thirst of the monsters who had done this.

My father was gone. They'd taken Montana to the other side of the country. I was being hunted like some kind of animal. And for what?

It wasn't right. I wanted them to pay. I wanted to make them feel an ounce of what I was feeling. I wanted to storm into their so-called kingdom, tear the walls down on top of their heads and let the sun burn them alive. Most of all, I wanted them all dead, turned to ash and rot and *nothing*. And there was only one way I could achieve that.

I turned towards Magnar who stood silently at my side and took his hand in mine. He raised his eyebrows in surprise as he caught sight of the determination in my gaze. There was only one way I wanted to grieve now, and that was through the violence of revenge.

"I'll take the vow," I said fiercely. "Tell me the words and I'll say them. I want my gifts unleashed. I want to be a full slayer like you. I want to kill the Belvederes."

Something sparkled in Magnar's golden eyes, and he wrapped his other hand over mine.

I waited for him to tell me what to do while Fury burned at my hip in excitement, urging me on.

Seize your destiny, Sun child.

This was what I'd been born for. It was what I was made for. And it was what it would take for me to claim the vengeance my heart desired beyond all else.

"No, Callie," Magnar breathed, shattering the moment of decision which burned through me, his words a slap to my face. "Not like this."

"What?" I stared at him in astonishment.

I'd thought he would have been pleased, thrilled even. He was the last of his kind. If I joined him, then there would be two of us just as dedicated to his cause as he was now. We could stay together and hunt down the monsters who had started all of this. I wanted to help him destroy the vampires. I *needed* to do it.

"Not like this," he repeated firmly. "This isn't a decision that you should make while you're feeling this way-"

"I'll never not feel this way," I hissed angrily. Who was he to tell me my own mind? "My father is dead! Don't you get it? They killed him!"

"You know I understand that pain better than anyone," he growled, and I remembered what Erik Belvedere had done to his father. He did understand, so why wouldn't he help me?

"So let me take the vow. Let me help you to destroy them," I demanded, my blood running hot.

"There are other implications, things that you don't understand. If you take your vow, I will have to train you and then we can never-"

"I don't care!" I yelled, snatching my hand from his grasp. "I don't care what the price is. I would give *anything* to get my sister away from them. I would give my soul, my life, anything at all."

Fury continued to grow hotter at my hip, seeming desperate for me to do this. It wanted me to realise my potential. It wanted me to become a true slayer.

I grabbed the blade from its sheath and a feeling like being submerged in warm water enveloped me. I gasped as a strange wind pulled at my hair and a power unlike anything I'd ever felt before surged around us.

I dropped to one knee, holding Fury before me before driving its tip into the frozen mud until it embedded itself there like a pillar of stone.

"Don't do this, drakaina hjarta," Magnar begged.

A small part of me felt his anguish like a punch to the chest, but it was nothing to the destructive power of the grief consuming me and the desperate need for revenge which urged me on.

I know the words, Fury breathed excitedly within the confines of my mind. *Let me guide your tongue.*

My eyes locked with Magnar's and a fresh kind of pain hit me as I looked into his desperate gaze, but I couldn't go back on my decision. I needed my gifts. I could feel it in every inch of my body. I had to say the words.

"I vow to always walk in the light," I said, and the power of the words locked my body in its position as my blood thrummed in my veins. "I will seek out those who dwell in the darkness."

Blinding light grew to the right of me, and though I couldn't turn my head, I could feel the presence of something far greater than any mortal or vampire as it turned its attention to me. The being moved closer, watching us and willing me on, its power seeming to flow into me as I spoke the words I shouldn't have known, Fury pressing them into my mind, my tongue bending around them without protest.

"My days shall no longer be my own. I give them to the cause."

Something immense slammed into my body, and I gasped as its power radiated through my blood. I couldn't move an inch. Each breath I took was laced with something that tingled and burned its way right down into my lungs before spreading further, finding every fibre of my being and moulding it into something new. I was being reborn as a creature of pure power, my human weaknesses leaving me and blowing away on the strange wind spiralling around me.

Magnar growled in resistance as the being spread its power towards him and he was slowly forced to his knees opposite me. His eyes were filled with rage and regret as his hands closed over mine where they clasped Fury's hilt. His rough palms were hot against my skin, and I sensed the same strange magic burning through his blood too. It flowed between us, forming a bridge from his soul to mine.

"Please stop, Callie," Magnar growled, his words a demand, though the plea in them was clear, but I doubted I would have been able to even if I wanted to. The power of the vow had me in its grasp and the only way out was onwards.

"I dedicate myself to my mentor," I said in a voice that didn't sound like my own anymore. "My life is in his hands. We will be bound by our cause, forfeiting all other ties. I will follow the path he sets."

The power in my chest surged from me to surround Magnar too, and his eyes burned fiercely as he fought against the urge to speak.

The seconds dragged as he kept his mouth shut and sweat beaded on his temple. His jaw ticked as he concentrated on resisting the power pushing against his will. His gaze burned with a desperate plea for me to end this and release him from the promise he was about to be forced to make.

A small part of me wished that I could. I wanted this for myself, but I hadn't meant to force him into something he clearly didn't desire. He'd already lost so much, and the look in his eyes made me feel like I was ripping the final piece of his happiness away from him. But there was no stopping it now that it had begun.

I could sense the being beside us growing displeased. The swirling vortex around us grew so bright that it became hard to see Magnar's face despite how close he was. The wind howled, sending our hair flying and whipping my coat out behind me. The being made a sound like an ancient gong ringing, and my ears pounded as it pushed its influence into Magnar until he uttered the words he had been fighting against, each one of them a growl as he tried to resist the immense power. I wondered if this was one of the gods Magnar had spoken of, come to bond us with their power and set the slayer vow in motion.

"I dedicate myself to this novice. Her life is in my hands." Magnar locked his jaw again, refusing to finish the oath, and his eyes flared with pain as the being forced her will into him again. "We will be bound by our cause, forfeiting all other ties. I will lead her into the light."

A sharp pain seared across the back of my left hand, and I gasped as I spotted a mark shaped like a five-pointed star branded into my skin. Magnar's grip tightened around my own and the same mark appeared on his hand. His shoulders slumped in defeat, and he dropped his gaze to glare at the ground while the power continued to billow around us.

"I will follow the way of the slayers until the last vampire is wiped from this earth or until death releases me," I swore, and the raging torrent of my grief rose in me again as I remembered exactly why I had to do this. It wasn't a choice. This was who I'd always been meant to be.

Power beyond measure hit me like a tornado. If I hadn't been fixed in place, I was sure I would have been tossed aside like a rag doll and dashed to death in the eye of the storm.

My vision wavered and I couldn't see Magnar, or the hill, or anything else that sat around me anymore. Instead, I could see slayers, hundreds of slayers living across thousands of years. Everything they'd ever learned poured into me. Every battle they'd fought, every passion they'd felt. I lived it all again and again. All of their memories tearing into me, filling me up and ripping me apart. I was them and they were me. I had lived a thousand times before. Always dying for the cause. Always taking the vow again. Their lessons became my own knowledge, their feats my memories, their lives my own.

Fury was thrumming with excitement and its voice rang out clearly in my mind. *Twins of sun and moon will rise, when one has lived a thousand lives.*

The power built in me like an angry wave carried on the tide of my grief, and I raised my head to the sky and screamed. I screamed for my father and my mother and for my sister trapped far, far away.

I reached for her, my soul clawing its way out of my skin and tearing away from me in a desperate bid to find her. I needed her more than I ever had in my life, and I would damn well find my way to her now.

And suddenly, she was there, our souls colliding with a force that stole all breath from me and made my heart stutter with shock. I was looking through her eyes at a hall full of monsters, and a surge of memories rushed between us like a tide crashing against a cliff face.

Monty? I breathed, but I had no body to speak the word, so it simply echoed through the space between the cracks in the world, snapping her attention onto mine. Somehow, the word itself had gotten lost along the way, nothing but a sense of self passing from me to her.

I felt her panic and confusion, my vision merging with hers, the hillside where I'd lain our father to rest swimming between the view of a hundred vampires who were all looking up at her in a room draped with finery. My grief flared and I felt her shock, her horror as she reacted to the memories slipping from my grasp and racing across time and space to reach her. I tried to convey all that had happened since the moment she'd been taken from me so brutally, showing her everything.

A hundred scenes flitted from my memory to her mind at high speed, the impossibility of this connection between us stalling my heart in my chest. It couldn't be real. Yet I knew it was, the power of the gifts I'd been granted with my vow unlocking this magical bridge between us.

I felt Montana's bewilderment as I showed her all I could, trying to explain in memories what I couldn't communicate with words. She balked at the rows of humans in those strange, glass coffins at the blood bank, the fear I'd felt in that place transcending this link between our minds. And once I was certain she'd seen that, I gave her more. Vampires snarling, biting, dying at my hands and his. *Magnar Elioson*. The mere thought of him had my mind relaying image after image, blood spilling at the feet of the frighteningly fierce slayer, vampires falling to ash and ruin all around him.

Montana flinched at the rush of information, the images moving so quickly between us that it was impossible for her to make sense of them, and the more I tried to take hold of the visions, the more they leaped about.

She blinked and the memories faded away, offering me a view out of her eyes, something telling me that what I was looking at was the present, the monster staring up at her the very same one who Magnar had warned me about.

Erik Belvedere's face was a mask of unblemished porcelain, his features cut from glass and radiant with ungodly perfection. Montana's eyes met his roiling gaze, and the hunger I found there set my heart racing with terror. He wasn't just looking at her like she was a meal to devour, his gaze was locked on hers like a creature set on utter destruction. But as I focused on the sense of Montana surrounding me, I didn't feel the world-altering terror which should have accompanied the sight of that beast. There was fear there, but it wasn't nearly so potent as it needed to be, like she didn't fully grasp the danger she was in.

I tried to cry out in the space between our souls, any words I might have been trying to push her way lost, but the grief which consumed me made its way between us, the final moments of our father's life flashing from my mind to hers as I dragged her into a vision of him lying in my arms, his bandages stained with too much blood. His face was deathly still, the truth of his suffering plain to see, the end of his life absolute.

My pain and grief tore through the void between us as Montana stood surrounded by the monsters who had done this, our dad's death ringing in her head like a gong. I felt the crack in her heart as it fractured at that truth, the power blazing between us roaring beyond the confines of my control. She took it in with a clarity that tossed her into a black pit of despair, one she would never be free of.

I tried to call out to her again, tried to tell her I was coming for her, that nothing in this world could stop me, and whether in reply to that or not, the tide of memories slipped between us again, her mind pressing against mine, showing me all she had survived since our separation.

I recoiled at the sight of the four vampires who called themselves royal, their beauty making my stomach knot with hatred as I saw flashes of humans being presented to them, wrapped up in fine clothes like playthings trotted out for the amusement of monsters.

Confusion tore at me, my mind lost as to why they would do any such thing and suddenly I was staring at a group of unnaturally beautiful children.

My heart stalled in my chest as I gaped at them, the truth of what they were and what those heinous creatures planned on using my sister for swimming through me with a cloying clarity.

No, I gasped, horror and grief colliding between us, more visions of our father dancing across the line which merged our minds.

It was too much, the power of this connection making my limbs quake and mind shatter as I tried to hold on to my twin with all I had, not wanting to leave her in that place. The mountainside flickered, becoming that room again, the vampires all staring as Montana began to fall, Erik's eyes widening as he lurched for her collapsing body.

My sister fell into an eternity of darkness, as pain splintered through her that was layered with grief, the truth of all that had happened overcoming her. Dad's death sliced into her heart, a jagged wound weeping as the horror of it surrounded her, cutting into me too.

My mind couldn't take it, my body close to breaking from the force it took to maintain that connection. Despite how desperately I wanted to stay with my sister, I felt my grasp on her slipping.

I fell backwards as I slammed into my own body once more, and like a switch had been flipped, everything went black before I even hit the ground.

As my consciousness swam in an eternal sea of darkness, one thing stayed with me among the abyss. Montana was alive. And we would be reunited.

Whatever it took.

WANT MORE?

To find out more, grab yourself some freebies and to join our reader group, scan the QR code below.

AUTHOR NOTE

Oh noooo, what a tangled mess of utter chaos we have plunged into. I hope I haven't caught you in your feels and that you're not currently in the midst of cursing our names and are instead ready to take a breath, drink a cup of tea, eat your bodyweight in chocolate and ask the moon why it has caused such woe to befall you.

If I have in fact interrupted such a scene of rage and trauma, then please don't forget to bottle those tears and send them on over to our pool of ever-lasting pain. We make good use of it by bathing in it daily and allowing the salt to burn our skin, once more awakening the need in us to hurt more of your beloved characters and get their pain onto the page for your next dose of torture. I mean, relaxing reading time.

Don't go getting your goose in a gander though, book three will make everything worse.

I mean worse.

I mean better.

In a worse way.

Well damn.

Don't blame us on this one though; blame those pesky gods, and while you're at it don't forget to bathe in the everlasting love we hold for you in our hearts as our most beloved of victims. I mean readers.

You're our favourite. Remember that next time we hurt you. This too shall pass.

Love, Susanne and Caroline XOXO

Printed in Great Britain
by Amazon